3397000100085- 05-1196

OCT 26 '78

F/C
CAMP
$30.00

or loan

An Unexpected Pleasure

*Also by Candace Camp
in Large Print:*

Secrets of the Heart
Winterset
Beyond Compare
Mesmerized

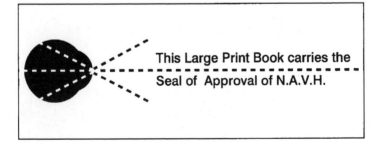

This Large Print Book carries the
Seal of Approval of N.A.V.H.

An Unexpected Pleasure

Candace Camp

Thorndike Press • Waterville, Maine

Published in 2005 by arrangement with Harlequin Books S.A.

Thorndike Press® Large Print Basic.

The tree indicium is a trademark of Thorndike Press.

The text of this Large Print edition is unabridged.
Other aspects of the book may vary from the original edition.

Set in 16 pt. Plantin by Carleen Stearns.

Printed in the United States on permanent paper.

Library of Congress Cataloging-in-Publication Data

Camp, Candace.
    An unexpected pleasure / by Candace Camp.
    p. cm.
    "Thorndike Press Large Print Basic" — T.p. verso.
    ISBN 0-7862-7917-6 (lg. print : hc : alk. paper)
    1. Women journalists — Fiction. 2. Nobility —
Fiction. 3. Brothers and sisters — Fiction. 4. Irish
Americans — Fiction. 5. Nannies — Fiction. 6. Large
type books. I. Title.
PS3553.A4374U54 2005
813'.54—dc22   2005014568

An Unexpected Pleasure

As the Founder/CEO of NAVH, the only national health agency solely devoted to those who, although not totally blind, have an eye disease which could lead to serious visual impairment, I am pleased to recognize Thorndike Press* as one of the leading publishers in the large print field.

Founded in 1954 in San Francisco to prepare large print textbooks for partially seeing children, NAVH became the pioneer and standard setting agency in the preparation of large type.

Today, those publishers who meet our standards carry the prestigious "Seal of Approval" indicating high quality large print. We are delighted that Thorndike Press is one of the publishers whose titles meet these standards. We are also pleased to recognize the significant contribution Thorndike Press is making in this important and growing field.

Lorraine H. Marchi, L.H.D.
Founder/CEO
NAVH

* Thorndike Press encompasses the following imprints: Thorndike, Wheeler, Walker and Large Print Press.

Prologue

New York, 1879

The shriek cut through the night.

In her bed, Megan Mulcahey sat straight up, instantly awake, her heart pounding. It took her a moment to realize what had awakened her. Then she heard her sister's voice again.

"No. No!"

Megan was out of her bed in a flash and running through the door. Theirs was not a large home — a narrow brownstone row house with three bedrooms upstairs — and it took only a moment to reach Deirdre's door and fling it open.

Deirdre was sitting up in bed, her eyes wide and staring, horrified. Her arms stretched out in front of her toward something only she could see, and tears pooled in her eyes before rolling down her cheeks.

"Deirdre!" Megan crossed the room and

7

sat down on her sister's bed, taking Deirdre's shoulders firmly in her hands. "What is it? Wake up! Deirdre!"

She gave the girl a shake, and something changed in her sister's face, the frightening blankness slipping away, replaced by a dawning consciousness.

"Megan!" Deirdre let out a sob and threw her arms around her older sister. "Oh, Megan. It was terrible. Terrible!"

"Saints preserve us!" Their father's voice sounded from the doorway. "What in the name of all that's holy is going on?"

"Deirdre had a bad dream, that's all," Megan replied, keeping her voice calm and soothing, as she stroked her sister's hair. "Isn't that right, Dee? It was nothing but a nightmare."

"No." Deirdre gulped and pulled back from Megan a little, wiping the tears from her cheeks and looking first at Megan, then at their father. Her eyes were still wide and shadowed. "Megan. Da. I saw Dennis!"

"You dreamed about Dennis?" Megan asked.

"It wasn't a dream," Deirdre responded. "Dennis was here. He spoke to me."

A shiver ran down Megan's spine. "But, Dee, you couldn't have seen him. Dennis has been dead for ten years."

"It was him," Deirdre insisted. "I saw him, plain as day. He spoke to me."

Their father crossed the room eagerly and went down on one knee before his daughter, looking into her face. "Are you sure, then, Deirdre? It was really Denny?"

"Yes. Oh, yes. He looked like he did the day he sailed away."

Megan stared at her sister, stunned. Deirdre had a reputation in the family for having the second sight. She was given to forebodings and premonitions — too many of which had turned out to be true for Megan to completely dismiss her sister's "ability." However, her predictions usually ran more to having a feeling that a certain friend or relative was having problems or was likely to drop in on them that day. The more pragmatic side of Megan believed that her sister simply possessed a certain sensitivity that enabled her to pick up on a number of small clues about people and situations that most others ignored. It was an admirable talent, Megan agreed, but she had her doubts whether it was the otherworldly gift that many deemed it.

Deirdre's looks, she thought, contributed a great deal to the common perception of her. Small and fragile in build, with large, gentle blue eyes, pale skin and light straw-berry-blond hair, there was a fey quality to her, a sense of otherworldliness, that aroused most people's feelings of protec-tiveness, including Megan's, and made it easy to believe that the girl was in tune with the other world.

But never before had Deirdre claimed to have seen someone who was dead. Megan was not sure what to think. On the one hand, her practical mind had trouble ac-cepting that her brother's spirit was walk-ing about, talking to her sister. It seemed much more likely that Deirdre had had a nightmare that her sleep-befuddled mind had imagined was real. On the other hand, there was a small superstitious something deep inside her that wondered if this could possibly be true. The truth was, she knew, that like her father, she wanted it to be true — she hoped that her beloved brother was still around in some form, not lost to her forever.

"What did he say?" Frank Mulcahey asked. "Why did he come to you?"

Deirdre's eyes filled with tears. "Oh, Da, it was awful! Dennis was scared and des-perate. 'Help me,' he said, and held out his hands to me. 'Please help me.' "

Frank Mulcahey sucked in his breath

sharply and made a rapid sign of the cross. "Jesus, Mary and Joseph! What did he mean?"

"He didn't mean anything," Megan put in quickly. "She was dreaming. Deirdre, it was just a nightmare. It must have been."

"But it wasn't!" Deirdre insisted, gazing at her sister with wide, guileless eyes. "Dennis was here. He was as clear to me as you are. He stood right there and looked at me with such pain and despair. I couldn't be mistaken."

"But, darling . . ."

Her younger sister gave her a look of mingled reproach and pity. "Don't you think I know the difference between a nightmare and a vision? I've had both of them often enough."

"Of course you have," their father responded, and turned to glower at Megan. "Just because there are things you cannot see or hear, it doesn't mean they don't exist. Why, I could tell you tales that would make your hair stand on end."

"Yes, and you have on many occasions," Megan responded, her tart tone of voice softened by the smile she directed at her father.

Frank Mulcahey was a short, wiry man, full of energy and a love of life. At the age

11

of fifteen, he had come to New York from his native Ireland, and he was always ready to tell anyone who would listen how his dreams had all come true in America. He had built a thriving business as a green-grocer, married a beautiful blond American girl and raised a family of healthy, happy children. Only those who knew him well knew of the hardships he had endured — the years of working and scrimping to open his grocery, the death of his beloved wife shortly after Deirdre's birth, the hard task of raising six children on his own and, finally, the death of his oldest son ten years ago. Many another man would have broken under the blows of fate, but Frank Mulcahey had absorbed them and moved on, his spirit wounded but never vanquished.

In coloring he resembled his daughter Megan; his close-cropped hair was the same warm reddish brown, though now liberally streaked through with gray, and if he had allowed it to grow longer, it would have curled just as riotously. The line of freckles across Megan's nose came from her father, too, and her eyes were the same mahogany color, their brown depths warmed by an elusive hint of red. They were alike, too, in their drive and determination — and, as Deirdre had pointed out more than once, in their sheer bullheadedness, a fact that had caused them to clash on many occasions.

"Clearly you did not listen to the tales well enough," Frank told Megan now. "Or you did not keep an open mind."

Megan knew she would never convince her father of the unlikelihood of her brother returning from the grave, so she tried a different tack. "Why would Dennis come back now? How could he need our help?"

"Why, that's clear as a bell," her father responded. "He's asking us to avenge his death."

"After ten years?"

"Sure, and he's waited long enough, don't you think?" Frank retorted, his Irish brogue thickening in his agitation. "It's me own fault. I should have gone over there and taken care of that filthy murderin' English lord as soon as we learned what happened to Dennis. It's no wonder he's come back to nudge us. The sin is that he had to. I've shirked me duty as a father."

"Da, don't." Megan laid a comforting hand on her father's arm. "You did nothing wrong. You couldn't have gone to England when Dennis died. You had children to raise. Deirdre was but ten, and the boys only a little older. You had to stay here and work, and see after us."

Frank sighed and nodded. "I know. But there's nothing holding me back now. You're all grown now. Even the store could get by without me, with your brother Sean helping me run it. There's nothing to stop me from going to England and taking care of the matter. Hasn't been for years. It's remiss I've been, and that's a fact. No wonder Denny had to come and give me a poke."

"Da, I'm sure that's not why Dennis came back," Megan said quickly, casting a look of appeal at her sister. The last thing she wanted was for her father to go running off to England and do God-knew-what in his thirst to avenge his son's death. He could wind up in jail — or worse — if his temper led him to attack the English lord who had killed Dennis. "Is it, Deirdre?"

To Megan's dismay, her sister wrinkled her brow and said, "I'm not sure. Dennis didn't say anything about his death. But he was so distraught, so desperate. It was clear he needs our help."

"Of course he does." Frank nodded. "He wants me to avenge his murder."

"How?" Megan protested, alarmed. "You can't go over there and take the law into your own hands."

Her father looked at her. "I didna say I was going to kill the lyin' bastard — not that I wouldn't like to, you understand. But I'll not have a man's blood on my conscience. I intend to bring him to justice."

"After all this time? But, Da —"

"Are you suggesting that we stand by and do nothing?" Frank thundered, his brows rising incredulously. "Let the man get away with murdering your brother? I would not have thought it of you."

"Of course I don't think he should get away with it," Megan retorted heatedly, her eyes flashing. "I want him to pay for what he did to Dennis just as much as you do."

Her brother had been only two years older than she, and they had been very close all their lives, united not only by blood, but also by their similar personalities and their quick, impish wit. Curious, energetic and determined, each of them had wanted to make a mark upon the world. Dennis had yearned to see that world, to explore uncharted territories. Megan had her sights set on becoming a newspaper reporter.

She had achieved her dream, after much

persistence landing an assignment on a small New York City rag, writing for the Society section. Through skill, determination and hard work, she had eventually made her way onto the news pages and then to a larger paper. But it had been a bittersweet accomplishment, for Dennis had not been there to share in her joy. He had died on his first journey up the Amazon.

"Aye, I know," Frank admitted, taking his daughter's hand and squeezing it. "I spoke in heat. I know you want him punished. We all do."

"I just don't know what proof can be found, after all this time," Megan pointed out.

"There was something more," Deirdre spoke up. "Dennis was — I think he was searching for something."

Megan stared at her sister. "Searching for what?"

"I'm not sure. But it was very precious to him. He cannot rest until he has it back."

"He said that?" Again Megan felt a chill creep up her back. She did not believe that the dead came back to speak with the living. Still . . .

"He said something about having to find

them — or it. I'm not sure," Deirdre explained. "But I could feel how desperate he was, how much it meant to him."

"The man killed Dennis for some reason," their father pointed out, his voice tinged with excitement. "We never knew the why of it, but there must have been one. It would make sense, don't you think, that it was over some object, something Dennis had that he wanted?"

"And he killed Dennis to get it?" Megan asked. "But what would Dennis have had that the man couldn't have bought? He is wealthy."

"Something they found on their trip," Frank answered. "Something Dennis found."

"In the jungle?" Megan quirked an eyebrow in disbelief, but even as she said it, her mind went to the history of South America. "Wait. Of course. What did the Spanish find there? Gold. Emeralds. Dennis could have stumbled on an old mine — or wherever it is you get jewels."

"Of course." Frank's eyes gleamed with fervor. "It's something like that. And if I can find whatever it is that he found and that murderer stole, it could prove that he killed Dennis. I have to go to England."

Megan stood up. Her father's excitement

had ignited her own. For ten years she had lived with the sorrow of her brother's death, as well as the bitter knowledge that his murderer had gotten away. Part of her passion as a journalist had come from her thwarted desire for justice for her brother. She had known she could not help him, but she could help others whose lives had been shattered or whose rights as human beings had been trampled. Among her peers, she was known as a crusader, and she was at her best in ferreting out a story of corruption or injustice.

She could not entirely believe that her sister had seen their brother. But her father's words made sense. The man who had killed Dennis must have had a motive . . . and greed had always been a prime motive for murder.

"You're right," she said. "But I should be the one to go." She began to pace, her words tumbling out excitedly. "I don't know why I never thought of this before. I could investigate Dennis's death, just like I do a story. I mean, that's what I do every day — look into things, talk to people, check facts, hunt down witnesses. I should have done this long ago. Maybe I can figure out what really happened. Even after all these years, there must be something I can find. Even if it's something that wouldn't stand up in a court of law, at least we'd have the satisfaction of knowing."

"But, Megan, it's dangerous," her sister protested. "I mean, the man has murdered already. If you show up there asking questions . . ."

"I'm not going to just walk up to him and say, 'Why did you kill my brother?'" Megan retorted. "He won't know who I am. I'll think of some other reason to talk to him. Don't worry, I'm good at that."

"She's right," their father said, and his daughters turned to him in astonishment. He shrugged. "I'm a man of reason. Megan has experience in this sort of matter. But," he added with a stern look at Megan, "if you think I'm going to let you run off and track down a murderer alone, then you haven't the brains I credit you with. I'm going, too."

"But, Da —"

He shook his head. "I mean it, Megan. We're all going. We'll track down Theo Moreland and make him pay for killing your brother."

1

Theo Moreland, Lord Raine, rested his hands on the railing and gazed down at the grand ballroom below, a look of discontent upon his handsome face. His green eyes, fringed by smoky lashes so long and thick they would have looked feminine on any face less ruggedly masculine, moved lazily across the floor below, crowded with dancers.

He wondered, not for the first time this evening, what he was doing here.

He was not the sort for elegant parties. He liked much more to be out-of-doors, preferably in some exotic locale, doing something more intriguing . . . and possibly dangerous.

Of course, Lady Rutherford's ball was dangerous in its own way — ambitious mothers and their daughters circling like sharks — but it was the kind of danger that he assiduously avoided. He wasn't sure why he had come here this evening. He had simply been bored and restless, as he had been many times lately, so much so that at last he had flipped through his stack of invitations, usually ignored, and settled on Lady Rutherford's party.

Once he got here, he had regretted the impulse. Besieged by flirtatious women of all ages, he had finally retreated upstairs to the card room. That, too, had paled, and he'd wound up here, gazing down moodily at the wide expanse of floor below.

"Lord Raine, what a surprise," a sultry voice behind him said.

Suppressing a groan, Theo turned. "Lady Scarle."

The woman before him was one of the beauties of London and had been for years. Her coloring was vivid, with jet black hair and deep blue eyes, and a strawberries-and-cream complexion. If the color in her cheeks was not entirely natural or a stray white hair or two had to be plucked out whenever they appeared, well, only her personal maid knew about it, and she was paid well to keep secrets. Most men, truth be known, found it difficult to lift their eyes above Lady Scarle's magnificent white bosom, which was, as was customary, spilling out lushly over the low neckline of her purple evening gown.

"Now, now," she said, smiling archly and laying a hand on Theo's arm. "I think that we know each other well enough for you to call me Helena."

Theo shifted uncomfortably and gave her a vague smile. He had never been good at dealing with rapacious females, and he found women like Lady Scarle even more unnerving than giggling young debutantes.

When he had left London on his last expedition, Lady Helena Scarle had been married to doddering old Lord Scarle, and while she had flirted with Theo, she had been interested in nothing more than a light affair, which he had avoided with little problem.

But when he'd returned a few months ago, he found that Lord Scarle had died, leaving the lady a widow. And the widow was interested in finding a new husband — as long as it meant moving up the social or economic scale. Unfortunately for Theo, he fit both requirements.

Lady Scarle had been on the hunt for him ever since.

"I was very disappointed not to see you at Lady Huntington's musicale last night," Lady Helena went on silkily.

"Mmm. Not my sort of thing," he replied, looking about, hoping to see some means of getting out of the situation without seeming rude. Lady Scarle, he had found out, was impervious to almost anything short of rudeness.

"Nor mine," she replied with a flirtatious glance. "But I had thought . . . well, when we talked last week, we discussed whether we might run into one another at the musicale."

"We did?" Theo blurted out, surprised. He did remember running into Lady Scarle when he was out riding in the Park one day last week. She had chattered on for some time before he could get away, but he had not really been listening to what she said. "I mean, well, I must have forgotten. I apologize."

Temper flashed in her blue eyes — she was not used to being forgotten by any man — but she hid it quickly, turning her eyes down and looking up at him beguilingly through her lashes. "Now you have wounded me, Raine. You must make amends by coming to my rout on Tuesday."

"I . . . um . . . I'm almost certain I have an engagement that day. My, uh . . . Kyria!" He spotted his sister walking across the room, and he waved to her.

Kyria, taking in the situation in a glance, grinned and walked over to him. "Theo! What a pleasant surprise. And Lady Scarle." Kyria's gaze swept over the other woman's overexposed chest. "My goodness, you must be chilled. Would you like to borrow my wrap?"

Lady Scarle gave her a stiff smile. "Thank you, I am perfectly warm, Lady Kyria. Or should I say Mrs. McIntyre?"

"Either is all right," Kyria responded calmly. Tall, flame-haired and green-eyed, Kyria was easily the most beautiful woman in the house. She had reigned as the leading beauty of London society since her coming out, earning the appellation "The Goddess" for her beauty and cool confidence. Even now, approaching the age of thirty and a wife and mother, there was no one who could match her.

Lady Scarle, several years older than Kyria, had been married by the time Kyria had made her debut, but it had put her nose out of joint to watch Kyria assume all the acclaim she had once held. The two women had never been friendly.

"Theo." Kyria turned to her brother and linked her hand possessively through his arm. "I had been wondering what had happened to you. I believe I promised my next dance to you."

"Yes." Theo brightened. "Yes, you did." He turned to the other woman and bowed. "Lady Scarle, if you will excuse us . . ."

Lady Scarle had little choice but to smile and murmur, "Of course."

Quickly Theo swept Kyria away down the stairs. She leaned closer to him and murmured, "Now you owe me."

"I am well aware of that. I didn't know what I was going to do. I was trying to wriggle out of going to some rout of hers next week. I cannot think what possessed me to come here tonight," he added feelingly.

Kyria laughed. "It isn't like you. I was very surprised to see you."

Theo shrugged. "I was bored, I think. I'm not sure what's the matter with me lately. I've felt . . . restless, I suppose."

"Ready to go off on one of your adventures?" Kyria guessed.

Theo, the eldest son of the Duke of Broughton, had spent most of his adult life exploring the globe. He had always been fascinated with new and exotic locales, and the physical work and even danger that his explorations entailed only added spice to his trips, as far as he was concerned.

He had returned only a few months ago

from his last trip, which had been to India and Burma. Usually he rested and recuperated, spending time with his much-loved family, for a while, before he began to itch to travel again.

"I don't know." He frowned. "Edward Horn is setting up a trip to the Congo. He wants me to go."

"But it doesn't sound as if you want to."

"Not really," Theo replied, puzzlement settling on his features. "I told Horn not to count on me. It's very strange. I've been feeling so restless, yet I don't really have the urge to travel anywhere, either. Perhaps I am getting too old for it."

"Oh, yes . . . the grand old age of thirty-four," Kyria teased. "You are quite decrepit, really."

"You know what I mean. Everyone has always told me that someday I would grow up and tire of travel. Maybe I have." He gave her a crooked smile. "All I know is that every time I think of leaving, something holds me back."

Kyria studied her brother's face, her puzzlement turning to concern. "Theo . . . are you all right? You sound almost . . . unhappy."

It was not an adjective she was accustomed to using to describe her brother, who had always entered into everything he did with great zest.

Theo looked at her, his expression serious. "You know me, Kyria. I'm not the sort to examine my life. I don't sit about thinking about what I'm doing, or whether or not I'm enjoying myself. I don't brood."

"No. You are more one to charge into things. You generally know what you want and go after it."

He nodded. "Which is why I think I'm so at loose ends. I feel as if there is something missing. But I don't know what it is. Something I should be doing? Some place I should go? I only know I want something else, something more."

Kyria thought for a moment, then began hesitantly. "Well, perhaps, have you thought that you are at an age where you want to settle down? Mayhap what you are missing is a wife — a home and family."

Theo let out a low groan. "That is certainly what they would all like to convince me of," he said, jerking his head toward the mothers and chaperones massed along the wall, watching their charges dance. "I think I have been introduced to every mother of an eligible girl tonight. I can't tell you how many have hinted that it's time for me to settle down. It's enough to make me run for cover. Are they always this voracious?"

Kyria chuckled, nodding. "Yes. There is nothing more dangerous than a mother out to make a good match for her daughter."

"Aren't these the very same women who have long complained that I am lacking in a proper sense of duty and consequence — always off gallivanting about the globe instead of staying here and preparing to take over the title? The ones who call us the 'mad Morelands'?"

"Yes. But surely you must know that it does not matter how mad one is if one is going to be a duke someday. A title makes up for a great number of sins, and the higher the title, the more sins it obviates. And if you possess a great deal of wealth in addition, well, you could have two heads, and it wouldn't matter."

"What a cynic you are."

"Only truthful."

"It isn't that I am against marriage," Theo mused. "It is simply . . . well, I cannot envision tying myself to any of these girls, even one as lovely as Estelle Hopewell."

"Estelle Hopewell! Good heavens, I should hope not. The girl hasn't a thought in her head."

"Do any of them? Perhaps it is just being under the watchful eye of their mamas, but every girl I spoke to tonight could do nothing but smile and agree with whatever I said. None of them seemed to have the slightest opinion of her own or the least interest in the world. And then there are eager widows like Lady Scarle, who frankly frightens me. Can you imagine any of them as part of our family?"

Kyria laughed. "Good Lord, no. Perhaps you need to find a country girl, as Reed did."

He smiled. "I think Anna is rare, even in the country."

"Yes. You are right. But I still hold hope for you," Kyria told him. "I have seen one brother find a wonderful woman for a wife. I have the utmost confidence that you will be able to, as well. Just think, four of us 'mad Morelands' have managed to find our loves. Your day will come."

"Will it?" A faint smile crossed Theo's lips. "Perhaps you are right. Perhaps what I am waiting for is the perfect woman. But for now, I'll just have to settle for a dance with the most beautiful woman in London."

And with those words, he swept his sister out onto the floor.

★ ★ ★

Megan Mulcahey stood at the window of the bedroom she shared with her sister Deirdre in the house her family had rented in London. With a sigh, she leaned her head against the cool pane of glass. It had taken her a month to get here, but now she wasn't sure what to do.

No matter how hard she had tried, she had been unable to dissuade her father and sister from accompanying her to England. She would have preferred to investigate this matter by herself, without having to worry about them.

However, Frank Mulcahey had had an answering argument for every objection she raised. Her younger brothers, Sean and Robert, were quite capable of taking over the store, so his presence was not needed there. And she would need his help. Women rarely traveled alone, he pointed out; the entire journey would go more smoothly if she had a male escort. Moreover, there might be places where a woman could not even enter. Both those things were true, Megan knew, much as she hated to admit it. And she had no argument against his major point, which was that he had a right to be involved in bringing his son's killer to justice.

Deirdre, despite her usually biddable nature and her general air of fragility that made everyone want to take care of her, had been just as stubborn. She had every bit as much reason as Megan to see their brother's killer brought to justice, she reminded her sister, and she was, after all, the one to whom Dennis had come in a vision.

"Besides," Deirdre had concluded, "if I don't go with you, who'll do the cooking and cleaning for you and Da?"

That had been a telling argument. Megan had never been one who liked doing domestic chores, and she had been quite content with their family arrangement for the last few years, in which she had gone out and worked each day as their father did, and Deirdre had taken over the household chores for the three of them.

Megan had expected her oldest sister, Mary Margaret, to agree with her that Frank and Deirdre should not go. The eldest of the Mulcahey children, Mary Margaret had helped their father raise all the younger children from the time she was twelve, and had always been the most responsible and levelheaded member of the family. Now married to a prosperous attorney and with three children of her own,

Mary Margaret was the very picture of a conservative matron.

Much to Megan's shock, Mary Margaret had agreed that Deirdre and their father should accompany Megan — or, as she put it, "go along to keep Megan out of trouble" — and had even offered to help pay for the trip.

So, finally, Megan had boarded the steamship to Southhampton with her father and Deirdre, and the three of them had arrived in London a few days ago. They had spent the first two days there finding a house and settling in. It had taken Megan another day to obtain Theo Moreland's address — something that would have taken less time if they had known his father's titled name.

This afternoon she had gone out to take a look at the house, just to get a sense of what she was facing. It was an imposing edifice, taking up all of a small city block, visible proof of the wealth and importance of the duke's family, as well as of their longevity. They had been dukes since long before Europeans settled the New World, and they had been earls for a couple of hundred years before that. The house itself looked as if it might have been standing there since New York had been New Amsterdam.

However, far from being overwhelmed by the imposing house, Megan was perversely roused to an even greater determination to take down the duke's son. She had taken on New York slumlords and powerful factory owners; she wasn't about to retreat just because this family had a longer history than the others she had gone up against.

However, it did cause her to wonder how in the world she was going to get inside the mansion to investigate Theo Moreland.

Megan turned away from the window and walked over to the small dresser. Opening the top drawer, she reached inside it and pulled out a small pink case. It was her box of treasures, a childish pink music box with a rose on top and a little ballerina rising out of the middle of the rose. Once the ballerina had danced when the top was opened, but the mechanism that propelled her had long since died. Still, Megan had kept the box, treasuring it as a link to her mother, who had died when Megan was only seven years old.

She reached inside the box and pulled out a small piece of smooth glass. Although cylindrical in shape, it was not perfectly round, but had several flat, smooth sides.

Megan had never known exactly what it was. She had found it one day years ago — it had been, in fact, not long after Dennis had died, when she had been filled with sorrow. While cleaning her room, she had stumbled across this piece of glass in the dusty area beneath her bed. Pulling it out, she had held it up to the light. It was clear glass, a prism, she thought, with the flat sides, and shot through the middle were tiny strands of silver. She had no idea how it had gotten there; she had never seen it before, and Deirdre, who had slept in the same bedroom with her at that time, had denied all knowledge of it.

Megan had stuck it in her pocket, and had carried it with her, changing it from dress to dress. It had become something of a lucky charm for her. She had found it soothing to rub the flat sides as she thought or worried about something, as she had been in the habit of doing before with the religious medal she had worn much of her life.

That, an oval silver medallion with the raised portrait of the Virgin on it, had been a present from her mother on the occasion of Megan's first communion, and it was all the more precious to her because her mother had died not long afterward. Megan had worn it always, putting it onto a longer chain as she grew older.

But a few weeks before she found the glass cylinder, she had lost the medallion. She was not sure what had happened to it. She had searched high and low, all over the house and even outside on the sidewalk and in her father's grocery, but she had finally given up. The chain, she thought, must have broken, and it had slipped off without her even noticing. The odd piece of glass had seemed, somehow, a replacement.

Though Megan no longer carried the good luck charm with her, she had not wanted to leave it behind, despite the limited space in their trunks. In facing Theo Moreland, she thought, she would need all the luck she could get.

Absently, she rubbed the piece of glass for a moment, then shook off her thoughts, and put it away. She left the room and ran lightly down the stairs to find her sister.

Deirdre was sitting at the kitchen table, peeling potatoes for their supper that evening, and she smiled at Megan's entrance. Megan sat down, and took up a knife and a potato to help her sister.

"Did you go to see Broughton House this afternoon?" Deirdre asked.

"Aye, I did, and it's as grand as you might imagine."

"Have you ever wondered about him?" Deirdre asked. "Theo Moreland, I mean."

"Wondered? Wondered what?"

"You know, what he's like. How he looks."

"Oh, I can imagine that perfectly," Megan responded. "He has English coloring, of course — blond hair and pale, lifeless skin — and doubtless a weak chin. He'll have that supercilious expression, as if he looks down on the rest of the world with all the arrogance and contempt of a man who's going to be the Duke of Broughton someday. His eyes are probably a cold blue."

"Do you think he feels guilty over what he did to Dennis?"

Megan shrugged. "I don't know. All I care about is that I make sure he pays for it till his dying day."

"What are you going to do? I mean, how are you going to find out what happened? How are you going to prove it?" Deirdre asked.

"Well, it's essential that I interview the other Englishmen who were there. Mr.

Barchester, of course, and the other one. Julian Coffey."

Their brother had set sail ten years ago on an expedition to the Amazon led by an American explorer named Griswold Eberhart. In the only letter they had received from Dennis after he left, he had told them that all the other men on the expedition had either fallen ill or given up by the time they had started up the Amazon, leaving only him and Captain Eberhart. Dennis had been exuberant, however, about their good fortune in coming upon a group from England, similarly depleted, with whom they had decided to join forces.

The English party had consisted of three men: Andrew Barchester, Julian Coffey and Theo Moreland. All of them were "excellent men," he had written, especially Theo Moreland, who was only four years older than he and, according to Dennis, "great good fun."

Some months later, Frank Mulcahey had received a short, formal note from Theo Moreland informing him of his son's death and extending his sympathies. But it had been Andrew Barchester who had written to give them a longer account of Dennis's death, revealing the unexpected news that Dennis had died at the hands of Theo Moreland himself.

"What he told Da wasn't very specific," Megan said now.

Deirdre nodded. "It's been ten years, too. Da's bound to have forgotten some things."

"Unfortunately, I imagine Mr. Barchester probably has, too. Still, I have to talk to him."

"What about Moreland?" Deirdre asked. "Are you going to question him?"

"I doubt he would even talk to me. He lives in a grand house, with a footman. I'm sure some unknown woman would not get past the door."

"I've known you to lurk about until someone you want to interview comes outside and then accost him as he's getting into his carriage," Deirdre reminded her, her eyes twinkling.

Megan grinned, a dimple deepening in her cheek and her eyes glowing with mischief as she agreed, " 'Tis true I'm not shy about throwing myself in his path. But for the moment, at least, I think it's better not to do so. He'll not admit that he killed a man. I need to use subterfuge here. I have to get inside his house and spy on him. If he took something from Dennis, as Da suspects, it's most likely that he has it in that house. If I can track it down, it will give me proof — and will be something I can use as leverage. If I'm lucky, I'll trick it out of him in some way."

"How?"

Megan shrugged. "A number of men are talkative when they're in their cups. I remember one fellow at Tammany Hall who let out quite a few secrets. He was a regular drinker at O'Reilly's Tavern, and I was able to get hired on as a tavern maid."

Deirdre shook her head in rueful admiration. "I remember the fit Da threw when he found out how you'd gotten that story."

"You'd think I had taken up walking the streets, the way he carried on. I did nothing but serve drinks — and I showed no more bosom than many an evening gown I've seen on an elegant lady."

"I don't know how you have the nerve. I'd have died of embarrassment — not to mention being too scared to go in the door. Weren't the men forward? Even, well, forceful?"

Megan shrugged. "Nothing I couldn't handle. It helped having been around newspapermen for several years."

Megan had had to fight for respect in her field — indeed, she had had to fight for everything she had gotten in her profession, from her first chance to write a story to her present job. She had known from the first that she could never reveal any weakness or others would seize upon it as proof that women were not competent to be reporters.

She had never told Deirdre about many of her experiences, knowing that they would have frightened her delicate sister — enough that Deirdre might even tell their father about them. And while Frank Mulcahey had been proud of her and ready to fight any man who dared suggest that his girl wasn't as good a reporter as anyone, he had also bombarded her with constant worries and warnings about her safety. If he had heard about some of her more dangerous exploits, she wouldn't have put it past him to come storming down to the newspaper to have it out with the editor for putting her in harm's way.

"But that sort of thing won't work this time," Megan told her sister now. "I have no idea what tavern Theo Moreland frequents — if he even goes to any place so plebeian. He probably drinks at some gentleman's club, with no women allowed inside. What I really need is to get inside the house. So I'm going to apply for a position as a servant there."

Deirdre dropped the potato she had been peeling and stared at her sister, then burst into a merry peal of laughter.

"What's so funny?" Megan asked indignantly. "It's a perfectly good idea."

"You? As a maid? Or maybe a cook?" Deirdre said after a moment, when she finally paused in her laughter and wiped away the tears her laughter had brought. "I should like to see that."

"You think I couldn't clean or cook?" Megan asked, putting her fists on her hips. "It's not as if I haven't done such things. I cooked and cleaned enough when you were growing up."

Deirdre tried, not entirely successfully, to compress her lips into a straight line. "Perhaps — when Mary Margaret was cracking the whip. But that has been years."

"I haven't forgotten how. I'm sitting here paring potatoes, aren't I?"

"Yes. But look at the pile of peelings in front of you." Deirdre gestured toward the newspaper spread on the table between them. In front of Megan, there was a handful of peelings. Across the table, before Deirdre, lay a mound three times that size.

"You started before I did," Megan

pointed out. At her sister's look, she went on, "Oh, all right, I'm not as fast as you. But they won't know that."

"You'd be fired in two days. For answering back, if nothing else. I know you, Megan Mulcahey, and taking orders won't sit well with you."

"You're right about that. But I will simply have to accept it. I don't see any other way to get into the house. Cleaning rooms will give me a perfect opportunity to look for something that Moreland might have stolen from Dennis." She paused and looked at her sister a little tentatively. "Umm, I wonder — about those things that Dennis, uh, was looking for . . ."

Deirdre sighed. "No, I don't know anything more about them. I haven't heard or seen anything from Dennis since that night. I have no idea what he wants back so badly." She paused, then went on, "I know you don't really believe that Dennis came to me."

"I don't think you're fibbing," Megan assured her hastily. "I know you believe Dennis appeared to you — in actuality or a dream or something. I just find it — well, it's —"

"I know. It's much too otherworldly for you. You believe in tangible things, and there's nothing wrong with that. You deal in facts, in the practical world. I know that. But, Megan . . ." Deirdre leaned forward, her brow wrinkled earnestly. "I'm not crazy."

"Deirdre, I never meant . . . !" Megan cried, reaching her hand to her sister.

"No, I know you don't think I'm insane. But there would be those who did if they knew some of the things I've seen and heard. But I know what I saw. It was Dennis, and he spoke to me — whether he was right there in the room with me or in a dream, I'm not entirely sure. But I know it was he, and I know he was desperate. He wants whatever was taken from him. It means a great deal to him. And he came to us for help."

"I don't know what to think," Megan told her honestly. " 'Tis hard for me to believe in such things, but I know you are neither crazy nor a liar, and as long as there is any chance that Dennis did come back from the grave, asking for our help, I shall strive to do what he wants. And I'll take any help you can give me, even if it does come to you in a dream."

"I only wish I *could* help you." Deirdre sighed. "I wish this sort of thing was not always so uncertain. Every night when I go to bed, I pray that I will hear from him again. That he will tell us how to help him."

Megan hardly knew how to respond to her sister.

Deirdre's unquestioning faith in her visions amazed her and left her feeling, frankly, a little envious. It must be comforting, she thought, to be without doubt or questions. It was not a state, she feared, that she would ever be in. Her entire life was built upon questions, it seemed.

They continued to talk as they finished peeling the potatoes, and afterward Deirdre put the potatoes on to boil and checked the roast in the oven as she continued to put the evening meal together. Megan went upstairs to wash up before supper, then sat down to record her notes about Broughton House in a small notebook.

It was her custom on any story to keep notes this way. It helped her to plan her actions, she found, as well as think about the story in depth, and it also kept her quotes as accurate as possible. Over the course of the years, it had become an ingrained habit.

She only wished she had more facts to go on.

Finally she went downstairs to supper,

finding, to her surprise, that her father had not come home yet. After waiting for him for some time, she and Deirdre sat down to eat, glancing now and again at the clock in the dining room, then at each other, their worry palpable.

He still had not arrived by the time they were through with their meal, and Megan helped Deirdre wash and dry the dishes as they talked, their vague concern growing.

It was with a great deal of relief that they heard the front door open a few minutes later, and then their father strolled in, whistling a tune.

"Good evenin' to you," Frank Mulcahey said, grinning and taking off his cap.

"Where have you been?" Megan asked. "We've been worried about you."

"Worried? No need for that. I've been out investigating."

"Investigating?" Megan cocked an eyebrow at her father as he drew closer, though she could not suppress a smile. "Is that what you call it?" She made a show of sniffing the air. "Smells more like ale to me."

"Aye, well, that was where I was investigating," he replied. "Is there a bite of supper left for your poor old da? I'm famished."

"So you've been investigating a tavern?" Megan asked teasingly as they sat down at the kitchen table and Deirdre took out the food from the oven, where she had been keeping it warm for their father.

"Nay, but that's where I made me inquiries." Frank winked at his daughter, looking pleased with himself.

Megan straightened, intrigued. "What do you mean? What inquiries?"

"I've been thinking about how you're to get inside that great house to expose the villain." He shook his head. "I went to see it, and it's an imposing looking place."

"You're right about that," Megan agreed. "I was telling Deirdre that I think my best chance is to get hired on there as a servant. It's such a grand house, they must need a lot of servants. I would think there are openings pretty often."

"And I told her she wouldn't last a week," Deirdre put in, sitting down across from Megan and their father.

Megan grimaced. "I could manage."

"That's if they'd even hire you in the first place. You don't look like a servant. You're much too attractive for one thing, and you haven't a servant's demeanor," Deirdre went on.

"I can put on an act," Megan said. "I'll

46

wear the drabbest dress I have."

"Ah, but nothin' can hide those sparkling eyes of yours," her father said, reaching out to pat her cheek fondly. "Don't worry, lass, I've a better idea for you."

"What?" Megan and Deirdre chorused.

"Well, I went to all the taverns last night that were close to Broughton House, and again this afternoon, and it happens I hit gold this afternoon. There's a footman from the place comes in for a wee nip every evening if he gets the chance to slip away. Name's Paul, and our Paul's an informative lad."

"Really? What did you find out?" Megan leaned forward.

"First of all, I found out that Lord Raine is in residence at Broughton House."

"Lord Raine? Who's that?"

"Seems that's Himself."

"I thought his name was Moreland," Megan said.

"Aye, well, 'tis, except it seems he gets a title, see, because he's next in line to be the Duke of Broughton. While his da's alive, he's another sort of lord. The Marquess of Raine. Don't ask me to explain it. It took me a bit even to figure out that our Paul was talkin' about the very villain I was interested in. Anyway, he's at home, which is our good luck — for I'll tell you, girl, I was worried we might get here and find that he was off in Timbuktu or some such place."

"Yes, it concerned me somewhat, too."

"But according to the gossip, the man's not looking to go off on one of his adventures for a few months yet."

"That's good."

"Even better is what else he told me. Seems they're in terrible need of a tutor for two of the boys of the family."

"A teacher?" Megan looked at him, puzzled. "Da! Are you saying I should go there as a tutor? You can't be serious!"

"Why not? You've a much better chance of convincing them you're a teacher than a scrub maid."

"You were always first in your class," Deirdre pointed out, adding, "Well, I mean, your grades were. It was just because you kept getting in trouble with the nuns that kept you from taking honors."

"Aye, and you went to the best convent school in New York," Frank added. "You learned Latin and history and all those high muckety-muck writers you're always quoting, didn't ye? All you need is enough to get by for a few weeks. 'Tisn't as if ye're actually going to *be* a teacher."

"Yes, but — I don't have any training, any experience. No qualifications, in short. They won't accept me."

Her father waved away her objections. "Easy enough to make up, now, aren't they, when all your references are thousands of miles away in America? It'd take weeks to get a reply from any name you put down. And they can't wait. They need someone now."

"But even if I made up the grandest qualifications for myself, why would they hire an American? There must be plenty of Englishwomen who would take the job — and who would have references right here in London."

Mulcahey grinned. "Seems they've already run through most of the lot. Got a certain reputation, these lads have."

Megan looked at him doubtfully. "What are you saying? They're such hellions they've frightened off all their other governesses?"

"Governesses, then tutors when they got too old for governesses."

"Too old? How old are they?"

Frank shrugged. "Old enough that Paul was saying any other family'd send 'em off to Eton soon, but the Morelands are an odd lot. I think they must be twelve or thirteen."

"Thirteen-year-old hellions? What am I supposed to do with them?"

"Ah, you'll have no trouble. You're no prissy Englishwoman. You grew up with boys. Just handle 'em like you did Sean and Robert — give 'em a good knock on the head when they get too rowdy."

"Da . . . they're English aristocrats. You can't just go knocking their heads together when you feel like it."

"Come, now, Megan. I'd back you against a couple of spoiled adolescents any day. You'll do just fine."

"They wouldn't hire a woman to teach their precious sons," Megan argued. "Not when the boys are that old."

"I'm tellin' you, they're desperate. Besides, it appears that the Duchess is an odd one. A free thinker, according to Paul. Believes in women's suffrage. Equality of the sexes and all that."

Megan cast her father a disbelieving look. "A Duchess? Da, I think this fellow was pulling your leg."

"Well, only one way to find out, isn't there?" Mulcahey smiled at his daughter challengingly.

Never one to ignore a dare when she saw it, Megan squared her shoulders.

"True. Well, I had best get to bed, hadn't I, if I'm going to be interviewing for a position as a tutor tomorrow?"

2

Megan arrived at Broughton House early in the afternoon the following day. When she reached the bottom of the steps leading up to the front door, she hesitated for a moment, gazing up at the grand edifice. Her stomach was a knot of nerves. Soon she would meet the man whom she had hated for ten years. All her grief, all her regret had been channeled into fury, and the fact that the villain had gotten away had only served to increase that anger. Megan wasn't sure how she would be able to face Moreland without revealing how much she despised him. It was going to take every bit of skill she had.

She clasped her hands together, pushing up her gloves in a nervous gesture. She would never have admitted it to anyone, least of all her father, but she could not help but be a trifle intimidated by the task ahead of her. She had bluffed her way through many a situation in search of a story, but no story had ever been as important to her as this one, and never had she felt so afraid of failing. She could not help but think that the duchess was going to take one look at her and send her packing.

She tugged down her dark blue jacket, quite plain except for its rather large silver buttons. She hoped it would be sober enough to make up for the small straw bonnet perched atop her head, which, with the brim curling jauntily to one side and the cunning cluster of cherries pinned there, was really too stylish for a tutor. Megan had a weakness for hats, and, frankly, she did not possess one that was dowdy enough to suit a governess. Standing here now, she wished that she had gone to a millinery this morning and bought the plainest dark bonnet she could find.

It was too late to do anything else now, she told herself, and, quelling the sudden flutter of nerves in her stomach, she reached up and brought down the heavy brass door knocker.

A moment later, a footman opened the door.

"May I help you?"

"I am here to see the Duchess of Broughton," Megan said calmly, looking the man squarely in the eyes.

Once she began, as always, her nervousness receded, turning into a sort of low-level hum that kept her alert and ready for anything.

She saw the footman sweep her with a quick, assessing glance, taking in everything about her and no doubt classifying her immediately as to social status, dress and country of origin.

"May I ask if you have an appointment?"

"Yes," Megan lied. She had always found it best to go on the offensive. Boldness generally won the day. "I am here concerning the tutoring position."

The man's expression changed from aloof and faintly forbidding to almost eager. "Yes, of course. Let me see if her grace is ready to receive you."

He stepped back, and Megan entered the house. She found herself in a large formal entryway. It was floored in marble, and across from her, elegant stairs rose to the second floor. A hallway stretched in either direction, with another leading toward the rear of the house.

"If you will be so kind as to give me your name?" The footman said politely, directing Megan toward a low velvet-cushioned bench that stood beneath an enormous gold-framed mirror.

"Miss Megan Henderson," Megan responded. She had decided that it would be too risky to use her real last name, as there was a chance that Moreland would connect it with the man he had known ten years earlier.

"Very good, Miss Henderson." The man turned to go, and just then a shriek echoed from down one of the hallways.

Both Megan and the footman turned toward the sound. As they watched, a young woman ran out of one of the doorways, followed a fraction of a second later by another, older, woman. Both were richly dressed — rather overdressed, to Megan's sense of taste — with intricately coiffed hair, and there was about them a tangible air of privilege and wealth.

That appearance was somewhat spoiled at the moment by the fact that both women were emitting high, piercing squeals, holding up their skirts and almost dancing about as they peered down at the floor around them.

Megan stared, and the footman let out a groan. As they stood watching, a number of small furry creatures scurried out of the doorway behind the women and raced off down the hall toward the front door, followed an instant later by two adolescent boys and a dog.

The women's shrieks grew louder and higher, if that was possible, and they ran and jumped up onto benches on either side of the hallway. The mice, obviously the object of all the hysteria, scampered along the elegant marble hallway, darting behind vases and under tables in their dash toward freedom.

The dog added to the noise, barking excitedly and jumping up to snap at the enticing ruffles on one of the women's skirts, then darting after the fleeing mice, then whirling back to leap again at the ruffles, which were fluttering as the woman jittered agitatedly atop the bench.

One of the boys dived under a narrow hallway table to grab one of the mice and knocked against one of the legs. The vase of flowers on top of the table wobbled and overturned with a crash, spilling blossoms and water. The boy let go of his quarry and whirled around, reaching out just in the nick of time to catch the vase as it rolled off the table. He let out a whoop of joy at this feat and jumped up, setting the vase back on the table and rejoining the chase.

As Megan watched in fascination, the

footman hurried into the fray, grabbing the frantically barking dog and pulling him away from the offending ruffles. The women, she thought, were abysmally silly; their screeching and dancing about were only serving to excite the dog even more.

"Hush, Rufus! Down!" the footman shouted.

His words seemed to have no effect on the dog, who whirled around, breaking the man's hold on his collar, and ran after the boys, barking like mad. His long tail caught a tall, slender vase standing on the floor as he passed, and it toppled over. At that, a wail went up from the footman, and he rushed to the vase to examine it.

Megan reached up to her hat, untying it and whipping it from her head. As the tiny mice ran toward her, she squatted down, putting her hat on the floor in front of her like a scoop, and quickly swept up several of the mice as they tumbled into it.

She folded the edges of the bonnet together, trapping the squealing, squirming mice inside. Turning toward the dog, now barking and jumping and whirling in delirious circles in front of her, she raised her voice, saying in a sharp, firm tone, "No! Rufus! Down!"

The note of command in her tone

reached the dog, and, amazingly, he stopped whirling and barking. Instead, tail wagging and tongue lolling out of his mouth in a foolish doggy grin, he gazed up at Megan.

"Good boy," she told him. "Sit." She pointed down at the floor.

Rufus promptly sat, and Megan reached down with her free hand and scratched the dog behind the ears. "Good boy, Rufus."

"That's wizard!" one of the boys said, sliding to a stop beside the dog. He held a box in one hand, and from the scrabbling noises issuing from it, Megan assumed that it held some of the mice. "Rufus did exactly as you said. He hardly ever does that."

The other boy let out a cry of triumph, pouncing on a mouse that had just emerged from the fringe encircling a gold settee. Sticking the little animal in one of the pockets of his jacket, he trotted up to join his brother.

Megan looked at the boys. These must be the charges who had run off almost every tutor in the city. They didn't look, she thought, like such monsters.

They were twins, identical in looks, and though they were a little messy — their black hair tousled, a smudge of dirt across one's forehead, the other's shirttail hanging out in back — they were undeniably handsome lads, and intelligence shone out of their green eyes. She had expected them to look arrogant and spoiled, but she saw neither of those qualities in their faces. Instead, she saw interest and an unabashed admiration for her dog-handling skills.

"It isn't that hard. It's the tone of voice one uses," Megan explained. "You see, Rufus wants to be good."

"He does?" The first twin looked surprised and glanced down at the dog.

"Yes. You just have to let him know how to do that. Praise him when he's good and let him know when he has misbehaved. A firm voice — you don't have to be loud, but he has to know you mean it." She bent over the dog, rubbing her hand back over his head. "Isn't that right, Rufus?"

The dog's tail thumped, and he leaned into her hand, gazing at her with a silly, infatuated look. With a final pat, Megan straightened up.

"I'm Alex Moreland," the twin holding the box said politely. "And this is my brother, Con."

"How do you do?" Megan extended her hand to shake each of the boys' hands. "My name is Megan M— Henderson."

"Miss Henderson. It's a pleasure to make your acquaintance," Con replied with exquisite politeness.

"Now, I believe these are yours?" She extended her other hand, still holding the bonnet edges firmly clamped together.

"Yes, miss. Thank you ever so much for catching them." Alex opened the lid of the box of mice, and Megan slid her catch into the box with the others.

Con quickly pulled another couple of mice from his pocket and smiled at her. "You didn't scream or anything. Most girls do."

He cast a contemptuous glance back down the hall, where the footman had helped the ladies down from their perch. The older of the women was now sitting on the bench, leaning back with her eyes closed, her hand to her head, moaning, while the younger woman fanned her vigorously.

"Not all girls are used to such things," Megan told him, grinning back. "I had the advantage of having three brothers, you see. But may I ask what you are doing, carrying all these mice about the house?"

"They're to feed our boa constrictor. That's where we were taking them. Would you like to see the boa?"

60

"We have a parrot, too. And a salamander and some frogs," Alex added.

"My goodness. I've never seen a boa," Megan said. "That does sound interesting."

Their words apparently reached the fainting woman, for she sat straight up with a little cry, her eyes flying open. "A snake! In this house?"

The younger girl glanced around her uneasily, and Megan wondered if she was going to climb back onto the bench. "A snake? Where?"

"He's upstairs. You needn't worry," Alex assured her.

"In a cage," Con added.

"That's horrid!" the older woman exclaimed, agitation propelling her to her feet. "Is the duchess aware of — of these wild animals?"

"They aren't wild," Con protested. "Well, I mean, I suppose they aren't tame, but they don't do anything. They're in cages. Well, the salamander and frogs are in a terrarium, but they can't get out."

"Or, at least, almost never," Alex added gravely, and Megan was certain that she saw a flash of amusement in his eyes as he spoke.

The girl let out a shriek and clapped her

hand over her mouth at Alex's words. "Almost!"

"You wicked creature!" the older woman cried, starting forward with such anger on her face that Megan instinctively moved to block her way to Alex.

Alex, however, seemed to need no help, for he squared his shoulders and came up beside Megan, as did his twin, facing the older woman's wrath.

"Someone should take you in hand!" the woman exclaimed. "You shouldn't be allowed in polite company. Bringing vermin like that into the room."

"Well, I wouldn't have if you hadn't insisted we come into the drawing room and see you," Con retorted heatedly.

"And the mice wouldn't have gotten loose if you hadn't kept on about wanting to see what was inside the box," added Alex.

"Oh!" The woman's face turned bright red. "How dare you speak to me that way?"

"I am sure that Alex and Con did not mean to be disrespectful," Megan said quickly, trying to head off further disaster. "They would never want to offend one of their mother's friends. Would you, boys?"

She cast a significant look at Alex, then at Con.

Con's chin jutted out obstinately for a moment, but then he heaved a sigh and said, "No."

"Now, I think you should apologize to these two ladies," Megan went on, giving the twins a little push at their backs, adding in a whisper to the two boys, "You wouldn't want them gossiping about how poorly your mother has raised you, would you?"

This notion seemed to have an effect on both the lads, for they were quick to step forward and give the women polite little apologies.

"Thank you, my dears," said a warm voice down the hall, and all the occupants of the hall turned to look.

At some distance behind the footman and the two visiting women stood a tall, slender woman of regal carriage. Her up-swept hair was a dark auburn, streaked at the temples with wings of white. She wore a plain blue dress, but the cut and material were clearly of the finest, and the color was a vivid reflection of the color of her eyes. She was a woman of great beauty and poise, and Megan was instantly sure that this was the Duchess of Broughton.

"Mother!" the twins exclaimed and went to her.

Megan noted that she smiled at the boys with warmth and affection, bending to give each a kiss on the cheek. Then she started down the hallway toward the rest of the group, while the twins seized the opportunity to hurry away.

"Your grace." The footman turned and bowed toward the duchess. "Lady Kempton and Miss Kempton."

The other two women turned to face the duchess, now smiling.

"Duchess. Such a pleasure to see you," Lady Kempton said, stepping forward, hand extended. "I'm sure you remember my daughter, Sarah."

"Yes, of course," the duchess replied coolly, shaking Lady Kempton's hand. "What an *unexpected* pleasure. Miss Kempton."

She looked past them toward Megan. "And to whom do I owe my thanks for bringing order out of this chaos?"

"Miss Henderson, your grace," the footman told her. "She is here about the tutor's position."

"Ah, yes, of course." The duchess smiled much more warmly than she had toward her other visitors, and she came forward to shake Megan's hand. "Miss Henderson. How nice to meet you."

"My pleasure," Megan replied, taking the duchess's hand. She was not sure how to address the woman. The footman had called her "your grace," but Megan's tongue balked at speaking such a reverential title.

The duchess turned toward the Kemptons, saying, "Please accept my regrets, Lady Kempton, but as you can see, I have a prior engagement. Had I but known you were coming, I would have arranged another time."

The other woman's face tightened, and Megan felt sure that Lady Kempton was insulted by the duchess choosing to interview a prospective employee over conversing with Lady Kempton and her daughter. Still, there was little she could do other than accept what amounted to a dismissal.

"Of course," she said through thinned lips. "Perhaps another time. Come, Sarah."

The two women walked past them, and the duchess turned to Megan. "Come. I think the garden would be a pleasant place to chat this afternoon, don't you?"

"Yes, certainly."

"We'll have tea in the garden," the duchess said to the waiting footman, then started down the hall, sweeping Megan along with her. "I am sorry about your hat," the Duchess said, a smile quirking at the corners of her mouth. "I shall replace it, of course."

"Thank you. That's very generous of you."

The duchess smiled at her. "It's the least I can do. You handled the twins expertly. I must say, it isn't something that most people are able to do."

Megan smiled. Unexpectedly, she found herself rather liking this woman. "I had two younger brothers. I learned a good bit about boys . . . and dogs."

"Ah, yes, Rufus. He is something of a handful. The boys found him in the woods, badly mauled. It is a miracle that he lived, and I fear that everyone has somewhat spoiled him as a result. He responds to the tone of authority in one's voice, and I fear several of the more timid servants have no control over him at all."

The older woman cast a sideways glance at Megan, the hint of laughter in her eyes. "I fear that a number of people would say that the same is true of Constantine and Alexander, as well."

"They seem like lively boys," Megan admitted. "But I don't think that they *willfully* misbehave."

They had reached the end of the hallway, and the duchess ushered Megan out the door onto the back terrace. A large garden lay behind the house, and beyond its carefully manicured walkways was an expanse of green lawn and trees, a quiet, verdant oasis in the midst of the city. The duchess led her down the wide, shallow steps and along the pathway to a graceful arbor. Shaded by the arching roof upon which roses tangled sat a small wrought-iron table and matching chairs.

"I often have tea out here," the duchess explained. "It is one of my favorite spots. I find it quite soothing to the soul."

"It's lovely," Megan agreed honestly.

"I hope that you will join me in a cup of tea," the duchess went on.

"Thank you," Megan answered, surprised by the courtesy. It was not one usually extended to employees. Or prospective employees, she reminded herself. She felt a trifle guilty at the other woman's kindness, and the feeling prompted her to say, "I am sorry you were not able to visit with your friends. I could easily have waited."

The duchess let out a little chuckle. "Oh, it was no hardship. I was glad of an excuse to get out of Lady Kempton's call. The woman is no friend of mine. She comes, as many ambitious mamas do, not to visit me, in whom she has no interest, but to ingratiate herself with the mother of a future duke. As if Theo would have anything to do with an insipid miss like Sarah Kempton."

"Oh. I see." Megan's pulse sped up at the mention of Theo Moreland, and she cast about for some way to keep the conversation about him.

However, the duchess was already moving on, saying, "Although I must admit that I don't remember having an appointment with you. Did the agency send you?"

Megan found it difficult to look into the duchess's calm blue gaze and tell a lie. So, hoping that her father had been correct in what he had told her of the woman, she said candidly, "No, ma'am, I am afraid that I was not entirely truthful with your servant. The agency did not send me." Skirting around the edges of the truth, she went on, "They did not feel that it would be appropriate to send a female candidate for the position of tutor to your sons. However, I feel that a woman can do an equally good job educating a child as a man can, regardless of whether the child is a boy or a girl. So I took it upon myself to make my application directly to you, for I had heard that you were a woman of progressive thought and a believer in the equality of the sexes."

"Bravo, Miss Henderson," the duchess said. "I couldn't agree more. You were quite right to approach me yourself. I could see quite clearly this afternoon that you are more capable of handling the boys than most of the male tutors that I have employed."

At that moment, a grave-looking gentleman arrived at the table, carrying a tray of tea things, and they were silent for a moment as the duchess went about the task of pouring tea for the two of them.

The duchess took a sip from her cup, then said, "I presume you have references, Miss Henderson."

"Oh, yes." Megan handed her the list over which she had labored for some time.

It was, she thought, artfully deceptive, listing her own education at the St. Agnes convent school, then adding a stretch of two years at a small, progressive women's college that she knew had gone out of business many years ago, and following that with several years of schooling the children of Mr. and Mrs. James Allenham, whose address happened to be that of her sister Mary Margaret.

After much thinking on the matter, she had decided that it would be better to go with a simple background that would stand up to the duchess's checking into it, rather than a tissue of more elaborate lies that would sound impressive enough for the children of a duke but would dissolve under the least scrutiny. She could describe the classes at the New England experimental college quite well, as she had done an article about the men and women who had banded together with high hopes to provide a superior education for young women. Megan was counting on the duchess's intellectual leanings, and the fact that the family was desperate to find a tutor, to get her a job.

"I am afraid that my references are all in the United States," she said apologetically.

"Yes, I noticed that you are American. But, frankly, I think it would be an educational experience for the boys to have a teacher from another country. Could I ask why you chose to come to England to seek employment?"

Megan spun a tale of a lifelong desire to see the country about which she had read all her life. Unable to afford a tour of the country, she had saved her money, she explained, to sail to England, with the hopes of then earning her way while she stayed here. Fortunately, Megan had always been an avid reader, so she was able to intersperse her story with praise for, and even quotes from, Chaucer, Shakespeare, and the more recent poets such as Byron and Shelley.

When she wound down, she braced herself for a more thorough examination of her knowledge in areas other than literature. However, somewhat to her surprise, after a passing reference to the duke's insistence upon a solid grounding in the classical languages, the duchess went on to a subject that clearly interested her more: the condition of workers in the United States.

Having written articles exposing the wrongdoings of a tenement landlord, as well as having investigated a factory that was notorious for its mistreatment of employees, Megan had no trouble fielding the other woman's questions, and they were soon absorbed in a lengthy discussion of the plight of the working class.

The scrape of a boot heel against the flagstone walkway interrupted them, and both women looked up.

A tall, broad-shouldered man was coming down the steps toward them. His hair was pitch black and thick, a trifle longer and shaggier than was customary, and it was shoved back carelessly, a lock falling waywardly across his forehead. His eyes were a light color in his tanned face — it wasn't until he was closer that Megan could make out that they were a clear, compelling green. He had a square jaw and prominent, sharp cheekbones, the strength of his face softened by the curve of sensuously full lips.

He was, Megan thought, the handsomest man she had ever seen. His gaze locked on hers, and a jolt shot through her.

She had never felt anything like this sensation before. It was stunning, paralyzing, slamming through her almost like a physical blow. Her nerves hummed, her muscles tightened, and for the briefest, strangest instant she felt as if she knew the man — not in the way she knew other people, even those she had known all her life, but in a deep, visceral way.

Even as she stared at him, the man halted abruptly and stood for a moment, staring back at her. Then, a little jerkily, he started toward them.

"Ah, there you are," the duchess said pleasantly, motioning him toward her. "Come here, dear, I want you to meet someone."

He reached them and bent down to kiss the older woman on the cheek. His eyes strayed almost involuntarily to Megan.

"Dear, this is Miss Henderson. She will be tutoring the boys," the duchess said. "Miss Henderson, this is my eldest son. Theo."

3

Megan continued to stare. This? This was the man she had hated for the past ten years?

"Miss Henderson." Theo sketched a polite bow to her. "It is a pleasure to meet you."

Megan murmured a polite reply, not even sure what she said. She was finding it difficult to bring her scattered thoughts together.

"So you are brave enough to take on the twins," he went on, his eyes twinkling. If he found it odd that a woman was being hired as a tutor for his adolescent brothers, he concealed it well.

"I — I'm not sure that I am their tutor — I mean —" Megan glanced toward the duchess. *Had the woman actually hired her?* She could scarcely believe it, but the duchess's words a few moments ago had certainly sounded as if she had given Megan the job.

"I am so sorry," the duchess said. "I did not give you a chance to refuse, did I? I confess, I was so eager that I was rude. Will you accept the position as their tutor, Miss Henderson?"

"Yes, of course." Megan could scarcely believe her good fortune. She had been certain that her father's plan would fail. Yet here she was, ensconced in the bosom of the family.

She stole a sideways glance at Theo and found his gaze on her, subtle lines creasing his forehead. She had the sudden, frantic notion that he knew who she was and why she was there. She told herself that was impossible. Ludicrous. It was merely her nerves making her see things that were not there.

Theo looked toward his mother, a smile forming on his lips, and Megan breathed a little sigh of relief. She had to get rid of this edginess.

"Perhaps Miss Henderson ought to see more of the twins before she makes her decision," Theo warned, grinning. "Has she visited their menagerie?"

"Theo, really," the duchess said repressively. "Don't scare Miss Henderson off. I have only just found her."

"I like animals," Megan replied sharply,

aware of a certain resentment that Theo Moreland was not at all as she had imagined him to be. "And I found the twins quite polite in a difficult situation. Indeed, they are lively lads who — who doubtless need a challenge in their schoolwork."

As soon as her sharp words were out, Megan regretted them. It was not part of her plan to antagonize Theo Moreland.

To her surprise, his dark eyebrows lifted in amusement. "Well done, Miss Henderson. I see the boys have a champion." He turned toward his mother, saying, "Perhaps it has been a mistake to give Con and Alex male tutors all these years. Given the way Olivia, Kyria and Thisbe feel about them, as well as Miss Henderson, it is obvious that women have a soft spot for the rascals."

The duchess let out an inelegant snort. "Not Lady Kempton and her daughter."

"The devil take it! Are they here?" Theo's face assumed a hunted expression, and he glanced around, as if the women might be hiding somewhere among the trees and bushes, about to jump out at him.

"Not any longer," the duchess assured him. "I was quite rude to them, I'm afraid. But they made me angry — criticizing Alex and Con in my own home! I hadn't even invited them. They simply came calling, hoping, no doubt, to surprise you at home — though, of course, they pretended that it was me they had come to call on. Abominable women."

"Thank heavens you sent them packing," Theo remarked. "I scarcely dare attend a party anymore for fear Lady Kempton will pop up with one or the other of her daughters in tow. Which did she have with her today — the silly one or the spotty one?"

"I'm not sure. I am afraid I didn't look at her closely," the duchess admitted.

"She was definitely silly," Megan offered. "As if those mice could do her any harm!"

"Mice?" Theo asked, a smile starting. "There were mice involved?"

"Oh, yes, and Rufus, as well," the duchess said with a resigned air.

"Rufus wouldn't have snapped at her ruffles if she had not jumped up onto the bench and danced about like that," Megan said, defending the dog.

Theo threw his head back and laughed. "This sounds like a scene I very much regret missing. No doubt it would have been worth even having to converse with Lady Kempton."

"Well, I would rather you had been

there," the duchess retorted. "I am sure then she would have been all honey and courtesy." She sighed. "Much as I love having you at home, dear, I must say it is easier when you are off on one of your travels. Then I don't have all these ambitious mothers trying to be friends with me."

"Shall I set sail tomorrow?" Theo joked.

"Of course not." The duchess rose and patted her son's cheek fondly. "Now, dear, if you will do me a favor and show Miss Henderson about the place . . . I really must get back to my correspondence. I am right in the middle of a very important point to the prime minister."

"Of course. It would be my pleasure," Theo replied, and his eyes went over to Megan.

Panic fluttered through her. She didn't want to have to face Theo Moreland alone right now. Indeed, she did not want to be around him at all, even accompanied by the duchess. She was feeling much too uncertain and confused.

She could not understand the feeling that had flashed through her when she first saw Theo — the visceral tug, the bizarre sensation that she knew him. It was like nothing she had ever experienced before.

But even putting that whole odd moment aside, she found Theo Moreland's presence distinctly unsettling. She had expected to feel something as soon as she saw the man — but she had not expected the something she felt to be attraction!

She knew logically that it was unreasonable to expect the man to look the way she had envisioned him for years. The fact that a man was a villain did not mean that he would look like one. A handsome face and form could hide all sorts of wickedness. She had met venal, cold, selfish — even evil — men before in the course of her work, men who had appeared to be quite ordinary or pleasant looking, even handsome. She knew better than to take someone at face value.

Yet she had trouble reconciling this square-jawed, handsome, smiling stranger with the weasely-faced murderer she had always imagined. It wasn't just his looks, she knew; it was his smile, his frank and open demeanor, the charming twinkle in his eyes — none of these things seemed to suit a murderer.

Most of all, she could not deny the sensations that rushed up in her in response to this man — the flutter in her stomach when he smiled at her, the strange heat that crept through her when his gaze settled on her. It was disturbing, even a little frightening, that a man she hated could make her feel so . . . so fizzy and unaccountably warm.

And why had he kept looking at her? After that first unnerving moment when she had been pierced by the sensation that he had somehow figured out who she was, Megan had noticed him sneaking glances at her as the three of them talked. There was a certain warmth in his eyes that she knew denoted an appreciation of her face and figure, but there was something else, as well, a questioning, considering quality that she could not quite understand.

She told herself that he was curious about her only because it was odd for a woman to tutor two boys. Even knowing his mother's espoused causes, he would have to wonder about Megan for applying for the position. It was unorthodox.

He could not suspect her true reason for being here. It had been ten years since he had killed Dennis; he surely would not connect her arrival with that.

As for the interest in his eyes when he looked at her, there was nothing remarkable in that. She had heard a number of tales of wealthy employers trying to seduce

— or even force their attentions upon — governesses and maidservants. It meant nothing other than that she could add *vile seducer* to his list of sins.

Theo presented his arm to Megan, smiling. "Well, Miss Henderson? Shall I give you the grand tour?"

Megan pulled herself from her worried thoughts and pasted a smile on her lips. "Of course, uh, my lord. I would appreciate it very much."

She hesitated for an instant, then stepped forward and slipped her hand into the crook of his elbow. His arm was rock solid beneath her fingertips, and even though she kept her hand as lightly on his arm as she could, it was impossible not to feel the firm muscle beneath his jacket.

"You have trouble with 'my lord'?" he asked as they strolled through the garden. "I find Americans often do."

Megan cast a look up at him. He was gazing down at her, not quite smiling, but his green eyes were alight with life and amusement. Megan realized that it suddenly seemed more difficult to breathe.

What was the matter with her all of a sudden? Why did this man affect her so strangely? She had never felt so tongue-tied and nervous, so unsure of herself.

"I always tell them just to call me Moreland if it makes them feel better. Or Theo."

"Oh, I could not do that," Megan said hastily, then mentally castigated herself for sounding so missish.

"As you like," he replied equably, guiding her around toward the side of the house, where they entered by a different door from the one Megan and the duchess had taken earlier.

"This is the gallery," Theo told her. One wall of the long hall was a bank of windows overlooking the garden. The opposite wall held portrait after portrait. "Countless generations of former dukes," Theo explained carelessly, gesturing toward the paintings. "Nothing much of interest here, although it makes a great long expanse for rolling hoops down or turning cartwheels."

"Activities of the twins?" Megan asked, smiling. She could well picture the boys using the grand, somber gallery for such occupations.

"For all of us at one time or another," Theo replied. "I fear Reed and I were rather like the twins when we were young. Of course, we were not able to communicate with one another without words as Con and Alex can, which I suppose put us at a disadvantage in the area of creating trouble. And we didn't have quite the number of animals to add to the mix — Mother blames me for that."

"Oh? Did you bring them Rufus?"

"No. Reed was responsible for him. Alex and Con found him in the woods near Reed's house last fall, rather badly torn up. An old farmer there patched him up for them and nursed him back to health. Then they brought him back here to terrorize the household. But I am the one who sent them the parrot and the boa and a number of other unseemly pets."

"Indeed? Those are rather unusual pets."

"I travel a good deal," Theo responded. "Only the fear of Mother's wrath keeps me from sending back more. I wanted to bring them a koala bear from Australia, but then I would have had to transplant eucalyptus trees for them to eat, as well, so I gave it up."

"That's fascinating. Where else have you been?" Megan kept her voice light and casual, though her heart sped up a little at finding herself so quickly on the threshold of the subject matter in which she was interested.

"Africa, China, the United States. India."

"South America?" Megan suggested.

He looked off into the distance, and something in his face changed subtly, hardened. "Yes. There, too. Went searching for the headwaters of the Amazon."

"And did you find them?" Megan watched him carefully, alert for even the most subtle signs.

Theo shrugged. Megan was about to ask him another question, but as they reached the end of the gallery and turned into the large open area of the foyer, Theo caught sight of a woman coming down the stairs, and he lifted his hand in greeting.

"Thisbe!" He turned toward Megan, saying, "Come. You must meet my sister Thisbe."

Megan swallowed her irritation at the interruption and walked with him to the elegant staircase. She studied the woman coming down the steps.

She was tall and slender, as the duchess had been, but her hair was the rich black of Theo's, and her eyes were an equally vivid green. Small spectacles perched on her narrow nose. She was dressed plainly in a dark skirt and white shirtwaist. Megan noticed that one cuff was ink-stained, and there was a smudge of something greenish on the blouse. She wore an abstracted look, but it vanished as she saw Theo, and she smiled broadly, her face lighting up.

"Theo!" She held out both her hands. "I haven't seen you in —" she frowned "— well, in a long time."

"That is because you have been locked in your shed out there for the better part of two days," her brother replied teasingly, taking her hands in his and smiling down fondly into her face. "What have you been doing?"

"Experiments," she replied. "I've been corresponding with a scientist in France regarding the effects of carbolic acid on —"

Theo raised his hands as if in surrender. "No. Please. You know I won't understand a word of what you say."

"Heathen," Thisbe retorted without heat.

Theo turned toward Megan, saying, "I am the only member of my family who dislikes education."

"No, not education. You merely dislike books," Thisbe put in. She smiled at her brother and then at Megan. "And writing. He is the most dreadful correspondent — which is really quite horrid, as he is off traveling most of the time." She extended her hand to Megan. "Hello, I am Thisbe Robinson, Theo's twin."

"I'm sorry," Theo said. "You can see that I am equally abysmal with social skills. Thisbe, please allow me to introduce you to the twins' new tutor, Miss Henderson."

Thisbe looked faintly surprised, then pleased, and shook Megan's hand heartily. "What a splendid idea. I am sure that a woman will deal much better with the boys. Have you met them yet?"

"Yes." Megan smiled at Thisbe. She could not help but like the woman, whose candid, unaffected manner was very refreshing, especially compared to the other upper-crust women whom Megan had met, both English and American.

Theo let out a chuckle. "Actually, she met them in a typical situation. They let loose some mice on Lady Kempton and her daughter."

"I am sure no one deserved it more," Thisbe commented dryly. She turned to Megan to say earnestly, "There is no harm in Alex and Con, really. They are merely —"

"Lively?" Theo supplied. "Isn't that how you described them, Miss Henderson?"

"Yes. There is nothing wrong with having energy," Megan said stoutly. "It simply needs to be directed."

"Quite right, Miss Henderson." Thisbe

beamed at her. "I say, I think you will deal nicely with the boys. Desmond — that is my husband — and I are always happy to help in the scientific areas. I find traditional texts quite lacking in that field."

"As are my skills, I am sure," Megan replied honestly. "I would welcome any help you could supply."

No answer could have pleased Thisbe more, it seemed, for she seized Megan's hand and shook it again with enthusiasm, promising that she would meet with her soon regarding her lesson plans. Then, with a quick smile for her brother, Thisbe was off down the rear hall, almost instantly deep in thought again.

"She and Desmond are excellent teachers in all things scientific," Theo told her. "It is only with such small practical matters as remembering supper that they have problems. So if you want her help, I feel sure you will have to seek her out. The twins can show you where her laboratory is located — it is at the back of the yard, since she set fire to her first one and not only alarmed the servants but did some damage to my father's workroom."

"Your father's workroom?" Megan asked, puzzled. She wouldn't have expected a duke to have a workroom. She could not have said what she thought a duke did all day, but she would have supposed it involved anything but work.

"There are those who would call it a junk room, I imagine," Theo explained. "It is a shed where he keeps his potsherds and the other artifacts he is working on. He sorts and identifies them, restores them if it's possible. The more important pieces, of course, he puts in his collection room in the house — he has one here and one at Broughton Park — but the overflow is consigned to shelves in his workroom."

"I see. He is interested in . . . antiquities, then?"

"Yes. Though only Greek and Roman. I am afraid he finds the rest of the world of little importance — the same can probably be said of everything since, oh, the time of Nero, as well."

"I see."

"Now, Uncle Bellard is interested in much more modern times — even as recent as the Napoleonic wars."

"Uncle Bellard?" Megan repeated.

"Great-uncle, actually. He lives here, too. But it will probably be some time before you meet him. He is somewhat shy and usually sticks to his rooms in the east wing." He grinned down at her. "Don't worry, that's about all the people present here at the moment. We are rather down from most years — we usually have a surprising number of relatives pop out of the woodwork when the season arrives. Fortunately, Lady Rochester has decided not to grace us with her presence this year — she chose to torment her daughter-in-law instead — or I would have to warn you to avoid her at all costs."

Megan could not help but chuckle. There was something infectious about Theo's smile. She looked at him and once again felt that strange tug inside her. The feeling was bizarre and unsettling, and she could not understand why she was experiencing it. She was not even sure what the sensation was.

However, she was sure that she should not be feeling it for this man. He was her sworn enemy, the man she had hated for ten years.

She put her hand to her midsection, as if to quiet the tumult there.

"I'll take you up to the nursery," Theo said. "It's something of a climb, I'm afraid. In general, Mother has never approved of the notion of sequestering children away in the nursery. However, given the twins' collection of animals, it seemed the most logical thing to stick them and their menagerie at some distance from the rest of us. So they are up on the third story."

Megan, never having lived in the sort of wealthy household that had a separate nursery area for the children, was not sure exactly what to expect. From tales she had heard and read, she half expected some sort of gloomy area tucked away under the eaves, but when they reached it, she found that the Moreland nursery was a pleasantly sunny place with a large schoolroom and several smaller rooms leading off from it.

Shelves filled with toys and books lined the two long walls of the rectangular room. Four desks lined up back to back stood in the center of the room, and at one end of them stood a large globe on a stand. A chart of the solar system and an astronomical map of the night sky were pinned to the wall, as were several smaller maps of England, Europe and the world. The world map, Megan noticed, was dotted with pins of various colors, the predominant ones of red. Along the far wall, in the sun streaming in through the windows, were several cages containing animals.

The twins were engaged in feeding their various animals, the dog, Rufus, beside them, gazing hopefully into the cages. Con and Alex turned at the sound of their entrance, and broke into smiles when they saw Megan and Theo.

"Theo! Miss Henderson!" they chorused.

Alex set the cup of fruits and nuts inside the large birdcage and closed the door, and the boys approached them.

"We've already fed the boa," Alex said apologetically. "I'm sorry. If we had known you would come up here, we would have waited."

"That's all right," Megan replied candidly. While she had grown up with boys and their variety of pets, watching a snake swallow several live mice did not appeal to her. "But you could introduce me to your other animals, if you like."

"But first," Theo put in, "I've brought Miss Henderson up here to tell you that she is going to be your new tutor."

The two boys stared at her in surprise, but she was pleased to see that their surprise was quickly replaced by excitement.

"Wizard!" Alex exclaimed.

"You'll be ever so much better a tutor!" Con added. "You're not at all stuffy."

"They usually are," Alex explained.

"Well, I shall try my best not to be," Megan assured them. "Now, why don't we look at your animals! That's a beautiful parrot."

She pointed to the vivid red-and-blue bird sitting on its perch of a dead branch inside its large cage. It was busily cracking nuts with its powerful beak, but it paused to turn its head and regard her with one bright eye.

Dropping the nut in its beak, the parrot let out a loud squawk. "Hello!"

"Hello," Megan answered, going over to him.

"Wellie. Treat. Wellie. Treat." The bird began to shift from one claw to the other on its perch, turning its head this way and that to watch Megan.

"What's his name?" she asked.

"Wellington. Everyone calls him Wellie," Con answered, coming up beside her.

"Don't put your finger through the bars," Alex warned, joining them. "Wellington sometimes takes a nip at one."

Behind them, Theo let out a snort. "Sometimes? Without fail is more like it."

"I don't think I've ever seen such a beautiful bird," Megan said. "Where is it from?"

"The Solomon Islands," Theo answered, coming up behind her. "I sent him to the boys, a fact for which much of my family never stops blaming me."

"It's not Wellington's fault he gets out sometimes," Con protested. "He only does what's natural to him."

"That's true. A strong argument for leaving him in the jungle," Theo responded. "There he can fly about all he pleases. I don't really believe in taking animals from their habitat, but sometimes I find it hard to resist — particularly in this case, where I found him already caged in a market."

"We're awfully glad you did," Con told him. "And Hercules, as well."

"Hercules?" Megan asked, raising her brows.

"The boa," Con replied, nodding his head toward the thick snake curled sleeping in another large cage.

"Come, see the others. Here are the turtle and frog."

Megan let herself be led from cage to terrarium to cage to aquarium, admiring a variety of fish, fowl and reptiles, and even a rabbit and a fuzzy creature that the twins informed her was a guinea pig.

"You must be very responsible," Megan told the boys.

They looked at her, slightly surprised. It was obviously not an appellation that they were accustomed to having attributed to them.

"Taking care of all these animals," she explained.

"Oh." The boys glanced at one another, and Alex said with a smile, "Yes, I suppose we are, actually."

"Did you hear that, Theo?" Con asked, turning to his older brother.

"I certainly did." Theo smiled at Megan. "I think Mother may have found the perfect tutor for you boys this time."

Megan felt warmed all through by Theo's smile. She could feel a blush rising up in her cheeks, and she looked away from him quickly.

It was crazy that she should react to him this way, she thought. Bizarre. She needed to get away and think this thing through by herself. Everything was different from what she had expected. She had not really thought of what she expected the Duke of Broughton's family to be, but certainly it was not what she had seen of them. Theo's sister, the twins, the duchess were warm and friendly, people who, if she had met them in any other circumstances, she would have liked immediately.

Even in these circumstances, she liked them, Megan had to admit. Of course, they were not responsible for what Theo had done. It was not beyond the realm of reason that they should be bright or concerned or humorous. Any family could turn out one bad specimen. Theo was not necessarily like his family.

The problem, though, Megan knew, was that Theo *did* seem like the rest of his family. He was charming and handsome and possessed a smile that she could feel all through her.

That was what she had to adjust to, she knew. She had to prepare herself to deal not with a cold and obvious villain, but with a man whose wickedness was concealed beneath a pleasant, appealing mask. She should have known that it would be too easy, too simplistic, for Moreland to be the way she had pictured him. After all, had not her own brother sent them a letter shortly after he joined up with Moreland's party in which he had declared Moreland a "capital fellow"?

The man was deceptive, and she had to guard against his deception. She had to guard against her own feelings. She could not let her liking for Theo's family color her judgment. Nor could she make the mistake of taking Theo Moreland at face value.

To succeed on her quest, Megan knew that she must be as deceptive as Moreland himself was. She had to pretend to like him, to be fooled by his easy charm, and all the while, inside, she must be like iron.

She had been in worse situations than this, she reminded herself, had faced worse enemies. She would get through this just as she had gotten through those other investigations, with determination and good sense. She had to. She owed it to Dennis.

"I should go now," she said, and gave the boys a smile, then turned one that was less genuine toward Theo. "I have a great many things to do in order to get ready."

"Are you coming back tomorrow?" Alex asked.

"No. I am afraid it will have to be the day after tomorrow. There are certain tasks that I must complete first."

Like talking to the other men who had accompanied Theo Moreland and her brother on their trek up the Amazon. She had not really expected to be hired on here — and certainly not so quickly. She would have to do her interviews with Andrew Barchester and Julian Coffey tomorrow.

She knew that once she began working at Broughton House, she would have very little time on her own to interview people.

Servants rarely got more than one day every two weeks off from work, and she suspected that it was probably even more difficult for governesses, who were probably expected to be with their charges every day, even if there were no studies pursued that day. It might be somewhat better for a tutor of boys as old as the twins, who did not need constant watching over as younger children did, but she could not count on that.

The boys insisted on coming down to see her off, a fact for which Megan was grateful. She frankly did not want to have to spend any more time alone in Theo's company. It was altogether too unsettling.

Alex and Con kept up a steady stream of chatter as they went down the stairs, eliminating any necessity for Megan or Theo to speak.

She turned to the others to say a quick goodbye at the front door. Theo extended his hand to her, and it was impossible not to take it. Megan's breath quickened as his hand engulfed hers. His palm was warm and a little rough, surprising her. She would not have expected an aristocrat to have worked enough to form calluses. Moreland must have been involved somehow in the menial tasks of his explorations.

She had always pictured him riding along on some conveyance or other, with plenty of native servants to do all the work.

Theo held her hand a fraction of an instant too long, releasing it just as her eyes flew to his in question. There was a certain heat in his gaze that sent an answering flame licking through her, but there was something else, a kind of watchfulness that reawakened the uneasy feeling she had experienced when she first met him.

The smile she gave him and the boys was a trifle unsteady. Quickly she turned and walked out the door and down the street, firmly refraining from breaking into a run. She could not shake the notion that somehow, impossible though it seemed, Theo Moreland knew who she was.

4

Theo barely heard the chatter of the twins as he stood in the doorway, looking after the retreating figure of Megan Henderson. Who the devil was she?

Con and Alex took off at their usual pace back up the stairs, and Theo turned and strolled through the hallway and out onto the terrace. He took the wide, shallow steps down onto the flagstone path that led to the arbor.

He stopped at the place where he had caught his first glimpse of Miss Henderson and stood, remembering the moment.

Recognition had jolted through him when he saw her, stopping him dead in his tracks. He could not believe it, and yet the fact of it was looking straight at him. Miss Henderson, the twins' new teacher, was the woman who had come to him in his dream years ago. The woman who at the time had seemed so real to him, but whom he had come to realize must have been a figment of his imagination, a product of his fevered, delirious dreams.

However, now he knew that his assumptions were not true. The woman was very real indeed . . . and about to be living in his own house.

Theo shook his head in confusion and walked over to the arbor where his mother and the tutor had been sitting. He sat down in the chair Miss Henderson had occupied. The odor of the first blooming roses mingled with the subtler, faintly lavender scent of Megan's perfume.

He had forgotten how beautiful the woman had been — no, not beautiful, exactly, in that sort of perfect, stunning way that his sister Kyria was beautiful. No, this woman was intriguing, enticing, with a soft, curvaceous body hidden and restrained by the plain dark clothes she wore, her hair warmly cinnamon in color and curling, seeming about to escape from its pins at any moment. And her smile . . .

Theo let out a groan, sinking his head onto his hands. He remembered that smile perfectly — the soft, wide mouth with its plump lower lip, slightly indented in the center, quirking a little to one side in an enchanting, eminently kissable way, her mahogany-colored eyes warm and inviting.

But she wasn't real. She was a dream! So how had she turned up here in the Broughton House garden?

It had been ten years, and he had been terribly ill at the time, Theo reminded himself. The odds were he simply did not remember exactly what the woman in his dream looked like, and when he saw Miss Henderson, she had resembled the woman enough that his mind attached the teacher's face to the image he had seen.

Even as he came up with the logical explanation for the odd occurrence, Theo knew that it was not so. That dream was as real, as vivid to him, as it had been ten years ago. He had only to close his eyes and he could remember the slab of stone hard beneath his body, and the sweat slicking his flesh and dampening his hair. He had been burning up with fever, his mouth constantly dry and parched no matter how much they poured that drink down his throat. The air had been stifling, heavy with the smoke from the incense burners on either end of the slab on which he lay. He remembered the low, rocky ceiling that arched over him, the rough walls, damp with the moisture of the cave.

He remembered, too, the dark, silent girl

who had tended to him, wiping the sweat from his face and urging the drink on him, the metal of the goblet cool against his fevered lips. Her low voice had chanted in some foreign tongue. Dennis had been there, too, most of the time, talking to him, urging him to return from the netherworld in which he floated.

But neither Dennis nor the black-haired maiden had been there when the woman had come to him. His fever had been burning more hotly than ever, and he had been assaulted by hallucinations — visions of animals and birds and strange, monstrous people had danced around him. And he had sweated and shivered, aware deep inside that life was slipping from him.

Then she had appeared at the end of the slab, a wondrously normal, heartening sight in his confused world. A plain white gown had fallen straight from her shoulders, and her hair had tumbled down around her shoulders, soft and riotously curling, a warm reddish-brown, slightly darker in the flare of the torchlight than it had looked today in the sun of the rose garden. She had been young, her cheeks pink with the blush of youth.

He had gazed at her then, having never seen her before, yet somehow viscerally *knowing* her, with an awareness that went much deeper than mental understanding. They were connected in a deep, intense way that he could not have explained yet he understood with every fiber of his being.

"You must not die," she had said to him, and walked around to stand beside his head.

He had looked at her, unable to speak, too weak even to raise his head. She had smiled down at him then, a wonderful, inviting smile that brought out the hint of mischief in her sparkling brown eyes.

"I won't let you," she went on. "Do you understand? You cannot die yet. I am waiting for you."

Then she had bent and softly kissed his lips. He could still recall the butterfly-soft flutter of her mouth.

Theo had spoken of his vision to no one, not even Dennis. It had been too real and at the same time too bizarre to share with anyone. He could not explain his certainty that he knew the woman even though he had never seen her before. Nor did he want to share the intense flash of hunger that had darted through him at the sight of her.

It was the same stirring of desire that had arisen in him today when he first saw

Megan Henderson. There was something about her, something that went beyond all notions of beauty or desirability, to an attraction so deep and elemental that it seemed a part of him. He had not felt anything like it with any other woman.

He remembered what his brother Reed had told him about the first time Reed saw Anna, the woman who would eventually become his wife. It had been like a blow to the chest, Reed had said, and Theo had thought the description overly dramatic. Yet today what he had felt had been as strong as that, as intense, though it had been more of a jolt all through him rather than a blow to his heart.

He had to wonder what that meant about the twins' new teacher. Not, he felt sure, that he was going to marry the woman. He had realized some time ago that he was apparently missing the romantic streak that seemed to run through the rest of his family. His parents, his brother, his sisters — even his twin — all had married for love. Theo, however, was sure that he had never felt the emotion. He had been attracted to many women over the years, had even indulged in affairs with those who were free and willing to engage in such relationships, both here in London and in some of the other places he had traveled.

There had been one woman — the clever, ambitious owner of a millinery store — with whom he had kept company happily every time he returned to London. That relationship had lasted almost three years, off and on, and had ended amicably when he'd returned from his trip to China to find that she had entered into a more permanent relationship with a man who stayed home. He had enjoyed her company, had found pleasure in her bed, yet he had never felt the sort of heart-thudding joy upon seeing her that he had witnessed on Kyria's or Olivia's faces when they saw their husbands.

He would have dismissed such happiness as a feminine trait had he not seen the same sort of besotted expression on his father's face every time he'd looked upon his duchess during the last thirty-four years. The fact was, obviously, that the Morelands loved deeply and for a long time — except, apparently, for him.

So he felt sure that what he had experienced today was not love at first sight. No, it was more likely astonishment at seeing his long-ago dream suddenly come to life in his mother's rose garden.

Still . . . whatever it was, he knew it was

something that he had to explore. He had to know why this woman was here in his life ten years after his "vision" of her. He had to understand that strange, intense feeling that had gripped him.

Theo remembered his reluctance to leave London despite the restlessness that had plagued him, as well as the odd sense of waiting that he had experienced. Was Miss Henderson the reason he had been "waiting"? And how the devil had he known it?

Theo stood up, shaking his head slightly, and started back into the house. In the midst of all these speculations, there was one fact he knew for certain: there was no way he would be leaving London any time soon.

He trotted up the steps to the terrace, unaware that he was whistling a merry tune.

Megan went to call on Andrew Barchester the following day, accompanied by her father and sister. She would have preferred to conduct the interview alone. Much as she loved her father, she was accustomed to doing her work by herself. Her father was all too likely to take control of the interview and send it shooting along some strange pathway. Nor did she really think that Deirdre was likely to be able to give them any pertinent information derived from the "feelings" Frank Mulcahey was sure Deirdre would receive on seeing this man, who was one of the last to see their brother alive. She would have liked to spare Deirdre the pain of hearing firsthand about Dennis's death. Megan was accustomed to hearing and seeing gruesome things in the course of her work; Deirdre was not.

Her father, however, had been insistent on accompanying her. And Megan could not deny that it would appear more natural for him to be the one making inquiries of the man who had told him of his son's death. Nor could she keep Deirdre from going along, as her sister seemed determined to do.

She would simply have to work around her family's presence, she decided, and hope that Deirdre did not hear anything that would disturb her.

They climbed the steps to the front door, and Frank used the heavy brass knocker. Moments later a servant answered the door, and Frank requested to see Andrew Barchester, explaining who he was. The footman, looking rather dubious, replied that he would inquire if the master was home and started to climb the staircase at a majestic pace, leaving the three of them standing in the entryway.

"What a beautiful home," Deirdre murmured, looking around her.

It was, indeed, quite lovely, and it was clear that no expense had been spared in creating the house. However, to Megan's eyes, it did not compare in magnificence to the stately Broughton House. While expensively built, there was a certain overdone quality to Barchester's house, and a newness that bespoke riches recently acquired. The elegant Queen Anne–style Broughton House, however, had a sort of lived-in air, a casual acceptance of its wealth that let one know that this house, this family, had been important long before any of its present occupants were born.

"Is Broughton House this elegant?" Deirdre asked.

Megan nodded. For some reason, which she had not herself examined, Megan had not told her father and sister much beyond the bare facts of her meeting with the duchess yesterday. She had not told them how engaging the twins had been, nor how easy it would be to like the Duchess of Broughton.

As for her meeting Theo Moreland, she had not even mentioned it. She knew that they would not understand the strange feeling that had assailed her when she'd met the man — indeed, she had not even understood it herself! Her father, she knew, would have lectured her about how dangerous it was to take a man like Moreland at face value. He would have pointed out that the man was deceptively charming, so she must keep her guard up at all times. She was fully aware of these arguments, as she had repeated them to herself all the way home. She did not want to have to listen to them from her father, as well.

She would deal with the unlikely tug of attraction she had felt for the man. She was certain that it had been a momentary aberration, a result of her surprise at meeting the man when she had not expected to, had not prepared herself for it. Tomorrow, when she returned to the house, she would have herself better in hand.

Her thoughts were interrupted by the sound of footsteps on the stairs, and she turned to see the footman coming back to them.

"Mr. Barchester will receive you," he said, looking faintly surprised, and led them up the stairs and into a spacious drawing room.

A man was standing by the windows, looking out, and he turned at their arrival and came toward them.

"Mr. Mulcahey," he said, reaching out to shake Frank's hand. "I am Andrew Barchester. I am so pleased to meet Dennis's father."

Mr. Barchester was a pleasant-looking man in his mid-thirties, with a high, wide forehead and even features. His eyes were a pale gray, and his hair was blond, and he was handsome in a nondescript sort of way.

"Mr. Barchester," Megan's father replied, and introduced Megan and Deirdre to him.

Barchester smiled at Megan and murmured a greeting, but when he turned to Deirdre, Megan noticed that his hand lingered on hers a trifle longer and his eyes took on an appreciative gleam. It seemed that Deirdre's fragile beauty was once again having its usual effect.

"What brings you to London, Mr. Mulcahey?" Barchester asked, showing them to a blue sofa and chair, and taking his own seat across from them.

"We're here to find out whatever we can

about my son's murder, Mr. Barchester," Frank replied.

They had had much discussion the night before over exactly what they should tell Barchester. Frank, not one to trust any Englishman completely, had been concerned that the man might balk at their intent of bringing a fellow Englishman to justice, and it was always Megan's policy in researching her stories to tell everyone as little as she had to in order to get them to talk. That way, she felt, there was less chance of their stories being influenced by her considerations. Deirdre, however, had been of the opinion that if Barchester did not realize the extent and gravity of their interest, he might very well smooth over details or even conceal some matters in order not to cause them distress. It was, she added with a significant look at her sister and father, something with which she had had a good deal of experience. Megan and her father had had to agree with the logic of Deirdre's argument, and they had agreed to be candid with Barchester.

Now Barchester stared at Frank Mulcahey for a long moment. "I will be happy to tell you everything I know, of course." He paused. "But I'm not sure I know exactly what you mean — are you hoping to *do* something about it? I mean, um . . ."

"I'm not going to take vengeance myself, if that's what ye mean," Mulcahey assured him. "Sure, and I'd like nothing better, you understand. But I've promised the girls I'll not harm the scoundrel. Still, we mean to bring Moreland to justice."

"Mr. Mulcahey . . . believe me, if there were any possibility of that, we would have done it ten years ago, when Dennis was killed." He frowned. "But it happened in the wilds. I'm not sure even what country we were in — Peru, perhaps. We had followed the Amazon River all the way up into the mountains. Where we were was uninhabited. And even when we returned to civilization, it was a foreign country, and we could not prove — I mean, we could not even speak the language, and it would have been just our word against his. Lord Raine's family is very old and wealthy. His father is a duke. And they are related to scores of influential people in one way or another. The government would have put such pressure on the local police that I am sure they would have let him go. And what government could we have gone to, anyway? We went back down the Amazon into Brazil before we reached a city of any size."

"Mr. Barchester, we are implying no wrong on your part, I assure you," Megan put in quickly. "Pray do not think we feel anything but gratitude to you for letting us know what happened to my brother."

"Aye. It's no slight to you, lad," Frank agreed. "It is just that we need to know. We need to do everything we possibly can for Dennis."

Megan stiffened, afraid that her father would launch into the story of Deirdre's visitation from Dennis. That, she was sure, would result in Barchester's being certain that they were quite insane. However, her father said nothing further and she relaxed.

"Thank you," Barchester said. "I am glad you feel that way. But it was not concern for myself that prompted me to speak. I was merely trying to explain how unlikely it is that you will receive any satisfaction out of this inquiry. We are in England. The crime did not even occur here. And it has been ten years since it happened. Besides, there is still the matter of lack of proof. It is one man's word against another's. And when one of those men is the eldest son of a duke . . . well, I can envision no way that you can receive satisfaction."

"He doesn't have to be tried in court,"

Frank replied. "It's impossible, I know. It will be enough for me if we can make people aware of what he has done."

"Newspapers have a powerful impact, Mr. Barchester," Megan told him. "I know. I work for one."

Barchester's jaw dropped. "You? You're a —"

"I'm a reporter. I have written stories that revealed terrible working conditions in factories, political corruption, the plight of slum-dwellers. I didn't have to go to court. Exposing their practices to the general public set demands for reform in motion."

"I — I see." Barchester still looked faintly shocked — more, Megan suspected, at the revelation of her job than at their plan to expose a member of the British aristocracy.

"I will dig into it, just as I do with any other story, and when I have found enough evidence, I can write a story. My newspaper will publish it, and I suspect there will be British papers that are eager to put out the story, as well. Nothing sells like scandal among the wealthy — I would imagine it is even truer when that person is not only wealthy but also titled."

"No doubt you are right." He hesitated for another moment, then said, "Well . . .

um . . . let's see . . . where shall I start?"

"Why don't you begin by explaining to us how you and Mr. Moreland — I mean, Lord Raine — joined up with Dennis and his group?"

"Of course." Barchester nodded. "I had not known Lord Raine before we went to Brazil together. Though we were of an age, we did not exactly move in the same circles. My grandfather made his money in trade, you see."

Megan nodded. She had started out on the Society Desk, where she had learned enough to be aware that old money did not regard the nouveau riche with respect. She could well imagine that in England the lines were much more distinctly drawn, and that money, new or old, could not cast one into the rarified class of the aristocracy.

"I was in my early twenties at the time. I had gone to university, as my grandfather had insisted. He wanted very much for me to be a 'gentleman.' So I did not go into the family business, as my father had. I was, quite frankly, a trifle bored with my life, so when my grandfather suggested that I go on the Cavendish expedition, I was more than happy to oblige the old chap. It sounded like quite an adventure."

He shook his head. "Unfortunately, it turned out to be far more of one than I would have liked."

"The Cavendish expedition?" Megan inquired, jotting the name down in her notebook.

"Yes. Old Lord Cavendish was quite interested in the cultures of other times and places. He turned his ancestral home in London into a museum. It was a huge old place, built shortly after the Great Fire, and it was no longer in a fashionable area. The family had built a new home in Mayfair. So he decided to house his collection of artifacts there, as well as whatever other ones he could get his hands on. He was particularly avid about the ancient cultures of South and Central America — Incas, Aztecs and all that — so that was the specialty of the museum. It wasn't much, really, just a wealthy old man's hobby, but he wanted to make it into something known all over the country, if not the world. So he hired a curator, and he started sending out expeditions to the Americas to find and bring back information and artifacts for the museum."

"I see. So Lord Cavendish financed your expedition?"

"Yes." Barchester nodded. "The curator

went along — well, frankly, he was the only employee of the museum at the time. His name was Julian Coffey. I knew him rather well. We had gone to school together and had been casual friends. My grandfather was also interested in artifacts, and he has corresponded and spoken with Lord Cavendish from time to time, and Grandfather had made one or two gifts to the museum, as well. Grandfather suggested to me that I might like to go. It sounded like an adventure, and as I knew Julian . . ."

"How was Theo Moreland involved?"

"Raine's father, the Duke of Broughton, was a friend of old Cavendish's, too. They were both collectors, you see — though the duke's field was the ancient Greeks and Romans. But I guess he told Lord Raine about the expedition, and he wanted to join. He had caught the exploration fever a couple of years before that after he finished university. Wound up in the Levant, then Egypt, and finally trekked into the Sahara. He liked the adventure, I suppose. He's been on a number of trips since, so I understand."

"What was he like?" Megan asked.

Barchester shrugged. "Actually, quite a regular sort of chap. Julian and I were rather surprised when we met him. We had expected him to be a lightweight, full of himself and thinking everyone else ought to do for him. But he was always the first to pitch in, never asked for special treatment. We hadn't been on the ship a day before we were calling him Theo. It was . . . well, we all thought it was going to be the trip of a lifetime."

The man's blandly handsome face saddened for a moment. "It was, I suppose . . . just not in the sense that we thought it would be." He seemed to shake off his moment of reverie and went on more briskly. "The head of our expedition was a chap name Thurlew. Howard Thurlew. He'd done a good bit of exploring and had worked for Lord Cavendish before — dug up some Aztec ruins some place in Mexico, and it was he who had proposed this trip to the old fellow. He wanted to follow the Amazon deep into the interior and perhaps find some Inca ruins. That was what Lord Cavendish was interested in, of course. I think Thurlew was in it more for the exploration — and Theo, too. Julian was a naturalist, and he was eager to see the wildlife and draw it and so on."

"How did you meet Dennis?" Frank asked.

"Well, Thurlew fell right after we

reached Brazil. Poor chap broke his leg —
quite badly. It was obvious that he could
not travel for weeks, even months. Even
once his leg was healed, he wouldn't have
been up to such rugged travel. So there we
were, with our equipment, all set to go into
the interior, and we had no guide. None of
us could have dealt with the native guides
and so on. We had no experience, didn't
know the language. But we hated to just
give up and turn around and go home —
nor could we wait for several months for
Thurlew to be up to the journey, as it
would have thrown us into the rainy season. Then, as luck would have it, we ran
into your son, sir. He and his friend
Eberhart, as it turned out, were all that
was left of their party. The others had either gotten ill or simply become disen-
chanted with the idea. Captain Eberhart
seemed a knowledgeable sort, and he had
already hired some native guides. So we
decided to throw our lot in with Dennis
and Eberhart."

"A doomed venture from the very start,
wasn't it?" Frank said, shaking his head.

"I suppose one could say that," the other
man conceded. "But it isn't all that unusual for some members of any expedition
to drop out along the way. Far too many

people set out expecting some fantastic adventure, with no realization of the hardships involved, or the dangers. Diseases, accidents — and all miles from civilization, of course."

"Where did you go?" Megan asked.

"We set out up the Amazon, as we had originally intended. It was a fantastic journey — utterly amazing." Barchester's eyes glowed as he remembered the trip. "The things we saw — the parrots, the vines, the trees, even the snakes were just . . . Well, it is impossible to adequately describe it. One has to see it, feel it, to really understand what it was like. Not pleasant a great deal of the time, of course. The heat was abysmal, and the humidity was almost unbearable. And, of course, there was danger. Anacondas. Jaguars. There was always the possibility that we might come upon unfriendly natives. Even a cut could become horribly infected, and we were miles from a doctor. But it was thrilling, nevertheless. We traveled upriver as far as we could go, and then we took out across land. Then Captain Eberhart died."

Deirdre let out a soft sound of distress, and Barchester turned toward her. His face softened. "I apologize, Miss Mulcahey. This is not a proper subject to be discussing in front of you."

"No, please, go on. I want to hear it — that is, I need to hear it. We must find out everything we can so that we can expose Dennis's killer."

She looked at him with her large, soft eyes, and Megan could practically see the man melting right in front of them.

"Miss Mulcahey," he said, his voice full of emotion. "I assure you that I will do everything I can to help you."

"It is very kind of you," Deirdre murmured.

Megan cleared her throat and pulled the conversation back to the subject. "What happened to Captain Eberhart?"

"It was one of those tropical fevers that felled him. As we traveled on, he became more and more ill. We stopped and made a semipermanent camp, then stayed there for a few days, hoping he would recover. But he did not. When he died, we were in something of a quandary, not sure whether we should turn back or go on, but finally we decided to continue. It seemed such a waste to turn back, as far as we had gone, and by that time, we had gotten to where we could communicate to some extent with the native workers. So we pressed on. Some of the natives abandoned us. They were a superstitious lot, and they viewed Eberhart's death as a sign that we should not go farther. We couldn't understand everything they said, but there was a lot of talk about Inca treasure and the ancient gods' displeasure and that sort of thing."

"Inca treasure?" Frank Mulcahey cast a significant look at his daughters.

"Yes. Oh, yes. We had heard tales of Inca treasure from Thurlew even before we left England." He shrugged. "Just legends, you know."

"What sort of legends?" Megan asked.

Barchester shrugged. "Oh, the usual sort of thing. I don't know how much you know about the Incas, but they had an enormous empire, centered in Peru but stretching throughout much of the Andes and up to Central America."

"They were very sophisticated, weren't they?" Megan asked, trying to remember some of the things her brother had told her. Dennis had been fascinated by the history of South and Central America. "Had a system of roads . . ."

"Administratively, they were quite advanced. But not able to withstand European weaponry. Pizarro and his lot came in and took the Inca emperor captive. Demanded a huge ransom from all his subjects. Of course, they killed him anyway, but gold and gems and all sorts of tribute poured in from all the outlying areas. Naturally, there are legends about the treasures — that there were Incas who hid the gold or part of the gold on their way to free their king. The natives said that the ancient gods were angry about what amounted to looting their temples. Much of their gold work, you see, was in the temples — statues of the gods and vessels for the priests and so on. So, of course, there are legends that the treasure is protected by the ancient gods, and that whoever finds it will be subjected to punishment by the gods. That sort of thing."

"Did you find any treasure?" Frank asked.

Barchester let out a short laugh. "No. Of course not. Julian found a few things — an ancient cup, a small statue, but no treasure trove, believe me. But the natives were scared — always talking about the land being protected by the old gods and all that. Just fear, really, I think, of going any deeper into unknown territory. But some of the natives stayed — we offered them more money. And we still had provisions. We wanted to see as much as we could. It was such an opportunity — an untouched land. But then . . ." He looked at them uncomfortably. "Then Lord Raine and Dennis . . ."

"What happened, Mr. Barchester?" Megan asked. "Exactly."

"They quarreled. And Raine . . ." His eyes flickered uneasily over to Deirdre again. "Well, Raine killed him."

"How?"

The man looked startled by Megan's blunt question. "What do you mean?"

"How did Lord Raine kill Dennis? Did he shoot him or —"

"He stabbed him."

A hush fell on the room. Megan had heard many sad and wrenching stories in her line of work, but she was unprepared for the stab of pain that went through her at Barchester's words.

"I'm sorry," Barchester said, looking wretched. "I should not have said that so bluntly."

Megan shook her head, shoving down her sorrow. " 'Tis not your fault, I assure you." She paused, struggling to put herself back into her reporter's role. "You said they quarreled. About what?"

"I don't know. I wasn't —" He paused, again with an anxious glance at Deirdre. "I didn't hear it."

"Could it have been over something Dennis had found?" Megan asked.

Barchester frowned. "Found? I'm not sure what you mean."

"Well, you said that Mr. Coffey came upon some artifacts. Had Dennis found anything? I don't know — some sort of object? An artifact? Even a jewel or something like that."

"Oh, well, yes, I suppose he could have. But if he did, I never knew of it." He paused, frowning. "But you know . . . now that I think of it, there was something in Raine's possession that he was rather secretive about."

The Mulcaheys glanced at each other, then back at Barchester, their interest clearly aroused. "Something?" Frank repeated.

"Yes. A pendant of some sort, I believe. I didn't really get a good look at it. As I said, Lord Raine was secretive about it. But as we were traveling back, I noticed that he was wearing something around his neck. It lay beneath his shirt, and I saw him pull it out once or twice to look at it. I never saw it up close. He didn't offer to show it to me, and I did not ask. I — we — well, obviously things were quite strained between us at that point. We did not speak much beyond what was necessary."

"Didn't you talk to him about the murder?" Megan asked in disbelief. "Didn't you ask him why? Didn't you put him in restraints or anything?"

"Of course we talked to him!" Mr. Barchester looked shocked. "Theo claimed it was an accident. And I, well, at first I believed him. I mean, I had never seen anything to indicate that he would do something like that. I thought surely it must have been an accident. It was only later that I began to realize the story didn't quite add up. Raine was evasive in his answers, and I could see that he was not telling me the truth. He was clearly uneasy, and he wouldn't meet my eyes. His story didn't really make sense."

Again sorrow tinged Barchester's features. "It was very hard for me, for both Julian and me, to accept that Lord Raine had murdered Dennis. We had grown to like him so, to think that he wasn't like other aristocrats we had met. But, finally, I could not deny any longer that he was lying. Julian and I talked about it. We didn't know what to do. As I said, we were miles from civilization, not even sure where we were. It was a matter of our word against his, and the Morelands are quite powerful. I — there was nothing to do but return."

His gaze went from Frank to Megan, then lingered on Deirdre's face. "I pray you will not think too badly of me. If I had had any idea what would happen, if I could have done something to stop it . . ."

"It wasn't your fault, Mr. Barchester," Deirdre assured him in her usual kind manner.

Megan was not quite as forgiving as her sister, however. It seemed to her that Barchester had given up all too easily in the face of Moreland's denial. However, she could scarcely afford to take him to task over it. His account of the events was the only proof they had against Theo Moreland at the moment, and she did not want to antagonize him. Besides, she reminded herself, it would have doubtless been unwise for Barchester to confront Moreland with his knowledge, given that he had already killed a man. Moreland could have done in the other two men also, and returned to civilization with no one the wiser.

"This other man who was with you — Julian Coffey? I'd like to talk to him. See if there is anything he can add."

"Oh, yes, I am sure that he could give

you more details," Mr. Barchester agreed. "Capital fellow, Coffey."

"Is he still the curator at the Cavendish Museum?"

Barchester nodded. "Yes. Julian makes regular trips to South and Central America to acquire new pieces for the museum. He has built up quite a collection over the years. Lord Cavendish died a few years back, but he endowed the place amply in his will, and his widow still supports it, as well. In fact, Lady Cavendish is holding a ball to benefit the museum in just a couple of weeks, I believe. I could talk to him, if you'd like," he added helpfully. "Set up something for you."

"Thank you, but that won't be necessary," Megan assured him quickly. She preferred to talk to the man without his being influenced beforehand by Barchester. "I should set up an appointment myself. I'm not sure exactly when I will be able to see him. In the meantime, I would appreciate it if you didn't mention any of this to Mr. Coffey."

He looked surprised. "Naturally, if that is what you wish."

"I find I get better results if I have the first thoughts out of one's head," Megan said by way of explanation. "You know, without their thinking it over a great deal. It's no longer fresh then."

"Of course," Barchester agreed politely, though he still looked faintly confused.

And well he might, Megan thought, since her glib response was not precisely the truth. She had found that the more witnesses to an event discussed it, the more alike their accounts of the event tended to become, but she had also found that telling people that fact often insulted them. In the same way, she also suspected that Mr. Barchester's story had probably been somewhat different than it would have been if Deirdre had not been present. The man had been clearly smitten by her sister. Megan wasn't sure how his story might have differed, of course; no doubt it was subtle. But she had also found that men were not inclined to be entirely honest when they were speaking in front of a woman they admired. She intended to arrange her visit with Coffey so that her father and sister were not present.

They stayed for a little longer after that, making polite chitchat with Mr. Barchester. He offered them tea and inquired about their trip across the Atlantic and their lodgings here, offering to help them in any way possible. He seemed a nice enough man, Megan thought, though a trifle bland. Her sister, however, seemed not to notice this defect, for she smiled and even, Megan realized, flirted with him a little.

For her part, Megan was barely able to sit still and be polite. She wanted only to go back to the house they had rented and talk over the tantalizing possibility of "treasure" that Mr. Barchester had raised. She could see, glancing at her father, that he was fairly twitching to discuss it, too.

Indeed, they had barely bade Mr. Barchester goodbye and walked a few feet from his front door before Frank burst out, "I knew it! Did I not I tell you? That murderin' English bastard stole that pendant from Dennis. That's what Den wants back, I'll warrant."

"Now, Da, we don't know that," Megan pointed out fairly.

"It's as plain as the nose on your face, girl," he retorted. "After Dennis was dead, that titled scoundrel was wearing this thing around his neck and being terribly secretive about it. How else did it suddenly appear? And why else would he have been hiding it?"

"It makes sense," Megan agreed. "But we don't *know* that Moreland took it from

Dennis, or that he killed him over it. The truth is, we don't even know what 'it' is!"

"A pendant," Deirdre offered. "That's what Mr. Barchester said."

"Yes, but what sort of thing was hanging from it? A jewel or a golden medallion or what? And what was it hanging from? A golden chain or a simple string? It could even have been a little pouch hung on a bit of twine. His description was very vague."

"Aye, that's true. It might not have been a necklace," Frank mused. "It could have been something small that he just carried close to him like that for safekeeping."

"But clearly it was something 'precious,' " Megan went on, emphasizing the word Deirdre had used in describing her brother's loss.

"And clearly Moreland did not want anyone to know about it."

"Well, at least it narrows down my search," Megan said. "I know that it's something small I'm looking for, probably a necklace of some sort."

Excitement rose in her, as it always did when she was chasing down a story. But this time, there would be a far greater reward if she tracked down the truth. All the little doubts that had been teasing at the back of her mind — the liking she had felt for the duchess and the twins, and her reluctance at deceiving them, the strange feeling that had gripped her when she first saw Theo Moreland — all vanished now. Such minor things scarcely mattered.

Tomorrow she would start stalking her brother's killer.

5

Megan presented herself at her new job the next morning with firm resolve. She was there to find her brother's killer, and she was determined not to be swayed by other feelings.

Barchester's story had brought back vividly her own memories of Dennis, making his loss once again a fresh hurt. She could well imagine how Dennis's imagination would have fired at the tales of the lost treasures of the Incas. She could picture his smile, his reddish brown eyes, so much like her own, lighting with eagerness. He had always been interested in the Inca civilization; she could remember him recounting with horror the bloody takeover of their lands and fortunes by the Spanish invaders centuries earlier.

Dennis would have loved to have found some piece of that empire, however small, some tangible link to that long-ago time.

Megan felt sure that he had diligently looked for treasure. What if he had found it? After all, Barchester had said that Coffey had come upon some artifacts. Surely Dennis could have, as well.

Thinking back on it, Megan wished that she had questioned Barchester more closely about Mr. Coffey's find. At the time, she had been more interested in digging more deeply into the quarrel that had set Dennis's death in motion.

Well, she reminded herself, she could talk to the man again — or, better yet, she would ask Julian Coffey himself when she interviewed him. It was even possible that he might have a better idea about the pendant that Theo Moreland had kept hidden beneath his shirt.

In the meantime, she could begin looking for the necklace. At least now she had a better idea what she should be searching for.

When Megan arrived at Broughton House, she was taken in hand by the housekeeper, a short, stout, grandmotherly looking woman with snow-white hair pulled back into a soft bun. Her name, she said, was Mrs. Brannigan, though the members of the family called her Mrs. Bee, a name given to her by the first set of twins when they were children. It was clear, from the softening of her face and the faint smile upon her lips when she mentioned this fact, that the housekeeper was sincerely attached to the family.

"The 'Little Greats,' now, they can be a trial," she said confidentially as she led Megan up the back stairs. "But you look like a sensible young woman. I think you can handle them."

"The who?"

"Oh. That's what Master Theo and Master Reed used to call them when they were little — the younger twins, Master Con and Master Alex. The 'Little Greats,' for their names, don't you see?"

"Oh. Of course. Alexander the Great and Constantine the Great."

"Aye, that's it. Never was much of one for history, myself, but in this household you can't help but pick it up. Lord Bellard, now, he's a wonder — all those tiny lead soldiers. I don't know how he keeps them all straight."

Tiny lead soldiers? Megan remembered Theo Moreland mentioning something about an uncle Bellard. But what was he doing playing with toy soldiers? "Is he, um, getting on in years?"

"Oh, must be in his seventies, yes. Sharp

as a tack, though I never know half of what he's talking about. But shy, you see. His suite of rooms is on the same floor as the nursery — so he can spread out. Right now he's working on Agincourt. Just got in a batch of knights the other day, don't you know? He keeps the old battles here and the modern ones at the Park. Too difficult to move around, now, aren't they?"

"Yes, I suppose so." Megan realized that the housekeeper must mean that the old man laid out his soldiers in re-creations of famous battles, not that he was living a second childhood with toys. Still, it seemed a rather odd occupation for a grown man.

"Here we are," the housekeeper said, stopping at a door along a wide, elegant corridor on the second floor. "These are the family's bedchambers. The duke and duchess are at the end of this hall." She pointed to their left. "With Master Theo — Lord Raine, that is — next, and Lady Thisbe and Master Desmond across the hall. Then these empty rooms — Lady Olivia's and Lady Kyria's — but they only come to visit now, don't they? They're married, you see, and, of course, the St. Legers have their own house in town, and Mr. McIntyre has purchased one, as well, for when he and Lady Kyria are both here. But her grace is hesitant to make them over into guest rooms. Perfectly natural, after all, and when there are so many rooms here, it scarcely matters."

"No, I'm sure not," Megan agreed, not sure why the voluble housekeeper was telling her all this.

"So you are down here," the older woman went on, going around the corner into a side hall. She stopped before the first door and opened it. "It's a pleasant room, I think, though a bit noisier, as it looks down on the street instead of back on the gardens."

Megan stopped on the threshold of the room, looking about her in astonishment. It was a spacious, well-furnished room, with a set of windows framed by heavy dark green velvet curtains. The dark green was reflected in the green-and-gold brocade cover atop the bed and the thick Persian rug that centered the room. A large wardrobe closet, vanity and dresser in mahogany, along with a small table and reading lamp beside a comfortable chair, completed the room.

The place was far larger and more elegant than Megan's own room at home and certainly was not what she had expected of a room given to a tutor of the family's children. An avid reader of the Brontë sisters and their successors, she had envisioned a cramped, dark room, sparsely furnished, among the servants' quarters or perhaps off the nursery.

"But I — this is my room?" Megan asked.

The housekeeper smiled. "Well, the boys' tutors usually stayed in a room off the nursery, but that wouldn't be proper, now, would it, what with you being a young lady and all. So her grace directed me to put you in here. In general, you see, she doesn't believe in separating the youngsters from the family." She shrugged, indicating the closest thing to disapproval that Megan had seen in her. "All the others' rooms have always been on this floor, and their governesses, too, when they were young."

"I — I see." A little dazed, Megan walked about the room, looking out the window at the view of the wide thoroughfare below and running a hand along the heavy bedspread. "It's beautiful."

"I'm glad you like it," a masculine voice said from the doorway.

Megan started, her heart leaping into her throat. She recognized the voice even before she turned to look at Theo.

He lounged in the doorway, one shoulder propped against the frame, his arms crossed, grinning at her. He was, she realized, every bit as handsome as she remembered him. She had been telling herself that her memory had endowed him with a more appealing face than he really had, but obviously that was not true.

"Mr. — I mean, Lord Raine. How do you do?"

"I'm doing quite well — now," he replied, uncrossing his arms and coming forward into the room. "I am pleased to see that we did not scare you off."

"I assure you, it would take more than what I saw the other day to scare me off," Megan replied tartly, annoyed by the fact that she even noticed how handsome the man was.

The acerbity of her statement seemed to bother Moreland not at all. His grin only grew. "Ah. Plucky to the end, I see. I always like that." He turned his attention to the housekeeper. "Mrs. Bee, you're looking as lovely as ever this morning."

"Get on with you, now," the housekeeper replied, but she blushed a little with pleasure and smiled as she said it, clearly not immune to Moreland's charm. "I can always tell when you're wanting something from me."

"Mrs. Bee! You wound me," he replied, laying a hand on his heart in a mock-dramatic manner.

"Same as when you and Master Reed were little and coming around trying to sweet-talk me out of a cookie."

"And here I was about to offer to take a task off your hands," Theo retorted. "I was going to show Miss Henderson up to the nursery for you."

"Were you now?" Mrs. Brannigan said, shooting him a speculative look. "Well, then, I'll take you up on that offer. It'll save a bit of wear and tear on these old joints, and that's a fact." She turned toward Megan. "The footmen will bring your trunk up later, miss. If you need anything else, just let me know."

With a bob of the head toward Moreland, she turned and walked out of the room. Megan, left standing alone with Theo Moreland in the middle of her bedroom, felt suddenly ill at ease. She could not remember when, if ever, there had been a man other than her father or brothers in her bedroom. It seemed far too intimate a setting.

"I, uh, thank you, but I feel sure that

there is no need for you to escort me to the nursery," she told Moreland stiffly. "I can doubtless find it on my own."

"Doubtless you can," he admitted easily. "But it would scarcely be gentlemanly of me."

"Certainly I cannot be responsible for that," Megan retorted dryly.

He extended his arm courteously to her as he had the other day, and Megan could think of no way not to take it without being rude. But she could not help but wonder why Theo Moreland was doing this. Employers did not customarily offer their arm to an employee any more than they put themselves out to show that employee to their workplace — certainly not when there was another employee around who could do it just as well.

She did not think that she was being conceited in thinking that Moreland was expressing an interest in her. But why? Megan could not help but feel that same breathless fear that somehow Theo Moreland was onto her, that he knew who she was and was looking for some opportunity to trip her up.

Megan told herself that she was being foolish. An employer flirting with someone who was not much more than a servant usually did so for the obvious reasons. Megan was not unaccustomed to men flirting with her — or even making quite unwarranted and improper advances. She knew that the plain businesslike shirtwaist and dark skirt she wore could not completely conceal her curvaceous figure, and her face, while not classically beautiful, was lively and appealing. And there was something about a woman on her own that seemed to all too often call forth the basest desires in men.

In all likelihood, she reminded herself, it was merely that sort of desire that impelled Theo Moreland to seek her out. He was undoubtedly the loathsome sort who used his position of power to impose his desires upon the women who were unfortunate enough to work for him. It was a little surprising, perhaps, that he would do so right under his own mother's nose, but, then, she thought with a mental sniff, why would she expect even that much gentlemanly reticence from the man who had killed her brother?

Well, she thought with some satisfaction, he would find out that she was not some helpless female whom he could seduce — or force himself on — with impunity. Megan Mulcahey was well able to take care of herself.

She laid her hand on his arm, pleased that not the slightest twitch betrayed her nervousness at doing so. As he led her down the hall and up the main staircase — rather wider than the servants' stairs that she and Mrs. Brannigan had climbed earlier — she remarked on the other halls that sprouted off from the main passage and all the rooms that lined them. Broughton House was enormous. She could see that the task of searching it would be almost overwhelming. Even the fact that she had gotten some faint idea of what she should be looking for made it very little easier — a pendant was a rather small item to find in this house.

"I can see why you thought I would need a guide," she said lightly. "There are an awful lot of rooms here."

"You should see Broughton Park," Theo responded wryly. "Some of its wings are a veritable rabbits' warren."

"Broughton Park?"

"The country seat," he responded. "My parents generally spend most of their year there. They only come here for the season. I can't think why, as neither of them likes it."

Good heavens, Megan thought with an

inner sigh, there was a whole other house in which this "precious" object might be hidden. She had to wonder how she would manage to hold up this charade of being a teacher long enough to explore everywhere.

As they neared the nursery, Megan could hear the sound of laughter, not only the childish tones of the twins, but also a deeper masculine chuckle and the lighter, higher notes of a woman. Theo's eyebrows went up, and he moved at a faster clip down the hall.

"Reed!" he exclaimed as he turned into the schoolroom. "I thought that was you I heard. And Anna! What a wonderful surprise. When did you get in?"

"This morning." The man who was seated on one of the desktops, his long legs stretched casually out in front of him, rose with an easy grace and came toward them, stretching out his hand to take Theo's in a firm shake. "I promised Anna a season."

He cast a warm look back toward the cluster of desks, where a well-dressed, attractive woman sat between Con and Alex. She stood up and came toward them, too, smiling at Theo a little shyly.

"Hello, Theo."

"Hello, Anna." Theo took her hand and

leaned in to lightly kiss her cheek. "You look radiant. It's hard to believe that you have been traveling."

Anna chuckled. "We have been up since five o'clock. We are still on country hours, you know."

She turned toward Megan, her wide gray eyes resting on her for a long moment. "Hello," she said, extending her hand. "I am Anna Moreland. You must be the new tutor."

"Why, yes, I am," Megan replied, faintly surprised.

"Anna always knows things," Alex told Megan in explanation.

"I beg your pardon?" Megan looked at the boy in confusion.

"She sees things," Con added matter-of-factly. "I mean, things other people don't see."

An icy finger ran up Megan's spine.

"Con! Alex!" Anna scolded, casting the two boys a dark look. "Stop. You'll make Miss Henderson think I am some sort of witch or something." She turned back to Megan, smiling. "I'm sorry. Con and Alex sometimes exaggerate a little. They had described their new tutor to me. That is how I guessed who you were."

"No, *I* am sorry," Theo put in. "You

should not have had to guess. I am lax in my introductions. You are correct, Anna. This is Miss Henderson, the newest sacrificial lamb on the altar of the twins' education. Miss Henderson, please allow me to introduce my brother, Reed, and his wife, Anna."

"How do you do?" Megan smiled politely at the tall man whom she thought she would have guessed was Theo's brother even without any introduction. Though he was not quite as handsome as Theo and his eyes were gray rather than green, his square-jawed face was similar enough to Theo's to mark him as a relative.

The woman beside him was quietly attractive, with thick golden brown hair and large, intelligent gray eyes. She was a trifle taller than Megan and slender, and there was about her an air of calm that drew one to her. Megan liked her immediately, and she sensed that if she had met this woman in any other situation, they would have become friends. As it was, she knew that she could not afford to let herself become close to anyone in this household.

"Is this your first day with these rapscallions?" Reed asked, smiling, reaching out to ruffle Alex's hair.

"Yes, it is," Megan replied. "I am looking

forward to teaching them." Looking forward with trepidation, if the truth be known, Megan thought, but she wasn't about to let anyone see that fact.

"I hope you still feel that way by this evening," Reed joked.

"Stop it. You and Theo both," Anna scolded her husband, shooting him a fierce look. She turned toward Megan, saying earnestly, "Con and Alex are really quite wonderful boys, and I am sure that you will enjoy teaching them. Their brothers simply like to tease."

"I am sure that I will have no problem with Con and Alex," Megan agreed, casting a smile at the boys. "We have already worked well together, haven't we?"

"Oh, yes," Alex agreed emphatically. "We told Anna what you did. It was just what she would have done, wasn't it, Anna?"

"Exactly," Anna said, and smiled at Megan. "I think it is time that we let you get down to work with your charges, don't you? We haven't even visited with the duchess yet. We came straight up here when we arrived."

"We knew these two would be the only ones in the family already up," Reed added. His hand slipped around his wife's waist, and he smiled down at her as he went on, "Come along, love. Mother will be very put out if she is the last to hear."

Reed and Anna nodded goodbye to Megan and started toward the door. Reed paused, glancing back at his brother. "Coming, Theo?"

"Yes, of course." Theo turned back to Megan. "I must take my leave, Miss Henderson." His mouth quirked up in a smile, and Megan felt an odd warmth rush through her.

She stiffened unconsciously and straightened her shoulders. "Goodbye, Lord Raine. Thank you for showing me to the nursery. I trust in the future I will be able to find my own way."

"No doubt you will." His green eyes danced, and Megan was aware of a sudden traitorous urge to smile at him.

He bowed slightly toward her before he turned and followed his brother and sister-in-law out the door.

Megan watched him go, then realized what she was doing and turned quickly back to the twins. She looked at the two lads, who were gazing back at her with interest.

Panic gripped her for a moment, and she was suddenly sure that the boys would realize in only moments that she was not really a teacher.

"Well . . ." Megan forced a smile. "I guess it is time for us to get down to work."

"All right. What do you want us to do?" Con asked. She was almost sure it was Con, anyway.

"What do you usually do?" Megan stalled.

The twins looked at her a little oddly, then Alex said, "Well, you know, our lessons. Which one we do first just depends on the tutor."

"What's your favorite subject?" Megan went on.

"Science," Alex replied promptly. "That's easy. It's the interesting stuff."

"Math, too," Con added.

"What's your least favorite?"

There was no doubt in that regard, apparently, for the boys chorused, "Greek and Latin."

"Ah." Megan nodded and smiled. "I never much liked them myself." The truth was, she had never so much as seen a word of Greek, but she had hated laboring over the Latin texts at the convent school, and Greek sounded even worse. "Then which shall we tackle first? The best or the worst?"

The boys gaped at her.

"You mean — you're asking us? Which lesson to do first?"

"Why not? You are, after all, the ones doing them. Personally, I like to take the hardest thing first and get it over with, then end the day with what I like best. That makes it easier to get through, don't you think?"

"Sure," Con agreed.

"Then why don't we all sit down and draw up our schedule?" Megan suggested. It seemed to her the most rational way to go about the matter, though she felt sure that the nuns who had taught her would probably be horrified at the idea of the students choosing any part of their studies, even the order in which they did them.

Alex and Con grinned at each other.

"Wizard!" Alex exclaimed. "I knew you were going to be the best tutor."

"Good. And I expect that you will be the best pupils," Megan tossed back with a grin, and started toward the desks.

The boys quickly followed her, and they settled down to the task of mapping out their days.

Reed Moreland turned to his wife as they walked away from the nursery and down the stairs. "You saw something when you looked at her, didn't you?"

Anna shot him a look. "No. I did not see anything."

"I was watching you," Reed retorted. "There was something about the way you looked . . ."

"Miss Henderson, you mean?" Theo asked, frowning and turning to look at Anna. "What are you talking about? Anna, did you have one of your visions?"

Like all the Morelands, Theo knew about the horrifying events that had occurred at Winterset, Reed's home in Gloucestershire, a few months earlier, before Reed and Anna were married. There had been a series of grisly murders in the area, and Anna had experienced eerie, terrifying moments during which she had envisioned the murders that had just taken place. The twins and Kyria, along with her husband, Rafe, had been visiting Reed at the time and had been there for part of the ordeal. But even they did not know the full extent of the shattering visions Anna had seen, visions that had made her doubt her very sanity. Reed had confided the whole story only to his older brother and closest confidant.

"No," Anna told Theo now, grimacing. "Really, you two are as bad as the twins.

You would think I went about seeing things every time I met a person. I did not have a vision. I didn't 'see' anything about Miss Henderson."

"But . . ." her husband said encouragingly.

"But I felt something," Anna admitted, frowning a little. "I — it was very vague. But I — I felt a little fear."

"Fear?" Theo's scowl deepened. "You mean you felt that Miss Henderson was afraid?"

"No. I don't think so. There was just a . . . a sense of turmoil, of . . . oh, I'm not sure what," she finished disgustedly. "It was very vague. I think it was more a general sense of fear — maybe something frightening looming in the future. Really, it was nothing to base anything on."

"You think that perhaps she is in danger? Or will be in danger?"

"Perhaps," Anna said somewhat reluctantly. "Please, don't speak of it to her. I am quite unsure about it, and I wouldn't want to frighten her. I quite liked her. And lately, well, the things I feel have been different. Ever since . . ." She cast a glance at her husband, a faint smile playing on her lips. "I — I feel things more easily now, more quickly, and I'm not entirely sure how much to trust my 'feelings.' "

"Ever since what?" Theo asked.

Anna glanced at him, a blush starting in her cheeks, and Theo's eyes narrowed speculatively.

"Are you saying — Reed?" He turned his gaze to his brother inquiringly, a pleased smile starting on his face.

Reed grinned. "Yes. Anna is — we are going to have a baby."

"Congratulations!" Theo reached out to shake his brother's hand, then turned to Anna. "My very best to you. I know how happy this must make you."

Anna smiled a little shyly. "Yes, I am very happy."

Theo knew from what Reed had told him that for several years Anna had believed that she could never marry and have children, and he felt sure that her pleasure at expecting a baby was even more than most women felt.

"Have you told the others?"

"No. We've seen no one but Alex and Con yet," Reed replied. "They were the only ones up and about when we arrived — well, except for Thisbe and Desmond, and they were already ensconced in their laboratory. We are going down to tell the duchess now. It is why we decided to come for the season. We would have stayed at Winterset, otherwise. There is still a great deal to be done there, getting the house in order, but Anna has never had a season, and once the baby is here, it will be much more difficult to come to London, so we thought that we must make it this year." He smiled lovingly down at his wife. "She has promised me that she will not overexert herself."

"I feel wonderful," Anna assured him, her gray eyes shining. "You needn't worry about me at all. Truthfully, I think that I will feel nothing but happiness the whole time. It is so much more than I ever hoped for."

"We are hoping to tell the whole family," Reed went on. "Are Olivia and Stephen in town? I am sure that Kyria and Rafe must be here."

"Oh, yes. Olivia and Stephen arrived a day or two ago, and Kyria and Rafe have been here for two weeks. Kyria isn't likely to miss a season." He turned to Anna with a smile. "I can assure you that you will have your fill of parties. If Kyria does not host it or go to it, then a party is generally not considered worth going to."

"Yes. I shall have to warn her not to wear you out," Reed agreed with some concern.

Anna chuckled. "My dear, I am quite capable of knowing whether I am about to be 'worn out.' I think it will be delightful."

Anna had lived a quiet life in the country, forced by circumstances to forego a London coming out when she was young, and clearly she was determined to attend as many of the glittering parties as she could.

"Come, let's go downstairs. I am sure that Mother and Father must be at breakfast by now," Theo said as they started down the stairs. "They will be so pleased by your news." He cast a grin at his brother. "And it will take some of the family pressure off me."

"Don't be absurd," Reed responded. "I am certain that neither of our parents has ever urged you to marry and produce heirs."

"No, of course not. I suspect that Father completely forgets about being a duke for months at a time. And Mother is somewhat embarrassed about it. But it seems that every other outlying relative reminds me of my 'duty' to my name every time I see them. Especially Great-aunt Hermione." Theo grimaced. Society generally regarded it as the eldest son's duty to ensure the succession of the family title and estate. It would at least reduce some of the expectation if he could point out that his brother had produced a son.

"No doubt." His brother chuckled. "Our great-aunt, Lady Rochester," he explained in an aside to his wife, "is the terror of the family. I can only hope that you will not have to meet her."

"Ha! No one could get that lucky twice in a lifetime," Theo stuck in. "You used up your share of luck when she was snowed in in Yorkshire and couldn't attend your wedding."

"One of the primary reasons for getting married in the winter," Reed replied.

Theo just smiled, well aware that it had not been concern for marrying without relatives that had prompted their wedding in December, but simply the couple's eagerness to be together after the years that they had been separated.

They reached the bottom of the stairs and turned toward the smaller, more intimate dining room where the family generally took their breakfasts.

"Theo . . ." Anna began, and there was something about the tone of her voice that made both Theo and Reed turn to look at her. "There was one other thing that I felt about Miss Henderson . . ."

"What?" Theo's gaze sharpened. "About danger?"

"No. About you. I had the impression that whatever the turmoil or danger around her is — that she will bring it to you." Anna's eyes fixed on his gravely. "Theo, I felt, I sensed . . . that she wants to harm you."

6

It did not take the twins long to lay out their schedule. Like Megan, they wanted to get through first with their least-liked subjects, so the reviled Latin and Greek led off their day, followed by something enjoyable — history — some easier but boring subjects such as grammar and spelling, then literature and math, and they ended the day with their favorite, science.

Megan looked over the proposed schedule. "You've left no time for lunch or a snack," she pointed out.

"Snack?" the boys repeated.

"Yes, you know — some milk and cookies or something. To take a little rest and get some energy. And outside time. You will need some time to go outside and play. Else you'll get restless."

"Outside? Play?" Now the twins were goggling at her. They glanced at each other, grins slowly spreading across their faces.

"Wizard!" Con exclaimed, and Megan began to think she could quickly tire of that expression.

"Do you mean it?" Alex added.

"Of course."

Megan felt on fairly firm ground here. She had done an article a few years back about an experimental educational program that had been started by a group in Massachusetts. The founders of the group had emphasized the value of allowing youngsters a break during the day in which they could burn off their youthful energy; it had been their contention that healthful exercise would also recharge the students' mental faculties. It had sounded wonderful to Megan, who had always suffered through the last part of the school day, longing to get outside and run, and she suspected that the duchess, with her unusual and forward-thinking views, would be willing to try an experimental program in education, as well.

Plus, she did not want to be stuck in the nursery for the entire day. She needed to move through the house, to become familiar with the layout of it and determine what areas she should explore further. She would be able to walk around a bit while the twins were out playing.

"You are the best tutor we ever had," Alex assured her solemnly.

She smiled. "I hope that means you won't put frogs in my bed or anything of that sort."

"We wouldn't do that," Con protested, adding tellingly, "not to you, miss."

Megan could not keep from chuckling. "But you have done it to others, I'll warrant."

Another look passed between the twins.

"That's all right," Megan told them. "You needn't reveal your secrets. Probably better if I don't know, actually. Now, let's put in thirty minutes for luncheon here, after spelling and grammar. And play — shall we call it exercise time? That sounds better, doesn't it?"

She quickly inserted the additions into the schedule. "There we go. So . . ." Megan's stomach tightened at the thought of facing the actual teaching. "I suppose I should see where you are in Latin and Greek. Um, where are your books?"

The twins pulled out their texts and composition books, and opened them. "Here is where we stopped with Mr. Fullmer," Con pointed out with a sigh.

"Good. Well . . ." Megan looked at the pages of Greek. She understood not a word of it. "The best thing, no doubt, would be to start reading where you left off. And are there exercises to do?"

"Yes. At the end of the reading."

"Very well. Read these pages, and then do the questions at the end." She had no idea how she would check their answers, she reflected, but she would deal with that problem when she came to it. "Why don't you do that after we do the Latin?"

She picked up the Latin text and flipped through it. At least she recognized some of the words, but since it had been almost ten years since she had studied it, her grasp of the language was severely lacking.

"Fullmer had us write out translations of what we read."

"How dreadfully dull," Megan commented before she thought. She caught herself at Alex's laugh. "That is — I mean — well, why don't you try reading it aloud?"

She realized her mistake as soon as she said it. If one of the boys didn't know a word, she would probably not be able to provide the answer. She could not take it back now, however. The twins obviously found this a less onerous burden than copying out the translation, and they grabbed their texts and started in on a letter from Pliny the Elder, Alex beginning.

Megan propped her head on her hand and listened. His reading brought back memories of afternoons in the convent school, listening to one of the other girls stumble through some translation while Megan had tried not to doze off, motivated to stay awake by sight of the ruler in Sister Mary Teresa's hands. She had, Megan realized now, forgotten how boring Pliny the Elder was.

Twenty minutes later, as she found herself nodding off, she stood up, stifling a yawn, and told the twins that it was time to move on to their Greek exercises.

The rest of the day was gotten through in much the same manner — asking the twins where they had left off in their studies, then setting them to work onward from there. She was on safe enough ground in spelling, grammar and literature, as those had always been her best fields, and she knew enough to get by in history, she thought, by reading ahead of her students a little. Math might be almost as severe a trial as Greek, she feared, but fortunately the twins both seemed to excel at the subject and asked no questions as they went about their exercises.

Her greatest good fortune was Thisbe's offer to teach the twins in science, for she quickly found out the first afternoon that the twins knew far more than she about plants, animals, the stars, chemical reactions and such. They were filled with glee when Megan told them that she was going to hand over their tutoring in the area to their eldest sister.

What made it even nicer was the fact that it would free up another hour and a half that she could use to search the house. Megan spent that time, as well as the twins' outdoor period, in wandering about the mansion, poking into nooks and crannies. She reasoned that if anyone questioned her about being somewhere, she could always claim that she had gotten lost in the huge house.

She started with the third floor and moved downward. There were several empty rooms just down from the nursery, but the next room she opened had an occupant.

A small, stoop-shouldered man with a shock of disordered white hair was bending over a large table, and he turned in surprise to look at her. A pair of spectacles rested on the end of his nose, and he pushed them up into his hair as he gazed at her.

"Oh!" Megan exclaimed. "I'm so sorry. Forgive me. I did not realize the room was occupied."

"No harm, my dear," the elderly man said with a shy smile. "You merely startled me. I was laying out my Welsh long-bowmen."

With a closer look, Megan now saw that what she had thought was a large table was in fact a large piece of thin wood propped up on two wooden sawhorses. On the piece of wood was a topographical layout of land, painted green. There were a myriad of little iron figures, some arranged in careful rows, but the majority still lying in a heap.

This was not the only such "table" in the room. Several flat pieces of plywood stood on sawhorses. All the others were finished products, with rolling land and flat land, and even small bodies of water. The landscapes were dotted with trees and hedges and brown roads. Miniature armies and navies were spread across the various tables, all laid out in precise order. It was all Megan could do to keep her jaw from dropping in astonishment.

This man, she realized, must be the great-uncle about whom Theo and Mrs. Bee had spoken. But the man's use of lead soldiers went far beyond anything Megan had imagined.

"It's Agincourt," Lord Bellard was saying now, looking at her hopefully.

"Ah, yes." Megan remembered that the housekeeper had said something about Agincourt. " 'Cry God for Harry, England and St. George!' "

History might not be her specialty, but she did know Shakespeare.

The small man's face brightened, and he quoted back, " 'We few, we happy few, we band of brothers.' "

Her bit of knowledge, apparently, was all it took to win over the twins' great-uncle, for he took her on a guided tour around his workroom, identifying all the battles and explaining the layouts to her. It was unfortunate, he told her with regret, that his favorite piece, the pièce de résistance of his collection, the Battle of Waterloo, was at home at Broughton Park, with the other more modern battles.

The old man did not seem to question her presence in his family's house — or, indeed, even ask her name. When at last she took her leave of him, she made a point of telling him that she was the twins' new tutor, just in case he might wonder later to whom he had been showing his collection.

He seemed only faintly interested in her words, saying merely, "Ah. How interesting. A woman. I see Emmeline's hand in that." He smiled at her. "Welcome to the house, Miss Anderson. If you need any help . . ."

Megan smiled, not bothering to correct her name. The old gentleman was a bit odd, but she could not help but like him. It was clear that questions of propriety or rank — or even identity — did not signify to him in the least. Scholarship, she suspected, was the only thing that mattered to the sweet old man.

She made her way through more of the house, peering into empty rooms and cautiously opening closed doors. Bedchambers predominated, although there were also various drawing rooms, sitting rooms, studies and a library, as well as a large and ornate ballroom. She encountered a few servants, and a time or two she saw a member of the family in the distance, but each time she quickly ducked back around a corner or into an empty room to avoid being seen.

She was most intrigued by the locked room that she found on the second floor next to the library. The door from it into the hallway was locked, and when she entered the library, she found a door in the middle of one wood-paneled wall that she felt must surely lead into the room next door, as well. When she tried it, she found that it was locked, too. Her curiosity was well up by then. A locked room in this open, friendly household was an unusual thing. It must contain something valuable, she reasoned, and it would therefore be the place where she was likeliest to find whatever rare and/or expensive item Theo Moreland might have taken from her brother.

Megan strolled back up to the nursery, where she took high tea with Con and Alex. The boys had returned from their science class with smudges of various sorts on their hands and faces, and smelling faintly of sulfur. They chattered animatedly about the chemical experiment, which had gone, according to them, "almost perfectly." Megan decided it was best not to inquire as to exactly what had not been perfect about it.

"Once you clean up a bit," she said, "I thought we might go down to the library and look for some books you might like to read."

When they were in the library, she thought, she could easily work around to trying the locked door, and then no doubt the voluble twins would tell her what lay behind it. However, her plans were dashed when Con and Alex shook their heads.

"Oh, no, miss, we have to clean up and go down to dinner. That's why our high tea is so small. We eat early, usually," Alex explained.

"You mean you take your evening meal with the family?" Megan asked, amazed. She had always understood that in wealthy families children ate early and alone with their governess or tutor, while the adults dined late, without the distraction of children.

"Unless there are guests and it's going to be boring. But with Reed and Anna home, I imagine the whole family will be here tonight," Con explained.

Alex swallowed the bite of cake he had just taken and added, "You will be there, too, miss."

"I will?"

Con and Alex nodded, and Con added, "Our tutors are always invited to eat with the family when we do. It wouldn't be polite otherwise, would it?"

"No. I — I suppose not." Megan thought about the wardrobe she had brought. She had nothing elegant enough for supper at a duke's table. Of course, no one would expect a tutor to look elegant. But still . . . she hated the thought of looking dowdy tonight in front of the entire Moreland clan. In front of Theo Moreland.

With a grimace, she suppressed the thought. What did it matter what she looked like to Theo Moreland? It was sheer vanity, and vanity was not going to help her discover what he had done to her brother.

Still, when she made her way down to supper with the twins later, Megan was wearing the least severe of her dresses, and she had added a softening bit of lace at the throat and cuffs, as well as putting on her best gold ear bobs. After all, she reasoned, not looking her best wasn't going to help her catch her brother's killer.

Supper at the Moreland household, she found, was a large and noisy affair. The long table was filled with people, and everyone seemed to talk at once, cutting across people and conversations. It reminded her, Megan realized with some surprise, of the evening meal in her own household growing up — lots of people and lively conversation ranging on all sorts of topics. It was enjoyable, and Megan could not help but join in, but it was not the sort of thing she had expected to find in an aristocratic British home.

Two more Moreland siblings were present this evening — a tall redheaded beauty named Kyria and a small, much quieter woman, Olivia, with soft brown hair and large, lambent brown eyes. They were accompanied by their husbands. Olivia was married to the handsome, dark-haired Lord St. Leger, who greeted Megan politely and with a sympathetic look. The other man, Kyria's spouse, was wickedly good-looking, possessed of compelling blue eyes, sunstreaked light brown hair and a flashing grin that Megan was sure could charm the birds out of the trees. His name was Rafe McIntyre, she was told, and, the duchess added with a pleased smile, as if she were handing Megan a real treat, he was an American.

Megan froze, her eyes flying to the man's piercing blue gaze, and her heart set up a galloping beat. She had not counted on meeting another American.

"Where are you from, Mr. McIntyre?" she asked, hoping that her trepidation did not show. It wasn't likely, she told herself, that he would know anything about the schools or made-up people whom she had given in her credentials to the duchess. But she could not help feeling that an American was more likely to trip her up in her lies.

"The West, Miss Henderson," McIntyre said, the warmth of his smile not quite reaching his cool blue eyes. "Before that, Virginia."

"But Rafe and I more recently resided in New York," Kyria put in, smiling at Megan.

Megan's heart sank, though she managed to keep a smile on her face. New York was a huge city, she reminded herself, and Lady Kyria would not have moved in the same circles as a lowly newspaper reporter. Even if, by some stretch of the imagination, the couple had read articles written by Megan Mulcahey in the newspaper, there was no reason to connect that woman with Megan Henderson, the tutor sitting in their dining room in England.

"It's a lovely city, New York," Lady Kyria went on.

"Yes, my lady, I have always thought so myself," Megan replied somewhat stiffly.

Megan wished she had thought to pretend that she was from some city other than New York. It had seemed best at the time, one less thing she would have to lie about, but in retrospect, it struck her as

171

foolish. What if by some strange chance one of the McIntyres *had* read her articles? What if the mere fact that they were talking about the city reminded Theo that it was where the man he had killed came from? What if Dennis had at some time mentioned his sister Megan?

She glanced over at Theo, who was sitting almost directly across the table from her. His eyes were on her already, their bright green color dark in the candlelight. She was aware, as she was every time their eyes met, of a sizzle along her nerves. Megan flushed and looked quickly back toward Kyria.

Kyria's gaze went from Megan to Theo speculatively, but she said nothing.

Beside Kyria, Rafe asked casually, "How did you happen to apply for the position of tutor for the Terrible Two?"

"Rafe! We aren't!" Con and Alex chorused in mock indignation, and Rafe grinned, sending the boys a wink.

"Well, I did not consider it at first, of course," Megan replied, aware of McIntyre's cool blue eyes studying her as she talked. "I assumed that no one would hire a woman as a tutor for two boys. But I had heard that the Duchess of Broughton was different, that she believed in the equality of the sexes, so I thought I would apply to her. I wanted to prove that I could handle the job as well as a man."

"Well done, Miss Henderson," the duchess put in warmly from her end of the table.

The conversation moved on as Theo asked Rafe a question about a horse he had bought a few days before, and Megan relaxed, grateful that the attention had been taken off her.

Olivia St. Leger, who sat on one side of Megan, leaned in closer and murmured, "I hope we are not overwhelming you."

"Oh, no!" Megan replied honestly.

While Rafe McIntyre and the fact that he and Kyria had lived in New York had raised a certain unease in her, she had otherwise thoroughly enjoyed the dinner conversation. The Moreland family was a trifle odd, but she found their eccentricities charming. None of them seemed to be snobbish in the slightest degree. Everyone, indeed, had gone out of his or her way to place Megan at ease.

She felt a flash of guilt at the way she was deceiving them all. She thought of how they would feel when she revealed the truth about what Theo had done, and she hated to think of how it would pain them.

They would, she knew, despise her.

When the meal was over and Megan was leaving the dining room behind the twins, it was Theo who caught up to her and bent near her to ask a similar question. "Ready to pack it in after a night of the 'mad Morelands'?"

"No, of course not," Megan replied, firmly quelling the traitorous twist of warmth that ran through her abdomen at the touch of his breath against her ear. "Who would dare to call your family that?"

"Oh, a number of people," Theo replied carelessly. "I fear that most of English society finds us distinctly odd."

"There are some," Megan responded, "who would say that they find *all* of English society distinctly odd."

He chuckled. "And they would probably be right." He paused, then went on, "Yet my mother says that you are interested in all things British."

"What?" Megan glanced up at him, puzzled, before she remembered, with a start, the lie she had told the duchess to explain why she had come to work in England. "Oh! Oh, yes, I am, of course."

She had spent hardly any time with him, and already he had caught her out in a lie! Megan reminded herself that she was going to have do much better than this or she would not last long enough here to find out the slightest thing about him or the secret of what had happened long ago with her brother.

"I have long been very fond of English poets," she went on, hoping to cover her mistake. "I wanted to see firsthand where they lived."

She all but winced at how syrupy her words sounded.

"Of course," Theo murmured.

Megan glanced at him sharply. *Had his voice been tinged with amusement? And did that mean that he suspected she was lying or that he merely thought her silly?* She found that she intensely disliked the idea of either.

Megan looked around them. Everyone else had disappeared up the stairs or down the hall into one of the sitting rooms. "You should join your family," she told him.

Moreland shrugged. "With everyone here, they will scarcely miss one."

"I doubt that." Theo, she thought, was not one who could be easily overlooked.

"If you are concerned, then let us join them." Theo offered her his arm.

Megan stepped back, clasping her hands together. It startled her how much she would have liked to slide her hand into the crook of his elbow. "I — I cannot. I should go up to my room."

"It is early yet," he protested.

"I must do some work," she replied. "I am unfamiliar with the texts the boys use, and I need to look them over. Plan my lessons."

She thought for a moment that he would protest or try to persuade her to skip her work, but he said only, "If you insist."

Perversely, Megan felt somewhat disappointed at his easy acquiescence.

"I will escort you to your room," he continued, once again offering his arm.

A little laugh escaped her. "I think I can manage to stave off the dangers between here and my bedchamber."

"Please, you must allow me to play the gentleman."

"Play?" she repeated, raising an eyebrow. "Is it only pretense, then?"

She realized, with some horror, that she sounded as if she were flirting with him. Megan looked away quickly, then started toward the stairs.

Theo walked along beside her, though he made no attempt to take her arm. "You neatly managed to avoid saying what you think of our family."

"Did I? I did not mean to. It is quite easy to say what I think of them — they are quite warm and kind, much more so than I would ever have expected. They have all been most generous and courteous to me."

"Mmm. There are those who find their behavior scandalously lax."

"I have never been attracted to snobbery, myself," Megan retorted.

"Neither have I," he agreed as they started up the wide marble-stepped staircase. "Perhaps that is why I have chosen to travel elsewhere."

"Avoiding your countrymen?" Megan asked, looking doubtful.

"Not avoiding, exactly. But I always wondered what other people were like. It seemed to me that there must be some who were not so stuffy. Less concerned with their rank or the proper form of address."

"And have you found them?"

He smiled. "Yes. And some of them have even been Englishmen."

"What about Americans?" Megan asked, sneaking a glance at him to see how he would respond.

"Oh, yes, I've met a few Americans here and there. I've been to the United States. Not New York. I traveled from the Orient to San Francisco three or four years ago."

"How did you like it?"

"A very interesting place. Raw and new and bustling. Rather like a lot of your country, I imagine."

"I have never been west, myself," Megan admitted.

"No interest in traveling?" he asked, slanting a look at her.

"No, it's not that. Lack of opportunity, I suppose. And I enjoy what I do."

"Teaching the children of wealth?"

"Oh. Well . . . it is always satisfying to impart knowledge." Megan tried to think of what enjoyment teachers would get out of their job, since she had spoken unthinkingly of her feelings about her own career. "To mold young minds."

"I see."

Megan also realized that she had let the conversation slip away from the topic of Americans whom Theo had known. "What did you think of the Americans you met? Less formal than the British, I imagine."

He nodded. "Yes. Quite friendly. At least most of them. Easy to get to know. Eager to help one out."

Megan nodded, hoping that he would expand on the subject, but he seemed content to let it drop.

"Were they explorers, like yourself?" she prodded.

Theo shrugged. "Some of them. Most, I guess, were off ships. Or there buying goods to import." He smiled. "Like Englishmen."

Megan gritted her teeth, wondering if he was being purposefully evasive. She wished she could just ask pertinent questions, as she did when she was researching a story. Of course, he would scarcely admit to having killed an American, anyway. She decided to try another tack.

"It must be fascinating, exploring far away places," she said. "You must have seen many wonderful things."

"Oh, yes." He smiled, remembering. "Temples, palaces, jungles. Extraordinary animals."

"Like the ones you sent back to the twins." He murmured agreement, and she went on, "I suppose you've probably brought back other things, as well. Silks from the Orient, for instance. Jade. Or precious stones. Artifacts from some ancient ruin."

"Yes, some things. Especially products of the country. Not artifacts, really. I disagree with many Europeans' habit of taking or buying the treasures of a country. Pieces of

179

history and culture are irreplaceable and belong to that country. My father and I disagree in that regard. He has numerous pieces of ancient Greek and Roman art and artifacts in that collection room of his."

"Collection room?" Megan repeated, interested. A collection room seemed like a perfect place to hide a treasure.

"Yes. If you're interested in such things, I am sure he would be happy to show it to you. Of course, his contention is that if he did not buy the objects and bring them to England, someone else would, or they would be left to ruin or be looted by local thieves. And there is something to be said for that. No doubt many of the ancient treasures would be destroyed or lost if left where they were, and the countries where they are located are often in no position to preserve and display them properly. Certainly it is the common practice of archaeologists and such to bring back what they find for the men who have financed their expeditions. Still, it is a practice I dislike."

"You have never brought back such things?" Megan asked, hoping that her question did not sound as skeptical as she felt.

He grinned at her. "I don't claim to be a

saint, Miss Henderson. Of course I have brought back some jewels and such. Kyria would never have forgiven me if I had not. But I have generally left any ruins I have traveled to intact. I don't believe in taking something that I consider a national treasure, especially as I have gotten older and gained more knowledge and experience." He shrugged. "Perhaps it is a meaningless distinction. Besides, I have to admit that, frankly, I am less interested in such things than my father. Far easier to be virtuous in that case."

As she was still trying to frame a question that would not give away her interest in what he had brought back with him from his trip up the Amazon, they reached the door of her bedroom. There was little Megan could do but turn to him and smile politely.

"Thank you for seeing me up to my room," she said.

"I can assure you with all honesty that it was my pleasure," Theo responded.

He looked down at her, his green eyes gazing deep into hers in a way that made Megan feel distinctly breathless. She could feel an unaccustomed heat rising in her cheeks, and she hoped that he could not see the betraying blush in the light cast by the wall sconces.

Theo reached down and took her hand in his. Megan's heart sped up. She wished that she could think of something, anything, to break the moment, but she could only stand numbly, watching him, as he lifted her hand to his lips and gently kissed her fingers. His lips were warm and soft against her skin, and her fingers trembled at the touch, heat corkscrewing down through her torso and pooling in her loins.

"Good night, Miss Henderson. Sweet dreams."

Megan had to clear her throat before she was able to answer. "Good night."

She snatched her hand away from his and hurried into her room, closing the door behind her.

7

During the next few days, Megan managed to avoid seeing Theo for more than a few fleeting moments. She chose not to inquire into her own reasons for being happy about that, simply accepting with gratitude the fact that for the next two evenings the duke and duchess and most of their family were committed to social engagements, which meant that the twins, and therefore Megan, had their supper upstairs in the nursery schoolroom. She pleaded illness the following evening, but the concern of the twins and even the duchess, who came to Megan's room to inquire after her health, forced her to decide that she would have to forego that scheme in the future.

Megan steeled herself the following evening to go down to the family dinner, only to find, to her relief and inexplicable disappointment, that all her effort had been for naught, since Theo had gone out to dine at a friend's.

That fact was, of course, quite fortunate, as she quickly reminded herself, since tonight she planned to search the duke's collection room.

Over the course of the last few days, in between the twins' schooling and her own hours spent in her room frantically studying in order to stay a bit ahead of them, she had finished searching most of the accessible areas of the house, even the servants' sleeping quarters and the kitchen area downstairs, the latter under the guise of seeking out a cup of hot chocolate. She had found only one other locked room, a small area off the butler's pantry, which she assumed was the storage place for the family's extensive silver serving pieces and flatware.

There were valuable items galore throughout the house, all of them sitting out in the open. Some of them looked exotic, but none appeared to her to be of South American origin — though she would be the first to admit that her knowledge in that area was limited. She realized more and more with each passing day the enormous task that she had set herself. She did not know exactly what she was looking for, other than that it was small enough to be carried on a chain about one's neck, possibly a medallion — provided, of course, that what Mr. Barchester remembered seeing Theo holding secretively was indeed something he had taken from Dennis when he killed him.

It could easily be in a safe in some wall that she had not located, or in a locked box. Or Theo could even have given it to someone else in his family — she could not help but remember his comment about bringing jewels back for his sister Kyria.

However, she realized that in order to actually accomplish any search, she needed to narrow it down to the most likely places where the mysterious object might be located. Those areas were Theo's own bedchamber and his father's collection room.

Searching both involved a certain amount of risk, since there was no reason for her to be in either one of those places. She decided to start with the duke's collection room in the hopes that she would get wonderfully lucky and find her quarry there, and not have to search Theo's room.

When Theo had mentioned his father's collection room the other night, Megan's mind had immediately leaped to the locked room beside the library. It seemed the right place for a scholar to have a room filled with the antique goods that interested him, and a valuable collection would warrant a lock. Besides, she was fairly certain that she had looked in every other room in the house and had found none that contained such a collection, which made it likely that it was the one room into which she had not looked.

It took only a trip to the library with the twins to confirm that the locked door in the library led into the duke's collection room. The boys had offered to open it for her, explaining that the duke kept the key for it in his study. She had declined, saying that they had best get on with their studies. Besides, she added, she doubted that the duke would want them all poking about his room.

"Oh, he doesn't mind," Con assured her cheerfully. "As long as we're careful."

"The lock is mostly to keep the servants from going in and dusting. One of his pieces got broken that way once," Alex explained. "And, of course, he wants to keep thieves out, though it's my opinion that a thief would take the silver and the jewels, not vases and broken statues and such."

"Well, those fellows did break into the house to get something out of the collection room that one time at Broughton

Park," Con pointed out.

"He has another one?" Megan asked, her heart sinking at this further demonstration of the enormity of her task.

The boys nodded. "Yes, at the house in the country. It's larger, actually. Papa spends more time there, and anyway, that house is bigger."

"But those men weren't really after anything of Papa's," Alex argued. "It was Kyria's reliquary they wanted."

"Your father keeps other things in his collection room?" Megan asked quickly. "Valuables that belong to you children?"

Con shrugged. "Sometimes. But nobody else collects much except Papa. Somebody just happened to give Kyria that box."

"Collapsed on the doorstep and died," Alex added.

Megan stared. "Are you serious?"

"Oh, yes. Lots of people wanted the box," Con said matter-of-factly. "Alex was abducted. They tried to get me, too, but I got away."

"I got away, too!" Alex protested.

"Yes, but it took you longer."

Megan intervened quickly to cut off one of the twins' lengthy debates. Close as they were, she had discovered that they were also each other's chief rival in sports, academics and seemingly every other aspect of life.

"Does this sort of thing happen often here?" she teased.

The boys considered her statement seriously.

"I'm not sure how much 'often' would be," Alex mused. "There were those murders near Reed's house. Con and Anna and I discovered one of the bodies." His face paled a little at the memory.

"And Olivia investigated those ghosts a few years ago," Con added. "But we didn't have anything to do with that. It all happened at Stephen's house."

Megan looked at the boys, not sure what to say. The Moreland family seemed to get into an inordinate number of scrapes.

Alex frowned a little. "I'm sorry. Perhaps we shouldn't have told you."

"You aren't going to leave because of that, are you?" Con asked.

"No, I won't leave because of that," Megan promised, smiling at them. "However, I do think it is time we got back to our studies."

Megan had to wait two days to break into the collection room, for both that evening and the next, several members of the family were out at social events of one sort or another. She had no idea at what time they would return, and it would not do to be caught rummaging around in a locked room when any of them came home. Some parties, she knew, lasted until the wee hours of the morning, and she would not be able to stay awake long enough to break in after all of them had come home.

The third evening, however, everyone spent quietly at home, with the exception of Theo, who had gone to dinner at a friend's house. Megan, too nervous to spend her evening as she usually did, reading ahead in the twins' texts, paced up and down in her room, going to the door frequently to open it a crack and listen for any sounds.

Gradually the house began to settle down. She heard the duchess's voice as she went down the hallway to her room, accompanied by a lower murmur that Megan identified as the duke. Later, there was the sound of the servants as they went about their late evening chores of turning down beds and helping the ladies of the house out of their difficult garments. Megan was sure that Thisbe and her husband had long since gone to bed, as they were in the habit of retiring early. Finally, a great deal later, she heard the sound of a heavy tread.

Theo, she thought, returning from his evening. Hurrying to the door, she opened it a crack and peered out. The hall sconces had been turned down to their lowest, casting much of the corridor into shadow. She slipped out into the hallway and edged around the corner to look toward the family's bedrooms. She was quick enough to catch a glimpse of Theo's back as he went into his room and closed the door behind him.

She continued to wait. It was good that Theo was home; now she would not have to worry about him returning to the house while she was in the collection room. Megan resumed her seat in her chair, a book open and unread on her lap as she forced herself to be patient until the hands of the clock drew close to midnight.

Surely everyone was in bed now. The only ones whom she had not heard were Reed and Anna, but she thought that they must be in their chamber. As Anna had mentioned the other day, they were still accustomed to country hours. Megan had noticed that the couple was usually up when she and the twins ate breakfast.

Slipping out of her shoes, she walked in her stocking feet across the room and opened the door. She paused, listening for

190

the faintest sound, and finally, when she heard none, she stepped out into the hallway. She slid around the corner and looked down the hallway. All the doors were closed, and no sound issued from any of the rooms. She looked the other direction. Everything was quiet and dark.

Taking a deep breath, she moved down the hallway to the servants' staircase, which lay farther away from the occupied rooms. She was not worried about the servants hearing her, as they retired early and slept soundly after their labors, tucked away on the top floor.

Downstairs, she eased along the dimly lit hallway to the door of the duke's study. The door was closed, and she turned the knob and pulled it open. It stuck for a moment, then came open with a pop. Megan froze, her heart in her throat.

The house was silent. No one on the floor above could have heard the sound of the door, she reminded herself. It had simply sounded inordinately loud to her ears. She pulled the door open and looked inside the dark room. In the faint stream of light from the hallway, she could make out the dark shapes of the furniture.

She had not been inside the duke's study, and she looked around the door for a light. She found a wall sconce beside the door, and felt around it for the key-shaped handle that turned the gas light on. Finally she found it and turned it cautiously, bringing up a pale yellow glow.

Megan stopped when there was enough light to see her way across to the wide walnut desk. The twins had not said specifically where their father kept the key in his study, but the likeliest place was the desk, so she planned to start there. She moved quickly, sliding open the top right drawer. When she saw no keys, she moved to the left top drawer.

Several keys lay in a shallow tray in the drawer. Fortunately, there were tags attached to each, and she sorted through them quickly, discarding those that read Workroom or Cabinet. She stopped at the tag that read C Room. Picking it up, she closed the drawer and straightened up.

Theo Moreland was standing in the doorway.

A shriek escaped Megan's throat, quickly cut off as she clapped her hand over her mouth. She stared at Theo, her brain as frozen as her muscles.

How long had he been there? What had he seen?

"Sorry," Theo said. "I did not mean to

startle you. I was in the library, and I heard a noise in here."

"I — that's all right. I — I just didn't expect to see anyone." Her fingers curled tightly around the key, hiding it in her palm. If he had not seen her take the thing from the drawer, perhaps she could get out of this without being fired from her job — or worse. The room seemed suddenly very dark and far away from everyone else.

"I am sure not," Theo replied sardonically. "Since you are in my father's study."

"I — I was looking for a book to read," Megan explained. "I could not sleep."

Theo came into the room, walking around the desk to stand in front of her. He glanced at the bookshelves filled with tomes that lined one wall of the study.

"I think you would have better luck looking in the library," he commented mildly. "Unless, of course, you are desirous of reading about Ionic columns or Mycenaean art or the layout of the Temple of Hephaestus."

Megan realized that her excuse was foolish, but it had been the first thing that had sprung into her head. She would simply have to brazen her way out.

"I was looking for something to put me to sleep," she pointed out with some asperity. She gestured with her empty hand toward the book that lay open on the desk beside her. "I thought this one looked as if it would do the trick."

As Theo glanced toward the open tome, she slipped the key into the pocket of her skirt.

"It certainly looks it," Theo agreed easily, adding, "Though I, of course, would find it difficult, as I'm no longer proficient in Greek."

Megan hid her dismay as she took another look at the book and saw that its pages were covered with indecipherable Greek letters.

"Yes," she agreed with a casual air. "I decided it would require too much effort to enable me to sleep. Although a text on Hellenic art and architecture might be just the thing."

"No doubt you are right."

Megan was certain now that a smile was tugging at the corners of his lips. They were exceedingly well-shaped lips, she thought, and she remembered what they had felt like brushing against her hand.

Firmly she pulled her mind away from such errant thoughts. She could not understand why he should be amused. One would think that he would be angry at catching one of the family's employees in such a compromising position. The notion that he was laughing at her raised her ire.

"I'm sorry. I fail to see what is amusing," she told him in her frostiest tone, raising an eyebrow for emphasis.

"I am generally amused at life, I'm afraid," Theo commented. "I have been told many times that my outlook is not sufficiently serious."

He took a step closer to her. He was only a foot away from her now, far too close for comfort, and Megan had to tilt her head back to look up at him.

"I — I had better get back to my room," she said.

"You know," Theo said, just as if she had not spoken, "there are those who would regard your presence in the duke's study at this time of night as somewhat suspicious."

"Suspicious?" Megan asked, drawing herself up and giving him her haughtiest look. "Suspicious in what way, I might ask?"

"Indeed you might." His lips curved upward as he gazed down into Megan's face. He put his hands on her arms and slid them up, sending tingles shooting through her. "There are a number of nefarious activities in which you could be engaged. If, of course, you were not such an honest person."

"Are you impugning my character, sir?" Megan snapped back, indignation coming to her rescue. "Tell me, what 'nefarious' thing do you think I am doing, standing here in a room full of books and scholarly papers? Do you suspect that I am going to steal your father's correspondence? Or perhaps abscond with his research?" She gestured toward the duke's desk, piled with papers and books.

"I don't know," he responded, his eyes lighting in a way that set her heart tripping in its beat. "I think, perhaps, you are guilty of ensnaring me."

Theo reached up and grazed his forefinger along the line of her jaw. Heat flowered low in her abdomen, unfurling and stretching out. Her breath was suddenly unsteady, and Megan could not look away from his face. She knew she ought to protest, ought to step back and break the contact. But something kept her rooted to the spot.

His other hand came up, cupping her face. Megan looked at him, knowing that he was about to kiss her, but still she could not move away. Indeed, deep down inside her, she knew that she did not want to move away.

He bent and kissed her, his lips grazing

hers gently, almost teasingly . . . once, then twice, then settling into a long, deep kiss. Megan shuddered as yearning and excitement exploded within her.

She had never felt anything quite like this before. Her senses were bombarded with the taste and scent and feel of this man. She felt achingly soft and yielding inside, and something so hot and sweet that it made her want to moan was pulsing between her legs. Almost without volition, her arms went around Theo's neck, and she clung to him tightly as desire thundered through her. His arm curled around her back, holding her to him like a band of iron as his mouth plundered hers.

Megan was enveloped by his heat. She could scarcely breathe. But she made no move to break away. She wanted nothing but to feel more of the passions raging through her.

Theo raised his head and for an instant looked down into her eyes. Then, with a little groan, he kissed her again. His arm tightened around her, pulling her up and into his hard body. His other hand slipped down her side, his thumb caressing the curve of her breast. Megan started at the unexpected touch, the heat between her legs expanding.

His hand was slow upon her body, moving downward and curving around to her back, gliding over her buttocks and onto her leg. Megan trembled under his fingertips, amazed and aroused. His hand slipped back up the side of her leg, caressing her, and he closed his fist in her skirts.

Megan swallowed a moan. She felt as if she might melt into him. She wanted to have his hands all over her body, stroking her as he had stroked her back and leg. Her breasts were full and aching, the nipples taut, and she was aware of a shameless desire to rub her body against him.

He pulled his mouth away from hers and buried his face in her neck. "Sweet heaven! Ah, Megan . . ."

His breath was harsh and panting. The brush of it against the tender flesh of her neck sent another twisting thread of heat through her loins.

"I — I'm sorry," he said haltingly.

He held her tightly for another instant, then let go abruptly and took a step back. Megan felt the loss of his heat and strength almost like a pain through her, and she tightened her hands into fists, her fingernails digging into her palms, to keep herself from reaching out to draw him back.

She struggled to bring her thoughts together, to pull herself back to reality. *Whatever was she doing? She had been standing here in Theo Moreland's arms, kissing him like a wanton!*

Megan's hand went up to her mouth in dismay. Her lips felt tender and moist, kiss-bruised. Heat flooded her cheeks. She looked at Theo. His face was soft and slack with desire, his eyes bright.

"I —" he began.

Megan threw up her hand in a halting gesture. "No! No, please! Don't speak of it. I am — oh, this is awful!"

She was appalled at what she had done. This man had killed her brother; she had hated him for years. He was the last person in the world she would ever have thought she would kiss. Yet she had just fallen into his arms as if she had no morals. And even less sense!

"I can't — you must not —" she began. "This can't have happened!"

Megan whirled and ran from the room.

Theo stood looking after her, his chest still rising and falling rapidly. He felt dazed and shattered, as if he'd just been picked up by a whirlwind. Desire choked him, lying heavy and hard in his loins. He hadn't expected their kiss to shake him like this.

With a sigh, he opened his hand and looked down at the key that lay nestled in his palm.

Now what the devil was the twins' tutor doing trying to steal the key to his father's collection room? And what the bloody hell was he going to do about it?

Megan ran down the hall and up the main stairs, heedless of the noise she might make. She rushed into her room and closed the door behind her, leaning back against it as though to hold it against all intruders.

What in the name of all that was holy had she done? She could not understand how she could have been so lost to sense, so disloyal to her brother and family. Her heart twisted as she thought of how she had betrayed him, kissing the man who had killed him, and not just kissing him, but thoroughly enjoying it — indeed, not wanting it to end. A few more minutes, she thought miserably, and she would have been loosening her clothes to the man!

With a groan, Megan threw herself onto her bed, burying her face in the cool sheets. She lay there, berating herself, wishing she could cry . . . wishing she could stop the heat that still coursed through her veins and throbbed in her loins.

He had caught her by surprise, she told herself. *And he was so devilishly handsome!*

Megan had never considered herself weak. No other man's blandishments had ever turned her head. Why, Timothy Doyle, who had the face of an angel and owned half the girls' hearts in St. Anthony's parish, had kissed her once when they were alone in her parlor, and she had felt little more than a pleasant tingling. She would have said that she was immune to seducers, and she had always held a certain contempt for women who were so weak they gave in to such men.

And then tonight, the man she hated most in the world had turned her into a trembling, quivering, helpless female, exactly the sort of woman she despised.

Megan knew that she had had no control over herself or the situation. Indeed, she had not even been the one who had called a halt to their kisses. It was Theo who had stopped!

With a sigh, she flopped over onto her back and stared up at the tester above her bed. As if the fact that she had kissed Theo Moreland was not bad enough, she had to face the fact that she had failed to do what she had set out to do. She had not gotten inside the duke's collection room.

It was then that she remembered she still had the key to the room. With a little cry, she sat up. Her thoughts raced. She could still get into the room — she just had to find another time to do it. However, there was a definite risk in keeping the key. The duke was bound to want to get into the room sometime soon, and when he went to his desk, he would find the key gone.

She did not think that Theo would say anything to his father about finding Megan in his study. He didn't know why she was there; she felt sure he had not seen her take the key from the desk, because he had said nothing about it. And he wouldn't want to say anything to his mother or the kindly duke that would lead to their finding out that their son was in the habit of kissing the servants. But if Broughton told him that his key was missing from his desk, then Theo was likely to guess why she had been in his father's study, and he would tell the duke. And she would very soon find herself out on the street, without having exposed Dennis's killer.

Megan knew that the only way she could save herself was to put the key back into the desk where it belonged without the duke noticing. She probably should not even risk waiting until she had searched the room to do it.

She slipped her hand into her pocket, feeling for the key.

There was nothing there!

Megan paused, unwilling to believe. She stood up and dug into her pocket, pulling until it was completely turned inside out. On the chance that she had put it in the other pocket — though she was certain she had not — she searched the other pocket in her skirt and found it equally empty.

She had lost the key!

Megan let out a groan. Somehow it had slipped out of her pocket.

Anxiously, she backtracked over her path from the door to her bed, but she found no sign of a key. Just to make sure, she lit a candle and went over the same path, bending over to light the area with the candle's glow. There was no glint of metal.

It was lost.

And she was in trouble.

8

Theo was sitting on a bench at the edge of the garden, waiting for the twins to come barreling past, heading for Thisbe and Desmond's workshop at the back of the property. He had noticed that they did so every afternoon. Thisbe had happily told him that their new tutor was letting her teach the boys science.

It made sense, he knew. Thisbe and her husband knew far more about chemistry, biology and physics than any tutor they could hire. But no tutor before had been willing to turn over even part of their job to someone else. What Theo wondered was whether Miss Henderson was wise enough not to let pride stand in the way of the boys' education — or was using Thisbe's willingness to help as a way to hide the fact that she was not a tutor.

Theo had found it difficult from the start to believe that the woman was actually a teacher. She was far too attractive, to begin with, and there was nothing in her demeanor that seemed like a governess. *Why would a woman apply to teach two boys with the reputation that Con and Alex had? And why would an American travel to England to tutor children?* Megan's explanations were not completely implausible, but they had not been convincing, either.

Most of all, there was the bizarre fact that she was the woman whom he had seen in his dream years ago. The whole thing was completely inexplicable, and Theo would not have told anyone about it, sure that they would think he was crazy. Of course, he supposed, the strangeness of it did not preclude her being a tutor, but the more oddities that piled up, the less inclined he was to believe the story Miss Henderson had told. The fact that Reed's wife, Anna, had had one of her premonitions that Megan was somehow dangerous had certainly done nothing to quiet his suspicions.

Last night, when he had found her in his father's study, slipping a key from the duke's desk into her pocket, his suspicions had solidified. He could think of no logical reason for the twins' new tutor to be trying to sneak into his father's collection room.

"Theo!" Alex's cheerful voice roused Theo from his reverie, and he turned to see Alex and Con running out of the garden.

"Hello, boys," he greeted them as they skidded to a halt beside him.

"Hallo," Con replied. "What are you doing here?"

"Waiting to talk to you."

"Really? Why?" Con dropped down onto the ground beside Theo's bench, heedless of the effect the grass and dirt would have on his clothes.

"You going down to see Thisbe, too?" Alex asked. Somewhat tidier than his brother, he sat down on the bench beside Theo.

"No. Actually, I was just — well, I wanted to see how you were liking your new tutor."

The boys' immediate grins told him how much they liked Miss Henderson.

"She's bang up to the nines," Alex responded, and Con nodded his head in agreement.

"Don't you like her?" Alex went on. "Why do you want to know about her?"

"Yes, I do like her," Theo replied candidly. "I just wondered . . . well, how she was as a teacher."

"She's ever so much better than all our old tutors," Con told him.

"Oh, yes. She lets Thisbe teach us."

"And she lets us have time to go outside and play. She says it burns off energy and makes it easier for us to study."

"I see. Well, I can see how that would make you like her. But what I wondered . . ." He paused, trying to think how to phrase his question so that the boys would not grow either suspicious or defensive about their new teacher.

"Whether she's really a teacher?" Alex prompted.

Theo grimaced at his own stupidity. He might have known that the twins would figure it out as quickly as he. "Yes. That's exactly what I want to know. Obviously she has made you wonder, as well."

"She's much too pretty," Con gave Theo his own argument.

"And much too nice," Alex added with a sigh.

"Why would anyone like her want to be a tutor?" Con went on, wrinkling his forehead in genuine perplexity.

"You must have noticed something more, though," Theo urged.

"Well, she's too practical. None of our

other tutors related anything we learned to life."

"She called Pliny the Elder boring," Alex added.

Theo suppressed a grin. "Honest, at any rate."

"And she doesn't know Greek," Con said.

Alex nodded. "She never corrects us when we get a word wrong, and she hasn't graded any of our exercises."

"What about Latin?" Theo asked.

"She knows that better," Con told him.

"She's good at literature and spelling and grammar," Alex put in.

"And history. She knows more than we do." Con frowned and looked at Theo anxiously. "You're not going to tell Mother, are you?"

"We can do the math just fine," Alex joined in. "And Thisbe is better at science than any tutor we ever had."

"And who cares about Latin and Greek, anyway?" Con argued. "I know Papa does. But it's not as if we are ever going to speak them, is it? We can do those things ourselves, anyway. She's not at all stuffy, and she lets us spend extra time on the subjects we're interested in."

"But she doesn't let us get away with

anything," Alex assured him. "We don't just like her because she lets us do what we please. We have been working much better than usual, haven't we?" He turned to his twin for confirmation.

Con nodded. "That's right. Really, Theo. It's easier to think when we've had a chance to be outside some, and I like arranging our classes the way we want them."

"Don't tell Mother to let her go," Alex pleaded.

"I won't. At least, not yet," Theo told his brothers. "I probably should, but I like her, too."

"Thanks!" Con bounded to his feet, grinning.

"You're the best," Alex added.

"I just wonder why she is pretending to be a tutor," Theo explained.

Alex nodded. "It *is* odd. I suppose, well, she must not have any money, don't you think? It would be better than being a maid." His expression made it clear that he had some doubts on that subject.

"Has she done anything else odd? I mean, aside from not knowing the subjects. Have you seen her doing anything? Has she asked you questions about — I don't know, anything tutors normally don't ask about?"

The twins frowned, thinking. Finally Con said, "I don't know. Not really. She takes books from the schoolroom back to her room — I think she's reading ahead in our texts."

"She'll feed our pets. And she even picked up the boa," Alex said in a tone of some awe.

"I think Henderson might not be her last name," Con said quietly.

"What?"

"You didn't tell me that!" Alex looked at his brother accusingly.

"I'm not sure." Con looked uncomfortable. "It might not mean anything. But I noticed her handkerchief one day. It had a monogram on it, only the big initial was an *M*, and the little ones were *M* and *C*. There wasn't an *H* at all." He looked at Theo pleadingly. "But there's probably a reason, don't you think?"

"Mm," Theo murmured noncommittally. He was sure there were any number of reasons for the discrepancy. Unfortunately, he could not think of a good one.

"She's not wicked," Alex said firmly, seeing his older brother's hesitation. "I'm certain of it."

"She's not," Con added.

Oddly enough, Theo thought, he agreed

with the boys. Despite the evidence to the contrary, he had trouble believing that Miss Henderson — or whoever she was — was deceiving them because she was wicked.

He nodded. "Don't worry. I will not say anything until I find out more about Miss Henderson. And don't you, either," he added, with a warning look. "Don't tell her we have spoken about any of this."

The boys promised solemnly, then took off at a run for Thisbe's laboratory. Theo settled back on his bench to think.

He was probably playing the fool, he told himself. Letting a pretty face lead him into thinking that the person who owned it was as attractive inside as out. All her actions pointed to the fact that she was deceiving them.

But what could be her purpose?

The most likely reason, he thought, was that she was planning to steal something from the duke's collection room. His father had one of the most extensive and valuable collections of early Greek and Roman artifacts in the country. Among the broken shards of pottery and lava-encased utensils were things of such beauty and age that collectors would pay a pretty price for them.

Still, they were not items Theo thought an ordinary thief would take. The statues and the large vases were not that easy to transport, for one thing, and, moreover, it would take knowledge of Greek and Roman artifacts to know which things were the most valuable. There were many other valuables in the house — jewels, silver and coins — that would be worth more and were more easily identified and carried than Papa's ancient vases and marbles.

Was Miss Henderson a connoisseur of classical art herself? It seemed unlikely that such a person would be sneaking about disguising herself as a tutor. More likely she had been commissioned by a collector — some jealous rival who wanted some piece or pieces for himself? Or a dealer, say, who knew that anything in the Duke of Broughton's collection was among the best pieces to be had?

But why wouldn't that person hire a male to masquerade as a tutor to the twins? It would be more logical. Their radical-thinking mother had been willing to hire a woman, but it had been a risky thing to try. Even the duchess might have felt it inappropriate to have a woman supervising two boys who were only a few years from manhood.

He shook his head. Obviously, he was going to have to get some answers. And until he did, he would be keeping a close eye on the duke's collection room . . . and on Miss Henderson.

A faint smile touched his lips at that thought. It would be no burden to keep an eye on Megan Henderson.

Megan kept her gaze on the floor as she went down the stairs to the dining room the next morning, searching for any sign of the key she had dropped. She saw it nowhere, either then or on her way back up the stairs after she and the twins ate breakfast.

Worry about the key gnawed at the back of her mind all through the boys' lessons. While the twins were taking their play break in the morning, she hastened downstairs to the duke's study, but much to her chagrin, the duke was seated at his desk, reading a book, so she had to beat a hasty retreat. Later, after the boys had gone for their science lesson, she once more started downstairs, but before she even drew close to the study, she heard Theo's voice in the hallway, so she whirled and ran back up the stairs.

The last thing she wanted was to run

into Theo. She had the awful feeling that she would blush as soon as she saw him, remembering how she had acted last night. Indeed, she hoped that he would not be at the table that evening at supper.

Her hopes were dashed as soon as she walked into the dining room with the twins. Theo was standing near the end of the table, chatting with Reed and Anna. The three of them glanced over when the twins clattered into the room, Megan right behind them, but only Theo's gaze went straight to Megan's face.

Just as she had feared, a flush rose up her throat, and she looked quickly away. She could not deny, however, that even in her embarrassment, she had felt a flash of heat ripple through her abdomen in a way that had nothing to do with embarrassment and everything to do with desire.

Megan dug her fingernails into her palms as she made her way to the table, determinedly not looking over again at Theo. She refused to allow him to unnerve her, she told herself. Whatever strange and awful power he had over her, she would fight it and win. She had to.

She was on edge, worried that Theo would come over to try to talk to her, alert every moment to where he was and what he was saying. So conscious was she of him that she could scarcely pay attention to the story Thisbe was telling her about Con and Alex's successful experiment this afternoon.

The duke and duchess finally entered the room, the signal for everyone to sit down and begin the meal. Megan took a seat between Thisbe and Alex. At the Morelands' unconventional table, no one bothered with the rules of social seating or the precedence of titles, but simply took their places wherever they wanted to. Tonight, much to Megan's dismay, Theo sat down in the chair directly across the long table from her.

"Miss Henderson," he said with a smile that would have melted a heart of stone. "How are you this evening?"

Megan tilted her chin up, determined not to appear disturbed by Theo's presence. "I am fine, sir. And you?"

"Never better." His eyes lingered on her face for a moment longer before he turned his attention to Anna, on his right.

They were a smaller group than they often were at supper that evening. Neither Kyria nor Olivia nor their spouses were dining with them this evening, and as a result, the family was all grouped at one end of the long table in a more intimate setting that encouraged conversation among all the occupants of the table together, rather than the scattered and noisy multiple conversations that normally reigned at the Moreland table.

A lull opened up in the conversation as they were finishing a delicately poached fillet of sole, and Theo tossed into the silence, "Father, Miss Henderson has not seen your collection yet. I am surprised you have been so remiss."

Megan's gaze flew to Theo in astonishment. He was watching her, his eyes unreadable, the faintest trace of a smile hovering about his lips. Her heart began to hammer in her chest. He knew!

Her mind raced. *Had he seen her at his father's desk last night? But why had he not said anything then? And even if he had seen her slip the key into her pocket, how had he known which key it was?* There had been several in the drawer.

The duke's head came up, and he looked at Megan with interest. "Is that so? Are you interested in Greek and Roman art, Miss Henderson?"

"Yes, of course," Megan lied. She imagined that there were few who could admit their disinterest in the face of the duke's gently pleased countenance. "I — I am afraid that I don't know much about it, though."

"I think you should show Miss Henderson around your collection room," Theo went on, his gaze steadily on Megan. "After supper, perhaps."

"Why, of course. I would be most happy to, if you wish, Miss Henderson?" The duke's voice rose slightly at the end of his sentence, making it a question.

"Thank you," Megan responded through stiff lips. "That would be very generous of you."

"I think you will find the collection fairly extensive for one of its kind," the duke went on happily and started to describe some of the pieces.

Megan scarcely heard him, though she kept a pleasantly interested smile plastered on her face. She could feel Theo's gaze on her as his father talked. She sneaked a glance at him and saw the challenge that lit his eyes.

She was certain now that he had seen her taking the key from the desk. She had underestimated him. Doubtless she had been right in thinking that he would not want to tell his father what had happened, as he wouldn't want the good duke to know exactly how Theo had happened to discover what Megan had done. But he had neatly manipulated it so that his father would discover that the key was missing. There would be questions asked. It wouldn't be at all unlikely if suspicion fell on her, the newest addition to the household. No doubt Theo presumed that the key was still in her possession, and, if they should institute a search of the place, that the key would be discovered there.

The heat of anger rose in Megan, shoving aside her nerves, and she looked straight back at Theo, her eyes as hard as his.

She had one thing in her favor, Megan knew. The key was not in the pocket of her skirt nor anywhere in her room. She had checked and rechecked that thoroughly. Even if Theo suggested a search, they would find nothing to incriminate her.

The rest of the meal passed with agonizing slowness. Megan had lost all hunger. She had to force down each bite of food. Pretending to listen with interest to the conversation, smiling and nodding at others' remarks, even answering when she had to, she fumed inside, her anger at Theo growing.

A man of courage, she thought, would

have confronted her last night. Instead, he had stolen kisses from her before he set her up to be discovered by his father. She should have known, of course, that he was the sort of man who would do such a thing. She knew better than anyone else the extremes of which he was capable.

When the meal was finally over, the duke escorted Megan to the study, along with Anna, who had not yet seen the collection, and her husband Reed, and Theo, who had elected to tag along. Megan felt his eyes on her, but she refused to look at him.

"I must just get the key, you see," the duke told them when they reached his study, and he walked past them into the room.

Megan tensed, waiting, as he crossed the room to the large desk and reached inside the top left drawer. He pulled out a key, closed the drawer and started back toward them. Megan stared, astonished.

He had the key? How had it wound up back in his desk drawer?

She whipped her head around to look at Theo. He gazed back at her, saying nothing, the same faintly amused smile playing about his lips.

Megan realized that he had known the key would be there. He had played out this little charade just to show her that he knew what she had done and that the key was once more in his father's possession.

The key must have fallen out on the floor right here in the study, Megan thought, and Theo had seen it after she left and had returned it to the drawer. She narrowed her eyes, meeting his bright green gaze. The light that she had seen in his eyes before was there again, intense and seductive. His eyes dropped slightly to her lips, and it was then that the realization struck her with all the force of a heavy stone dropped on her: Theo had taken the key from her.

She remembered how he had kissed her until she was dizzy. She remembered how his hand had crept down her side and onto her leg, sliding up and down, clenching her skirts in his fist. She had felt only the wild, delirious passion that had thrummed through her in response to his touch. But he had used the opportunity to slip his hand into her pocket and retrieve the key.

Looking into his knowing eyes, Megan was certain that it had happened as she thought. *He had kissed her just to retrieve the key!*

She flushed hotly in a combination of embarrassment and anger. *He had de-*

ceived her, used her own desire against her to get what he wanted. And she — she had been a fool to respond as she had, desiring him, believing that he desired her.

Megan felt as if she might choke on her fury. It was all she could do to stand there and keep silent, not to turn on him and vent all her hatred. She ached to reveal to his family what kind of villain he was and what he had done ten years ago.

But she would wait. When she revealed his wickedness, she would have the proof to back it up.

Whirling around, Megan followed the duke down the hall, carefully keeping Anna and Reed between her and Theo. She refused to look at him again. She would not give him the satisfaction of letting him see that he had upset her.

Broughton unlocked the door that lay just beyond the library and stepped into the room, turning up the gas lights. Anna and Megan followed him, the other two men bringing up the rear.

"Oh, my!" Megan said, looking around the room in some astonishment.

She knew that the duke was an avid collector, but she had not expected this museumlike room. Small tables and pedestals of varying height were scattered throughout, and on them stood statues and vases and other pottery. The walls were all lined with shelves, about half of them open, the rest closed with glass doors and locked. She did not know much about any of the periods of Greek art, but even she could tell that the duke's collection was impressive.

"I had no idea. . . ." Anna said, echoing Megan's own thoughts.

The duke beamed, his pleasant face alight with joy. "It is only part of my collection. The rest is back at the Park. I have a much larger storage area there, of course."

Megan trailed around the room, looking at the various artifacts carefully. The duke obligingly opened the locked cabinets for them, showing the smaller and more valuable pieces that lay within. Megan poked her head into each one, looking for something that might have come not from Greece or Macedonia or Italy, but from South America.

Of course, she admitted, she knew even less about South American art and culture than she did about Greek. But it seemed to her that something from South America should stand out among the classical

Greek jewelry and bowls and beads.

But nothing did. Everything fit with the duke's obsession with classical antiquities.

Megan had more or less expected that, given the way Theo had engineered their tour. He would hardly urge her into a room where there was something that would incriminate him.

Megan took a last, careful look at a collection of jewelry — necklaces made of glass beads or chunky, semiprecious stones, carved broaches, wide metal bracelets for wrists and upper arms. She turned away, swallowing her disappointment, and found herself looking straight at Theo.

He had obviously been watching her. She wondered what he had hoped to see. Surely he could not know who she was. It made her wonder what he had thought she was up to when he caught her with the key. Did he think her a thief? That she wanted to steal what lay in the collection room?

Indignation spurted up in her at the idea. She had to admit that that would the logical thing to assume, but, still, the thought stung.

Megan turned to the duke, who was watching her and Anna like a proud father showing off his offspring.

"This is so amazing, sir," she told him

honestly. "I have never seen a private collection like this."

Broughton beamed. "Thank you, my dear. I have spent a number of years building it."

"It's wonderful," Anna agreed. She looked over at Megan, and the faintest of shadows touched Anna's eyes.

Megan felt the same shivery sensation along her nerves as she had the first time she had met Anna. There was something about the way the woman looked at her — not always, but every once in a while, like now, or the moment they met — that made Megan feel nervous and unsettled. Anna was a perfectly nice woman; indeed, she had been quite friendly with Megan, and Megan liked her. But she could not help but feel that Anna knew more about her than she should.

"Do you ever collect anything else?" Megan asked, as much to distract Anna as anything else. "Other than things from Greco-Roman culture, I mean?"

The duke looked faintly surprised. "More modern things?" He shook his head. "I am afraid not. No interest, you see. The Middle Ages, the Renaissance — there were lovely things, of course, but they just haven't the same appeal."

"Nothing from other parts of the world?" Megan asked lightly. "China, say, or India?"

"Oh, no. Theo here is more likely to have that kind of thing. He has been all over the world." The duke said the words with the faint astonishment of a man who had rarely seen any reason to stir from his home.

"You have a collection, too?" Anna asked Theo, and Megan was grateful for the words, which saved her from having to ask.

Theo shrugged. "No. Only a few things in my room. I don't usually bring a great deal home. My primary interest is in seeing the places."

His room. Megan knew that was where she would have to look next. She didn't want to. Even the thought of being in his room did strange things to her insides. It wasn't fear, she knew . . . or, at least, not exactly. It was a combination of emotions that roiled in her in a way she did not even want to contemplate.

She would have to go there eventually, she knew. She would wait until some evening when she knew he was gone for several hours, and then she would sneak in and search the place. But if she didn't find anything there, she was not sure what she would do.

There was the Morelands' house in the country, of course. The evidence she needed was just as likely to be there. But she knew that the family would not be retiring there until after the season was over. She could not wait that long — and she was certain she would be unable to carry off her pretense of being a teacher for that long, anyway.

The twins were bound to realize that she hadn't the slightest idea what they were doing in their Greek lessons, and she wasn't a whole lot better when it came to Latin and higher mathematics. There had even been a few times when she had looked at Con or Alex and wondered if they already knew that she was floundering, completely over her head, in those subjects. The boys seemed to like her and her teaching style; it was quite possible, she thought, that they had guessed she was not competent as a tutor and were simply keeping quiet about it.

But some other family member would be bound to notice, sooner or later. And, indeed, she felt a trifle guilty, knowing that because of her, the boys might very well lag behind their peers in certain subjects.

She needed to discover something, and soon. Megan wished that her father and

Deirdre could go to Broughton Park and search the place. She didn't know how it might be accomplished, but next Sunday, when she had the day off, she would visit them and discuss the matter of the second house.

In the meantime, she would have to do something else to further her case.

The group, having finished their tour, was beginning to drift out the door, and Megan moved along with the others, her mind worrying at her problem.

When she reached the door, she turned to the duke, saying, "Good evening, your grace, and thank you again for showing me your collection."

"No trouble at all, my dear," Broughton assured her, smiling. "But aren't you coming back to the sitting room? Con and Alex have a dandy puzzle going."

Megan smiled. Her pupils had informed her that the duke was almost as fond as Con was of jigsaw puzzles, and he spent many an evening working on them with his sons.

"Thank you," she replied honestly. "But I fear I am rather tired. I should retire early, I think."

The fact was, she was rather fond of puzzles herself and would have enjoyed working on one, but she was coming to realize that the less time she spent with this family, the better. She was already liking them far more than was good for her. There was no point in making it any more painful when she had to reveal to them what Theo had done.

"Come, Miss Henderson, surely a little time spent relaxing would be good for you," Theo said persuasively. "A card game, perhaps. Or Anna might be persuaded to play a few tunes on the piano. Or, if you prefer, Mother has been reading up on the educational ideas of Bronson Alcott, and I am sure she would love to discuss them with you."

There was a twinkle in his eye as he said this, and Megan knew he was hoping once again to trip her up.

"Oh, yes," she said, looking him straight in the eye, her chin going up challengingly. *Thank heavens for that article she had written on the New England experiments in education.* "The conversational method. It is quite interesting."

"Hardly relaxing for Miss Henderson, Theo," Reed put in. "Since she has spent her whole day educating the twins. No doubt she would welcome a few hours sans Morelands."

"Of course," Theo agreed easily. "I apologize, Miss Henderson. No doubt you have been staying up too late preparing the twins' lessons."

Megan shot him a daggerlike look, well aware of his jibe at her late-night activities, though she knew none of the others would be.

"Yes," she replied smoothly. "And I have a long day planned tomorrow." She turned back to the duke. "I would like to take the twins on an educational outing tomorrow, if that is all right with you, sir."

The idea had just occurred to her, and it was, she thought, perfect. She had been longing to get out of the house. Used as she was to being out and about, chasing down her stories, the walls of Broughton House, elegant as they were, were beginning to feel rather restrictive. Besides, she needed to interview Julian Coffey, the other Englishman who had gone on the trip with Barchester, Theo and her brother. A trip to the museum where he was curator would serve both purposes, and she could do it under the guise of tutoring the twins.

"An outing, eh?" The duke smiled. "That sounds interesting."

"Yes, it does," Theo added, studying her.

"Where are you planning to take Con and Alex?"

"To a museum," Megan answered shortly.

"Museum?" Broughton's smile grew. "That sounds quite jolly. I am sure the twins would enjoy it." He paused, then added, his smile fading, "Um . . . are you quite sure you are up to it? The twins, you know, well . . . and you're unfamiliar with the city."

"Don't worry, Father," Theo said pleasantly. "I will volunteer to go along and keep an eye on Con and Alex."

The older man's face cleared. "That will be just the thing." He smiled widely at Megan. "You should have no problem."

"Thank you, your grace," Megan replied with a smile for the kindly duke, but she turned a stony stare on Theo as she went on, "but it really won't be necessary. The twins and I will be fine on our own."

"No, I insist," Theo replied, his affable tone underlaid by steel. The face he turned to her was as implacable as his voice. "Really, Miss Henderson."

Megan's smile was more of a grimace as she shot back, "No, please, Lord Raine, I will not allow you to put yourself out. I am quite capable of finding my way about a city."

"I am sure you are. But as a gentleman, I cannot allow you. We shall take the carriage."

"No doubt Con and Alex and I could take the carriage without your accompanying us. You needn't bother."

The other three people with them stood watching Theo and Megan with interest, their heads swinging from one to the other throughout their sharply polite exchange.

"Now, now, Miss Henderson," the duke said, patting her arm and smiling benignly at her. "You must let Theo accompany you. It takes at least two people to keep an eye on Constantine and Alexander."

"Of course." Megan gritted her teeth and gave in with as much grace as she could muster. She could scarcely refuse her employer's order, even one given as graciously as the duke's. "Thank you."

The look she turned toward Theo was anything but grateful. "We shall leave early."

His eyes dancing with inner amusement, Theo gave her a short, precise bow. "I shall be ready."

Damn the man! How could he manage to thwart her at every turn when he didn't even know what she planned?

It was excessively frustrating. She didn't

want Theo to know that she was going to the Cavendish Museum, let alone have him accompany her there.

Megan itched to slap Theo's smug face. Instead, she turned on her heel and swept away.

9

Megan hurried the twins through breakfast the next morning, hoping to get out the door before Theo appeared. Much to her chagrin, when she and the boys came down the stairs, Theo was standing by the front door waiting for them, arms folded.

"Theo!" Alex cried out gleefully. "Are you coming with us?"

"Do!" Con urged.

"Yes, I'm coming. Didn't Miss Henderson tell you?" He cast a wicked grin at Megan.

"I was not sure that you would be able to accompany us," Megan retorted in a frosty tone.

"You doubted me?" Theo's green eyes danced, and he leaned closer, murmuring, "Or did you just think that you could sneak away without me?'

"I'm sure I don't know what you're

talking about." Megan swept toward the front door, and the footman jumped to pull it open for her.

Theo and the boys followed.

Con cast an eye up at Theo and whispered, "Is she in a snit? She's acting just like Kyria when she's in a snit."

"I'm not sure," Theo replied. "Do you think an American snit looks the same as a British one?"

The three glanced at Megan, then back at each other, and nodded, bursting into laughter. Megan cast a sharp glance back at them.

No doubt Theo was enlisting her charges against her, she thought darkly. Well, let him. Perhaps she would be able to saddle him with the twins so she could slip away to talk to the museum's director.

The ducal carriage stood in front of the house, the coachman waiting patiently to open the door and hand Megan up into the vehicle. The twins bounced in after her and plopped down side by side in their usual way on the seat across from her. This left Theo to sit down beside Megan. She managed with some effort not to turn her head to look at him.

"Where are we going?" Theo asked cheerfully. "The British Museum?"

"No!" Con and Alex chorused. "The Cavendish!"

"The Cavendish?" Theo repeated in surprise.

Megan turned. "Yes. The twins said they had never gone, and I thought it better to start out on a lesser scale than the British Museum." She lifted her brows a little. "Is there some problem?"

Theo shrugged. "No. Of course not. The Cavendish it is."

He leaned out to tell the driver, and the carriage rumbled off.

"It will help a lot to have Theo with us," Alex confided to Megan.

"Indeed? Why is that?"

"He knows all about the stuff at the Cavendish," Con explained. "Don't you, Theo? He's been there."

"To the museum?" Megan asked, as if she knew nothing about it.

Alex and Con chuckled. "No. To South America. That's what the Cavendish has — South American things."

"The Cavendish specializes in objects from Central and South America," Theo said, his voice blank of any emotion. "Ancient civilizations, primarily — Aztec, Maya, Inca."

"I see." Megan looked at Theo. His face

was as unrevealing as his tone of voice. "It is an unusual specialty, don't you think?"

Theo shrugged. "The director is something of an expert in the area."

"I take it you must be one, as well," Megan said, still watching him for any change of expression.

"Con and Alex tend to exaggerate, I'm afraid," Theo said, his gaze flickering to the boys. "I have been up the Amazon once, that is all."

"That must have been quite exciting," Megan remarked. "When did you go?"

"Ten years ago." Something changed in his face, hardened. He turned his head to look out the window.

Guilt, Megan thought. It was obvious that he did not want to talk about his trip. *Who would, if they had done what he had done?* Her heart squeezed a little in her chest at this confirmation that she was right, and she realized, with some surprise, that somewhere deep inside her, she had been hoping that she would be proved wrong, that some other explanation for what had happened to Dennis would arise. She did not want Theo to be guilty.

She, too, turned to look out the window, not wanting her emotions to show. It was foolish and wrong, she told herself, even to wish that Theo Moreland would turn out not to have killed Dennis. She felt as if she were betraying her brother by entertaining such a thought.

Theo Moreland was her enemy. Just because he had not revealed to his father that she had tried to steal the key to his collection room did not make him kind or a friend. He was merely playing some game of his own. Look at the way he had grinned at her last night, taunting her with his knowledge of what she had done — and look at how he had forced his way into this field trip. And it didn't even bear mentioning that he had kissed her the other night just as a means to slip the key from her pocket.

She told herself that the problem was that she had unexpectedly liked all the Morelands so much. She did not want the duchess or the twins or any of the others to have to learn that their beloved heir was a murderer. Her desire to absolve him had nothing to do with the fiery heat of their kisses the other evening or the way her heart turned over when he smiled at her. She was not that weak, that ruled by the flesh.

Megan unconsciously straightened her shoulders. She would do what she had to do. She would follow through with this investigation and not falter, no matter how likeable the Moreland family was — and no matter how treacherously heat quivered through her body when Theo was near.

In keeping with her resolve, she ignored Theo during the remainder of the drive to the Cavendish Museum. When they arrived, however, she could not completely ignore him, as he stepped down from the carriage before her and offered his hand to help her down. It was a gesture that she could not politely refuse, so she was forced to slip her hand into his as she emerged from the carriage. However, she steeled herself against any sensation and turned her attention quickly from Theo's face to the structure that lay before them.

Cavendish House, though perhaps no longer in a fashionable area, was a magnificent structure. Built of massive gray stone in the baroque style, it was reputed to have been designed by the master English architect Sir Christopher Wren, along with a great many other buildings during the vast rebuilding of London after the Great Fire. Megan had found a guidebook of London in the large Moreland library, as well as a thick volume on the work of Wren, and she had read everything about the Cavendish, as it was called. She had learned that it was quite a bit larger even than Broughton House, and there was still a good bit of grounds around the house itself, including a pleasant garden behind the museum.

They entered the building behind the twins and were greeted by a slender young man who apparently recognized Theo and seemed overcome by the prospect of meeting him.

"Lord Raine," he gushed. "What an honor to have you here. Please allow me to get Mr. Coffey. I am sure that he would wish to show you around the museum personally."

Meeting Coffey in the presence of Theo was the last thing Megan wanted, so she was glad when Theo said shortly, "No. Don't bother him. I am sure we will be able to find our way about ourselves."

The young man continued to bow and babble as they started down the hall, and Megan was afraid that he would follow them all through the house, but, much to her relief, after a few more obsequious questions and comments, he disappeared.

The twins darted from exhibit to exhibit, which ran the gamut from stuffed jaguars, parrots and monkeys to re-creations of narrow native crafts used to navigate the mighty Amazon, to ancient gold and silver artifacts locked in glass cases. To Megan, who knew little about South America or its indigenous ancient tribes, the place was fascinating.

The museum, having originally been a house, was composed of a number of rooms, some small and some large. The first two rooms they went into contained stuffed animals, including a long-necked llama, and a number of drawings of the flora and fauna of South and Central America. On the walls hung several small blankets and ponchos in bright colors and geometric designs.

The next room displayed a number of odd-looking masks, stylized in design, several made of gold, silver and copper. One was of a man's face, wide and square, with large almond-shaped eyes and huge rings in his earlobes, with an arcing headdress across his forehead. The mask appeared to be silver, with the headdress and the round earrings done in gold. Another mask, also made from metal, was, she realized on second glance, the wide-open jaws of a jaguar, with nose and eyes above the gaping square of the mouth, large, wicked-looking teeth jutting up and down at the corners of the square. Inside the opened mouth was the stylized face of a man, the two faces melding together in such a way that they appeared to be one creature.

She leaned forward for a closer look. "How curious. What is that?"

"The jaguar god," Theo said flatly.

Megan glanced at him. His face was devoid of expression. "Also the sun god. When he passes through the day, he is the sun god, the supreme god, then he descends into the darkness of the underworld, where he is the jaguar god. The god of war."

Megan could not suppress a little shiver. The mask was, frankly, a little bit unnerving. She strolled around the room, looking at all the masks, some of metal and others of cloth or ceramic, some topped with feathers. All were of human or animal faces, often a blending of the two. There were long-beaked birds and openmouthed serpents, deities and warriors.

In the center of the room stood a large, glassed-in display case containing a variety of small figurines. Several were gold and silver, a veritable garden of plants and trees in gleaming metal, and others were carved from some sort of black stone. There were painted pots, and also a short instrument of some kind, with another headdressed figure on top, and below it a rounded piece of metal that looked rather like a miniature spade.

Megan glanced again at Theo. He stood in silence, gazing down into the display case, and there was a look on his face, distant and melancholy, that clutched at Megan's heart. It was the face of a man staring into bitter memories, and once again she felt the sharp stab of certainty that Theo lived with guilt.

Her heart felt immensely heavy, and tears welled suddenly in her eyes. She turned away, swallowing the fierce emotion that threatened to swamp her.

Seizing on any diversion, she wondered where the twins were. With the house laid out the way it was, it had not taken the boys long to outstrip them as they went from room to room. But she realized now that she did not even hear their voices any longer.

"Oh, dear," Megan said. "Where are Con and Alex?"

She crossed the room to the hall and looked out. "Boys? Con? Alex?"

There was no sign of them and no reply, and anxiety sharpened in her chest. She went to the next room and peeked in, only to find the boys were not there, either.

Consternation on her face, she turned back to Theo, who had followed her out into the hall. "Where did they get to?"

Theo shrugged with a notable lack of concern. "The twins have a knack of disappearing wherever they go. Don't worry. They also have a way of turning up just when you're sure that something dreadful has happened to them."

"I must say," Megan told him crossly, "you seem rather cavalier about it."

"The twins are good at taking care of themselves," Theo responded with a smile. "At least here I know they're enclosed in a house. It's a great deal more unnerving to lose sight of them in the midst of the city, which I have had the misfortune to do before. With the Greats, it's best to save one's worry until you find that they're actually in danger. Otherwise you'll be gray before your time."

Megan knew it was true that the twins were able to take care of themselves quite well, and she had little doubt that in a few minutes they would come pounding back, full of excitement and babbling about something that she and Theo should see. Still, Theo's attitude seemed one more irritation in an already annoying day, and she was just about to snap back a heated comment when she was distracted by the sound of footsteps.

She turned and saw a man approaching them from the rear of the house. He was of medium height, with light brown hair that was receding in a dramatic V from his forehead. He made up for the lack of hair atop his head with a wide set of muttonchop sideburns. He was dressed plainly in a dark suit and white shirt with stiff collars and cuffs, but both the cut and cloth of the suit were expensive and stylish, and his black shoes were polished to a mirror shine. A pearl stickpin nestled in the dark gray silk of his ascot.

He smiled as he approached them, saying, "Lord Raine, this is indeed an honor."

"Coffey," Theo responded shortly, giving a brief nod.

"I am so pleased that you and the lady have chosen to visit the museum today." He turned with a faintly questioning look toward Megan.

"Allow me to introduce you to Miss Henderson," Theo said without enthusiasm. "Miss Henderson, Mr. Julian Coffey, the director of the Cavendish."

"How do you do, Miss Henderson?" Coffey said, taking the hand she extended and bowing politely over it.

His eyes, a light gray, looked at her assessingly, and Megan had the feeling that he had quickly summed up the quality of every bit of her attire, from her straw hat to the sturdy black laced shoes on her feet.

"I am a tutor with the Moreland family," Megan explained, not wanting the man to think that she was Theo's companion. "Constantine and Alexander are with us, as well, but I fear that they have forged ahead."

"They will find a great deal to interest them here, I hope," he replied smoothly. "But I do hope that you and Lord Raine will allow me to show you around my little domain." He offered them a quick, deprecating smile. "The Cavendish, you see, is not only my employment but also my obsession."

"Yes, I know," Theo responded, his voice crisp and cool.

Megan looked at Theo, interested by his almost discourteous response. His face was smooth and unexpressive, his eyes, usually twinkling, now devoid of any emotion. Clearly, she thought, he did not like Mr. Coffey. But of course he would not, considering what Coffey knew about him.

"That would be very nice," Megan said quickly to counteract Theo's rudeness.

Simply the fact that Theo did not want the man around was enough to make her want Coffey to stay. Besides, she wanted to see what else transpired between the two men. Perhaps Theo's horning in on their excursion to the museum would turn out to be a useful thing. While she could not question Coffey with Theo around, she just might learn something from the way Theo reacted to him. She could always come back later to see Coffey on her own — or maybe she could get a few moments alone with him if she could convince Theo to go look for the twins.

"I was curious about this figure," Megan said, leading him back into the room where they had just been.

She did have a question or two, but primarily she was curious to see what Coffey would say about the items that had sent Theo into his quiet reverie.

"Ah, yes," Coffey said, looking at the miniature spade-like instrument. "That is an Inca ceremonial knife." He shot a sideways glance at Theo before he went on, "Even though it is rounded, the blade is quite sharp. They used it, I believe, in ritual sacrifices."

"Sacrifices?" Megan repeated, surprised.

"Yes. Usually of a llama or some animal.

However, the Incas also engaged periodically in the sacrifice of young children."

"Children?" Megan paled a little. "How awful!"

"Yes, to our Western minds, it doubtless was. However, they were not simply blood-thirsty savages, you know. The sacrifices were done to please or appease their gods, and they were not routinely of children. That occurred only when they were trying to escape the god's anger, manifested, no doubt, in some sort of cataclysmic natural event — an earthquake, say, or a very long drought, or something of that sort. And on the succession of an emperor, in a ritual called the *capac hucha*. It was considered a great honor to be one of the chosen children. Only the healthiest and most beautiful were accepted as good enough."

"An honor I think most of us would decline," Theo commented.

Coffey gave Megan a small smile and shrugged. "It seems bizarre to us, of course. But one must remember that this was their worship, as sacred to them as our churches are to us. As best we can tell, the Incas believed that their emperor was a god himself. They built each successive holder of the title a grand palace, and the dead emperor was mummified and treated with great reverence. The mummy remained in his palace and was attended by servants and surrounded by his possessions. Rather like the Egyptian burials, except that the servants were not entombed with the mummy but lived and worked in the palace as they always had."

It seemed a grisly custom to Megan, but she said only, "You must know a great deal about the Incas."

"I hope I will not appear immodest when I say that I am something of an expert in the field. I was more a naturalist when I went on my first expedition to South America." He gestured toward the framed ink drawings of jungle scenes that lined one wall of the room. "I sketched those depictions of the flora and fauna of the Amazon. But I became fascinated by the culture and art of the ancient Incas, and gradually, over the years, it was the ancient artifacts of their culture that became my subject of study. The other civilizations are, of course, quite interesting, too — we have rooms devoted to the Mayan culture and the Aztec civilization, as well. But Peru and Ecuador and the Incas have remained my favorite."

"We are very fortunate, then, to have you as our guide," Megan replied politely.

"When did you first go to South America?"

"About ten years ago," Coffey replied, and again his gaze flickered over to Theo and back to Megan. He hesitated, and Megan wondered if Theo would say anything about his own presence on the trip.

Theo was silent, and after a moment, Coffey went on, "I went on an expedition up the Amazon. It was fascinating. And, as you can see, it became my all-consuming passion." He gestured around the room. "Please, let me show you some of the other pieces."

He led them into the next room, where he pointed out a long knotted string, from which a series of other knotted strings dangled. "This is known as a *quipu*. It is how the Incas kept records. They had no written language, you see. It's really quite amazing how they managed such a vast empire — they ruled more than ten million people and their territory covered several modern countries. They were excellent administrators. Their road system was highly developed. They built bridges and shelters a day's journey apart, where travelers could find lodging. They kept it all in repair. They built temples and palaces, using huge blocks of stone, which they carved and transported — all without the use of the wheel. They did not use mortar, yet the stones fit so well together that they were able to withstand earthquakes." He stopped and smiled self-deprecatingly. "I apologize. I get carried away, I'm afraid."

"No, don't apologize," Megan told him. "It's fascinating."

She looked around the room they had entered. There were numerous shelves containing all sorts of pottery, and once again masks hung on the walls. A glass-fronted cabinet contained a long cloak, brightly colored. Megan realized as she moved closer that it was composed entirely of feathers.

"Oh, my!" she breathed. "This is beautiful."

"The natives of Peru are skilled craftsmen," Coffey told her. "This is of much more recent vintage, of course, but I believe that it is similar to garments actually worn by the Inca priests. There were also tunics in which the material was flecked with gold or which were decorated with various gold pendants. They made much use of gold and silver. They called them the 'sweat of the sun' and the 'tears of the moon.' In Cuzco, the capital city, the temple walls were decorated with sheets of gold. Can you imagine how it must have glittered in the sun?" He sighed. "Unfortunately, most of their gold work was lost when the Spaniards invaded. They tore down the gold decorations and melted them down to ship back to Spain."

He shook his head sorrowfully. "Greed and religious intolerance destroyed irreplaceable art."

Megan murmured a sympathetic reply and strolled over to one of the open shelves of objects. There was a cup made of gold, with a whimsical handle in the form of a laughing monkey. There were brightly colored pots, bowls and vases, some with geometrical markings and others with stylized scenes of human and animal forms.

"Look at this, Theo," she said, turning toward him. She stopped abruptly, swallowing her next words as she realized that his first name had slipped out of her mouth in a far too familiar way. A blush flooded her cheeks.

"They're lovely, Megan," he responded. She saw in his eyes a little twinkle of mischief, and she knew that he had noticed not only the slip of her tongue but also the embarrassment that followed it. And he was perversely enjoying both.

Megan's eyes flashed, and she would

have liked to make a heated remark in response to his annoying smile. But she reminded herself that she could not in front of this stranger. So she merely pressed her lips together firmly and turned back to the display.

"The Incas were adept at pottery, then?" she asked to get the conversation back on track. She directed her question to Coffey, keeping her shoulder firmly turned away from Theo.

"Oh, yes. They did not use a wheel but rolled long ropes of clay, then coiled them around into the shape of the pot. The smooth surface was achieved by rubbing them with some sort of flat object. They dried them by simply setting them out in the hot sun. This pot is a very popular form with the Incas. It is called *aryballo*."

The vessel to which he pointed was a round, fat pot with two small handles low on the pot and a long neck. It was painted black, with orangish lines running around it and orange geometric shapes.

"Did you find many of these on your first trip to the area?" Megan asked.

Coffey smiled. "Oh, no. That was more an exploratory expedition. Most of these have come from my most recent journeys to Peru, when I sailed to the western coast and journeyed inland from Lima. I would not recommend the passage up the Amazon. Fascinating, of course, but very hard, and, of course, at the end, one is still faced with the Andes. The wildlife is magnificent, however. Many of my drawings that you see here are from that trip."

Megan admired the display in the center of the room, where personal jewelry was laid out. There were necklaces of gold and silver, and wide gold armbands, as well as large round ornaments, which Coffey identified as ear spools. Megan examined the necklaces with the most interest, remembering Barchester's words about Theo having possessed a pendant of some sort.

Some of the necklaces were large gold links with a heavy pendant in the middle, rather similar to Egyptian pectorals that she had seen. There were also some single ornamental disks, which she guessed could once have been attached to a chain or leather thong. Was it something like this that Barchester had seen in Theo's hand?

She glanced over at Theo to see if he had any reaction to the necklaces, but there was no change of expression on his face as he gazed at them. Nor, she thought, was there any great interest. He looked, she thought, impatient or restless, as though he were ready to leave the room, and she wondered if this implied merely boredom or a wish to get away from things that reminded him of what he had done.

She turned back to Coffey, who had started on an explanation of the hierarchy of the Inca governmental system. Keeping a polite expression on her face, she let her mind wander. *Had Mr. Barchester said anything to Coffey about her and her quest?* She had asked him not to, but she was well aware how often people ignored such requests. She wished that she could think of some way to get rid of Theo and ask Coffey more searching questions about the expedition and her brother's death.

"Perhaps we should look for the twins," she said, turning toward Theo, hopeful that he would offer to do it himself.

"I'm sure they will turn up," he replied. "Why don't we continue? What's upstairs, Coffey?"

Swallowing her irritation, Megan followed Coffey out the door and up the stairs to the next level of the museum, Theo behind her. There were more exhibits in the rooms upstairs, many of them featuring articles from Mexico and the other Central American countries, along with a small library of books focusing on various aspects of South and Central America. Coffey kept up his explanation of the ancient artifacts of the Aztec and Mayan cultures, as well as the more modern exhibits of clothing, jewelry and such.

As time passed, Megan began to really worry about the twins. It was all very well and good for Theo to say that they were contained in the house, but there were doors leading outside, after all, and she knew Con and Alex well enough by now to know that their curiosity might lead them anywhere. It seemed clear that the two of them were not on this floor, either.

"Is there another floor of exhibits?" she asked, interrupting Coffey in the midst of another monologue. "Could the boys have gone upstairs?"

"We have some offices there, and some storage, but little that they would find of interest, I'm sure," Coffey replied and looked around, a frown forming on his forehead. "I was sure that we would find them up here. Perhaps at the diorama . . ."

He started down the hall, but at that moment, there was a clatter on the stairs behind them, and the twins appeared. In the mysterious way that Megan had grown accustomed to, the boys had acquired a liberal smattering of dust and stains on their clothes and persons, and even in their hair. She didn't want to think about where they had been. She only hoped that nothing had been broken on their travels.

"Ah, boys, there you are," Mr. Coffey said in the hearty sort of voice adults often used with children. "Having fun, were you?"

"Yes, sir," Con replied. "It's quite interesting."

"Especially the animals," Alex added. "I've never seen a jaguar before. I should like to see a live one."

"I hope you will save that for a trip that does not include me," Megan told him, smiling. "You missed a most interesting tour. Mr. Coffey is the curator of the museum, and he told us about all the exhibits."

They made their way back down to the ground floor, the twins pelting Coffey with questions all the way. Con was quite enamored of the feathered cape and the tall, elaborate headdresses on many of the figurines. Alex, as always, was more interested in the various animals.

Megan could see that there was little possibility now of her being able to ask Coffey any questions in private. She would have to return at some other time. Perhaps she could send him a note and arrange to meet him on a Sunday when she was off work. Not this Sunday, though — she was much too anxious to see her father and Deirdre.

They took their leave of Mr. Coffey and walked down the steps to where the Moreland carriage waited. Megan took out her handkerchief and made a largely futile attempt to clean off some of the accumulated dust on the twins.

"Wherever did you go?" she asked. "You must have been crawling about in the dirt."

"Upstairs and downstairs," Con replied. "There was a lot of interesting stuff in some of the storerooms."

"Some of them were locked, though," Alex added with a grimace as he and Con brushed at their hair and clothes. "There was an enormous room down in the basement."

"We didn't get to look at all of the basement," Con said with regret. "We thought you'd get cross if we were gone too long."

"I *was* a little worried," Megan admitted.

"We're sorry," Alex assured her. "Theo should have told you we'd be all right."

"I did," Theo hastened to tell them. "And Miss Henderson was admirably calm. She appears to have figured you two out."

Cook had packed a lunch for them, and they took their well-filled basket to Hyde Park and spread out their picnic on a blanket on the ground. They ate, laughing and talking, and afterward the twins raced off to fly kites, and Theo and Megan watched them, calling encouragement.

Megan could not help but enjoy the outing. The food was scrumptious, the day balmy, and the twins made her laugh. She told herself that it was only the boys' company that she enjoyed, but she knew she was lying.

It was Theo's presence that made the picnic more than pleasant. She could not sit there beside him on a blanket without feeling a stirring of excitement. It seemed to her that if she could single out the one particular thing that made him so appealing, she could dismiss it — and him. But it was not one thing, she realized as she tried to analyze what it was and only wound up feeling more and more enthralled. It was the flash of his smile, the way his green eyes lit with laughter under the dramatic slash of black brows. It was the low timbre of his voice, a vibration that seemed to rumble right through her whenever he spoke. It was the whisper of breath against her cheek when he leaned closer to murmur a sotto voce comment. It was the size and subtle strength of him as he sat beside her, the heat.

It was, perhaps most of all, the touch of something wild and untamed about him. It was there not just in the careless tousle of his just-a-little-too-long hair or the small scar that cut dangerously close to his eye, or the taut muscle beneath the smooth material of his jacket. It was in the hint of rawness not far below his surface, the faint hum of restless energy, the sharpness of that clear green gaze. There was power in him, a little frightening even as it drew her.

"What drives you?" Megan asked.

He looked at her, faintly surprised. "What? What do you mean?"

"The boys say you have been all over the world. Why? What is it you're looking for?"

"I'm not sure." He gazed off into the distance, thinking. "Excitement, I suppose. At least, that is what most people would say."

"What would *you* say?"

He shook his head. "I'm not entirely sure. I just . . . want to see other things. Do other things." He lay back on the ground, pillowing his head on his crossed arms and gazing up at the lacy tangle of branches above them. "I never wanted to be Lord Raine. Lord knows, I have no desire to be the Duke of Broughton, either. Reed, now, Reed is the sort who would be an excellent duke. Responsible, careful, concerned." He cast her a laughing glance. "All the things that I am not — as my great-aunt Hermione will be happy to tell you. I want to know what else is out there."

"It can be dangerous, can't it?"

"It can get exciting." He shrugged. "I can't deny that there is some appeal in that."

Theo turned his head and looked up at Megan. His voice softened a little as he said, "Isn't there something in you that feels the same way?"

Megan looked into his eyes, feeling the pull. Was that what drew her to him? The excitement? The danger? She knew that she responded to that; it was part of what sent her out in pursuit of her stories. But she had met other dangerous men in the course of her work, and none of them had held any allure for her. There was something more in Theo, something as elusive as smoke and as searing as fire.

"Isn't that why you're here?" he went on.

"At least part of it?"

She jerked back. *What did he know about why she was there?* "What do you mean?"

"You could have taught just as easily in America," he pointed out, watching her steadily. "Why travel here? To someplace unknown? There is something more exciting about it, isn't there? Not knowing what you'll find? Or even whether you will be able to get a job."

"Oh." Relief trickled through Megan, and she relaxed, telling herself not to be so silly. *He didn't know. There was no way he could guess.* "Yes, I suppose so. I've always wanted something that most other women don't seem to care about."

"What is that?"

She smiled a little. "Maybe just not to be what was laid out for me. Like you. Not to assume a woman's place and marry and settle down — raise children and run a household."

The corner of his mouth quirked up. "I presume a number of people have told you that that is what you should want?"

"Oh, yes. That is what my sister did. And it's a perfect life for Mary Margaret. But just the thought of it gives me the shivers."

261

"You don't want to marry?" He tilted his head, studying her.

Megan colored a little under his regard. "I'm not sure," she replied in a low voice. "It's not so much that I don't want to marry. It's that marriage isn't my life's goal."

He smiled. "Then you have nothing against men, as such." He reached across the grass that separated them and touched his forefinger to her hand, braced against the ground. Slowly, idly, he traced down each finger, leaving a sizzling trail in his wake.

"I — ah, no, I've nothing against men." Megan tried to focus on something, anything, other than the sensations his touch created in her. "In general, I mean."

"Then there are specific men you've something against?" he asked lightly, his forefinger sliding up onto her wrist and arm.

Megan looked at him, knowing that she should pull her hand away, should, in fact, shift farther away from him or stand up, ending this tête à tête. But gazing into his eyes only seemed to immobilize her further. It seemed as though she could fall into their clear green depths, submerge and never surface.

Almost unknowingly, she leaned toward him. Slowly Theo sat up, closing the gap between them. He was going to kiss her, she thought, and she knew, moreover, that she would not resist. Indeed, she realized that she was moving forward to meet him.

At that moment Con's laughter soared across the park toward them, breaking the trance Megan found herself in, and she realized with a guilty start exactly what she had been about to do. She sucked in her breath, cheeks flaming red, and scrambled to her feet.

"We should go," she said quickly. "We have been here far too long."

"Have we?" Theo responded wryly. "I would have said it hadn't been nearly long enough."

But she was already moving away, packing up the remnants of their meal and calling to the twins. "Con! Alex! It's time to go!"

Resignedly, Theo moved to help her. He knew she was right; the middle of Hyde Park with his two younger brothers in tow was scarcely the time or place. But one day, and soon, it would be. He was going to make sure of it.

10

It took some time to get their things packed back up and into the carriage — and even longer to persuade the twins that it was time to pull down their kites and go. So it was drawing close to teatime when they finally returned to the Moreland mansion.

Con and Alex ran down the hallway and into the drawing room, followed more slowly by Theo and Megan. The boys were already into the middle of an excited recitation of their visit to the museum when Theo and Megan stepped into the room.

Megan came to an abrupt halt, somewhat surprised by the number of people in the room. Normally, by teatime, most afternoon callers had gone, and only the duchess, and sometimes Anna and Reed, took tea with the boys and Megan.

This afternoon, however, sitting with the duchess were her two daughters, Olivia and Kyria, as well as Anna, Reed and

264

Thisbe. There was also another woman whom Megan had never seen before. She was strikingly beautiful, with raven-black hair and eyes of an odd blue shade that was almost lavender. Her skin was a creamy white, and her curvaceous body was clad in an elegant purple afternoon dress that deepened the color of her exotic eyes. Although she was not young, perhaps in her mid-thirties, she was one of the most beautiful women Megan had ever seen, one who could almost rival Kyria in looks.

Beside her, Megan heard Theo let out a soft, wordless groan.

A smile spread across the lovely woman's face, and she nodded to Theo. "Lord Raine, what a pleasant surprise to see you here."

"Not such a surprise, perhaps, since it is his home," the duchess put in dryly.

Megan looked at the Moreland women with interest. All of them wore an expression of determined politeness, and there was the faintest air of tension in the room. Megan was immediately intrigued.

"Lady Scarle," Theo said, giving the woman a polite bow. "Please allow me to introduce you to Miss Henderson. Miss Henderson, Lady Helena Scarle."

The other woman gave Megan a frosty nod, her eyes sweeping down Megan's plain brown dress. "How do you do, Miss Henderson?" Her attention went immediately back to Theo. "How kind of you to take your little brothers to a museum."

"It was Miss Henderson's idea," Theo replied cheerfully. "They just allowed me to tag along."

"Indeed?" The purplish blue eyes returned to Megan assessingly.

"Miss Henderson is our new tutor," Con explained. "She took us on an 'educational excursion.' " He flashed a grin at Megan as he repeated the phrase she had used.

"Ah, I see." Lady Scarle's face relaxed, and she turned from Megan, obviously dismissing her as unimportant. "You must tell us where you went, Lord Raine." She addressed Theo again and patted the seat of the chair beside her invitingly. "Come, sit down and tell us all about it."

"Oh, I think Con and Alex were already doing an excellent job of that," Theo replied, ignoring her suggestion to sit.

"Yes," Kyria said. "Do go on, dear." She smiled brightly at Con, then at Megan. "Please sit down, Miss Henderson." She gestured toward the empty chair between Lady Scarle and herself. "Mother was about to ring for tea. We can hear all about your adventures at the museum while we have it."

There was a certain light of amusement in Kyria's eyes that Megan suspected was directed toward Lady Scarle, who appeared rather put out at Kyria's suggestion that Megan take the seat the other woman had offered Theo. Having taken an immediate dislike to Lady Scarle, Megan was happy to put the woman's nose out of joint by sitting down next to her.

"Why, thank you, Mrs. McIntyre," she responded and sat down, flashing a grin at Kyria.

"It seems a trifle unusual," Lady Scarle stated, "for the children and their governess to take tea with the family, does it not?"

Her words earned her a swift glance of dislike from most of the other occupants of the room. If the woman had an eye for Theo, as Megan suspected she did, she had certainly taken a misstep with the Morelands in this regard, Megan thought.

"We don't believe in excluding our children from family gatherings," the duchess told her crisply. "I believe that the way the aristocracy has traditionally handed the care and education of their offspring into the hands of others is a poor way to raise children and has a certain unnatural coldness that is harmful not only to the family but to society itself."

"You are quite right, Mother," Thisbe agreed and turned to Lady Scarle, saying flatly, "We were all raised by Mother's precepts, beginning with Theo and me, and I think we are all most grateful to her."

"Indeed, I did not intend any criticism, Duchess. It was merely surprising to me, having been raised much more traditionally." Color flamed high on the other woman's cheeks, and Megan could almost feel sorry for her. But then the woman shot a look of cool contempt at Megan, and Megan decided that she was not sorry, after all. "Even when we children were allowed at tea, our governess was rarely involved."

"She's not our governess," Alex put in, his jaw set in a mutinous way.

Megan knew that Lady Scarle had earned the twins' implacable enmity by implying that they were young enough to have a governess.

"She is our tutor," Con added. "And she is the best one we have ever had, too."

"I am sure that is most remarkable," Lady Scarle replied coolly. She smiled in a girlish way at Theo, her eyelashes sweeping down provocatively. "Personally, I have never been much of a bluestocking. I find that men rarely prefer a woman of great education."

"I cannot imagine why a man would wish to marry a numskull," Thisbe retorted. "Unless, of course, they intend to deceive them and find it easier with a woman of limited understanding."

Megan sneaked a glance at Theo and found him gazing off into the distance, his lips pressed tightly together. He glanced at her, as if feeling her gaze, and his eyes danced devilishly. He turned quickly away.

Fortunately, at that moment the servants wheeled in the tea cart, and the next few minutes were taken up with the serving of tea and cakes.

Megan watched Lady Scarle as she sipped daintily at her cup, her gaze often turning to Theo. The woman kept up a determined line of chatter, often calling Theo by name to draw him into the conversation. As most of her conversation consisted of talk about people and places Megan had never heard of, she found it terribly boring. Her attention wandered to the other occupants of the room. Con and Alex were busily stuffing themselves with cakes. Most of the others looked bored. Kyria, Megan noted, was watching Lady Scarle speculatively.

"Why don't you tell us more about your trip to the museum, Miss Henderson?" Kyria said into a brief silence in the midst of Lady Scarle's patter.

"It was quite interesting, Mrs. McIntyre," Megan began. Lady Scarle glanced over at her disdainfully. She was, Megan thought, a thoroughly disagreeable woman — and her opinion had nothing to do with the fact that Lady Scarle was obviously pursuing Theo Moreland. "It primarily holds a collection of artifacts from the Inca, Mayan, and Aztec cultures."

"There's a replica of an Aztec pyramid. And this feathered cape," Con put in. "You'd like it, Kyria. They have jewelry — these peculiar big earrings. Men wore them, and they played these games —"

"You're talking about the Cavendish?" Lady Scarle asked, surprising Megan. From her earlier comments, Megan would not have expected the aristocratic woman ever to have set foot inside a museum.

"Why, yes, I am. Have you been there?"

"Of course." Lady Scarle barely glanced at her as she answered. "It is a lovely place. It was one of Lord Scarle's pet charities, you know, and of course I continued his patronage after his death. Lady Cavendish and I are holding a benefit for it next week. I am sure that you have received invitations to it."

That explained it, Megan thought sardonically. There was a party involved.

"I hope you will come to our little ball, Lord Raine," Lady Scarle went on, casting a flirtatious look at Theo. "We have decided to hold it at the museum itself, so that everyone can see the excellent work that Mr. Coffey has accomplished there."

"Um, I — I had not really thought . . ." Theo began, and cast a quick look around as if for inspiration.

"Of course he is coming," Kyria spoke up. "We are all coming, are we not, Olivia? Anna?"

Both women looked faintly surprised, Megan noted, but they nodded gamely.

Kyria went on, a devilish twinkle in her green eyes, "Miss Henderson is accompanying us, as well, of course."

Megan choked on her tea, but Kyria ignored the interruption, smiling blandly at Lady Scarle.

"Miss Henderson?" the other woman said, her eyebrows rising. "But, really, Lady Kyria, this is a ball, not an excursion to the museum. It is by invitation only."

"Oh, I'm sorry. I was under the impression that all of us had received an invitation. Is it only Theo?"

"No, of course not." Color touched Lady Scarle's cheeks. "Of course you are invited, and the duke and duchess. I am sure all of you received invitations."

"If the Moreland family is coming, then of course Megan will, as well. We consider her quite one of the family, don't we, Mother?"

"Of course, dear." The duchess favored her daughter, so much like her in looks, with a gracious smile. "The duke and I would not think of attending without Miss Henderson."

Lady Scarle looked chagrined, but she said only, "Of course. Miss Henderson must come as well."

She did not spare a glance at Megan as she said this, and a few minutes later, when Reed and Theo excused themselves and left the room, Lady Scarle took her leave, as well.

For a long moment, the women remaining behind said nothing. Then Kyria exchanged a look with Thisbe, who responded with a grin, and a moment later, they were chuckling.

"Kyria, you wicked thing," the duchess said without heat.

"Lady Scarle looked as if she had swallowed a bee," Olivia added.

"I cannot like the woman at all. She is so blatantly pursuing Theo. Can't she see he is not interested?" Kyria exclaimed.

"Lady Scarle is the sort who sees nothing but herself," Thisbe retorted. "I am sure she would never believe that any man might not be interested in her. She certainly had her choice of beaux when she came out."

"Yes, and she married the oldest and wealthiest of the lot," Kyria added dryly. "Now that he's gone, she is hoping to move up to duchess."

"She's very beautiful," Anna commented.

"Hmph." Kyria raised an eyebrow. "Did you like her, though?"

Anna laughed. "No, not at all. I certainly would not choose her for Theo."

"No, nor would I," Olivia agreed in her soft voice. A small woman, with soft brown hair, large, intelligent eyes, and a surprisingly mischievous smile, Olivia was a warm person whom Megan could not help but like. Quieter than her two sisters, she struck Megan nevertheless as having a great strength of will.

She went on now, "But, you know, Kyria, perhaps you should have asked Miss Henderson before you committed her to going to the charity ball."

"I'm sorry." Kyria turned toward Megan contritely. "I did not mean to be impolite. Sometimes I get a little carried away."

"But I — surely you do not mean for me to actually go with you," Megan said, surprised. "I thought you only said that to put Lady Scarle's nose out of joint."

Even as she said it, Megan realized that her words were far too blunt for an employee to deliver to a titled lady, and she clapped her hand over her mouth. "I'm sorry. I should not have said that."

Kyria laughed, joined by the other women in the room. "Don't apologize. You are exactly right. I did want to put her nose out of joint. But I certainly intended for you to come. Please say you will. It should be quite lovely. Lady Cavendish is getting rather old, but she still has a wonderful sense of style. Her parties are always quite fun. You would enjoy it."

Megan was a little surprised by how much she would indeed like to go to the party. She had never been one who had envied the wealthy their glittering galas and elegant balls, but as she thought now of sweeping out onto the floor in a lovely ball gown, she was aware of a rush of longing. She decided not to consider why the man in whose arms she saw herself dancing was Theo Moreland.

With an inward sigh, however, she pushed aside that dream. "I'm sorry. I would love to go, but I have nothing appropriate to wear to a ball."

"Don't worry about that." Kyria waved away her objection. "We shall come up with something for you. My maid can alter one of my dresses. She is a wizard with a needle."

"No, one of mine," Olivia put in. "We are nearer the same size."

"We are, as well," Anna said. "And I just bought a whole hoard of gowns when I came to London. You are most welcome to wear one."

"There, you see?" Kyria said triumphantly. "I am sure we will be able to find something quite lovely." She studied Megan, her head to one side. "A warm color, gold or — no, perhaps that rust-colored satin that you wore last summer, Livvy."

Megan looked at them, warmed by their generosity. "I — I don't know what to say. You are so kind."

"Why, say you'll come. That is all," Olivia told her.

Megan smiled at her, unable to resist. "All right. I will go with you."

Megan spent much of that evening pacing in her room, worrying about what she was doing. She felt increasingly guilty. She hated the fact that what she was planning to do would hurt the Morelands. They had been terribly kind and generous to her, and she knew that when she revealed what Theo had done, they would all regard her as a traitor.

On the other hand, she felt as if she were letting down her own family by even worrying about Theo's family — and how could she let herself join in their activities, even enjoy them? She should be searching for evidence about Dennis's death, not eating meals that melted in her mouth with the family of his killer, or jaunting off to charity balls in a dress that probably cost more than her entire year's salary.

On the other hand, she argued with herself, going to the charity ball was not without purpose. She could get Julian Coffey alone and talk to him there, something that was obviously difficult to do while she was staying at Broughton House.

With a sigh, she sank down into the chair beside her bed. The fact was, she knew, she could bring this whole problem to a close quickly. She might not even have to talk to Julian Coffey again or remain as the Morelands' tutor if she could put her hands on the pendant that Barchester has seen Theo holding after Dennis's death. And she knew where she was most likely to find that pendant — in Theo's bed-chamber.

She was holding back only out of fear. Not just fear of getting caught. Megan felt that, of course, for there was absolutely no reason for her to be in Theo's bedchamber, and if someone walked in on her there, it would probably lead to her immediate dis-missal.

But more than that, she knew, she was afraid of finding the pendant, for it would be more evident that Theo had killed her brother. No matter how sure she was in her head that Theo had been responsible for her brother's death, something in her heart stubbornly refused to accept it. Even today, when she had seen the look on his face as he stared at the exhibit, she had struggled against the obvious interpreta-tion of his moody gaze. She had wished for some other explanation for the crisp, almost unfriendly way he spoke to Julian Coffey, or the way he turned aside questions about the trip he had made, or his knowledge of South America. Could it not be that he was simply remembering the sorrow of her brother's death? she urged in her inner dialogue.

Still, she knew she had to look for the pendant. She could not simply go on not knowing the truth. She had to sneak into Theo's room and search it thoroughly. And the sooner she did it, the better. She needed to bring this to a close before her tangled emotions got even more confused.

But when? Megan rose and began to pace again, chewing at her lower lip in thought.

There were always servants about, and she had no idea when Theo might be in his room — or when some other member of the family might be coming out of one of the other rooms and would see her slip into Theo's. She could try, of course, late at night, when the servants and family were in bed, but then she would have to wait until some night when she knew that Theo was out. Even then, she would have no idea when he might return, and she couldn't have him walking in on her.

Of course, there was one time when the

servants were all downstairs in the servants' area and the family was also away from their rooms — the evening meal.

If they were home, every member of the family was there, which was not the case with luncheon or breakfast or high tea. There would be no one to see her enter Theo's room. And as the meal took some time, with all its courses and the Morelands' lively conversation, she would have a good thirty minutes or so in which it would be safe to search.

Of course, she would be expected to be at the meal, as well, but surely she could take care of that problem by pleading illness. She could get a tray from the kitchen or even go without food, if she had to.

The more she thought about it, the more the idea grew on Megan. It would be the perfect opportunity, and she could seize it tomorrow night. There would be no waiting around to learn when Theo was going to be out in the evening. She could do it and get it over with. And if she could find the pendant, then the whole thing would be over with quickly. She would not have to stay with the Morelands, growing fonder of them every day. She would not have to wrestle any longer with her wayward feelings for Theo.

It would be done with.

And though the idea put ice in her stomach, she was certain it was what she must do.

Megan went through the twins' lessons distractedly the next day, the search she planned preying on her mind. Her frequent frowns and distracted air caused Alex to inquire if she was feeling quite all right.

Seizing on the opening his remark offered, Megan admitted that she had a headache and planned to lie down with a lavender compress on her forehead after the end of the day's studies.

When she sent Alex and Con off for their science lesson with Thisbe, Megan went to her bedroom, closed the curtains and did as she had told the boys she would, lying down in her bed with a lavender-sprinkled warm cloth on her head. Later, when one of the maids came in to see if she needed help with her buttons as she dressed for dinner, she raised her head from the pillow and offered the girl a wan smile.

"I am afraid I won't be able to come down for dinner, Millie," she told her, hoping that the nerves dancing in her stomach made her look ill.

"I'm sorry, miss," the maid said sympathetically. "Is it the headache? Cook brews up a good tincture. Take it and go to sleep, and you'll feel right as rain tomorrow."

"That would be very nice," Megan responded. If she was lucky, she would not have to drink it in front of the girl. She sat up slowly. "Would you take a note down to the duchess for me, saying I won't be there?"

"Of course, miss. Would you like for me to bring you a tray of food?"

"That would be very sweet of you," Megan told her. "I'm not sure how much I can eat, but perhaps later . . ."

She penned a brief note excusing herself from dinner and gave it to Millie to carry to the duchess. Then she lay back down to wait for the sounds of the rest of the family going downstairs.

Millie brought her back a tray of cold cuts, bread and fruit, and laid it on the dresser for Megan to eat later. She also left a small brown bottle with instructions for mixing it with water and drinking it.

Megan assured her she would, and after the girl left, she poured a bit of the brown noxious-looking mixture in a glass, then tossed the contents out the window. She nibbled at the food as she listened to the footsteps outside her room.

Finally the corridor fell silent. Going to her door, Megan leaned her ear against it, listening, then eased open the door and peered out. The hallway was empty. After a glance in either direction, she tiptoed out of the room and moved quietly down the hall and around the corner. The door to Theo's room stood ajar, and she carefully peeked inside.

There was no one, so with another quick glance around at the empty corridor, Megan stepped into the room and closed the door softly behind her. If by chance some servant or other family member did come down the hallway, it would not do for them to see her moving about inside the room.

It was a pleasantly large room, befitting, she supposed, the heir to the family title. An expanse of windows across one wall looked out over the back garden. Dark green velvet drapes decorated the windows, drawn back with ties to let in the last faint glow of daylight.

A large bed dominated the room. Four dark walnut posts supported a high tester the same dark green velvet of the draperies, and the wide, thick mattress was covered with a heavy gold-and-green-patterned brocade bedspread. The rest of the furniture was also black walnut, massive, but with clean, elegantly simple lines. A leather chair and hassock stood next to a standing lamp, a small table beside them, piled high with books. It was a comfortable-looking place, with jumbled bookshelves and odd masculine bits and pieces of things stacked in corners and on shelves — an old cricket bat, a fishing rod propped in one corner, a flat dish in which lay a hodgepodge of coins and keys and an old, dented metal pocket watch.

Megan's eyes went first to the bed. It was, after all, impossible to miss. She thought of Theo lying in it at night, and an unexpected heat curled through her abdomen. Telling herself not to be foolish, she walked forward into the room. She made a quick circuit of the chamber, noting the odd foreign-looking piece here and there. A small jade statue sat on his dresser, and an oddly twisted walking stick leaned against the walnut wardrobe. A straw mask of a demonic creature hung on the wall, along with a graceful watercolor of a white heron picking its way through bamboo plants.

She saw nothing that reminded her of any of the objects they had seen at the

Cavendish the day before, nor did she spot any pendant. But, then, she had not really expected Theo to have left it sitting out in plain sight.

She would have to look inside the drawers and chests and compartments, something that went against her grain. Steeling herself to snoop, she turned first to the small desk.

It did not take long to check through all the drawers, finding little except pen nibs, papers, pencil stubs and the like. She turned to go to the large chest that lay at the foot of the bed. It was intriguingly carved with the figures of exotic animals, and it looked like the sort of place where one could stash all sorts of items.

Megan went down on one knee before the chest and placed her hands on its rim, starting to lift it. Suddenly, behind her, there was a loud metallic groan, as of hinges moving. Megan jumped, the lid of the chest slipping from her hand and crashing back down, and whirled around.

Theo Moreland was standing in the doorway of his room, looking at her.

11

Megan jumped to her feet. She could feel the blood flooding her face in embarrassment, and she clasped her hands together in front of her, unable to speak.

"Miss Henderson, what a surprise," Theo said calmly. "I had been told you were sick, but when I came up to see how you were feeling, I found your room empty. And this door, which I had left open, was closed."

He paused. Megan cast about wildly for something she could say to explain herself, but her mind was a blank. What could possibly excuse her being in his room, snooping into his things?

When she said nothing, he smiled faintly. "Cat got your tongue?"

Theo strolled into the room, closing the door behind him. "This is indeed an unusual moment. I can only assume that, feeling ill, you must have been searching for a headache powder. I am sorry to disappoint you, but I fear that I have no such remedies. I rarely get headaches."

"Theo — I mean, Mr. Mor— Lord Raine —" Megan stumbled over the words.

His smile broadened into a grin. "You are quite alluring when you're flustered, Miss Henderson — or shall I call you Megan? I think we could dispense with the formalities, don't you, seeing as how we are standing in my bedchamber?"

"I — I can explain. . . ."

"Can you?" His eyes danced. "I would truly enjoying hearing it."

Megan's eyes flashed. "All right. I cannot explain it. You know I cannot."

"Well, a mystery is better than a lie," Theo mused.

He strolled over and stood looking down at her. He was too close, but Megan stubbornly refused to back away from him. It would seem too much like cowardice. Instead, she tilted her head back and looked up at him, defiance in every line of her face and posture.

"I am left to wonder . . ." he said as he reached out to trace the line of Megan's jaw with his thumb. "What reason would there be for a woman to enter a man's bedroom?"

Megan could feel his touch all through her as he moved his thumb along her jaw and up onto her cheek. She could not hold back a quiver of response.

"There are doubtless prosaic sorts who would assume that you had come in here to steal something from me. In that case, I suppose I should search you." His eyes swept down her body, lingering on her breasts. "You might have something concealed about your person."

He stroked his thumb across Megan's full lower lip. Her eyes fluttered closed as a damp heat blossomed between her legs. Theo, watching her, sucked in his breath sharply at the obvious stamp of desire on her face. His hands came up to cup her face.

"I prefer to think 'tis something else that brought you here," he went on in a husky voice, his breath sharper and faster now. He bent and pressed his lips against hers, softly tasting, nibbling, teasing at her lush mouth.

Megan shuddered and let out a quiet, involuntary noise, her hands coming up to clutch at the lapels of his coat. His arms went around her, pressing her into him so hard she could scarcely breathe — if, indeed, his kiss had not already taken her breath away.

She trembled, a hot, fluid ache growing within her, spreading and filling her, as his kiss deepened, the testing turning hungry and demanding. Desire surged in him, and Megan could feel it in the tightening of his arms, the insistent pressure of his flesh against her, the sudden, uneven rasp of his breath.

"Megan . . ." Her name was part sigh, part groan in his mouth, as he tore his lips away from hers and kissed his way across her face to nibble at her earlobe.

His hand caressed her hair, fumbling at the pins that held it, then sinking into the springing mass. His fingers twined through her curls, popping loose all the last restraining pins, so that her hair tumbled down around her shoulders. The warm red-brown curls were as soft as silk, tugging at his calloused hand, wrapping around his fingers. He clenched his hand in the lush strands, as he had been aching to do for so many days now.

Desire thundered in his head, drowning out all other sounds, all other thoughts. The doubts he held about her, the questions he had asked himself, all fell away, thrust aside in a passion that made any other thought unimportant.

Theo's hands slid over her, caressing

Megan through the barrier of her clothes. Her breasts were soft and yielding beneath his hands, her body warmly inviting. He yearned to feel the texture of her skin under the clothes, to taste her heat and sweetness.

His mouth moved down the tender flesh of her throat, sipping, nibbling, tracing patterns of delight with his tongue. Passion jolted through Megan, stunning her. She melted against him, letting her head fall back, giving him easy access to her throat.

The cloth of her dress impeded his progress, and impatiently his hand went to the buttons that marched down the front of her dress, unfastening them with fingers that trembled slightly. He slipped his hand inside her bodice, skimming over the lush tops of her breasts and delving beneath her simple cotton chemise. Megan jerked, sucking in her breath at the feel of his fingertips upon her skin.

His finger slid over the tight, prickling flesh of her nipple, and Megan quivered at the touch, heat flooding her loins. She had never imagined a man caressing her this way, never dreamed how her body would respond. She wanted to moan, wanted to move against his hand. She wanted, she realized with some astonishment, to feel his hands all over her body.

She opened her eyes and looked up at him, and found him gazing at her. His eyes stared deeply into her own, holding her as surely as if his hand had gripped her face, as he caressed her breasts, shoving down the thin cotton of her chemise and lifting each orb from its confinement. His thumb circled one nipple lazily, his eyes darkening. He saw, Megan thought, the desire that swelled in her as he teased at the small bud of flesh, and her hunger stirred his even more.

Her breath came hard and fast in her throat. She wanted to touch him, she knew, wanted to slip his buttons from their fastenings and slide her fingers inside his shirt. Her fingers ached to feel the texture of his skin, the heat that burned her flesh even through their clothing.

"Megan," he murmured, his breath a caress on her cheek, and just the roughness of his voice spiraled her passion.

Startling them both, she moved up and kissed him. A small moan escaped him, and he kissed her back hungrily. His hand moved restlessly over her body, sweeping down and bunching up her skirts, pulling them up until he could slip beneath them.

Megan quivered at the touch of his hand

against her leg, separated from her flesh by nothing more than cotton. He moved up her leg and over her buttocks, smoothing and squeezing, his fingertips digging into her flesh. Then his fingers slipped between her legs, pressing against the very center of her desire. Megan shuddered, lost in a maelstrom of sensations.

He tore his mouth from hers, kissing his way down her throat and onto the soft tops of her breasts. His fingers moved rhythmically between her legs, rubbing the cloth against her sensitive flesh, even as his mouth closed gently around her nipple.

Megan choked back a groan. The heat inside her coiled and tightened with each lash of his tongue, each pull of his lips. Her loins ached, and she wanted to move against his hand, to rub herself wantonly against him.

In another moment, she knew, she would be sliding down to the floor with him, opening herself to him, and the thought shook her. This was her enemy, the man who had killed her brother, and she was on the verge of giving herself to him like a wanton!

With a gasp, Megan tore herself from his grasp. She grabbed the sides of her bodice and held them together over her bared breasts, staring at Theo in horror. His eyes were fiery, his skin taut over his facial bones. His nostrils flared, his mouth tightening, and he took a step toward her.

Megan stepped back with a low, wordless cry, holding up her hand as if to stop him, and he halted, frustration stamped on his features.

"Megan . . ."

"No. No. I cannot. We cannot."

He cursed softly and turned aside. "I am sorry. Go. Now."

He shot a glance at her, and Megan saw in his blazing eyes the effort it took for him not to reach for her.

She whirled and ran blindly from the room, not stopping until she had gained the sanctuary of her own bedchamber. There she collapsed in a heap upon her bed and thought with dismay of what she had almost done.

Her body still throbbed with the passion he had aroused in her, the pulse hot and deep within her. She drew a finger across her nipples, still hard and aching from his touch. She could not understand how she could have responded so to him, knowing what he had done to her brother. It was wicked, worse than wicked, she told herself, and still she could not turn aside the yearning that twisted through her. There was nothing she could do, she realized, but lie there as the passion gradually ebbed from her body and wonder what she was going to do next.

She did not know how she could face Theo again. Indeed, given the way she felt right now, she did not know how she could look anyone in the house in the eyes again. She felt as if shame must be stamped clearly upon her face.

Megan got off her bed and went to the mirror above her vanity, peering into it. Her hair was tumbled about her face, wild and curling. Color stained her cheeks, and her lips were lush and faintly bruised looking. Her bodice hung open down the front, exposing a strip of her white cotton chemise. She could feel the scrape of the material of her bodice against her sensitive nipples, each breath gently abrading her flesh.

She looked wild and foreign to herself, someone she hardly knew. She remembered the feel of his hand between her legs, and the ache there throbbed into life again. With a soft groan, she turned away.

This could not continue, she knew. She had to get control of herself. The only question was how.

Sighing, she undressed and stood for a moment, savoring the feeling of the air on her naked flesh. It was distinctly unnerving, she thought, to know that she wished Theo were there with her. Heat pooled deep in her loins at the thought of him watching her.

Feeling decidedly wanton, she did not pull on her nightdress immediately, but moved about the room as she was, putting away her clothes and brushing through her hair. Finally she slipped on her nightgown and lay down. The window was open, admitting the soft summer breeze. Moonlight slanted in, silvering the furniture and carpet, and Megan lay staring at it, thinking of what had happened tonight.

It was a long, long time before she slept.

Megan was careful to keep out of Theo's way the next day. She oversaw the twins' lessons, which were always light on Saturday, giving them the afternoon off to do as they wished. The duke and duchess were attending the opera with Reed and Anna, and they were all four dining beforehand at Kyria's house, so the twins were eating supper in the nursery, and Megan was able to join them there. She worried throughout the day that Theo might come into the nursery to visit with the twins, but as it turned out, he did not — a circumstance that, she admitted to herself, left her feeling both relieved and perversely disappointed.

The next morning she ate a hurried breakfast and left, walking briskly to the house her father had rented. It would be wonderful, she told herself, to be out and free of responsibility. To be able to be herself again. It was somewhat disconcerting to find that as she walked, she spent most of her time thinking not about being with her family again, but about what she was going to tell them about the Morelands — more specifically, Theo.

Of course, she could not let them get a hint of anything that had happened between her and Theo. Da would explode and Deirdre would worry. And, she told herself, it wasn't really pertinent to what she had learned, anyway.

A few blocks from Broughton House, as she cut through a small park, Megan became aware of an odd sensation, a sort of prickling along the nape of her neck. She told herself not to be foolish, but she could not dismiss the feeling that she was being watched.

She picked up her pace, crossing a street

and walking rapidly to the major thorough-fare that ran perpendicular to the one she was on. There she turned and slowed down, idling along, looking into the win-dows of the shops along the way. She stopped at a millinery store and sneaked a look back down the street. There were one or two people strolling along the street be-hind her, as well as a man who was gazing into a store window himself. None of the people looked out of the ordinary, and cer-tainly none of them were looking at her.

It was nonsense, she told herself, just her nerves. After all, who would be following her? No one in London knew her except the Morelands and their servants, and she was certain that none of the people behind her were any of the residents of Broughton House. She knew that Theo had suspicions about her — how could he not, after the other night? — but he was nowhere around.

Megan turned and started down the street again, relieved to find that the odd feeling had dissipated. When she arrived home, she found her father and sister sit-ting in the kitchen, tucking into a hearty breakfast, having just returned from early mass.

"Megan!" Deirdre cried, jumping up

from the table and coming to hug her. "I've missed you. It's been so long."

Megan smiled fondly at her younger sister. She had never before been away from Deirdre for as long as two weeks. "I know. I missed you, too." She hugged Deirdre and turned to her father. "Da."

"Ah, Megan, me love, it's good to see you again. I cannot help but worry about you in that den of vipers."

"They're not all vipers, Da," Megan felt compelled to say. "The duchess is a very nice woman. They all are, really. And I truly like the twins."

"Megan, me love, what are you saying?" Frank Mulcahey regarded his daughter with something akin to horror. "Have you let those British bastards corrupt ye?"

"No, of course not. Don't look at me like that," Megan replied, and sat down at the table with a sigh. "Deirdre, I would dearly love some coffee, if you have it. I am heartily sick of tea."

"Of course you are. Here." Deirdre patted Megan's shoulder sympathetically and went to pour her sister a cup of coffee, saying over her shoulder, "Da, stop badgering Megan. I am sure she has a good reason for saying what she did. After all, just because Theo Moreland is wicked, it doesn't necessarily mean his whole family is."

"His father's an English duke," Mulcahey replied, as if that settled the matter.

Megan rolled her eyes. "That doesn't make him wicked, Da. Trust me, I am sure that the Duke of Broughton has never done anything to harm anyone, including the Irish. He is a sweet man who is interested in nothing but his ancient pots and statues." At her father's doubtful look, she said, "I promise. If you met them, you would realize that it's true. They are not at all what I expected. They don't act like aristocrats. They are friendly and down-to-earth. I feel wicked deceiving them — and it's going to be even worse when I expose Theo."

"Are you still planning to do that?" Mulcahey asked.

"Da!" Megan's eyes flashed. "How can you ask that? As if I would give up on our plan."

"It's soft you sound about these people. I figure the next thing you'll be telling me is Theo Moreland is innocent."

"No," Megan said, with an unconscious sigh. "I don't think he is innocent. But I have not been able to prove it yet. I haven't found a trace of a pendant or anything else that he might have taken from Dennis. I have tried to ask him a few questions about the trip, but he's very close-mouthed about it."

She related their trip to the museum and the way he had acted there, the few things he had said about his trip up the Amazon.

"Where have you looked in the house?" her father asked.

"Everywhere," Megan replied dispiritedly. "Well, everywhere I could get in. There is a locked room by the butler's pantry where they keep the silver, I think, and there is a safe in the duke's study, but I don't know how to break into either of those. I did check the duke's collection room, which seemed the likeliest place to me, but everything there is Greek or Roman."

"What about his bedroom?" Deirdre asked.

Megan looked at her sister, hoping that no blush would creep into her cheeks to betray even a hint of what had happened in Theo's bedroom. "Yes, I looked there, but I found nothing. I — I didn't have much time. It's difficult to find a chance to go in there without getting caught. But I will go back some night when he is out of the house. I just wish we knew more about what I'm looking for." She paused, then asked, "Have you had any more dreams?"

Deirdre nodded. "Yes, Dennis has come to me twice more. But he said nothing more than what he's already told me."

"Couldn't you ask him a question?" Megan asked. "What this thing is we're looking for, maybe?"

Her sister gave her a disparaging look. "Megan, it's not like that. I'm not even conscious. Mostly I just feel these emotions coming from him — grief and loss and a need for our help. Believe me, I wish it was all clearer."

"I wish I could talk to Mr. Barchester again," Megan mused.

"Why, we can ask him," Frank said. "Next time he comes over. What is it you want to know?"

Megan looked at her father in surprise. "Mr. Barchester has been here?"

"Yes. He has come to call three times now." Frank smiled, casting a glance over at his other daughter. "I'm thinking 'tis Deirdre he's coming to see, not me."

Megan's gaze went to Deirdre. "The man's courting you?"

Deirdre blushed. "No, of course not. Da . . . don't exaggerate."

"What? Exaggerating, is it? Why else

would he keep popping in?" Frank Mulcahey's eyes, so like his daughter's, twinkled merrily.

"Are you interested in him?" Megan asked Deirdre, happy to be diverted from the subject of Theo and the search for incriminating evidence.

"I scarcely know the man," Deirdre protested, but the small smile that played about her lips belied her attempt at indifference.

"You *are* interested in him!" Megan cried and leaned closer to her sister. "All right. Tell me everything."

Deirdre chuckled. "There is nothing to tell. Really. He's come over here a few times, and he is very nice and polite. But he's done nothing to indicate any particular interest in me."

"I should think not, with your own father sitting right here," Frank said.

"His coming here three times when there was no reason for him to come even once is a pretty clear indication of a particular interest in you," Megan retorted. "What I want to know is whether you have any particular interest in him."

"Of course not. Don't be silly," Deirdre admonished.

"What's silly about it?"

"He lives in England, for one thing," Deirdre pointed out. "I'll be going back to New York soon, and that will be the end of that. So 'twould be foolish to have feelings for the man."

"Sometimes you have feelings whether it's foolish or not," Megan responded, and was aware of a sudden small stab of pain at her own words. She knew all too well how difficult it was to control one's feelings.

"Well, I don't and I won't," Deirdre said firmly. "But I will ask him something for you, if you like. What is it you want to know?"

Pulled back to the subject of Theo's crime, Megan said, "I'm not sure. I would like him to think it over again and see if any more thoughts occur to him. Any more memories. If I just had some idea what the pendant looked like, or any more details of how Dennis was killed, maybe I could ask Lord Raine some pertinent questions. It would help a great deal if I knew exactly what I was searching for."

"I will ask him," Deirdre promised. "Now . . . let's just put all this away and have a nice afternoon together. It has been so long since I've seen you."

"I know. I've missed you terribly," Megan agreed. "Both of you."

So they settled down to a hearty meal, followed by an afternoon spent talking. The time passed quickly, and all too soon Megan had to start back to Broughton House. She bade goodbye to her father, and Deirdre followed her out the door.

As soon as they stepped outside, Deirdre laid a hand on Megan's arm and said in a quiet voice, "I have to tell you something."

"What?" Megan turned to her, concerned by the tone of her sister's voice. "Is something wrong? Is it Da?"

"No, he's fine. I just didn't want him to hear." Deirdre cast a quick look back inside the house and moved a little farther away from the door. "I have not told him, because I didn't want to worry him. But I have been having dreams — about you." She looked at Megan, her blue eyes dark with worry.

"About me? What do you mean? What kind of dreams?"

"Frightening ones," Deirdre replied, frowning.

Megan's heart sped up a little. "Deirdre . . ."

"I don't know what they mean," Deirdre said quickly, taking hold of her sister's hand. "I'm not sure whether they are visions or just nightmares. But they scare me. I am worried about you. I think you are in danger, or will be. And knowing that you are there in that house with the man who killed Dennis scares me. What if he discovers who you are? What would stop him from hurting you?"

"He doesn't know who I am," Megan told her firmly. "How could he?" She paused, not sure if she really wanted to know, then went on, "What did you dream? What did you see?"

Deirdre sighed. "I'm not sure. There was a fire burning in a sort of brazier and — a hideous face, bright . . . glowing. I cannot describe it, but it terrified me to see it. You were there, and — and Dennis was there, too. And there was an odd instrument. I'm not sure what it was. There was a hand holding this thing and slashing at you with it, but it wasn't exactly a knife. It was a figure of some sort, and at the end of the figure there was a small, rounded thing that looked like a miniature shovel. A sort of semicircular shape."

Ice crept up Megan's spine. She stared at her sister, speechless. How could Deirdre know what that knife looked like? Megan had never seen anything like it before she saw it at the Cavendish, and she was sure that Deirdre had been equally ignorant of it.

"What?" Deirdre's voice rose in anxiety. "Why are you looking at me like that? Do you know what it is? Is it in that house?"

"No. No. It isn't at Broughton House. It sounds like something I saw at the museum."

"The museum?"

"Yes. The Cavendish Museum, where Julian Coffey works."

"You have been there?"

"Yes, and there is a ceremonial Inca knife that is shaped like that."

"But what does it mean?" Deirdre asked.

"I am sure it doesn't mean I am going to get stabbed with it," Megan said flatly. She had no intention of letting Deirdre see how badly her sister's tale of the dream had shaken her. She had never really believed in Deirdre's visions, though she loved her sister too much to completely discount them. But this dream defied rational explanation, and she could not suppress a shiver.

"You said Dennis was in the dream, too," Megan went on, searching for an explanation that would allay Deirdre's fears — and perhaps her own, as well. " 'Tis much more likely that it relates to his death. Maybe a knife like that is what killed him. Maybe that is the thing I should be looking for at Broughton House."

"Instead of the pendant?"

Megan shrugged. "I don't know. Perhaps both of them are there."

"Megan . . ." Deirdre reached out and wrapped her hand around her sister's wrist. "I am worried about you. About your being there."

"Nothing is going to happen to me," Megan assured her. "I promise you, I will be very careful. But I have to go back. You can see that. How else are we going to find out what happened to Dennis?"

"I'd rather we never found out what happened to him than to have you hurt!" Deirdre snapped back.

"That won't happen. I can handle myself. Besides, the house is filled with people — the family, the servants. No one would risk doing anything to me there. I will be perfectly safe."

Deirdre looked at her, not entirely convinced. Megan leaned over and gave her sister a quick peck on the cheek.

"Don't worry," she said firmly. "I'll come back here on my next day off — or sooner, if I can find anything."

"Write to me if anything worries you," Deirdre replied. "Promise me."

"I promise."

Giving her a bright smile, Megan set off down the street. She hurried, looking neither right nor left, her mind too occupied to even think about her earlier eerie feeling of being watched. She did not stop to look behind her.

Deirdre's dream had unnerved her, and she found herself walking ever faster, eager to get home. It did not occur to her to wonder that she thought of Broughton House as home, and when at last she saw its elegant white facade rising up before her, the windows glowing warmly in the encroaching dusk, she smiled and hurried toward it, her heart lifting.

Late that evening, Theo trotted down the front steps of Broughton House. He strolled down the block and hailed a hansom, giving the driver an address that was some distance from the elegant Mayfair section in which Broughton House was located.

He went into a humble tavern there, stooping a little to enter the old door, and stood for a moment, looking around the low-ceilinged room, smoky from the pipes and cigars of its patrons, and smelling of ale and the sweat of workingmen. It was not a gin mill, but neither was it the sort of place that his peers generally frequented. That was one of the principal reasons Theo liked it.

He nodded toward the barkeep behind the counter, and the man nodded back, familiar enough with Theo that he moved to the tap to draw him an ale. Theo strolled to a table nestled in the corner of the room and sat down to wait.

Shortly after the barkeep brought the tankard of ale and placed it on the table before Theo, the door to the tavern opened again and a young man walked in.

Slender and lithe, the young man had a shock of blond hair, untidily cut, and piercing blue eyes. He moved with noiseless grace toward Theo's table, signaling to the barkeep, and pulled out a chair. His name was Tom Quick, and he had been an employee of one Moreland or another for a number of years.

"Yer grace," he said in greeting, grinning, his eyes alight with mischief.

Theo grimaced. "You can't plague me with that title yet, Quick."

He watched as the barkeep brought another tankard and Quick took a long pull from it. He knew better than to try to hurry Tom. He was his own man, more given to insolence than subservience.

Quick had grown up in the slums of the East End and had made his living as a child as a pickpocket. He did not know his father or mother; his last name was one given to him by the man who ran the gang of pickpockets, and it referred to his speed at lifting items from strangers. Doubtless he would have ended up as most of his accomplices had, in Newgate, but for the fact that one day he had attempted to steal the wallet of Reed Moreland. Theo's brother, recognizing Tom's innate intelligence and abilities, had not turned the boy over to the authorities but had taken him in, feeding and educating him, and giving him a job.

Quick had worked for Reed, then for their sister Olivia in her business of debunking mediums, and now generally worked for Kyria's husband, Rafe, in whom he had found a kindred spirit. He had, however, been happy to take on a small task for Theo on his Sunday off.

He let out a sigh of pleasure as he set down his ale and leaned back in his chair. "I followed your Miss Henderson, just like you asked. She went to a house — a snug little place. Then I followed her back to Broughton House. She didn't go anywhere else. So I returned to the area where she visited, and I talked with a few people in a tavern or two."

"And what did you find out?" Theo asked.

"The house where she went is being rented by an Irishman. Nobody knew his name, or they weren't telling. But he visits the taverns — well, he would, wouldn't he, being Irish?"

Theo considered Tom's news for a moment, aware of a fierce surge of jealousy. *Who was this man to Megan? Husband? Lover? Or simply a business associate?* It disturbed him to realize how much the answer mattered.

"Did anyone know what he does for a living?" Theo asked finally.

"Not that any of them could tell me. He's full of Irish stories and the like, but they didn't know anything about his work. Seems that, on reflection, they realized that he didn't talk much about himself, really, except for long ago things about Ireland."

"Indeed? Interesting."

"That's not the most interesting thing," Tom went on. He took another swig of ale and sat back in his chair, looking quite pleased with himself.

"All right. I'll play along," Theo said.

"What is the most interesting thing?"

"When I was following your lady . . . I realized I wasn't the only one. There was another fellow trailing her."

12

Theo stared at Quick in astonishment. "What?"

"After walking along after her for a little ways this morning, I noticed this other chap in front of me. He was taking all the same turns I was, and once when she stopped to look in a store window, he stopped, too. I realized that he was following her, just like me."

"Who the devil was he?" Theo asked, his brows drawing together thunderously.

Quick shrugged. "Don't know. Never saw him before today. But I'm sure I was right, because while I was idling about, waiting for her to come back out of the house, I saw him doing the same."

"Did he spot you?" Theo asked.

Tom shot him a scornful look. " 'Course not. I may not be in the game anymore, but you won't find any better than me. I know how to stay out of sight. He was clumsy, or I wouldn't have noticed him — followed too close behind her."

"Is he in the game, do you think?"

Quick shrugged. "I don't know. I been out of it too long — don't know anybody in it anymore. But usually, following somebody around — you got to figure one or both of 'em's up to no good." He paused, then added, "Who is this woman, guvnor? Is she going to hurt your family?"

"Not if I can help it," Theo replied. He sighed, then said, "I'm not sure. She is the twins' teacher, but I can't help thinking there is more to her than that. I have found her in a couple of places where she had no reason to be. I suspect she may be a thief — or working for one."

He saw no point in mentioning that she was also someone who had come to him in a dream ten years earlier.

"Chuck her out — that's what I would do," Tom offered.

"I'm keeping my eye on her," Theo promised.

"Aye. Well, she's worth keeping an eye on, all right." Tom grinned, then added seriously, "But not worth letting any harm come to your family."

"No. Of course not. I won't allow her to hurt them."

But Theo knew it was already too late for that. The members of his family liked her, had taken her in and treated her as one of their own. If Megan was there to steal from them, just the knowledge that she could betray them would hurt them far more than whatever she might steal.

"I could look into it some more, if you want," Tom said. "I could probably find one or two of my old mates. Check if she and the Irishman are thieves. Though it seems an uncommon roundabout way of stealing something, if you ask me — especially if it means taking on the Greats."

"She has no problem with the twins," Theo said in some wonderment. "I have never seen them as well-behaved — or as happy with their tutor."

"I'd guess they're not the only ones who like her," Tom replied shrewdly.

Theo shot him a sardonic look. "Don't get cheeky."

"Me?" Quick feigned innocence.

"Do whatever checking you can on her and the Irishman." He frowned. "And on the chap who's following her."

Whatever Megan's game was, the fact that someone was following her could not be good. Whether the follower was an accomplice who did not trust her or someone from whom she had stolen or had crossed in some way, it seemed very clear to him that the man represented a danger to her.

Theo knew, with a fierce, sharp pain in his gut, that he had to protect her from whoever threatened her. It came as an unwelcome surprise that the need to protect her was greater than his concern for whatever she was planning against him and his family.

"Right you are, guvnor," Quick said cheerfully. "What about Miss Henderson?"

"I will keep an eye on her," Theo replied flatly. "The lady won't be going anywhere this week unless I am along."

Megan dreaded seeing Theo again after what had happened in his bedroom the other night. However, there was little way to avoid being in his company — especially, she found, since he seemed to pop up at every turn for the next week.

He dropped by the nursery to chat with the twins or check on their animals. When she took a stroll about the garden after classes, he was there, sitting on the terrace and reading a book, his gaze on her more often than on the tome in his lap. He ate every dinner at home, and not an evening went by that he didn't suggest that Megan join the family after the evening meal for a round of games or an hour of music or simply the free-flowing conversation that often occupied the Morelands.

There was nowhere that Megan particularly wanted to go, but she felt certain that if she left the house, with or without her charges, Theo would turn up before she had gotten ten steps from the door. He was, she knew, trying to find out what she was doing, why she had tried to get into the duke's collection room, and why she had been prowling around his own bedroom.

It made her a little nervous that he did not simply ask her what she was doing. It seemed the obvious course. It was even odder, she supposed, that he had told no one else in the family, even his parents, about her strange nocturnal visits to places she had no right to be. It was as if he was protecting her from his family's anger.

The thought made her feel warm and tender inside. It was foolish, she supposed, to feel that way; he was not doing it, after all, because he wanted to protect her. There were bound to be reasons — selfish reasons — behind his actions.

He could intend to hold his knowledge over her head, to coerce her with the threat of revealing what she had done. But she could think of nothing he could want to coerce her into doing besides giving herself to him, and she had already proved herself embarrassingly close to bedding the man without any sort of coercion at all. Besides, Theo had made no move in that direction since the other night.

He had not tried to be alone with her at any time. His conversation and manner were perfectly gentlemanly. Except for a time or two when Megan had glanced up and found his gaze on her, a quickly veiled heat in his eyes, she would have wondered if he even remembered the ardor they had shared the other night.

She moved through the next week, puzzling over Theo's actions and attitude, and wondering how she could get back into his bedroom to search it. She could not risk entering it again unless she was absolutely certain that he would not walk in on her. She would have to wait until he was out for the evening, preferably very late at night when no one else would be up or on some night when the rest of the family was out, as well.

The evening of the museum benefit, for instance, would have been perfect — if it had not been for the fact that she would be attending it, as well.

She had half hoped that Kyria and the others would forget about their promise to take her, but those hopes were dashed on Monday afternoon when Kyria, Olivia and Anna swept her out of the nursery and down to Anna's room, where Kyria's maid was laying out a number of dresses.

Megan's eyes widened when she saw the display of sumptuous ball gowns. "Mrs. McIntyre! My lady!"

She turned from Kyria to the other two. Kyria wore a broad smile on her face and Olivia looked pleased and encouraging. Megan glanced at Anna, whose expression was more guarded. There was in her gray eyes the same faint darkness, even suspicion, that Megan had seen there when they first met. Reed's wife, she thought, did not completely trust her. And there had been that disturbing thing about the woman's seeing things that others could not. . . .

Megan turned from the women back to the bed, where a wealth of jewel-toned satins, velvets and laces were draped across the spread. There were also gowns lying across chairs and every other available surface.

"This is too much," Megan protested feebly.

"Nonsense," Kyria said. "Now stand there and let me look at you. Joan . . ."

Kyria's maidservant obligingly held up one gown after another in front of Megan as she chatted with Kyria and Anna about the possibilities. Golds and greens and blues followed deep red and chocolate brown and pale yellow.

"Olivia's colors suit you best," Kyria said thoughtfully. "If only she didn't insist on such plain things."

"Not plain," Olivia protested. "I just don't like a lot of fussy decorations."

"Elegantly simple," Anna said, compromising. "I agree. The shades that look good on me aren't as good on Megan, though I think I am a little more the same size."

"I like the rust-colored satin," Anna went on, picking up one of the gowns and holding it up to Megan.

Anna might be suspicious, but she seemed willing enough to help her, Megan thought. Perhaps she was simply more reserved than Kyria. *Or perhaps she was simply waiting for her to take a misstep.*

"It's a beautiful color on her," Kyria agreed. "Why don't you try it on, Megan, and Joan can see where she needs to alter it?"

It didn't take much urging for Megan to try on the dress. It was a beautiful rich satin in a dark russet that picked up the red of her hair and warmed her pale skin. She had had her eye on it the whole time. The low neckline curved slightly up to the short, puffed sleeves, and a darker lace trimmed the edge, making the neckline more modest.

Olivia was a trifle more slender than Megan, she found, and she had to suck in her breath sharply to let Joan fasten the hooks up the back.

"Oh, yes!" Kyria exclaimed. "That looks lovely."

"I can scarcely breathe," Megan commented, but Kyria waved away that protest.

"We'll lace up your corset more tightly," she told her. "I think this is definitely the one."

Joan tucked the lace down inside the dress, startling Megan with the familiarity that the aristocratic ladies seemed to not even notice.

"Much better," Kyria almost purred. "We'll take off the lace at the neckline. You can add a bit of copper lace as decoration at the hem. I have some earrings I made last year that would be absolutely perfect.

Copper-and-turquoise dangles." She paused, thinking, her head tilted to one side. "Or perhaps just plain ear bobs and a cameo choker with a copper-colored ribbon."

"The choker, I think," Anna said, hopping up and going to her jewelry box and returning with a cameo on a ribbon. "We can exchange these ribbons." She wrapped it around Megan's throat and held it, looking toward Kyria for confirmation.

"Simple and elegant," Kyria said with a nod.

Megan, looking at her reflection in the mirror, could not help but agree. Even with her hair twisted into its usual plain knot, she looked more attractive than she could ever remember looking. The rich material and the warmth of the color made her skin glow, and her eyes were lit with pleasure. Her waist was infinitesimal in this tight dress, well worth, she thought, a little discomfort. Her bosom, larger than Olivia's, swelled above the lowered neckline, full and soft, beckoning the eye.

"Um . . . don't you think it's, well, a little low cut?" she asked doubtfully. "I mean, I am only a tutor. It seems, well . . ." She shrugged.

"Nonsense," Kyria said firmly. "There is no need to look like a governess at a ball, is there? It isn't as if you're going to be teaching anyone."

"Besides, it's simple," Olivia put in. She cast a look at Kyria. "Plain, in fact. No one could say it was inappropriate."

Megan suspected that her father and the nuns would probably argue about that, but she wasn't about to let that stop her from wearing this dress. It was sheer vanity, she knew, but she could not wait to see Theo's face when he saw her in this dress.

Joan fussed about the skirt of the gown, pulling it up here and there, and telling Kyria that she could drape the hem over the copper lace, as well as add a little more padding to the modest bustle. Kyria was quick to agree.

Puzzled, Megan looked at Kyria. "I have to wonder — why are you doing this?"

Kyria raised an elegant brow in a gesture that was designed to quell impertinent questions. "I'm sorry. Do you not wish to attend the museum benefit?"

Megan was too accustomed to asking unwelcome reporters' questions to be turned aside by the other woman's manner. She merely smiled and said, "It's not that I am not grateful for your kindness and generosity, Mrs. McIntyre. Or that I'm not looking forward to being Cinderella at the ball. It is just, well, I cannot help but wonder why you are going to so much trouble to take me to this party."

Kyria's snobbish expression dissolved into a grin. "All right. I do have an ulterior motive. Surely you know what that is — I would like to put Lady Scarle's nose out of joint."

"She has had her tentacles out for Theo for months now," Olivia put in, surprising Megan a little. She would have thought Lady St. Leger was as unobservant as her father of all things social.

"He doesn't have any partiality for her, though," Anna said. "Does he?"

"Oh, no. He has never been more than polite to her," Kyria replied. "It's just . . . well, I worry sometimes that she will keep after him so long that she will wear him down. Or that she will manage to trick him into some compromising position. You know Theo. He would marry her if he thought honor demanded it."

"She is just the sort who would do something like that," Olivia agreed.

Megan could understand Theo's loving sisters' motives. She would herself relish irritating the obnoxious Lady Scarle.

"But why — I mean, what does that have to do with me?" Megan blurted out, then blushed to her hairline.

Kyria let out a throaty chuckle. "My dear Miss Henderson, surely you have noticed that our brother spends an inordinate amount of time with the twins these days."

"And he is not usually inclined to scholarly pursuits," Olivia stuck in with a smile.

"Lady Helena saw it as soon as the two of you walked into the drawing room the other day. Her back went up immediately. Even she isn't usually quite that rude. She was livid when I said you were coming with us to the ball." Kyria smiled at the memory of the other woman's discomfiture. "I intend for her to be even more upset when she sees you this Friday evening."

Megan could not understand Kyria's satisfaction at the thought of her brother's interest in a mere employee. The Morelands were abnormally egalitarian for aristocrats, of course. Kyria herself had married an American and was quite happy to be addressed as Mrs. McIntyre instead of Lady Kyria. But Rafe McIntyre was at least enormously wealthy, whereas Megan was nothing but a tutor.

It was not, she supposed, as bad as her real occupation — she could think of little an aristocratic family would like less than one of them marrying a muckraking careerwoman. But even so, she was not only a commoner and a foreigner, she was someone who worked for them. And while a daughter might marry outside their group of peers, as Kyria and Thisbe had obviously done, it was an altogether different thing for their firstborn son, the heir to the ancient title, to do so. *A tutoress as the next duchess?* It would be, Megan guessed, unthinkable.

Then she realized that that very fact was the answer to her question. Kyria and Olivia knew that Megan was so unacceptable as a wife that Theo would never consider marriage to her. It would not be the same as falling into the clutches of a woman of good birth, whom he might have to marry. An employee, and an American at that, would never be anything to Theo but a passing fancy — a mistress, at best.

Megan was aware of a pang of hurt and disappointment at the thought. She liked Kyria and Olivia, and it wounded her to think that they did not consider the consequences for her in their scheme to keep their brother out of Lady Scarle's clutches.

Somewhat subdued, she stood, letting Joan crawl around her skirt, pinning it up here and there, while the other women chattered about ribbons and jewelry and the dreadful Lady Scarle. When the maid finally finished, Megan quickly got out of the elegant gown and back into her own plain clothes, and left the ladies with a polite smile and thank-you.

She went through the rest of the week careening back and forth between conflicting emotions. Part of her did not want to go to the benefit, didn't want to face Theo — or Lady Scarle. Yet she knew that she had to; it was a perfect opportunity to see Mr. Coffey again and question him privately about the trip he had made with Theo and her brother.

However, she knew that it was not simply this opportunity that made her a little breathless with anticipation every time she thought about the ball. She wanted to see herself dressed in the beautiful gown; she could not help but imagine how Theo would look when he saw her — the smile that would curve his mouth and the heat that would light his eyes. She wanted to put that hot glow of passion in his eyes; indeed, she melted a little inside just thinking about it.

But the thought scared her as much as it excited her. She did not want to have to face the man's passion again. Did she?

Surely she did not really look forward to having to fend off his advances — or the guilty shame that would assail her if she gave in to his drugging kisses.

By the time the evening of the museum benefit arrived, Megan's stomach was a ball of nerves. Joan had brought the dress to her that afternoon, altered and pressed, and had hung it carefully in her wardrobe, pushing all other clothes back so that nothing would crease the ball gown. Hanging there in solitary splendor, it was even more magnificent than Megan had imagined. Joan's touch of scalloping the skirt, with lace inserts peeking through between, added richness and sophistication, as did the drapery over the heightened bustle.

She had also brought the simple cameo, tacked with Joan's infinitesimal stitches onto a grosgrain ribbon that matched the copper color of the lace, and it now lay spread out on Megan's vanity. Beside it lay the simple onyx ear bobs that matched the background of the cameo.

Megan had just sat down to begin her toilette when there was a knock on the door and Joan entered. When Megan looked at her, surprised, Joan said, "Her ladyship sent me over to do your hair, miss."

The maid looked, Megan thought, a trifle miffed. No doubt she preferred to be at her mistress's side, putting the final touches on Kyria's beauty. However, she went to work on Megan's hair with deft efficiency, sweeping it up into a knot, then separating it and winding each strand around her finger, so that the ensuing curls fell in a cascade. Artfully, she arranged delicate feathery curls around Megan's face. To complete the hairdo, she wound a coppery satin ribbon around the knot and through the curls.

Joan helped Megan into the petticoats and bustle, cinching her up in her corset so tightly that Megan wondered if she would be able to breathe at all that evening. Carefully, Joan lifted the dress over Megan's head and brought it down, hooking it up the back and arranging the folds of her skirt so that they fell exactly right. She finished her work of art by fastening the cameo on Megan's neck and putting in the simple earrings.

She stepped back, allowing Megan to look at the finished product. Megan drew in an involuntary gasp. Kyria's sense of style had been unerring. The stylish dress complemented the color of her hair and eyes, and her pale skin glowed against its satin richness. The cameo around her neck was at once simple and devastating, showing off the elegant line of her neck and drawing the eye without distracting from the expanse of her bosom swelling up from the neckline of the dress.

Megan had always known that she was pretty in a casual way, but never had she imagined that she could look striking. Somehow, she marveled, Joan and Kyria had managed to make her look both desirable and unattainable.

She smiled blindingly at Kyria's maid. "You are an artist, Joan. Thank you."

Joan nodded, accepting Megan's praise as her due. "Her ladyship said that was just how you would look. She's a canny one." She stepped forward and pinched Megan sharply on both cheeks, startling her. "There, now there's a little color in your cheeks. Just perfect. Press your lips together and put a little color in them, too."

She stepped back, grinning. "Everybody'll be wondering who the new American beauty is at the ball tonight."

Megan could only laugh, excitement bubbling up in her. She swept from her room and walked down the stairs, where several of the Morelands already waited, including Theo. He looked up at the sound of her footsteps, and the stunned expression on his face was everything she could have hoped for.

"Miss Henderson, how lovely you look," the duchess said, moving forward to take Megan's hand and smile down at her. "Doesn't she, Henry?"

"Yes, yes, lovely, my dear." The duke smiled benignly and rather vaguely at Megan, then back at his wife, adding, "Not as lovely as you, of course. You are stunning, as always."

It was the truth, for the duchess, with her regal height and still slender figure, the dramatic streaks of white in her vibrant red hair, made a striking figure, despite the unostentatious lack of jewelry at her throat and ears, and the almost severe cut of her peacock-blue dress.

Theo stepped forward as his parents turned away, and took Megan's hand in his, raising it to his lips in formal greeting. She glanced away, struggling to suppress the flicker of nerves inside her at the touch of his lips upon her skin.

"You are beautiful," he murmured, and the flicker of heat in his eyes as he looked down into hers underlined his words. "I can see that I will have to beat your admirers back if I hope to have a dance with you."

Megan smiled. "I am sure that is not the case."

"Will you promise me your first waltz?" he asked.

"I would not think that is appropriate, surely," she said, casting an unabashedly flirtatious glance up at him through her lashes. "The future Duke of Broughton, taking the governess out onto the floor for the first waltz."

He grinned. "It will doubtless scandalize the old biddies. Now I am determined to do it."

She chuckled, though she shook her head.

His fingers tightened on hers. "You cannot abandon me to all those ambitious mothers and their daughters. Please, say you will save me."

"Don't be absurd."

"You would not say that if you had seen them."

Megan could not keep from smiling. "All right. I will give you my first waltz." She paused, then added, "But only to save you from the overbearing mamas."

"Of course." He turned and picked up a white box from the nearby table. Turning back, he held it out to Megan, saying, "I did not know the color of your dress. . . ."

She took the box, surprised, and opened it with suddenly fumbling fingers. Inside, nestled on a bed of green tissue, lay a delicate white gardenia, framed by its waxy dark green leaves.

"Theo — I mean, Lord Raine . . ." Megan had not expected this. She reached into the box and pulled out the fragile white flower, breathing in its heady scent. "I — I don't know what to say. It is beautiful."

"It pales in comparison to you," he murmured, taking the small corsage from her hand and fastening it around her wrist. Then he raised her arm so he could smell the flower. Turning her hand, he brushed his lips against the tender flesh inside her wrist.

Megan jumped a little, startled, and cast a swift glance toward his parents. The duke and duchess, fortunately, were engrossed in each other and paying no attention to anyone else.

"Please . . . you should not," Megan told him a little breathlessly and took a step back from him. She lifted her head and looked into his eyes, saying softly, "Thank you."

There was the sound of footsteps at the top of the stairs, and they turned to look up, moving a step farther apart as Anna and Reed came down the stairs to join them. The duke and duchess turned and came over, and for a while they all chatted casually. Megan moved subtly away from Theo, directing most of her comments to the others.

Kyria and Rafe arrived a few minutes later. Kyria was stunning in a gown of pale green silk, pulled back in the front and falling from a bustle in three puffed tiers. Silver lace decorated the hem of the dress and made an inverted V below the tiers of material in the back. Around her neck was a magnificent emerald necklace that would doubtless have outshone anyone less stunning than Kyria.

Kyria gave Megan a swift, assessing glance, and a small smile touched her lips when she saw the corsage on Megan's wrist. Stepping forward, she greeted Megan with a peck on the cheek, murmuring, "You look beautiful, just as I thought you would."

Linking her arm through Megan's, Kyria said, "Theo, why don't you and Miss Henderson come with us? Papa's carriage will be too crowded with all of you."

As they walked out to the carriage, Kyria leaned closer, confiding to Megan in a whisper, "I want to make sure I am there when you arrive. I am anticipating with great glee the look on Lady Scarle's face."

"I cannot imagine that anyone will look at me much, Mrs. McIntyre, when I am standing beside you."

Kyria let out a light laugh. "Don't underestimate yourself, Miss Henderson. Besides, everyone is quite accustomed to seeing me, whereas you are someone new and different. Everyone will be wondering who you are."

"Theo and I will be considered the luckiest men there tonight, to be with two women as beautiful as you," Rafe put in diplomatically in his lazy drawl.

"I feel a little like Cinderella at the ball," Megan confessed.

Theo smiled at her, kicking up a clutch of nerves in her stomach. "Just so long as you don't disappear at midnight."

"I think I can guarantee that I will not." Megan could not keep from smiling back. How could this man be a murderer?

But he was, and she had to remember that. Theo Moreland was her enemy. She turned her head away, breaking their locked gazes, and kept it that way for the rest of the ride.

13

The McIntyres' carriage pulled into a long line of carriages that rolled down the driveway to the front door of the Cavendish Museum. People were streaming up the steps and into the house, the men in formal black and the women decked out in the finest satins and laces, gems glittering at their throats and ears.

Megan looked out the window at the sight of the richly dressed crowd, unable to suppress her excitement. She was not one who yearned for the glitter of wealth and sophistication, but she had to admit that it wouldn't be bad to participate in this sort of life every once in a while.

Inside the house, many of the exhibits had been removed or pushed back against the walls, opening up the large rooms to the crowd. The largest of the rooms had been emptied completely, and a small group of musicians were set up at one end to provide music.

They had scarcely entered the house when Megan felt the same uneasy feeling of being watched that she had experienced the other day as she walked home. A quick survey of the place provided the reason. Lady Helena Scarle was standing on the stairs — the better, Megan suspected, to be seen by all — staring down at Megan with hot, angry eyes. Her lovely face was transformed for an instant into a grotesque mask of fury before she managed to pull it back into a cool, politely smiling facade. She turned to the man beside her and gazed raptly into his eyes, letting out a sparkling laugh at some witticism.

If the lady was playing this little scene for Theo's benefit, Megan thought, she had miscalculated badly. Theo, his head turned to listen to a remark Rafe had made, was not even looking at Lady Helena.

Megan turned toward Kyria, who cast her a devilish grin. Obviously she, too, had witnessed Lady Scarle's reaction.

"Come, let me introduce you around," she told Megan, taking her hand and leading her toward a group of women.

Megan could see the interest and speculation in the other women's eyes as Kyria introduced her, saying only that she was a friend of hers from America.

"Another American?" one of the women said, lifting an eyebrow. "How unusual. You are the second American I have met tonight."

"Really?" Megan replied, not sure what she could say to that.

"Yes. What was that girl's name — you remember, the one with that banker fellow, Barchester."

"Oh, yes. Quiet little thing — can't say I remember," the woman on her left replied.

"Barchester?" Megan repeated, her stomach knotting. An American girl with Mr. Barchester?

She glanced around the room, hoping that she looked only mildly curious.

"Yes. Can't say as I see them right now."

"Some sort of Irish name, wasn't it?" her companion added.

Megan had little doubt now that the women were talking about Deirdre. Mr. Barchester must have brought her to the ball with him. The thought made her a little panicky. *What if Theo heard Deirdre's last name and remembered it as Dennis's last name?* At least, she thought, she and her sister were very different in coloring, so with luck Theo would not guess that they were related, even if he met Deirdre.

As she and Kyria strolled around the room, Megan glanced about unobtrusively, looking for her sister. Perhaps she should go to the stairs, as Lady Scarle had done, she thought, so that she could look over the crowd better.

They had covered most of the downstairs when Theo and Rafe rejoined them. Rafe swept his wife off for a dance, and Megan was left alone with Theo.

"I have been besieged by chaps wanting an introduction to you," he told her, his eyes warm on her face.

"They probably think I am an American heiress since I am with your family. Just tell them I am the tutoress, and they will melt away."

He grinned. "Perhaps I should try that — although I fear it would scare off only a portion of them. I told most of them that your dance card was full."

"So now I shall be a wallflower?" Megan asked with mock indignation. In fact, she had little desire to get out on the dance floor, unsure if her adolescent practicing with Deirdre in their room at home would hold up to British Society's standards.

"Credit British men with a little more

perseverance," he retorted. "They will wangle an introduction from my parents or sisters. I have no doubt that you will be bombarded with invitations to dance." He paused, then added, "Which is precisely why I intend to take that first waltz you promised me before any of the others show up here."

He extended his hand to her. Megan hesitated, then put her gloved hand in his. "All right. But I must warn you — American teachers are not well versed in such social arts as dancing."

"Then it is fortunate that British peers are," he responded, giving her fingers a little squeeze. "Just follow my lead and it won't be so dreadful."

He led her to the ballroom, where a lively dance was already in progress. "A quadrille," he told her. "One of Rafe's favorites. He says it reminds him of the Virginia Reel."

Megan spotted Rafe and Kyria dancing down the line of couples, flushed and smiling, and she felt a little pang clutch at her heart. Love and happiness were evident on the couple's faces, and Megan could not help but feel a longing for the same emotion. Her mind had always been on her career, not the dream of husband

and family shared by most of her school-
mates. She had never regretted the direction in which her life had gone, but
sometimes there were moments, like now,
when she wondered if she had given up too
much to become a reporter.

But then, she reminded herself, she had
never met a man who made her feel the
way Kyria seemed to feel. Unconsciously,
she glanced up at Theo, standing beside
her. An increasingly familiar warmth
stirred in her loins.

The dance ended, and a moment later
the musicians struck up the beginning
strains of a Strauss waltz. At least it was familiar, Megan thought. Deirdre had played
the tune many times on the family piano.
Still, her stomach quivered a little —
though she was not sure whether it was
from dread or anticipation — as she put
her hand in Theo's and let him lead her
onto the floor.

They faced each other, his hand on her
waist, the other hand curved gently around
hers. With a slight pressure, he swung her
into the flow of the dancers. The little jitter
of fear vanished. It was easy to dance in his
arms. Her feet remembered the steps well
enough, and his grip was firm, yet relaxed,
guiding her effortlessly through the move-

ments. She looked up into his face, letting the exhilarating music pour over her as they circled the room.

It was easy to dance with him, to let herself go and move with the music. To feel his arms about her, holding her, guiding her. To gaze into his eyes until she saw nothing, thought nothing, felt nothing but him. It was dizzying, exciting, terrifying, all at once.

It ended all too soon. They walked from the dance floor, Megan's heart pounding, her face flushed. There was a giddiness inside her that made her want to laugh and whirl about. She smothered a smile at the thought of the reaction of the staid guests if she were to break out spinning like a top.

Theo offered her a cup of punch, and she accepted, trying her best to tamp down her eagerness. Slipping her hand through his arm, she walked with him out into the hall and down to the refreshment room. He brought her a cup of punch, his fingers grazing hers and sending a sizzle straight down to her abdomen.

Megan drew a shaky little breath and sipped at her drink. It was beyond foolish, she knew, that she should react this way. They had done nothing but dance; he had handed her a drink. Both were such ordinary things, and yet they sent her insides skittering around crazily.

Theo looked down into her eyes, and Megan swallowed, her heart pounding. He reached up and drew a finger down her cheek, smiling at her in a way that closed out the rest of the world.

"Who are you?" he murmured.

Megan gave a little laugh, hoping it sounded more natural than it felt. "I don't know what you mean, sir. I — I am the twins' teacher."

"I think you are far more than that." He sighed, shaking his head. "When I am not with you, I have so many questions, and I tell myself that I will get the truth from you yet. And then the next time you're near, the questions just fly from my head, and all I can think about is the way you look, the scent that clings to your hair, the way your eyes change color in the sunlight. . . ."

He moved closer to her as he spoke, leaning down a little, creating an intimate space around them. Megan's fingers trembled, and she closed them in her skirts to control the shakiness. She thought for one mad, breathless instant that Theo was going to kiss her right here, in this public place.

A woman's brittle voice sailed across the room, shattering the moment. "Lord Raine! There you are! Whatever are you doing, shutting yourself away down here?"

Megan stepped back guiltily, and Theo cursed under his breath as he turned. Lady Scarle was moving toward them, a smile fixed on her face, though it did not quite reach her stormy eyes.

She wore a royal-blue satin dress that deepened the blue of her eyes, though it was ornamented with far too many ruffles, bows and bits of lace for Megan's taste. Her waist was cinched into nothingness, and her full bosom swelled above her dress, seeming ready to pop from its bounds at any moment. A diamond-and-sapphire necklace was wrapped around her throat, and matching earrings hung from her ears. Megan noticed that the same jewels winked out from her intricately up-swept hair.

Lady Helena was, Megan thought, everything she was not: rich, titled, seductively beautiful, entrancing to men. She knew exactly how to walk and talk, how to address the myriad array of British titles or order a servant. She had grown up in the same world as Theo. There was no dusting of cinnamon-colored freckles across her cheeks, and her hair was not a common brown with an irritating tendency to curl wildly out of control. Watching her approach, Megan was aware of an unusually fierce stab of dislike.

Lady Scarle swept up to Theo, not even glancing toward Megan, and laid a hand on his arm, saying in a low, intimate voice, "I saved a waltz for you."

Theo's mouth twitched in something close to a grimace, Megan saw, and he replied coolly, "Did you? How kind of you."

Now was the perfect time, Megan knew, for her to slip away and find her sister. Lady Scarle would keep Theo tangled up for some time. But Megan's feet stayed rooted to the spot. She was not about to let Lady Scarle think that she had chased Megan away.

"Lady Scarle," Theo went on now, "you remember Miss Henderson." He turned slightly toward Megan, smiling.

"Lady Scarle," Megan said in greeting, her tone polite, and nodded toward the other woman.

Lady Helena's gaze flickered over to Megan, barely touching her, and she gave her a short nod, then turned back to Theo. "Raine, the orchestra has been playing the most divine waltzes."

Her rude action stiffened Megan's back, and she jumped in, saying, "Yes, they have. Lord Raine and I were just dancing to one of them."

The look Lady Scarle turned on Megan this time was killing. "Indeed?" she said in a chilly voice. She looked back to Theo. "How gracious of you, Raine, to dance with your servants. Though usually one would expect you to confine such things to occasions like Boxing Day, say, or —"

"Oh, but Lord Raine is not my employer," Megan said sweetly. "Perhaps you did not understand. I am employed by the Duchess of Broughton."

"Miss Henderson is not a servant," Theo said flatly, his green eyes as hard as marbles. "She is an educator."

Lady Helena's mouth lifted on one side, as if she were faintly amused. "Yes, of course. Your family has always had . . . unusual ideas. One of their charms, of course."

"I am surprised you find it charming," Theo replied. "I would have thought quite the opposite."

She let out a lilting laugh. Megan wondered if it sounded as practiced to Theo as it did to her.

"You naughty man," Lady Helena said

playfully, reaching out to rap Theo's arm lightly. Her eyes glowed as she gazed up at him. "You are such a tease. You must know how much I enjoy your mother's company. And your sisters are quite delightful."

"Mmm, Mrs. McIntyre speaks of you often, as well," Megan put in, meeting Lady Scarle's sharp glance with wide-eyed innocence.

Beside her, Theo pressed his lips together tightly and turned to look out across the room. Lady Scarle narrowed her eyes at Megan sharply.

"Miss . . . Henderson, was it?"

"Yes."

"Perhaps you would be so good as to allow Lord Raine and me to conduct a private conversation," Lady Helena went on, her voice sharp as cut glass.

Megan's brows sailed upward in astonishment at the other woman's arrogance. She clenched her fists unconsciously, anger spurting up in her.

Something of what she felt must have shone in her face, for Theo reached over and wrapped a hand around Megan's arm, holding her in place. Looking at Lady Scarle, he said, "Excuse me, my lady. I was unaware that you and I had anything we needed to discuss in private."

Lady Helena's eyes widened at his dismissive words. Bright spots of color stained her cheeks, and she shot Megan a glance of venomous dislike. "Indeed, Lord Raine. Perhaps I was mistaken."

"Perhaps so. Now, if you will excuse us . . ."

Still gripping Megan's arm, he steered her away from Lady Scarle and out the door. "Temper, temper," he murmured as they walked.

"You needn't hold on to me," Megan told him sharply. "I am not going to hit her . . . however much I would like to."

"I wasn't sure. You looked as if your Irish was up."

"My what?" Megan whipped her head around to look at him. Her heart began to pound in her chest. *Why had he used that term? Did he know somehow that her name was false — that her real one was Irish?*

He returned her gaze blandly. "Isn't that the right term? Does it not mean one is angry?"

"I — yes, I guess it does. But I wasn't that angry — only irritated."

"Lady Scarle is an irritating woman," Theo agreed. "However, you seem to have inspired her to new heights."

"I wasn't properly servile," Megan said. "I think she believed I should curtsy and fade away to let her pursue you."

"Thank God you did not," Theo replied feelingly.

Megan had to laugh. "Needed protection, did you?"

He gave an elaborate shudder and looked at her with laughing eyes. "Desperately. Now that Lord Scarle is dead, she has her eye on a higher title."

Megan suspected that the title was not all Lady Scarle found appealing in Theo. Looking at him, she thought that almost any woman would be attracted to him, titled or not.

"She is a beautiful woman," Megan pointed out.

"She has a number of admirers," Theo agreed. "I, however, am not one of them." He looked down at her. "I prefer a woman of a different sort."

"Indeed?" Megan knew that the smile she turned up to him was flirtatious, and that it was wrong of her smile at him that way, but somehow she could not seem to stop herself.

"Yes." His face sobered as he stopped and turned to face her. "If we were not in this place, I would show you what sort of woman appeals to me."

Megan's breath came faster in her throat. "Then it is just as well that we are here, is it not?"

"I find it quite the opposite," he responded, his gaze drifting down her face to her mouth. "Megan . . ."

Heat flickered deep within her. Megan clasped her hands behind her as though to make certain that they did not move of their own volition to touch him.

"My lord, as you said, this is a public place." She turned her head away; it was too difficult to think when she was looking at him.

"Yes, dammit, I know," he ground out. His face knotted in frustration. "I need to talk to you. I need to know —"

"Theo, darling, there you are," a woman's voice sounded, and they turned to see the Duchess of Broughton walking toward them. "Hello, Miss Henderson. Are you enjoying the party?"

"Yes, ma'am, very much."

"Good, good." The duchess smiled, then turned to her son. "I have been looking everywhere for you. Lady Rochester is here and asking about you."

Theo let out a groan. "Mother, no . . ."

"She insists upon seeing you. Says you

haven't paid her a visit since you came to town this summer."

"Indeed I haven't," Theo retorted with heartfelt emotion. "All she ever talks to me about is settling down and doing my duty."

"Yes, dear, I know, it's terribly tiresome," the duchess sympathized, patting his arm. "But she was threatening to come stay with us for a few days just so she can see you."

"So I am to be the sacrificial lamb?" Theo asked, cocking an eyebrow.

"Yes, I am afraid so," the duchess agreed serenely. "Your father nearly swallowed his tongue when Lady Rochester suggested visiting us. He cannot abide his aunt, and one can scarcely blame him." She turned to Megan with a smile. "Now, my dear, I have been absolutely deluged with requests to be introduced to you. I fobbed most of them off, of course, but there are a few young men who aren't entirely silly, so I thought I would introduce you to them. Unless, of course, you would prefer not to dance — I am sure they will all ask you."

"Thank you. That is very kind of you." Megan ignored the ill-natured grunt Theo let out behind her and smiled at the duchess, letting her lead her back toward the ballroom.

The duchess introduced her here and

there, and before many minutes had passed, Megan found her dance card filling up. She danced with several young men, all the while keeping her eye out for Mr. Barchester and for Mr. Coffey.

She managed to catch sight of Julian Coffey two or three times, but he was always talking to someone, and she had little time to spare before another man came to lead her out onto the dance floor. It was going to be harder to get a chance to talk with the director of the museum than she had thought. She decided to tell anyone else who asked her that her dance card had been filled, so that she would have some time alone to interview Coffey.

As luck would have it, she was just walking off the floor after a lively waltz with a young man who danced expertly but had trouble saying anything but boring pleasantries when she came face-to-face with Mr. Barchester and her sister. Megan drew in her breath sharply, and her companion glanced at her with vague curiosity.

"Miss Henderson," Deirdre exclaimed. "How very nice to see you again. You know Mr. Barchester, I believe."

"Yes, of course."

The two men seemed to be acquaintances and they shook hands politely. Megan wrapped her hand around her sister's arm, saying, "Will you walk with me? It has been an age since I have talked to you."

Megan bade her dancing partner a polite goodbye, and whisked her sister through the crowd and into the hallway.

"What are you doing here?" she whispered. "Why didn't you tell me you were coming?"

"I didn't know," Deirdre replied. "Mr. Barchester did not ask me until after you came to visit us. Isn't it grand?" Her blue eyes sparkled. "Do you think my dress looks good enough? I didn't have anything fancy, but I so wanted to come. So I threw some lace and bows on my best dress and ripped out the lace fichu. Da was scandalized." She let out a little giggle.

"You look lovely," Megan replied, which was the truth, despite the fact that Deirdre's gown was not as elegant as most of the others in the room. Deirdre's fragile beauty was what drew the eye. "It's just — I don't know — it seems dangerous. Is he introducing you as Deirdre Mulcahey? What if Theo hears your name and remembers?"

"He won't. Why would he? Andrew —

Mr. Barchester, I mean — will not introduce me to him. He said that he and Lord Raine rarely speak to each other. Well, he would not want to, would he? Where is he? Lord Raine, I mean. Mr. Barchester hasn't been able to point him out to me yet."

"I'm not sure." Megan cast a glance up and down the hallway. "But I cannot let him see me chatting so chummily with you — I'm not supposed to know anybody here."

"That's all right." Her sister gave Megan's hand a squeeze. "I just wanted to see you — and I couldn't resist the idea of going to a grand ball like this. I have never seen anything like it."

"Deirdre . . . has Mr. Barchester . . . I mean, he seems to be paying particular attention to you. Is he — are you . . . ?"

Deirdre smiled, her eyes twinkling. "He is a nice man. Very polite and quite handsome. I — I think he is probably just being kind, coming to call so often. But I cannot help but think sometimes that he does have a certain partiality for me. Do you think it's possible?"

"Of course it's possible. Haven't you looked in a mirror recently?"

"I know. But there is a definite difference in our fortunes, our stations — not to mention the fact that he is English."

"There." Megan spotted Theo seated on a couch beside an old woman with an elaborate coiffeur that sat in a strangely crooked manner on her head. She pulled Deirdre into the nearest doorway, whispering, "That is Theo Moreland out there, sitting with the woman in the red wig."

Deirdre's mouth opened in an *O,* and she stuck her head out the door, then ducked back inside. She stared at Megan.

"That is Theo Moreland? But he — he's so handsome," Deirdre whispered.

"I know. It surprised me, as well."

"I thought — I don't know, I thought he would look evil and twisted, like Iago in the *Othello* we went to see."

"Well, he doesn't . . . and neither does he act it." Megan sighed.

Deirdre studied her sister's face. "You wish he were not who he is, don't you?"

"I wish he were anyone else!" Megan admitted, the words rushing out of her. She looked at Deirdre, her eyes filled with unhappiness. "If you could only talk to him, be around him — he is nothing like I thought he would be."

"I'm sorry." Deirdre laid her hand on her sister's arm, gazing into her face with sympathy. "Perhaps there is some other way."

"What?" Megan asked resignedly and shrugged her shoulders.

She cast a quick glance at the other occupants of the large room, who were standing chatting in the far corner beneath an array of Inca masks, then moved closer to her sister.

"What else can we do?" Megan whispered. "You are the one who has nightmares of Dennis. Can you countenance not doing anything to avenge his death?"

Deirdre frowned. "No. I — we are duty bound."

Megan nodded. "I have to go ahead. The fact that he is . . . pleasant cannot matter in this." Unconsciously, she squared her shoulders. "The sooner it's done, the better. I need to speak to Julian Coffey."

"Andrew introduced Mr. Coffey to me," Deirdre told her. "He seemed a very nice man. I am sure he will help you in any way he can."

"Look out and see if Theo is still there," Megan told her, nodding toward the door.

Deirdre stepped into the doorway and looked down the hall, then turned back to Megan. "He is walking toward the stairs with that odd-looking old woman." She turned back, keeping up a running commentary in a hushed tone. "They are going up the stairs. Almost gone . . . they are out of sight."

She and Megan stepped out into the hall.

"I am going back to the ballroom to look for Mr. Coffey," Megan told her. "I — it is probably best if we don't spend any more time together."

Deirdre nodded. "I will remain here for a little while."

Megan nodded and moved off down the hall. It felt strange to leave her sister without a hug or even squeezing her hand. She glanced back at Deirdre, who smiled and turned away. Megan went on. Her sister would be fine, she told herself. She would find Mr. Barchester, and he would take care of her.

Of course, that was another worry. Was Deirdre falling in love with the Englishman? Mr. Barchester seemed an honorable, upstanding man, but still, Megan could not help but worry about Deirdre. She was such an innocent, and this was the first time that Megan had not been around to protect her. *What if Deirdre fell in love with him? What would she do when it came time to go back to New York?*

Megan walked around the edge of the crowded ballroom, searching for Coffey and hoping that she would not run into any of the Morelands. Just as she reached the middle of the room, she cast a glance over her shoulder and caught sight of the museum curator walking through the doorway into the hall.

Hurriedly she changed course and retraced her steps, weaving through the crowd, excusing herself. She reached the hallway and glanced first one way, then the other. A man was turning the corner into the back hallway. She caught only a glimpse of him, but she thought it was Coffey.

She followed him as rapidly as she could without causing comment and turned as he had done. A short hallway stretched in front of her, leading to a set of stairs. It must be the old servants' staircase, she thought, and it provided an easier way to get to the next storey than the crowded staircase in the front.

Lifting her skirts to keep them from dragging, she went lightly down the hall to the stairs. Just as she started to go up the steps, she heard the distinct clatter of feet on the stairs below her. She looked down, surprised. Had Coffey gone down into the cellars?

It seemed odd, but she turned and

started quietly down. She reached the bottom and paused, looking cautiously about her.

She was in another hallway, this one much less well lit than the one upstairs had been. Candles burned in infrequent sconces up and down the hall, casting a flickering light and leaving much of the hallway in shadow. Megan was tempted to turn around and go back upstairs, but then she saw a man emerge from a room down the hall and turn the other way. It was Mr. Barchester.

Her curiosity piqued, she started after him. What in the world was he doing down in the basement? she wondered. He should be upstairs, looking after Deirdre. *Had it been he she had glimpsed turning the corner, instead of Coffey?*

Far in front of her, Barchester turned left into another room and closed the door after him. Megan slipped down the hall and paused a little way from the door, wondering what to do. Her curiosity was fully aroused now. What was one of the guests at the party doing wandering about in the basement?

As she stood there, she heard a noise. She stiffened, listening. It sounded . . . it sounded almost like someone crying softly.

Megan frowned, turning slowly. Was it coming from behind her? From one of the closed rooms she had passed?

She started down the hall, moving as quietly as she could, listening for the faint sound. With all her attention on the soft crying, the sudden scrape of a heel behind her made her jump, and she started to whirl around. But before she could do more than glimpse a flash of black at the corner of her vision, something thudded hard into the back of her head. Pain exploded inside her, and she crumpled to the floor.

14

"Megan?"

The voice came from far away, and Megan turned her head, wanting to bury her face in her pillow. But the voice would not let her sleep.

"Megan? Can you hear me?"

A hand stroked over her cheek, then picked up her arm and began to chafe her wrist. Megan realized that her head was throbbing violently. She let out a groan.

"I think she's coming 'round," said another voice, feminine, this time. A breeze touched her face, cooling her.

The masculine voice once again said her name, adding, "Wake up."

"What happened to her?"

"Why is she here?"

Those were two more women's voices.

And now a man said, "You know, if any of the women of my family were proper ladies, you would have smelling salts about you."

Megan wondered how many people were here. *And what were they doing around her bed?*

Reluctantly, she opened her eyes. Theo was beside her on one knee, holding her hand in one of his, his other hand around her wrist, and he was looking down at her, frowning.

"Thank God!" he exclaimed, adding unnecessarily, "She's awake."

Megan blinked and looked cautiously around. She was not lying in her bed at all, but on the hard floor in some hallway. The duchess and Kyria were standing behind Theo, and most of the other Morelands were grouped around her, as well, all staring down at her with worried frowns. Anna was bent over her beside Theo, wielding her fan so that the air cooled Megan's face. The odd woman in the red wig to whom Theo had been talking earlier was standing at her feet, leaning on a cane and peering down suspiciously at Megan.

"What the devil is she doing up here?" the old lady said querulously. "Queer start, I must say."

"I don't know, Aunt Hermione," Theo replied shortly. "I think perhaps she fainted."

"But what is she doing up here?" the old

woman persisted. "There is no one else about."

"I — I'm sorry," Megan said, not sure exactly why she felt the need to apologize. Something about the old woman seemed to call for it.

"Lady Rochester," Rafe said in his molasses-tinged voice, sliding a hand around the old woman's arm. "It must have been very tiring for you to have climbed these stairs."

"Yes, you really should not have," the duchess put in flatly.

"Let me escort you back downstairs and get you a seat. And maybe a nice glass of punch?" Rafe went on smoothly.

"Hmph. Don't think you can work your way around me, young man," the old lady groused, but she let him turn her gently around. "I would take a cup of punch. Can't imagine what the world's coming to, young women running about fainting all over the place."

Her voice went on, listing complaints, punctuated by the thud of her cane on the floor, as she and Rafe went down the hall.

"Sorry you had to meet Lady Rochester this way," Theo said, smiling down at Megan. "Can you sit up?"

"Yes, of course."

She started to protest as his hand slid under her back to help her, but as she sat up, her head swam. She closed her eyes, sucking in her breath, and it took all her concentration to keep her suddenly pitching stomach from tossing up all its contents.

Theo stopped, his arm around her back, bracing her. "Are you all right?"

Her stomach settled enough for her to breathe, "I — I feel a little ill."

"Of course you do," Anna said soothingly, squatting down beside her and wafting the fan.

The breeze it created was cooling, reviving, and after a moment, Megan felt well enough to open her eyes again. "What happened?"

"We were rather hoping you could tell us that," the duchess told her.

"I found you here," Theo said. "No one had seen you in quite a while, so I started looking for you. You were nowhere downstairs, so we began a search of the rest of the house. I found you here."

Megan looked around her, careful not to move her head too suddenly. "Where is here?"

"A back hallway on the second floor," Theo replied, his green eyes studying her.

"Do you not remember how you got here?"

"No. I have no idea." Megan raised a hand to her head. "My head aches."

"I think you must have fainted," Anna told her, "and hit your head when you fell. You may have been unconscious for quite some time. I don't know how long it was before Theo found you."

"The last thing I remember was talking to, uh, a woman. I don't recall coming upstairs at all." Megan's brow furrowed.

"Don't worry about it," Anna said. "It is often so with head injuries. People forget what happened right before. It will come back to you later, perhaps."

"Perhaps," Megan agreed somewhat doubtfully. She felt as if her head was stuffed with wool batting.

"I'll take you home," Theo said, and slid his other hand beneath her knees, as if to pick her up.

"No! I can stand," Megan exclaimed and started to rise.

"Stubborn," Theo said beneath his breath, and helped her up, his arm around her back.

Megan swayed a little, and he steadied her.

"I'll carry you," he told her firmly.

"No. I won't make such a spectacle of myself in front of everyone," Megan protested, blushing. "Just give me a minute."

She could not keep from leaning against Theo as she stood there, gathering her strength. The Morelands all gathered around her, gazing at her with such concern on their faces that she felt tears prick at her eyes. She hated deceiving these kind people.

"We shall go home with you," the duchess said.

"Oh, no! Please, stay. I don't want to ruin your evening," Megan protested.

"It's all right. I will take her home," Theo told his parents. "I'll send the carriage back for you."

The duchess agreed somewhat reluctantly, and they started down the stairs. Megan was determined to walk on her own, but every step sent pain jarring through her head, and she was grateful for the support of Theo's arm.

When they finally reached the front door and were able to step outside, away from the crowd of partygoers, Theo swept Megan up into his arms and carried her to the Morelands' waiting carriage, despite her feeble protestations that she could walk.

"You pride has been maintained," he told her. "Now hush and just let me take care of you."

Her head ached too much to protest, Megan decided, and she leaned her head against his chest gratefully.

The coachman jumped to open the door of the carriage, and Theo bundled her inside. Megan leaned back against the leather squab of the carriage seat, wincing a little as her head touched the material. Theo swung into the seat opposite her, and the carriage set off at a sedate pace. Her forehead ached, a continual pounding that was in counterpoint to the sore spot on the back of her head. She closed her eyes and tried to pull together her scattered wits.

What had happened to her? She had been looking for Julian Coffey, hoping to talk to him; she remembered that much, though she had not, of course, revealed that to Theo and the other Morelands. She remembered winding through the ballroom, searching for Coffey, then spotting him and starting after him. Everything after that was a blank.

One thing she was sure of: she had not fainted. That was something she had never done in her entire life, even during the most tension-filled or gruesome moments she had gone through covering her newspaper stories. She had been cinched up more tightly at the waist tonight than she was accustomed to, but she did not remember feeling faint.

If she had not fainted, it followed that someone had intentionally knocked her out. That would account for the sore spot on the back of her head. She reached up and gingerly wound her fingers into her hair until she touched her scalp. There was a lump forming there, and she could feel dampness, too, as well as the rougher texture of dried blood.

But who had hit her? And why?

She opened her eyes and looked across the carriage at Theo. He was watching her silently, his eyes shadowed in the dim light. He was the obvious suspect.

There was some stubborn part of her that did not want to admit it, but that was what made the most sense. He was the person who had found her. It was easy, after all, to find a person if you were the one who had felled her.

Theo knew she had been poking her nose into things. Perhaps he had seen her following Julian Coffey. He might have known that Coffey could give her the information she needed. So, to stop her from questioning Coffey, he had sneaked up behind her and cracked her over the head.

She remembered opening her eyes and finding Theo bending over her. There had been fear in his eyes, something she had attributed to concern for her. But wasn't it more likely that it was fear that she had seen him when he attacked her and would identify him? Or simply the fear of discovery that had led him to hit her to begin with?

There had been something else in his gaze, she remembered as she thought about it. Despite the expression of concern on his face, there had been a watchfulness in his eyes, a certain shrewd consideration.

It occurred to her that it was perhaps very foolish of her to be riding alone in a carriage with the man. Her stomach tightened. She reminded herself that everyone in Theo's family knew that she had gone back to Broughton House with him. He could not risk harming her, not with everyone aware that she had been alone with him.

She laced her fingers together tightly and leaned into the corner of the carriage, closing her eyes once again, in a pose of resting. Inside, every part of her was on alert, poised for defense.

The time passed slowly, but eventually the carriage rolled to a smooth stop in front of the Moreland mansion. Theo climbed out and turned to help Megan down. She put her fingers in his to step down, and his hand closed possessively around hers.

"Your hand is cold," he said, and peered down into her face.

"I'm fine." She knew it was fear that had sent the blood rushing from her extremities, not shock, but she did not want to say so.

"Let's get you inside, so I can look at your head."

"I only want to go to bed," she said, hating the weakness in her voice.

He shook his head. "Not when you have been out cold like that. You need to stay awake."

He whisked her through the front door and down the hall to a cozy, masculine room paneled in oak and furnished with dark maroon leather chairs. It smelled pleasantly of tobacco, and against one wall was a cherrywood sideboard on which sat glasses and decanters of liquor.

Theo rang for a servant and sent him for the supplies he wanted. Then he turned and went to the sideboard, where he poured golden brown liquid into two short glasses. He took a hearty drink from one glass and handed the other one to Megan.

She looked doubtfully at it.

"Don't be missish. Drink it down," he ordered her. "It will warm you up."

Cautiously, Megan took a sip. She shuddered at the strong taste, but it did warm her throat as it slid down. She took another, larger, sip.

The footman returned with a tray containing a bowl of water, a bowl of ice and a tin of medical supplies. Theo turned up the gas sconces to their brightest and lit a kerosene lamp, which he placed on the small table beside her.

Dismissing the footman, he dipped a rag in water and squeezed it out, then gently parted her hair and dabbed the rag against her wound. Megan sucked in her breath sharply at the pain.

"Sorry." He continued to clean the wound, touching it as lightly as he could. "Someone cracked you a good one."

"What?" Megan's eyes widened, surprised at his blunt statement. "What do you mean?"

"Come, come," he retorted. "Surely you don't expect me to believe that you fainted."

Finished cleaning the area, he dabbed a bit of ointment on her wound and pressed a small pad to it.

"That is what everyone said."

"It seemed the most likely explanation. And they didn't look at the location and severity of that bump on your head. I did. It split the skin and was a little high and to the side — not a likely place for your head to hit the floor when you fell. Looks more like someone knocked you out."

"Oh." Megan didn't know what to say.

Theo wrapped up a few small chunks of ice in a towel and handed it to her. "Here. Hold this against it. It will help the swelling."

He sat down in a chair across from her. "Who was it, Megan? Who hit you?"

"I don't know!" she blurted out honestly. "I don't remember. The last thing I remember is leaving the ballroom."

Even as she said the words, a wisp of a memory came into her mind — a shadowy corridor lined with walls of stone, lights flickering in wall sconces. She had been in the basement, far from the place where she was found.

"You're lying," Theo said dispassionately.

"No. I mean — yes, I just remembered

that I was in the basement. But it is the very vaguest memory. I don't know why I was down there or how I came to be upstairs when you found me."

She wasn't about to tell him that she had been following Julian Coffey or that she now remembered seeing Andrew Barchester in front of her in the basement. She had followed him, she thought, but beyond that, her mind was still a blank.

"I think this has gone on long enough. What is going on, Megan? Who are you and why are you masquerading in our home as a tutor?"

Megan opened her eyes wide, saying, "What are you talking about?"

"Come now, Miss — I don't know what your real name is, but I would hazard a guess it isn't Henderson. So I shall just call you Megan. I think we have moved beyond protestations of innocence, haven't we? It is clear you are up to something — stealing the key to the collection room out of my father's desk, sneaking into my room when you are supposed to be too ill to come down to supper. . . . I cannot flatter myself that your purpose was to seduce me, since you assumed I would be in the dining room with everyone else."

Megan set her jaw. She had no explanation she was willing to offer for either of the incidents, so she decided it would be best to say nothing.

"You and I both know that you are no teacher. The twins are aware of it, as well, even though they both pleaded with me not to reveal that fact to our mother. But you know less Greek than they do, and your Latin is a trifle rusty. As for science and mathematics . . ." He shrugged eloquently.

Again Megan said nothing. As a reporter, she had long ago learned that people were usually better off to remain silent. It was their inability to keep from justifying their actions or making up lies to cover what had really happened that led them into saying much more than they ever wanted to.

When she did not answer, Theo grimaced and swung out of his chair, pacing about the room. He turned back to her and shot out, "Who is the Irishman you went to see on your day off?"

Megan's eyes widened in astonishment. "What? How did you —" Then, as it settled in on her how he must have found out that she had gone to see her father and Deirdre, anger spurted up in her. "You followed me? How dare you?"

She jumped to her feet, fists clenched, letting the bundle of ice fall unheeded from her wound. "You have no right to follow me. I am an employee here, not a slave! What I do on my day off is my business, not yours."

Megan remembered the eerie feeling that she was being watched. She had seen no one when she turned around, but, then, she had not really known what she was looking for. Still, surely she would have noticed if Theo was lurking somewhere behind her. "No, of course, it wasn't you. You wouldn't dirty your hands with work like that. Doubtless you hired someone."

There was no guilt on his face, only a faint amusement, and that spiked Megan's anger even higher.

"You find this funny?" she snapped. "You dare to laugh at me?"

"My dear Megan, what I find humorous is your self-righteous indignation at my having someone follow you. It sits a little oddly on a thief. Did you seriously think that I would sit back and do nothing to protect my family? That I was so besotted by you that I would let you hurt —"

"Your family!" Megan exclaimed. "I would never endanger your family! Are you mad?"

"No, I don't believe that you would yourself physically harm the twins or my mother and father. No doubt you mean only to take things from them, things that you feel they can live without — indeed, will scarcely notice are gone. In that respect, you are right — material things being stolen will not cut deeply with them, although my father is exceedingly attached to his collection. However, surely you could not believe that your betrayal of their trust would not hurt. Constantine and Alexander admire you. So does my mother, who thinks you are forging forward in the fight for women's rights. Kyria and Olivia have —"

"I know! I know how much they have done for me. I don't want to hurt them."

Theo was pleased to see the real regret and sorrow that lay in Megan's eyes. He had worried that he was somehow mistaken in her, that she was only playing a part, the feelings he had seen in her merely acting, not reality.

However, he could not hold back now, could not let her slide away. He had to make her tell him the truth.

"Just because you intend them no physical harm does not mean that your cohorts feel the same. I don't know who they are or what they intend, but obviously someone who is involved with you has no compunction about hurting people."

"What?" Megan looked at him, confused. "What are you talking about?"

He gestured toward her head. "Someone obviously tried to harm you tonight. And someone else was following you the other day, someone besides my man."

Megan stared at him, suddenly speechless. She could barely take in the meaning of his words. "What? There was another man following me?"

"Yes. Tom Quick — he is the man I hired to follow you — told me that he saw another man trailing you, as well. Who was it, Megan? One of your associates who doesn't trust you? A rival? Or perhaps someone whom you have deceived in the past and who is seeking revenge?"

"What? You're mad. He was mistaken."

"I think not. Tom is clever, and very loyal to this family. He would not lie to me, and I doubt he made any mistake. Someone wants to harm you, Megan. That's clear enough from what happened tonight. What is to stop him from trying again — or doing worse? If you have no care for yourself, you might think of the boys. What if the twins are with you the next time he decides to attack you? I cannot be with you every moment. No matter how close I've stayed to you for the last week, I could not prevent that attack on you tonight."

"No! It's not true. You are just trying to scare me away from here!" Megan responded. She wasn't about to add that he was doing a very good job of it. "No one is trying to harm me. The only enemy I have is you!"

"Are you suggesting that it was I who knocked you on the head tonight?" Theo's eyes flashed with a hard, bright fury, and his jaw set, color flaring on his razor-sharp cheekbones. "Do you honestly believe that I sneaked up behind you and cracked you on the head? Why would I do that?"

"To stop me — you've just been talking about stopping me. How you won't let me hurt your family."

"I must say, if you thought I was the one who hit you on the head tonight, you were remarkably foolish to ride home alone with me," Theo retorted heatedly.

Megan opened her mouth, then closed it, aware that she had no response for that. She had thought about the very thing he mentioned, but she had dismissed it, rationalizing her actions by saying that he would do nothing with all his family knowing he had been alone with her. It occurred to her now that deep inside she had not really had any fear of Theo.

He cocked an eyebrow at her. "You see? You were not frightened of me. You know I didn't hurt you. Let us say I were the sort of person who would hit a woman over the head in order to get her out of my house. It would still be a most roundabout way to do it. However much the duchess likes you, don't you think she would let you go if I wanted her to? All I would have to do is reveal the fraud you have been committing against our family, and you would be out the door immediately."

"Then why haven't you?" Megan retorted, with a little stab of hurt at his words. "Clearly you despise me. You want me gone."

"Want you gone?" Theo let out a short laugh, raking one hand back through his hair. "Are you that blind?"

He crossed over to her in two long strides, his hands coming out to grasp her shoulders. Megan set her jaw mutinously and looked up at him, determined not to let him see how he affected her.

It made her blood pound in her veins to be this close to him. She could feel the heat of his body, and memories of the other times he had been this close flooded her mind. She could not keep out the images of him wrapping his arms around her and crushing her against him. She remembered the feel of his long, muscled body, his heart thudding so fiercely in his chest that she could feel it through her own flesh. She remembered the taste of him on her mouth, the soft insistence of his lips, the passion pulsing and burgeoning inside her until she thought she would explode.

She saw the desire darken his eyes now, and he lowered his head, resting his forehead against hers, his shoulders moving as though to draw himself around her, enclose her. Megan trembled, her breath coming hard and fast. She wanted to lean into him, to melt against him and feel his arms tighten around her. She closed her eyes, trying to will away her treacherous feelings.

"I don't want you out of this house," he said quietly. "Why do you think I have protected your secret — at a risk to my own family? All I can think about, all I want, is to have you here . . . to have you in my bed. Good God, Megan, you fill my head . . . my senses . . . everything inside me."

His words, uttered in that husky, passion-thickened voice, resonated all through her. Her body yearned for him, her breasts full and aching, her loins melting. Desire for him was a need within her, a desperate hunger.

"Megan . . ." he murmured, his lips brushing her forehead, her cheek, trailing down across the soft skin, as he whispered her name over and over, in plea or incantation.

Her skin tingled wherever his lips touched it, anticipation building, throbbing within her. She knew the feel of his lips on hers, and she wanted it again, with a deep ache, until it seemed as if the world hung motionless, waiting . . . yearning . . .

And then his mouth was on hers, and their lips were melding together. Megan made a low, moaning noise deep in her throat as she moved the last few remaining inches closer. His arms wrapped around her tightly, and he lifted her up into him, their mouths locked. She wound her arms around his neck, clinging to him, uncaring that her feet dangled inches off the floor or that she was crushed so hard against him she could scarcely breathe.

She was dizzy with the taste, the scent, the feel of him, her senses exploding in a paroxysm of delight. Her fingers dug into the cloth of his coat, wanting to feel his flesh, his heat. Heat throbbed between her legs, and she was aware of a wild urge to wrap them around him, to press herself against him and ease the ache within her.

He tore his mouth from hers, kissing his way down the side of her neck, nibbling at the cord and sending heat spearing down through her to explode in her abdomen. Letting her slide back down his body to the ground, he allowed his hands to roam over her, cupping her buttocks and pressing her into the hard evidence of his desire.

"Megan . . ." he panted. "Let me help you. Tell me. Trust me. Please."

His words pierced the haze of her desire. Megan stiffened, appalled at what she was doing, what she was allowing him to do.

With a low cry, she wrenched herself away from him. "Trust you? Is that what you are doing? Is that what this is about?"

He blinked, stunned by the sudden change in her. "What?"

"You think that you can get around me like this?" Megan shook with her anger, all the more incensed because she was aware of how easily he could sway her, make her forget everything except the feel of his lips on hers. "That you can make me throw everything away? Give it all up for the sake of your kisses?"

He let out a low groan. "Dammit, Megan, what are you talking about? I am not trying to get around you. I want you. I can help you. Whatever you are involved in, I can —"

"No! No!" She turned away, raising shaking hands to her head. "It's not that easy. *I'm* not that easy." She turned to face him, her hands clenched at her sides, her whole body quivering under the force of her emotions. "You cannot turn me away from this. I know what you are. What you have done!"

Theo stared at her, bewildered. "What I have done? What are you talking about? I've done nothing except offer you my protection —"

"I don't want your protection!" Megan shot back, indignation stiffening her resolve. She knew very well what it meant when a gentleman offered to take a woman of common background, a woman he could not marry, under his "protection." "What gall you have! You think that you can make me your mistress and I will keep quiet?"

Theo's eyes widened, and he started toward her. "Megan! No! I did not —"

Megan backed up a step, holding out her hand as if to stop him, the words rushing out of her in a torrent of guilt and anger. "It makes me ill to think that I let you touch me! I hate you!"

He came to a quick halt, and his face paled, the hand he had been reaching toward her dropping to his side. "You made a damn good pretense of feeling otherwise, then," he said in a tight voice.

Pain pierced Megan at the look on his face, and she wanted suddenly to cry.

"I could not feel anything else," she said, her voice cracking on the words, "for the man who murdered my brother."

15

There was a moment of profound silence. Theo gazed at her as blankly as if she had spoken in a foreign language. He started to speak, then stopped, and finally said, "What?"

There was no calling it back now, Megan knew. She straightened and said, "You were right. Henderson is not my real name. My name is Mulcahey, Megan Mulcahey."

"All right," he said slowly. "But who —"

"Do you not even remember his name?" Megan snapped. "My brother was Dennis Mulcahey."

"Dennis!" He stared at her. "You are Dennis's sister?" Suddenly, incredibly, a faint smile touched his lips. "Yes, I can see it now. Your eyes . . . So that was why you came —" He stopped abruptly, and his face changed from astonishment to outrage. "Wait! What the devil are you talking about, murdered your brother? You think I *murdered* Dennis?"

"I know it."

"That's impossible," he declared. "Since it didn't happen. Where in the name of all that's holy did you get that idea?"

"From a reliable source."

"Not very," he shot back. "I was there. I know what happened, unlike this 'source' of yours." He turned away, pushing his hands back into his hair, and paced away from her, then swung back. "I wrote your father. I told him what happened. Did he not receive it?"

"Oh, yes, he got your note informing him that his son had died in an 'accident.' "

Theo looked abashed. "I'm sorry. I should have written something longer. I was ill, tired, but I felt I needed to let Mr. Mulcahey know about Dennis as soon as I could. So I sent that short letter with the bare facts. I should have written a more detailed letter after I recovered." He sighed. "It was wrong of me. My family will tell you how poor I am at letters. I tried — many times — to write again. To explain what had happened and what sorrow I felt at losing Dennis. But nothing ever seemed adequate. I was — I confess I could not bear to think about Dennis's death."

"That is not surprising," Megan retorted tartly.

He frowned. "But did not Andrew write you? I saw him not long after we returned, and he told me that he had written to your father, as well. I was a coward, I admit, and felt relief that he had explained it in more detail. That is one reason why I did not send any of the letters I wrote."

"Yes, he explained it. He has explained it to me in person, as well."

Theo looked at her, understanding dawning in his eyes. "Are you saying that *Barchester* told you I killed Dennis?"

"That is exactly what I'm saying."

Theo gaped at her. In any other situation, she would have found his expression comical.

"He told you I murdered Dennis!" Shock gave way to anger. "That bloody son of a bitch! Why would he have told you such a thing? Dammit all, he wasn't even there!"

"What? You're saying Andrew Barchester wasn't even on the trip with you and Dennis?" Megan asked skeptically.

"No. I mean, yes, he was on the expedition with us, but he was not there when

Dennis died. He would have had to make this up out of whole cloth."

Hope stirred in Megan's chest. *Had Barchester lied to them all along? Could Theo be telling the truth?* Firmly she tamped down her emotion. She was not going to let Theo deceive her just because she wanted to believe that he was innocent. It was vital that she remain objective.

Crossing her arms across her chest, she said, "Then why don't *you* tell me what happened."

He regarded her for a moment, then said, "All right. As I suppose you know, I was in Brazil on an expedition for Lord Cavendish — the chap who started the museum. Julian Coffey and Mr. Barchester were with me. The man who was to lead our expedition could not. Then we met up with your brother and his companion, a Captain Eberhart, who was an experienced guide. So we joined together and started up the Amazon."

"Mr. Barchester told me how Captain Eberhart died and the rest of you forged ahead."

"Yes. We had gone so far that we did not want to abandon the expedition. Coffey was thrilled with the variety of flora and fauna he was able to sketch. We were all young and enthusiastic." A faint smile touched his lips as he remembered. "We were enjoying the adventure. Dennis — well, he was ready for anything. He and I grew quite close."

"It seems unlikely. A lower-class American, a British aristocrat."

Theo looked at her. "No more unlikely than you and I."

Color stained Megan's cheeks, and she looked away. "We are not talking of — of physical attraction."

"No. We are talking of friendship," he replied soberly. "And Dennis and I became friends. I do not choose my friends on the basis of their birth or their bank accounts. Neither did Dennis. He was a great fellow, always full of stories and laughter and good cheer."

Tears filled Megan's eyes at the accurate description of her brother. "Yes. He was."

"I am sorry, Megan." Theo came closer to her, reaching out as though to touch her arm, then halted halfway there and let his hand fall. "I know how much you must have loved him. I remember him talking about you. He said I would like you." He paused, then added softly, "Obviously he was right."

Megan swallowed against the emotions

that rose in her throat. She straightened her shoulders and faced Theo squarely. "What happened then?"

"After Eberhart's death, the native bearers and guides grew more and more reluctant to travel farther inland. They were full of fears and superstitions. They talked of the ancient gods wreaking vengeance on all who dared disturb their sacred places. They whispered of treasures and curses. We had all heard stories about the gold that Pizarro demanded from the Incas —" He paused, asking, "You know, do you not, about the Spaniards conquering the Inca empire? How Pizarro and his men captured the Inca emperor and held him ransom for a vast amount of gold?"

Megan nodded. "Yes."

"There were legends, as there always are in such cases, that some of the Incas who were bringing the gold decided not to turn it over to the Spanish but to hide it somewhere in the mountains. Hidden treasure, protected by the curse of the old gods. Pretty irresistible stuff, especially to several young men. Naturally, we hoped we would stumble upon it. The native bearers feared exactly the same thing. Some of them left, sneaking away in the night — with some of our supplies. Of course, with the number of natives dwindling, as well as our supplies, we had to be very careful not to get lost. There was a vast amount of territory — uncharted territory. That is why we set up a system of searching."

He stopped and sat down on a chair, sighing. He rested his elbows on his knees and his head on his hands, thrusting his fingers back into his thick hair. "God. You don't know how many times I have wished that we had simply turned back at that point." He rubbed his hands over his face, then dropped them to his lap and looked at her.

"But we did not. We set up a base camp, where we stored the majority of our supplies, our tents and pack animals. One of the four of us stayed at the camp with the natives at all times. We took it in turns. The other three of us would venture out in short exploratory trips, taking only a couple of donkeys to carry our supplies. Our last trip out, Barchester stayed at the base camp, while Dennis, Julian and I set out to explore. I fell ill about a day or two into the journey. I think that I must have caught the fever that felled Eberhart. As we hiked on, I grew more and more feverish and weak. Then it began to rain. We took refuge in a cave that we found partway up a hill."

Theo stood up and began to pace restlessly. "That is where Dennis died. Barchester was not even there."

"How did he die?" Megan asked quietly, watching Theo.

"He fell. The caves went deep into the base of the hill. He was exploring, and he fell."

Megan's heart sank, and tears clogged her throat. "You are lying to me."

She stood up and walked around to stand in front of Theo. He looked at her, and she could see the misery and pain in his eyes.

"I can see it in your face," she said, unaware that her eyes filled with tears as she spoke. "In the way you stand. The way you turn your head. You are a dreadful liar, Theo."

"Megan, I swear to you that I did not kill Dennis," he told her, gazing straight into her eyes.

Megan felt, with the same certainty in her midsection that had told her the moment before that he had lied, that now he was speaking the truth. "Then look me in the eyes, right now, and tell me how my brother died."

Theo stared at her for a moment, then

broke away with an oath. "Bloody hell, woman. I swore never to reveal this to anyone."

He stopped and stood, gazing into the distance at something only he could see. Finally, with a sigh, he turned. "All right. Nothing will satisfy you now but the complete truth. I suppose it no longer really matters, anyway."

He came back to her and, taking her hands in his, led her to the small couch, pulling her down to sit with him. They turned toward each other, her hands still in his, and Theo looked into her eyes as he went on, "We went deep into the cave, carrying our lanterns. There were other smaller caves and tunnels branching off from it. We were curious — even I, despite my growing fever — and we searched them. One tunnel narrowed and then emerged into a large, high cave deep in the mountain. It was very much like a vaulted room, empty except for a tall, flat stone that lay in the center of the cave. The stone was carved and looked like an altar."

"An altar?"

"Yes, I know. It sounds fanciful. But if you could have seen the place — there were soot marks on the walls at intervals, as if something had burned close to them.

It wasn't hard to imagine torches flickering around the cave and people gathered around an altar. But what was even more astounding was what we found in some of the other caves. In two, there were stores of golden objects."

Megan drew in an involuntary gasp.

Theo nodded. "Exactly. Hidden treasure."

"But this is fantastical."

"I know. It was like something out of a story. There were small statues and sheets of worked gold. Replicas of all sorts of animals and trees. Bowls and trays and goblets of gold and silver. Gold and silver masks, bracelets, necklaces, earrings. Boxes and chests, some all of gold and others of wood with inlays of worked gold. You cannot imagine the sight of it, all piled up, gleaming in the light of our lanterns. We could scarcely believe our eyes. If the others had not been there, I think I would have thought it was a fever dream."

"And is that what you fought over?" Megan asked softly. "The treasure?"

"Fought over?" Theo grimaced. "No. I told you, I did not hurt Dennis. Someone else killed Dennis."

"Who? Are you saying Mr. Coffey —"

"No, no. I don't know who it was."

"But there was no one else there."

"Yes, there was. You have to hear all my story. There was another cave, long and low. At one point we had to crawl through it. We got to the end, and we found — well, it opened on the other side of the hill. There was a beautiful enclosed valley. And in this valley was a village. It was lovely, untouched, closed off from the rest of the world. We were uncertain what to do, what our reception would be, so we crawled back into the main cave. My fever continued to grow worse. Dennis did what he could for me, but he was very worried. Finally he felt he had no recourse but to go down to the village."

Caught up in the story, even knowing that Dennis did not survive, Megan could not help but feel the clutch of worry and fear. "What happened to him? To you?"

"Somehow he communicated with them. I'm not sure how, for they did not speak even Spanish. They spoke in a tongue none of us had ever heard or dreamed of hearing. They were, we think, descendants of the Incas. From what Dennis could gather from their attempts at communication and from some drawings on the wall of the cave, we came to believe that a group of Inca warriors and their families fled from the Spaniards, carrying as much as they could of the treasures of their temple. They found this secluded valley and settled down there. And the people there now are the descendants of the ones who fled."

"This is unbelievable."

"Yes. But it is the truth." Theo looked unwaveringly into her face. "I did not kill your brother, Megan. But I —" Sorrow filled his face. "The truth of the matter is that I did not save him, either. I tried — I swear to you that I tried, but I was still so weak. . . ."

The raw emotion in his voice tugged at Megan's heart, but she struggled not to let it overcome her reason. "What happened?"

"The villagers seemed friendly, at least at first. Dennis made them understand, I think, that he had a sick companion. A young woman came back with him to the cave. I don't know who she was. She had long, straight black hair, and she was quite lovely. She gave me a bitter brew to drink. I resisted. It tasted foul, but she insisted, time and again. She tended to me. She lit bowls of incense, and set them at my feet and head. I'm not sure what else happened. I was so feverish that I was delirious half the time. I saw things that —"

He broke off and shook his head. "I woke up one time. I'm not even sure if it was day or night. Everything seemed the same there in the cave. There were torches around the room, casting light. And I saw Dennis struggling with a — a creature."

"A creature! What do you mean? An animal?"

"No. A man . . . I think. Frankly, in my delirious state, I took him to be one of the statues of their gods come to life. His face wide and gold, glittering, rising in a high headdress of feathers. His eyes glowed green in the dark. And his body was gold, as well. I cannot explain it. He scarcely seemed human. He was wide and rather boxy, not shaped like a man, and he had scales, golden scales all over him."

Theo shook his head. "To tell you the truth, I don't know exactly how he looked, how much was real and how much was the product of one of my fevered hallucinations. But it was clear that he was fighting with Dennis. He had a knife, and he slashed at Dennis with it, cutting his arm, his chest. I let out a shout — or at least, I meant to, but it came out as little more than a hoarse whisper. I got to my feet and staggered over there to help him. He had stabbed Dennis, and Dennis fell to the ground. I fell on the fellow. He was hard, and I think he was somehow covered in metal, like golden armor. He shook me off and hit me in the face with his arm, and I tumbled backward.

"The next thing I remember is waking up and finding Julian bending over me, shaking me and telling me to wake up. I sat up and looked over at Dennis. He was lying there dead. There was blood all over his chest and on the ground around him. Julian helped me up, and he told me that one of the priests had killed Dennis. Julian said the villagers were gathering and were coming toward the caves. We had to get out of there. I wanted to take Dennis's body with me. I couldn't bear to leave it there. But Coffey pushed me out into the tunnel. He told me we could not wait. The villagers would be there any moment, and we must hurry. We stumbled through the tunnel and out to our burros. He put me on one of the pack animals, and we fled."

Theo let go of Megan's hands and stood up abruptly. "I didn't help Dennis. I left him there. You have ample reason to despise me. I shouldn't have let Julian rush me out. I should have stayed. We should have brought him out with us, not left him there for his enemies."

Megan sat in silence for a long moment, then said, "That is the most bizarre story I have ever heard."

Theo sighed. "I know." He turned. "I can understand why you would have trouble believing it. But I swear to you that it is the truth. I would never have hurt Dennis. In that short time he had become like one of my brothers." He ground his teeth in frustration. "If I had had any idea what your family believed, I would have come to your father and told him the tale in full." He paused, then said quietly, "I am not a murderer, Megan. I could never have killed your brother."

Megan sighed, looking at him for a long moment. There were doubtless a hundred reasons why she should not believe Theo's story. Her father, she knew, would simply assume that Theo was a smooth liar.

But deep inside, Megan knew that Theo was telling her the truth.

No matter how peculiar or unlikely the story he told was, he was not lying. It was there in his face, in his eyes.

Theo was not a murderer. She had known that, really, on some level, from the moment she'd met him. That was why she had had to struggle so hard to remember that he was a villain.

"I believe you," she told him simply.

Theo's brow went up in surprise. "Just like that? Really?"

"Yes."

"Why?"

"For one thing, you are a terrible liar. For another, no one would ever have made up a story like that. If you were going to lie about it, you would have invented something much more plausible."

The beginning of a smile tugged at the corner of his mouth. "Perhaps you are right about that."

"But why did Mr. Barchester lie about it? Why did he tell us that you killed Dennis?"

"I don't know." Theo looked as puzzled as Megan felt. "It makes no sense. He wasn't even there when it happened. He was back at the base camp. All he knows is the story I told him — that Dennis had fallen, that he had died in an accident."

"He did say that he couldn't believe your story, that he questioned you and he was certain you were lying. Having seen you try to tell that story, I can understand why he thought you were lying."

Theo grimaced. "But why make the leap from that to my murdering Dennis?"

"He was quite definite about it. He told

us that you and Dennis had quarreled, and that you had stabbed Dennis," Megan told him.

Theo stared at her. "He is lying. I cannot imagine why, but he made up that entire story." He paused, shaking his head in disbelief. "I thought Andrew was a good man. He had been my friend. Even though we are no longer friends, I wouldn't have thought he would spread such lies about me. And to what purpose?"

"I agree. It makes no sense. I plan to question him about it."

Theo gave her a sharp look. "Not without me, you won't. I was furious and sad about Dennis's death, but I was certain that the priest who had killed him must have believed that Dennis was harming the village somehow. They were a peaceful, gracious people, and they had not harmed us. Indeed, they had taken care of me. I knew that whatever caused the fight, it had to have been a mistake. Besides, the whole village did not deserve to be punished for one man's sin."

"So you kept silent to keep the village's secret."

Theo nodded. "We agreed not to tell anyone, even Barchester, about what we found. We made up the story about the accident, and that is what we told Andrew. We used my illness as an excuse for packing up our camp and leaving immediately. And we returned to civilization."

He stopped and turned to look at her. "You cannot know how much I have regretted what I did. I wished I had never taken that trip. I failed Dennis. I could not save him, and then I left him there. I should have brought his body back. I could never forgive Coffey for making me leave. I couldn't forgive myself either. And now, I see how much I failed you and your family, too."

Megan ignored the comment. "But I don't understand. Why *did* you lie to Mr. Barchester about what happened? Why didn't you just tell the truth?"

He sighed. "Looking back on it, maybe we shouldn't have made up that story. I wasn't thinking very clearly. My fever was still high, and even when it subsided, I was weak as a cat. It was all I could do to stay on my mount. Julian and I talked about it as we rode back to the base camp. The thing was, we didn't want to reveal anything about the village. If you could have seen it — it was so pure and untouched by the modern world. We did not want it to be destroyed, as it surely would have been if word had gotten out about the fabulous treasure they had concealed in their cave."

Theo came back to sit down beside her and took her hand in his. "Dennis was dead, and whatever we did could not bring him back."

Megan curled her fingers around his. "You did your best, Theo. You were ill and weak. What else could you have done?"

He shook his head. "I don't know. But it seems as though I should have done something." He sighed. "That is why I had so much trouble writing to your father about it. Just to think of it was like a knife in my gut. It pained me to even see Andrew or Julian. We had been friends, but . . ." He shrugged. "It was never the same after that. I resented Coffey for making me leave. I could barely stand to talk to him after that. Unfair, I know, but . . ." He shrugged. "Every time I saw one of them, I thought of Dennis and his death. And how I had let him down."

"No one could have expected any more from you," Megan told him firmly. "It was not your fault."

"Perhaps not. But it always felt as if it was."

They were silent for a moment, each thinking their own thoughts. Finally

Megan said, "Why did the villager turn on Dennis and kill him?"

"I don't know. He was a priest, Julian thought — what I had seen on him was a golden mask and a cloak made of linked pieces of gold. Julian said that he and Dennis had seen it before in the storage room. Julian thought perhaps the man had found Dennis taking something from the storage area."

"Stealing?" Megan asked indignantly. "Dennis would not have stolen anything!"

Theo gave her a rueful smile. "Most people, my dear Megan, scarcely regard it as stealing if they take some of a treasure hidden in a cave, especially when it is ancient artifacts that belong to what we Europeans consider a primitive society. Just look at the way we have looted Egyptian tombs. Or the ruins of Troy."

"Yes, but those are just sitting there, buried by people long past. These things obviously were the property of that village."

"I know. And I am certain that Dennis would not have taken anything that belonged to the village. When he was sitting, watching over me while I was ill, he had talked about the villagers. He had great liking for them and their way of life. I think, perhaps, he was even a little in love with the girl who gave me the medicine and chanted over me."

"Really?" Emotion clogged Megan's throat even as she smiled. "So then Dennis was happy those last few days of his life?"

"Lord, yes. The only dark cloud on his horizon was my illness. He was worried about me, I think, and whether I would make it out of there. But he was delighted, fascinated, by the village and its people, the way they had survived and prospered there, passing down a way of life unchanged from three hundred years ago. He talked to me about the need to conceal their presence from the outside world. It was of great concern to him. That was one of the reasons Coffey and I wanted to keep the place hidden and unknown — it had been so important to Dennis."

A reminiscent smile curved Theo's mouth. "And he told me quite a bit about my healer's beautiful dark eyes and lustrous hair." He paused for a moment, thinking about his friend, then went on, "So I do not think that Dennis had taken anything from the storage area. I suppose the villager could have thought that Dennis had stolen something or was about to. I thought about it quite a bit, as you might imagine, on that long trip back home. I decided that the most likely thing was that Dennis inadvertently stumbled upon the villagers in some sort of ceremony. Why else would the villager have been wearing that mask and cloak? They were engaged in a secret ritual, and if Dennis intruded, they might have been so angered that the priest killed him — felt that his gods demanded it or something."

"I suppose." It seemed a flimsy reason to kill someone, Megan thought, but she knew that many people had killed in the name of religion, even one like her own, which espoused peace and love for one's fellow man. How much more likely would it be if one worshipped a bloodthirsty god who demanded the sacrifice of children? "It just seems so terrible that Dennis should have died because of a simple mistake."

"There is no good reason for him to have been killed," Theo pointed out.

"That's true. I cannot understand why Barchester lied to us. I have to find out."

"Did he tell you this recently?" Theo asked. "Perhaps it was some wild idea he had years ago, just because he was so upset over Dennis's death, and over the years he has realized that it wasn't true."

"No. He told Deirdre and me just a few weeks ago — right before I came to work here."

"Deirdre?" Theo looked at her questioningly.

"My sister."

"Your sister is here? Oh . . . and the Irishman? Is that your father?"

Megan nodded. "Yes. The three of us came over to . . ." she met his gaze squarely ". . . to find proof that you killed my brother. To bring you to justice for it."

To her surprise, he smiled a little. "And exactly what did you hope to find in my bedroom?"

Megan blushed, but tilted her chin and said, "Something that you and Dennis might have quarreled over. Something precious to him that you might have taken from him. A pendant, perhaps."

"A pendant?" His brows flew upward, his body stiffening a little. "What do you mean, a pendant?"

"I'm not sure." Megan studied him, aware of the subtle difference in him. Why had his demeanor changed when she mentioned the necklace? "It seemed to us that if it was an object, it would have to be something rather small and easily carried, yet still valuable. Jewelry seemed a likely thing. And when we asked Barchester if he had seen you hiding anything after Dennis's death, he mentioned a necklace of some sort. A pendant. He said he saw you take it out from beneath your shirt and look at it from time to time."

"I see." Theo's eyes were unreadable. "Interesting."

Doubt quivered in Megan. "Was there a pendant? Did Dennis give you anything like that?"

"No. I had nothing of Dennis's. I did carry something . . . that was of importance to me." He paused, looking at her consideringly, then shook his head. "It was nothing to do with Dennis."

Megan's curiosity was fully aroused now. "What was it?"

"Something given to me by someone else. A woman."

"Oh. I see." Megan's voice turned frosty.

She did not care, she told herself, if Theo had carried some token from a woman he had loved. It was, after all, many years ago, and in any case, it made no difference to her.

Theo was still regarding her steadily, and Megan felt suddenly uneasy at what he might read in her face. She stood up and strolled away, stopping and looking down at a piece of statuary as though it held her interest.

"What will you do now?" Theo asked, and Megan turned to look at him, surprised.

"What? Oh. Yes, of course. I — I no longer need to pretend to be the twins' tutor," she said, her spirits sinking at the thought.

What *was* she to do now? she wondered. If what Theo said was true — and she was certain in her heart that it was — there was no reason for her to continue to spy on him. She knew now how her brother had died, and that the man who had killed him was a world away in a remote village. Her family would never really know the reason why he had been killed, and his killer could scarcely be brought to justice.

She squared her shoulders, swallowing something that felt very much like tears. "I shall tell the duchess the truth, and of course I will resign."

Megan hated the thought of facing the duchess's dislike almost as much as she hated the idea of leaving this house.

Theo, seeing her expression, smiled. "My mother can be a bit daunting. She doesn't like lies. However, I think you will find that she can be quite understanding, as well. And of more importance to her than your qualifications will, I think, be the impression she has formed about you from being around you. I will accompany you when you have your interview with her, if you like."

Megan looked surprised, and it touched her that he would help her in that way, despite what she had thought about him.

"Thank you. That is very kind. But I think that I should deal with the duchess on my own."

"Of course." Theo was too accustomed to independent women to object. He would simply talk to his mother on his own. "You know, there are still some loose ends you need to tie up. For instance, the man who was following you or having you followed."

"Besides your man, you mean?" Megan quirked an eyebrow. It still aggravated her that he had had her followed — almost as much because she had not seen the man as because Theo had done it.

"I must find out why Mr. Barchester lied to me, as well," she went on. She hesitated, then added, "I did not tell you quite all I remember about being hit on the head tonight."

"Really? You shock me," Theo responded dryly.

Megan grimaced at him. "When I came to, I didn't remember anything past leaving the ballroom. I was following Mr. Coffey. But later I remembered that I went after him and then I heard someone on the back stairs going down to the basement. So I followed him. I didn't see Coffey anywhere, but I did see Mr. Barchester walking down the hall. I thought it was strange that he was in the basement."

"There seem to have been a number of people down there," Theo murmured. "You are sure it was the basement?"

"Of course I'm sure. The blow didn't rattle my brains enough that I don't know down from up," Megan retorted tartly. "I don't know how I ended up on the second floor. I may have followed him up there. Or maybe whoever knocked me out carried me up there. I still can't remember being hit on the head. But it is possible, I suppose, that Barchester could have seen me, then doubled back and hit me over the head."

"Or that someone else took advantage of an opportunity to get rid of a troublesome snoop."

Megan sent him a quelling look. "At any

rate, it is enough to make me wonder exactly what Mr. Barchester is up to. And I still want to interview Mr. Coffey. I will need someone else's word to convince my father that you are not Dennis's murderer. He has believed it for so many years, and he does not know you as well as I do. And he —" She shot him an apologetic glance. "My father tends to be somewhat prejudiced against the English, especially English noblemen."

Theo grinned. "Having been acquainted with some other Irishmen, I am not really surprised. And you are right. It would help if you had some corroboration from Coffey." He paused, then added, "I would like to accompany you when you talk to both of them, if you don't mind."

Megan's heart grew immediately lighter. "All right. That would . . . I would like that."

Theo's smile was slow, and Megan's heart took a hard, slow thump at the sight of it. "I would like that, too."

She felt suddenly breathless and ill at ease, and she had the irritating suspicion that she was beginning to blush. She glanced toward the door. "Well . . . I should . . . rest now."

"You have had a busy evening," Theo

concurred. He watched her as she walked to the door and opened it. "Megan . . ."

She turned and looked back at him, brows lifting slightly in inquiry.

"Did you mean what you said earlier . . . ?" he asked, his eyes intent on hers. "About despising my touch?"

Color bloomed on her cheeks, matching the warmth that filled her loins. "No," she said, the words coming out in a hoarse whisper. "I didn't mean it at all."

She turned and hurried from the room.

16

Megan was surprised, the next morning, to find that her interview with the duchess was neither as long nor as difficult as she had expected. The duchess was an imposing woman, but she listened to Megan's explanation with a quiet attentiveness and an astonishing lack of rancor that led Megan to suspect that this was not the first time Theo's mother had heard the story.

She knew she should resent the fact that Theo had obviously stolen a march on her and told the duchess all about her deception, but, frankly, Megan was glad that she was not having to face the older woman's first reaction. She suspected that the duchess's cool blue eyes could light with a temper to match her red hair, particularly if danger threatened one of her beloved children.

When Megan at last finished her statement, pleased that her voice had trembled only slightly, and added a final, heartfelt apology, the Duchess of Broughton regarded her for a moment, then sighed.

"I am sure you are aware, Miss Mulcahey, that I abhor lying," she told her calmly, rising from her chair and beginning to pace. "However, in this instance, I suppose there was a certain amount of reason to your charade. Not knowing my son, you could not have realized before you came here that any tale of his murdering someone was bound to be nonsensical. And I cannot disdain the sort of love and loyalty for your brother that impelled you to try to bring down his murderer."

"Thank you, your grace," Megan said, making a point of getting the troublesome form of address correct. "You are very generous."

"I am merely truthful," the duchess responded. There was a twinkle in her eye as she went on, "I must confess that I was not entirely convinced of your qualifications, as Rafe had cabled the school where you received your training and received the less-than-reassuring news that it had closed down. Also, Anna experienced some . . . troubling feelings regarding you. Not, let me hasten to assure you, that she did not dislike you. She does like you, which made her doubts all the more upsetting to her. However, I trusted my instincts and those of the twins enough to let you continue for the moment. I was rather pleased, quite frankly, when Theo told me this morning what you were really doing here. It is so much more pleasant than thinking you were perhaps a thief."

Megan struggled to keep from looking as astonished as she felt. "I — I don't know what to say." She smiled a little ruefully. "Obviously I must not have been as clever as I thought."

The duchess smiled back at her. "Oh, you were clever enough, Miss Mulcahey. However, it is a mistake sometimes to confuse an easygoing manner with carelessness."

"I can see that. I want you to know, ma'am, that I have been much torn, knowing the pain that what I believed was the truth would have caused you and your family. I am extremely fond of Alexander and Constantine."

"As they are of you, my dear. Of course, I will begin to look for another tutor for the twins." The duchess looked somewhat downcast at the thought. "In the meantime, I do hope that you will continue to stay with us as our guest."

Megan stared, completely caught off guard by the request. "You want me to stay here? After what I have done?"

"Why, yes. We are all quite fond of you, not just the twins. And Theo tells me that you and he are going to look into the matter of this Mr. Barchester's lies about Theo. It would seem the easiest thing for you to remain here. I do hope that your father and sister will come to meet us. Theo has told me how close he was to your brother."

"Of — of course," Megan agreed, her mind boggling a little at the thought of suggesting to her father that he call on the Duchess of Broughton.

"And if it would not be too much trouble . . . the twins seem to be doing so well under your tutelage. They are much more willing to work on their studies and stay out of mischief when you are overseeing them. If you could simply check on their work, keep them going in the right direction — only a few minutes a day, really — while I look for another tutor?" The duchess paused, looking hopeful and a little worried.

"Of course," Megan agreed readily. "I will be more than happy to work with them."

She started to take her leave, only to have the duchess hold up a hand and say, "By the way, my dear, if you are not a teacher, I confess I am rather curious. All those things that we talked about — the experimental teaching, the problems in the slums. What exactly is it you do, then?"

Megan smiled. "I work for a newspaper."

"A newspaper? Really? How fascinating. Then the things we discussed —"

"I have written stories about them."

The duchess brightened considerably. "I would so love to hear about them. Come here, my dear. Sit down and tell me about what you've written."

Megan left the study a good thirty minutes later, feeling somewhat dazed. Things never went as one expected with the Morelands, she reflected.

Eager to atone for her deception with the duchess, she put in a full morning tutoring the twins. A good portion of it was spent going over the same territory she had covered with the duchess that morning. The twins, however, were far more interested in her brother's death in the jungles of South America and her own plan to unmask his killer than in any of the social ills she had uncovered as a reporter.

She did not ask how they had so quickly

found out about the matter. The twins were never far behind any news in the family. Megan suspected that it had much to do with their habit of hanging about in the kitchen, cadging snacks from the cook and listening to the servants' gossip.

Their suspicion, they were quick to tell her, fell on Andrew Barchester.

"Sounds like a wrong 'un," Alex confided. "I bet that it's him who really killed Dennis."

"But how? He was back at the base camp," Megan pointed out.

Con shrugged. "Why else would he lie about Theo that way? He must be covering something up."

"Maybe he followed them," Alex suggested. "Maybe he didn't like being left behind while the others went off on the adventure."

"I wouldn't," Con agreed.

"Yeah, and so he sneaked out after them. Spied on them."

"And dressed up like a priest and killed Dennis?" Megan asked skeptically. "Why would he do that?"

Con shrugged. "Don't know. That's what you and Theo'll have to figure out. My guess is he was stealing stuff, and your brother caught him."

"Maybe he dressed up like that so they wouldn't know it was him," Alex supplied triumphantly. "You know, when he was stealing the stuff."

"And that's why they figured it was a priest."

"He doesn't really seem like a killer," Megan opined.

"Well, they don't, do they?" Alex answered unarguably. "Like that chap that tried to kill Kyria. Seemed regular enough."

"Someone tried to kill Kyria?" Megan asked, astonished.

"Oh, yes," Con answered, as if it were quite an ordinary event. "Before she married Rafe."

"I never knew life in England was so risky," Megan commented.

"It's not, usually," Con assured her.

"It's something about our family," Alex added. "We have a bit more fun, I think, than most of the peerage."

They spent another good portion of their study time regaling Megan with stories of the adventures that various members of their family had embarked upon. It was some time before she was able to pull them back to the subject of medieval history.

After lunch, Theo arrived in the schoolroom. His gaze slid over Megan, and heat began to spark along her veins even though he said nothing. She moved a cautious step back from him as he turned to the twins. Megan had spent far too much of the largely sleepless night before contemplating her relationship with Theo, and none of the answers she had come up with had given her any optimism.

She was far too attracted to him. Even though she no longer believed that he was responsible for her brother's death, there were too many obstacles between them. A future duke, even in a family as unconventional as the Morelands, did not go about marrying an American nobody. There had been marriages between English blue bloods and American heiresses, where the American money made up for the woman's lack of appropriate ancestors. But Megan was no heiress, and Broughton had both too much fortune and integrity for the title to be up for sale in that manner.

The truth of the matter, she knew, was that Theo Moreland could not, would not, marry a New York newspaper reporter. And she was not the sort of woman who would settle for anything else. The passion that all too often flared between them, therefore, was destined to go no further.

Megan was too honest not to admit that

Theo had an effect on her that no other man had ever had. It took only the sight of him to arouse a heavy ache deep in her loins and a tingling all over her skin. She wanted him. She might even be skating perilously close to falling in love with him. But she was not foolish enough to let that happen.

After all, she was not a starry-eyed dreamer like her sister. She was a woman who knew how the world worked. And she had no intention of getting into a situation she could not handle. She had kept her heart — and her virtue — intact this long, and she intended to continue that way.

Therefore, when at last Theo got the twins shuffled off to their class with Thisbe, Megan turned to him with a businesslike air, ignoring the smile he aimed at her.

"I am ready to talk to Mr. Barchester," she said briskly.

He raised an eyebrow at her abrupt manner, but said only, "Yes. I've sent for the carriage."

Megan got her hat and gloves and busied herself with putting them on as they went down the stairs, thus neatly avoiding the arm Theo offered her. He looked at her a trifle warily, but again said nothing.

But when she stepped up into the carriage without putting her hand in the one he offered, he swung in quickly after her and asked, "Have you changed your mind about me? Have I become the villain again?"

"What?" She looked at him, but her eyes dropped before his penetrating gaze. "No, of course not. Don't be absurd."

"Then why are you acting as if I have the plague?"

"I am not. That's nonsense."

"Then why can you not look at me?"

Megan lifted her head in response and looked directly into his face. She didn't like the way her insides quivered when she looked at him, but she ignored the sensation.

"We are going to interview Mr. Barchester together," she said firmly. "That doesn't mean . . ."

She faltered as he turned a politely inquiring gaze upon her. It occurred to her that there was no way to express her thoughts on the matter of their relationship without revealing how foolishly attracted to him she was.

"Yes?" he urged her. "It doesn't mean what?"

"It doesn't mean anything," she finished

lamely and turned to look out the window. She continued after a moment, "You are still Lord Raine, and I am still Megan Mulcahey from New York."

An annoying twinkle started in his eyes. "I cannot argue with that."

Megan grimaced, refusing to share his amusement. "It isn't as if we are friends."

"Are we not?" The amusement grew, now tugging at the corners of his mouth. "I had hoped that we were. Then what you feel for me is solely animal attraction?"

Pink stained her cheekbones, and Megan shot him a fierce look. "That is not what I meant, and you know it."

"I am afraid that I don't know. You are being unaccustomedly unclear," he responded mildly, still with that irritating amusement in his eyes that told her he knew exactly how she felt about him and was rather smugly pleased with it.

Megan narrowed her eyes, but Theo was spared her hot retort by the fact that the carriage pulled to a halt in front of Andrew Barchester's redbrick townhome.

With a flash of a grin at her, Theo exited the carriage and held up his hand to help her down. She could not avoid taking his hand without obvious rudeness, so she put her hand in his and stepped down. Even through her glove, his hand was warm and she was more aware of it than she was of the ground beneath her feet. His fingers closed around hers with just the briefest of pressures and then were gone. Megan could not resist looking up into his face, and the warmth she saw there in his eyes left her a little breathless.

Foolish, she reminded herself. Dangerous.

Neither warning seemed to weigh much against the flutter of her heart.

Theo knocked at the door, and it was opened promptly by a haughty-faced man-servant, whose expression changed subtly at the sound of Theo's name. He whisked them into the same elegant drawing room where Megan and Deirdre had visited Barchester, then bowed out of the room and went in search of his employer.

Megan's thoughts turned to her sister as they waited for Barchester to appear. She feared that Deirdre had become attached to Mr. Barchester, and that whatever they found out in the next few minutes would hurt Deirdre. Mr. Barchester had been, at best, careless — and at worst, villainous — in what he had told her family about Dennis's death. For Deirdre's sake, Megan hoped that they would find out that Barchester was innocent of any ill intent.

A few minutes later, Barchester strode into the drawing room, whatever surprise he felt at their visit carefully concealed behind an expression of polite welcome. Only his eyes as they went to Megan betrayed his curiosity.

"Miss, umm . . ." Barchester fumbled for the false name under which she had been introduced to him at the museum party.

"Mulcahey," Megan told him, returning his gaze with a cool, steady examination.

"Uh, yes, of course," he replied, though his face looked more bewildered than ever. "And Lord Raine. How do you do?"

"I am quite well," Theo replied, his voice as hard and flat as his eyes. "And my memory, it seems, must be quite a bit better than yours."

Barchester's eyes widened. "Excuse me?" He glanced from Theo to Megan, then back.

"Lord Raine and I have been discussing the expedition you and he took up the Amazon," Megan said. "And I find his version is significantly different from yours."

He looked at her, faintly puzzled. "Yes, well, it would be, wouldn't it?"

"What I am wondering is why?" Megan went on.

"Miss Mulcahey . . ." He frowned at her a little and cast a glance toward Theo. "I, um . . ."

"He knows what you told me," Megan explained. "There is no need for any of us to dance around the matter."

Barchester looked shocked. "He has gotten around you? He has made you believe him?"

"I didn't 'get around' Miss Mulcahey," Theo retorted. "And if you knew her better, you would realize that no one could make her believe anything. But she knew the truth when she heard it. What we are here to find out is why you lied to Megan and her family." Theo's face was dark with anger, and he took a step closer to Barchester.

To Barchester's credit, he did not back up, but faced Theo squarely. "I did not lie, my lord."

"You told them I killed Dennis." Theo's eyes flashed, and his fists knotted.

Barchester swallowed, but continued to stand his ground. "I did not lie," he repeated.

"Bloody hell! How do you have the nerve to stand there and tell me to my face that that is not a lie? You were not even there!"

"No. I was not. But anyone could have seen that you were lying. You could scarcely get the words out. Every time I asked you about the details, you were vague and obviously uneasy. You avoided conversation. Hell, you avoided me. It was clear that you were lying."

"You *are* a terrible liar," Megan conceded, turning to Theo. "I knew last night that what you said about Dennis having an accident was pure poppycock."

Theo's mouth twitched in irritation. "All right, yes, I am not adept at lying. I admit it. Dennis did not die the way that we said. But why the devil would you make the leap from that to saying that I killed him?"

"Because Julian saw you!"

Theo's jaw dropped.

"Ah, you didn't realize that, did you?" Barchester went on triumphantly. "While you were struggling with Dennis, you did not see Julian come into the cave. He saw you stab Dennis, and he hid, afraid of what you would do to him if you knew that he had witnessed the whole thing."

"Coffey told you I killed Dennis?" Theo asked carefully. "He told you that he saw me murder him?"

"Yes. I questioned him about the story you had told me, because it didn't ring true. At first he tried to back up your version, but when I told him that I knew you were lying, he admitted what really happened. He thought you must have been delirious from a fever, that you mistook Dennis for an enemy or something."

"I see." Theo contemplated the other man for a moment, then said, "Interesting that neither of you did anything about this murder you think I committed."

Barchester shot him a scornful look. "As if our word would have meant anything against that of a marquess!"

"You didn't even confront *me* about it."

"What good would it have done?" Barchester asked him, bitterness tainting his voice. "I asked you what happened, and you lied to me. Why would that have changed if I told you I knew the truth? You would tell any official I might go to the same lie. And we had no proof to back it up."

"You could have given me the chance, instead of believing I was guilty!" Theo shot back.

Barchester's mouth twisted. "I had thought you were different, that you weren't the kind of aristocrat's son that I had gone to school with. But then you lied, and I realized that whatever egalitarian facade you put up, it was only skin deep.

Scratch, and the aristocrat came out soon enough."

"I had thought you were different, too," Theo retorted coldly. "I thought you judged a man on who he was, how he acted with you, not on the arbitrary matter of his birth. Scratch you, and your prejudices come out clearly enough."

"You expect me to believe that Julian lied about it? Why would he do that?"

"You tell me. I will point out one thing, though, that you might think about with your intellect instead of your prejudice. You saw me when Coffey and I came back into camp. You saw how weak my illness had left me. I wasn't even completely over my fever. How the devil do you think I was able to overcome a fellow like Dennis in my condition? Eh? And why did Coffey hide and watch instead of coming to Dennis's aid? Two men against one feverish one? I would think they could have brought me down."

Barchester's eyes shifted away from Theo. "Madness can give people inhuman strength. Delirium would be the same."

"No doubt you would like to believe that," Theo responded tightly. He turned toward Megan. "I think it is time for us to leave."

Megan nodded. She gave Barchester one last long look, then swept from the room, Theo right behind her. They said nothing until they were out of the house.

Megan looked up at Theo. "Do you think he's telling the truth? That Coffey is the one who lied about you?"

Theo shrugged. "It's anybody's guess. He seems convinced of what he says."

"Yes, he does." Megan frowned. "But why did he tell us without reservation that you did it? As if he had actually witnessed Dennis's death? Why did he not say that he heard it from another?"

Theo shook his head. "I don't know." He handed her up into the carriage. Then he spoke quietly to the coachman and swung up onto the seat across from her.

The carriage pulled out into the street, went smartly down the road and turned left, then left again, coming up on the other side of the small park that lay across from Barchester's house. The carriage pulled to a stop.

Megan, who was still ruminating on Barchester's words, looked over at Theo questioningly. "Why are we stopping?"

"I think a little walk in the park would be of benefit to me right now." He nodded toward the strip of greenery and trees that separated them from the street in front of Barchester's house.

"We are going to spy on him?" Megan asked eagerly.

"I would suggest that I do it myself and send you back safely to the house, but I have a good idea what you would say to that."

Megan grinned. "You are a smart man."

She scrambled out of the carriage after him and took his arm to stroll into the park as if they were simply out enjoying the afternoon. They walked across the width of the park until they could see the front door of Barchester's house.

"Let us hope that he has not left the house yet," Theo said as he turned and began to walk parallel to the iron fence that separated the trees of the park from the street.

"Are you sure he is going to leave it?" Megan asked.

"No. But I think it is a strong possibility," he replied. "If he was telling the truth — that Coffey is the one who lied about my having killed Dennis — then I would think he would go to question Coffey about it. It is certainly what I would do."

"And if he doesn't leave, then you think

he was lying to us again? That the lie is his alone?"

"It seems more likely."

"Unless, of course, they are in it together," Megan pointed out. "Then he would go running off to see his partner in the lie."

"True."

They had reached the end of the park and stopped. Sheltered by the trees, they were able to look at a slant across the street and down to Barchester's door without being seen themselves from his house.

"But what exactly is this 'it' they are in together?" Theo mused as he gazed through the fence railings. "What is the purpose of the lies?"

"I don't know why they would be in it together," Megan replied. "Or, indeed, why Mr. Barchester would be the one who made up the lie. While it is possible, I suppose, that Barchester could have done as Alex and Con surmised and followed your group, then killed Dennis, it seems an unlikely scenario. It makes more sense to me that Barchester simply accepted Mr. Coffey's lie."

"I agree. Which leaves us with only the question of why Coffey would have made up the lie."

"It makes little sense for him to lie to Barchester if a villager killed my brother, as he told you. I would think that means Coffey lied because he killed Dennis himself." Tears glittered in Megan's eyes, and Theo put his hand over hers on his arm.

"I am sorry."

Megan offered him a weak smile. "It is foolish, I suppose, for all this to make the wound fresher. But somehow it does. It seems so much more horrible that a man Dennis knew and trusted killed him."

"I know. It is hard for me, too, to believe that Julian killed him."

"The twins' rationale makes more sense with Mr. Coffey," Megan reasoned. "He came upon all that treasure with you. It wouldn't have been strange for him to want some of it — many men would have. But Dennis opposed that. Perhaps Mr. Coffey tried to sneak some of it out and Dennis caught him."

"He was stealing the treasure while dressed up in a priest's garb?"

"Perhaps Dennis caught him in the garb and realized what he was doing — I don't know."

"Or perhaps I confused the scene with one of my dreams," Theo admitted. "Aside from the delirium I suffered, I think that the healing tea they gave me to drink may have induced hallucinations. I read more about the Incas after I returned, and I learned that the priests often ingested plants that gave them visions. So I'm not entirely sure that what I saw was accurate. Dreams and reality could have blurred. It was all so vague and strange. . . ."

"Mr. Coffey could have taken treasure out of the cave. You wouldn't have known if he loaded some of the objects on your pack animals. You were too ill. But Dennis might have caught him. They fought, and he killed him. Then he lied to you about what happened. And when Barchester didn't buy the accident story, he made up a different lie for him."

"But why make up that second lie? Why not just stick to what he and I had agreed upon?" Theo pointed out.

"Well . . ." Megan thought for a minute. "Barchester, feeling that the story you two told was a lie, might very well have kept on questioning you, and after a while, you might have explained the truth to him. And in talking about it, one or both of you might have begun to see holes in Coffey's story. The best thing to do was to keep the two of you from thinking about the story, from talking about what happened. If

Barchester believed that you killed Dennis, he would not keep on questioning you."

"That's true. I wanted to put it out of my mind, but if Barchester had continued to plague me about it, I would soon have admitted what I thought was the truth. As it was, I closed it off. I avoided Barchester because of the painful reminders, and he avoided me just as assiduously. Moreover, he wrote to your father and repeated the lies, so your father never contacted me about it." Theo grimaced. "And I fell right into the plan — not writing to your father again, being relieved when Barchester told me that he had done so."

"Coffey must have thought that he had gotten away with it long since," Megan agreed. "He wouldn't have suspected that Dennis's family would turn up after all these years, stirring up the whole matter again."

"Look!" Theo interrupted, nodding toward Barchester's front door. "His carriage is pulling up in front of the house. He is leaving."

Megan turned to Theo, excitement rising in her chest. "Shall we follow him?"

A grin was his only answer as he took her arm and started back across the park toward their own carriage.

By the time they reached the carriage

and climbed in, then circled around, Barchester's carriage was almost a block ahead of them.

But it was easy enough for the coachman to keep it in sight, and they followed at a leisurely pace. Inside, Megan kept twitching aside the curtain impatiently to look for Barchester's carriage.

"I can't see it at all," she grumbled.

"Neither can I, but we are headed toward the museum," Theo told her, satisfaction in his voice.

Their suspicions were confirmed a few minutes later when they drove slowly past the Cavendish's entrance. Barchester's carriage sat in the driveway. On Theo's instructions, their coach turned into the next street and parked at the corner, where they had an excellent view of the museum's driveway.

"I would love to hear what they are saying to each other," Megan mused, peering out past the edge of the curtain.

"Somehow, I suspect we could not sneak close enough to hear. But at least we know now that it was not merely Barchester lying. Either Coffey lied to him, or he and Coffey are in it together. There is no reason for him to go running to Coffey otherwise."

"What shall we do now?"

"I think we certainly need to talk to Coffey. And another visit to Barchester might be in order." Theo's jaw tightened, and his green eyes grew cold and hard. "If it was Coffey who killed Dennis . . . All these years, and I did nothing. . . ."

"You didn't know."

"I did not try hard enough to find out. I was too busy trying to escape my grief and guilt."

"You are too hard on yourself." Megan leaned forward and closed her hand over his.

His skin was warm beneath her palm, and suddenly she was very aware of the small, confined nature of the carriage. It was an intimate setting, shut away from the world by the closed curtains, cradled by the soft, buttery leather of the seats. Megan's heart tripped in its beat.

Theo looked at her, his eyes dark and deep in the shuttered space. He turned his palm over, his hand curling around hers. Megan drew a shaky breath, reminding herself of all the reasons why nothing could ever happen between the two of them.

"I — we should probably go back," she said quickly. "It is growing late."

His eyes narrowed, but he released her hand slowly and said, "No doubt you are right. I think the best thing to do would be to set Tom Quick up to watch the museum — see if Coffey goes anywhere, what he does."

Megan nodded. "Yes. No doubt."

It was best not to think about what might have happened just then. Or why Theo had let the moment go so easily. Most of all, it was best not to consider why his letting it go engendered such a flat feeling of disappointment in her.

They rode home, speaking little, wrapped in their own thoughts. As Theo handed Megan down from the carriage in front of Broughton House, he clasped her hand for a moment longer than necessary.

"I did not hurt your brother," he said fiercely. "Whatever it takes, I will prove it to you."

Startled, Megan looked at him. "I know."

"Do you? I wonder."

"Yes," Megan replied calmly. "I am certain of it."

He gazed at her for a moment longer. "And if Coffey did, I promise you, he will pay for it."

Taking her arm, he propelled her into the house.

Megan dreamed that night.

She was in a cave, a vast, cavernous place with rough walls of stone. It was lit by torches shoved into iron braces spaced regularly around the walls. Torchlight flickered on the stone, uneven and gleaming with a dampness that had an almost satiny look. The ceiling of the cave was high, and if she looked up, she could see the faint glitter of rock that seemingly dripped down from the roof, barely touched by the light from the torches.

In the center of the room was a large stone, waist high, and so flat on top that it seemed almost a table. On this slab of rock lay a man. A sheet of white cloth covered his legs and torso, extending midway up his chest, which was bare. His hair was thick and black, shaggily falling almost to his shoulders, but swept back now from his face and spread over the gray rock.

His eyes were closed; she could not see their color. But she could see the handsome features — the full lower lip and high, wide cheekbones, the firm thrust of jaw and chin, the straight nose, the thick black sweep of eyebrows and eyelashes. His skin was darkened from the sun, but

439

she could see the flush of blood beneath the tan. His flesh, damp with sweat, gleamed in the dim light.

There was a woman standing beside him, a small woman with delicate features and velvet-brown eyes. Thick black hair fell in a sweep down her back. She wore a white gown that fell straight from her shoulders, belted at the waist with plates of gold fastened end to end. A wide band of gold encircled her head, cutting across her forehead, and above it rose more narrow plates of gold, shorter at the ends and tapering to the longest plate in the center. Fastened behind the plates was a small fan of feathers, long, bright sweeps of yellow, red, blue and green. A gold armlet banded one upper arm, one end of it the stylized head of a snake, the body zigzagging to the other end, which was its tail.

She held her arms out, palms up, over the man on the slab, and her eyes were closed, her face raised. She chanted in a strange tongue, her words nonsense to Megan. A bowl lay on the table in front of her, beside the man, and next to it lay a cloth and a golden goblet. At either end of the table sat metal bowls, and in them incense burned, its pungent smoke curling up toward the ceiling and perfuming the air.

Megan was looking down upon the scene as if she were floating above the man and his companion. She stared, fascinated, as the woman ceased her chant and picked up the cloth, dipping it into the bowl and mopping his face and chest with it. The man stirred and muttered, then coughed, a long, wracking cough that shook his large frame.

The woman put her hand behind his neck and lifted his head a little, bringing the goblet to his lips and pouring some of its contents into his mouth. He drank a little, and she laid his head back down. Picking up his hand, she slipped something into his palm and curved his fingers around it. She inclined her head, her lips moving in prayer or incantation; Megan was not sure which.

Megan moved closer, drawn to the man, floating down from the heights to stand on the rock floor. It was cool beneath her feet, and she realized in that instant that her feet were bare. She glanced down at herself. She was wearing one of her nightgowns, a simple, straight, white cotton shift with a rounded neck and one frivolous row of ruffles across the bosom. The air was chilly on her skin, but it did not bother her.

She walked closer, and the woman on the other side of the table lifted her head and looked straight into Megan's face. She smiled slowly, with satisfaction, then turned and walked out of the cave into the darkness beyond, leaving Megan alone with the man on the rock slab.

Megan went to his side and looked down at him. The heavy incense filled her nostrils, the smoke stinging her eyes. He moved restlessly on the stone, coughing again. His face was flushed, and she could hear the rasp of his breath in his lungs. She touched his forehead, and his skin was searing with heat. He was dying. She knew it as certainly as she knew that she loved him.

"You can't die!" she exclaimed, her voice cracking with emotion.

His eyes flew open at her words, and he stared at her. His eyes were dark in the dim torchlight, and he seemed to gaze deep inside her.

"You cannot die," she repeated. "I won't allow it. I am waiting for you."

She slipped her hand in his. His palm opened to her, revealing the clear crystal that the woman had laid there. Megan curled her hand around his, the crystal trapped between them, and squeezed, holding onto him fiercely.

"Live!" she whispered. "You are mine."

The crystal between them flared with heat, sending it shooting up Megan's arm and into her body. She trembled with the intensity, her gaze locked with that of the man before her. For an instant they were melded together; her veins, her nerves, her flesh connected to him, humming with the same piercing vibration.

Then the moment was gone, and she went limp. She had to grab the edge of the stone table to remain standing. She looked at the man. He gazed back at her for one long moment, then placed the crystal in her palm.

Megan closed her hand around it tightly, not caring that its edges bit into her flesh. She laid her other hand upon his forehead. It was noticeably cooler, and she smiled. He would live now, she thought.

Reaching up, she took the chain she always wore out from beneath her nightgown. She slipped it off over her head and kissed the medal, warm from lying against her skin. Then she put the medallion and its chain into his palm, replacing the crystal, and curved his fingers around it. She lifted his fist to her mouth and brushed her lips against his knuckles.

"Remember me."

"Always." His word was a mere breath on the air, but she heard it.

He smiled.

Theo.

17

Megan shot bolt upright in her bed. She stared into the darkness, her heart racing. The man in her dream had been Theo.

She had had the dream before. She remembered it now, with that eerie sense of reliving a moment.

She had dreamed it when she was sixteen, a few weeks after Dennis had left on his expedition. It had been erased by time — and, she thought now, by a certain reluctance to recall it. It had been too piercing, too vivid, too at odds with the world she knew, to be retained.

But now she remembered. Remembered each word, each movement. A shiver ran through her.

Megan slipped out of her bed and hurried to her dresser. Lighting a candle, she opened the top drawer of the dresser and pulled out her little box of treasures.

She set the box on the dresser and lifted

the lid, reaching in to take out the chunk of glass that she had kept as a lucky charm for so many years. Ten years, she thought now, remembering how she had found it lying underneath her bed one day when she was cleaning.

It seemed strange, thinking about it now, that she had never questioned how it had come to be there. She had simply pocketed it, keeping it, she thought, because it was intriguing.

Megan held the thing up to the light. Though the candle cast only a dim glow, it lit the silver lines inside the glass. Not glass, she told herself. She realized that now. It was a crystal. She gazed into its depths, scarcely believing the thoughts that were whizzing around in her head — incoherent, unbelievable ideas that she could not dismiss.

Her fingers closed around the crystal, and, picking up the candlestick, she turned and left her room. She hurried down the hallway, hand held up to shield the flickering flame of the candle, heedless of the fact that her feet were bare upon the runner of carpet or that she had not even thrown on a dressing gown over her night robe.

She did not pause at Theo's door, but

turned the knob and rushed in, calling out his name in a low, urgent voice.

He sat up, coming awake with a start. "Megan!"

Theo shoved aside the covers and leaped out of bed, realizing a moment too late that he was wearing nothing beneath the sheets. Megan gasped, blushing red to the roots of her hair, at the sight of his lean, muscled body. Yet she could not look away, could not close her eyes, fascinated by the smooth musculature of his hardened body, the dark hair that sprinkled his chest and tapered down to the flat plane of his stomach and abdomen . . . and lower. . . . Heat curled through her own abdomen and pulsed along her veins.

Muttering an oath, Theo grabbed the sheet and yanked it from the bed, quickly wrapping it around his waist and tucking the ends in to secure it. Thus covered, he came forward.

"What is it? What's the matter?" he asked, reaching out to her.

He laid his hand on her arm, and his touch was like a kiss of fire to Megan's already heated skin.

"I . . . um . . ." Megan gathered her scattered wits together. "I dreamed tonight."

Theo looked puzzled. "A nightmare?"

"No. A dream I had a long time ago. One I had forgotten. I — I think I put it out of my mind because it was so unbelievable. But tonight it came to me again. A man in a cave, lying there flushed and ill with fever. A woman standing over him, chanting. She was wearing a feathered headdress, and she gave him something to drink."

Theo's eyes widened, intent on her face, but he said nothing.

"I was there, although I did not know either one of them. I walked over to him, and I — I took his hand. There was this flash of indescribable heat between us. Something . . . happened to me. I cannot explain it."

"It is difficult to," Theo agreed.

"It was you, wasn't it?" Megan asked. "How can that be?"

Theo shook his head. "I don't know. But I recognized you the moment I saw you in the garden with Mother."

"Why didn't you tell me?"

"What was I to say? You are the woman I saw in my delirium ten years ago? You came to me and touched me, and I didn't die? You told me I could not go because you were waiting for me? You would have thought me mad."

"Perhaps we are both mad." Megan held out her hand to him, the crystal nestled in her upturned palm. "I found this in my room not long after that dream, and I kept it, even though the dream had left my mind. It has been my lucky charm throughout the years. Whenever I felt hurt or tired or lonely, I would take it out and hold it. Somehow, it seemed to help."

Theo's gaze flicked down to the crystal in her hand, then back up to her face, astonishment beginning to dawn across his features.

"This is the crystal that was in your hand, isn't it?" Megan asked. "The one that you gave to me."

He looked at her for a long moment, then, saying nothing, he turned and crossed the room. Opening a wooden box that sat upon his dresser, he took something out of it and came back to her, his fist clenched tightly.

He opened up his hand. A silver medal on a thin silver chain lay in his palm, small and delicate in his large, roughened hand. On the front of the medal was a raised figure of the Virgin Mary.

With trembling fingers, Megan reached out and picked up the familiar religious medal. She knew it, had worn it for years.

It was hers, the one her mother had given her and she had believed she lost. But she had not lost it; she had given it away.

Her stomach flip-flopped, and her knees went weak, her eyes blurring.

"Megan!" Theo's arm lashed out, catching her around the waist and holding her up.

She leaned against him, and quickly he bent, scooping her up in his arms and carrying her over to set her down on the side of the bed. He sat beside her, his arm around her shoulders, propping her up. Megan leaned her head on his shoulder, letting the buzzing in her mind and the lights dancing behind her eyes fade away.

"I am not going to faint," she murmured. "I never faint."

"I am sure you do not." Amusement threaded through his voice.

"This is my medal," Megan said, lifting her head and looking at him. "My mother gave it to me years ago. It was my most treasured possession." She paused, then asked, "Is this what Barchester saw you taking out and looking at?"

"Yes. I turned to it whenever I was tired or troubled." The corner of his mouth quirked. "When I needed to reassure myself that what I had seen had really happened."

He lifted her hand, folding it closed over the medal and bringing it to his lips, gently kissing her knuckles. "You saved me."

The soft touch of his lips on her skin sent tingles through Megan. The heat, still heavy in her loins, expanded, heightened. Yearning began to throb deep within her.

Destiny, she thought, gazing up into Theo's face. It was no wonder that she had had trouble believing him a villain. He had lived in her heart for ten years, even though she had not been aware of it.

Megan lifted her other hand and curved it around his cheek, looking into his eyes. It did not matter anymore that he was a lord with centuries of aristocratic English breeding behind him. It did not matter that he could never marry an ordinary Irish girl from New York City.

Theo belonged to her and she to him. She loved him. She knew that now. She loved him with every ounce of her being, with every breath she took and every thought she had. Titles, families, the censure of society, could not measure against that love. If it meant that she would be his mistress, then she would live with that. She could live without a ring upon her finger.

She could not live without Theo.

A smile trembled on her lips as her eyes drank him in. With a little sigh, she stretched up and touched her lips to his. And in that small joining, she gave herself up to him. To fate. To love.

Theo went very still for an instant, and then his arms came hard around her. He kissed her, long and deep, hunger shimmering through them. His mouth teased and satisfied, his hands exploring, arousing. Theo felt as if he had been waiting for this half his life. He wanted to taste her all at once, to gulp her down like water to a thirsty man. At the same time, he wanted to savor her, to linger over every kiss, every touch.

Megan slid her hands into his hair, letting the silky strands slip across her skin. She was bombarded by new sensations, greedy to taste every one of them. Her hands slid down his neck and across the expanse of his shoulders, exploring the thick pad of muscle and the bony outcroppings of his shoulders and collarbone. His flesh was smooth and hot beneath her fingertips, and it spurred her own excitement to hear the quick intake of his breath when her fingers brushed over the sensitive skin, arousing him.

His chest was hard, the hair prickling against her fingers. Something coiled and tightened deep in her abdomen as she trailed her hands down over his chest and back up, and the warm ache between her legs blossomed.

He could feel the faint trembling of her fingers as she touched him, and both the touch of her skin and the evidence of her own urgency aroused him. Fire washed out across his skin and tightened in a ball in his belly. He ached to be inside her, to sink into her soft, welcoming warmth. But first there was the journey, the slow, drifting exploration, and that made it well worth the wait.

There was little that separated her flesh from his — a loose cotton gown that crumpled in his searching hands, easily pushed up until his fingers could roam beneath it over her bare flesh. His palms slid up the smooth line of leg and hip and onto her side. He felt the hard cage of her ribs beneath her skin, and he ran his fingertips along the lines of the bones, then up until he touched the satiny curve of her breast.

Megan drew in her breath in a sharp gasp, shaken by the wave of intense desire that swamped her. Her breasts turned swollen and heavy, the nipples tightening in a sudden, intense ache of passion. She dug her fingers into his shoulders and, turning her head, nipped gently at his arm. He let out a groan, and his hand moved more urgently across her breasts, stroking and squeezing.

His mouth left her lips to roam down her throat, nibbling and kissing the sensitive flesh, until he ran into the obstruction of her gown. With a soft oath of frustration, he pulled back and grasped her nightgown, pulling it up over her head and tossing it away. Gently he eased her back down on the bed, then paused for a moment, his eyes roaming over her naked body, washed by the flickering golden glow of the candle-light.

"You are beautiful," he murmured hoarsely. "So beautiful . . ."

Slowly he caressed her, watching his hand as it moved across her creamy skin, delighting in the sight of her nipples prickling in response to his touch. He stroked down across the soft skin of her stomach, and Megan twisted beneath him, her body thrumming with passion. He ran his fingertips down over her hip and along the side of her thigh, then moved back up, sliding them between her legs. She clamped her legs together, startled, but at the same time suddenly, intensely, aroused.

Theo smiled down into her eyes as his hands moved slowly up, separating her legs. Her breath rasped in her throat, and her legs fell apart, opening to him. Megan closed her eyes, giving herself over to the sensation.

His fingers were on her, slipping across the slick flesh, opening, teasing, stroking. Megan gasped, and her heart seemed to wobble in her chest as heat rolled and twisted through her.

She was all feeling now, every inch of her alive to each new pleasure that rippled through her body. With every moment, she was sure that she had reached the height of sensation, that she could feel nothing more intense than what she felt right then, and in the next instant, she was trembling under the force of an even greater pleasure.

As his fingers caressed her, found and explored her most intimate flesh, Theo's mouth trailed across her chest and onto the supremely soft skin of her breasts. With tongue and lips and teeth he teased, stirring them both to an almost painful pleasure. When at last he took her nipple into his mouth, Megan let out a small whimper of delight.

She wanted, and with every stroke of his

tongue, each pull of his mouth, she wanted more. Megan dug her fingers into his shoulders, her wordless moans urging him on. He murmured her name against her skin, his voice thick with passion.

Desire was building in him, pounding like fury with every beat of his heart. The mists of passion clouded his brain as he struggled to maintain control.

Megan let out a low sob of pleasure, reason seeming to hang by a tenuous thread. Something was building in her, so forceful and stunning that her limbs trembled, tightened. She ached with the sweetest longing she had ever known. It was as if she were racing, racing toward her destination, fear tickling in the back of her mind that somehow the moment would end before she reached it.

His fingers slipped inside her as his mouth feasted on her breasts. And she shattered.

Before she could even gather her scattered wits or relax into that deep satisfaction, he was gently stoking her passion again, caressing her sensitized flesh into a renewal of hunger. Limp, exhausted from the storm of her release, she lay in a haze of pleasure, as he coaxed from her still more desire.

His hands went to her hips, lifting her as he slipped between her legs. Slowly he slid into her, filling her, astonishing her yet again with a new pleasure, a deep satisfaction at this final completion that far outran the brief slash of pain as he entered.

His mouth covered hers, his hunger compelling hers, as he began to move inside her. Megan's hands fisted in his hair, and she moved beneath him, driven to match his rhythm, to meet him passion for passion. This, above all else, was what she wanted, she knew. To be melded to him, to move with him, breath and heart surging as one.

She was his and he hers and, as they flung themselves higher, harder, faster, until they teetered on that last, fierce precipice, then tumbled over in an explosion of release, she knew that whatever else might happen, they would never again be apart. Where it mattered, in the center of them, they were united.

Megan awoke the next morning in her own bed. She stretched and lay still for a moment, a smile hovering about her lips, letting herself luxuriate for a little while in the pleasure that permeated her body.

She felt a little sore and bruised, used in

a wickedly delightful way. And she had never felt quite such satisfaction and happiness in her life.

Her smile widened to a grin as she stretched and sat up, pulling the sheets up to cover her nakedness. Her nightgown, she noted, was laid across the foot of her bed. Theo must have carried her in here sometime in the night, she thought. She had been so deeply asleep, she had not even known it.

Megan would have liked to have awakened in his bed, cuddled up to his long, hard body. Then they could have held one another as they had last night after they had made love, talking about nothing and everything, lazily caressing one another until the need had overtaken them and they had made love all over again, more slowly and thoroughly this time, but with no less cataclysmic pleasure.

But it wouldn't have done, she knew, for her to still be in his bed when the rest of the household got up. It would be a tremendous scandal if one of the maids had come in upon them, or if Megan ran into the duchess in the hallway as she made her way back to her room, still clad in her nightgown.

Secrecy, she knew, would have to be a

watchword of their relationship, however much it pained her. The fatalist in her knew that Theo was her destiny, that her heart was his for the rest of her life. The realist in her knew that she could be no more than a beloved mistress to a future duke. And if that knowledge ate a little at her happiness, well, that was simply something she would have to overcome, just as she would have to overcome the fierce disapproval of her family.

The important thing was that she had found her love, her life, and she had no intention of letting him go.

She rose and bathed, then dressed, in a quiet hum of happiness. She was late to breakfast, for the twins were long finished and already up in their schoolroom, so she grabbed only a quick bite and a cup of tea before she joined them.

"Miss Henderson! I mean, Mulcahey," Alex hastily amended. "You look beautiful."

"Why, thank you, Alex," Megan replied, her grin springing up again.

"What happened? Did you find out something about your brother?" Con asked, leaning forward, interested.

"A little," Megan admitted. "But I found out more about myself. And it's very nice."

The boys looked puzzled, but shrugged it off and returned to their studies. Megan tried to settle down to their schoolwork, too, but she found her mind wandering off with regularity, hopping from Theo to her future to the Cavendish Museum to speculation of just what had taken place on the day her brother died.

She was afraid she blushed later in the morning when Theo strolled in, and, after one dazzling smile for him, she struggled to keep her distance and an aloof manner.

She realized that she must not have done a very good job of it when, after Theo left, Con asked her bluntly, "Are you in love with Theo?"

"What? Don't be absurd," she said repressively.

Con and Alex rolled their eyes at one another, and Con went on, " 'Cause he's silly about you."

Alex nodded. "Just like Rafe was with Kyria." He screwed up his face in a puzzled look. "Are grown-ups *always* like that?"

Megan could not help but laugh. "I'm not sure. Perhaps they are. It's . . . fun to be silly about someone."

Con shook his head, and the boys bent their heads once again to their schoolwork.

She was going to have to be more careful, Megan thought. It would not do to let everyone see how she felt about Theo.

After lunch, when the boys were released for their science lesson, Megan went down to the garden to walk. It had become a habit with her during the time she had been here at Broughton House. Today she found Theo waiting for her.

They walked through the garden, talking and laughing, even sneaking a few heart-stopping kisses in the shadowed secrecy of the rose arbor. And for those few hours, she thought not at all about Julian Coffey or Andrew Barchester or the Cavendish Museum.

It wasn't until that evening, after the family supper, when the problem of Coffey intruded on her again. As she sat with the rest of the family in the piano room, chatting while Anna played a few popular tunes, Megan saw a young blond man stop outside in the hall. He looked into the room, and when Theo's head turned in his direction, he raised his eyebrows significantly. Theo rose, turning to look at Megan.

"Miss Mulcahey? I believe we have a matter that concerns you?" he said politely,

461

ignoring the interested glances of the rest of the family.

"Yes, of course." Megan rose, excusing herself to the duchess and the others, and followed Theo out into the hallway.

"Megan, this is Tom Quick," Theo introduced her.

"Ah, yes, the man who followed me," Megan replied tartly. "It's nice to actually meet you face-to-face."

Tom Quick shot her an unrepentant grin. "My pleasure."

"What brings you here, Tom?" Theo went on. He had set Quick to watch the museum after they had followed Andrew Barchester there the day before. "Did you learn something about Coffey?"

"I'm not sure, sir," Quick told him. "But there is something strange going on over at that museum."

"What?" Megan asked quickly. "Did Coffey do anything?"

"Not as I've seen, miss. I took a tour through the place today and poked about wherever I could without being obvious. Wandered about the grounds a bit. Didn't see anything untoward. But after it closed, I hung about where I could watch the entrance. Nothing happened. The clerk left, but your Mr. Coffey never did. Then, a little while ago, these two fellows came up to the place and somebody let them inside. Two or three more came, and one of them was that chap Barchester. A couple of them were women."

"Really? Interesting. What do you suppose they're doing there at night?" Theo mused.

"It could be nothing more than a meeting of the museum's trustees," Megan proffered.

"With women present?'

She shrugged. "I presume Lady Cavendish is one of the trustees."

"Maybe." Theo shrugged.

"But I think we ought to take a look," Megan went on.

Theo grinned at her. "I couldn't agree more."

So it was that, a few minutes later, they were sitting in a carriage outside the walls of the museum, gazing at its front door from across the street. There was nothing to indicate that anything was occurring inside — or even that there were any occupants. No lights shone behind the curtained windows. None burned outside.

"Let's look a little more closely," Theo suggested.

They slipped out of the carriage and

across the street, melting into the shadows as they moved toward the house. Tom Quick ran lightly up the front steps and tried the door. It was locked. They moved around the house, looking for a chink in a curtain, an open window, an unlocked door. They found none.

"Locked up tight," Theo concluded as they turned away from the back door. He looked at Tom, who grinned back.

"I could probably get the locks to tumble," Quick said in answer to Theo's unspoken question. "Have to improvise. Don't have any of my tools with me."

Theo hesitated, glancing at Megan. Her chin went up.

"Don't back out of this because I'm here," she told him. "I want to find out what's going on here as much as —"

She broke off at a noise inside. The three of them glanced at the doorway, then jumped away from it, slipping in behind a flowering bush a few feet from the door. They were silent, barely breathing, waiting.

The back door opened with a crack that made Megan's stretched nerves jump. There was a low murmur of voices, then the sounds of steps on the flagstone walkway. Several men walked out, followed by a woman. All were dressed in black, with hats pulled low on their heads. The woman was heavily veiled. Megan peered through the branches of the bush.

There was a pause, then a few more people emerged. There was no light from the house, and none of them carried a lantern, moving with the ease of familiarity in the darkened yard. In the dim light, it was difficult to see the faces of the dark figures.

Finally two more people exited the door, closing it behind them. One was a woman, heavily shrouded in a veiled hat. The other Megan recognized, even in the faint light, as Julian Coffey.

The two of them walked close together, her arm linked through his, and there was something about them that spoke to Megan of lovers. She exchanged a glance with Theo. He bent close and whispered in her ear, "I suggest we follow the woman."

Megan nodded emphatically, and as soon as the couple was out of sight, they slid out from behind the shrubbery and moved around the house after the dark figures. Sticking close to the shadows of trees and shrubbery, they trailed the couple out to the street.

There they paused, looking after the dark figures disappearing along the street in different directions. Tom nodded toward one of the men and took off after him, silent as a wraith. Theo and Megan slipped across the street and into the carriage. After a few whispered instructions to the coachman from Theo, the carriage began to roll slowly down the street.

They stayed well behind the couple, keeping them in sight. Before long, Coffey hailed a passing hansom and handed the woman up into it, kissing her hand before he closed the door.

Theo glanced at Megan. "Follow the woman?"

She nodded. "Yes. I want to find out who she is. Maybe she is a lever we can use against Coffey."

"I agree." He pushed aside the curtain and spoke to the coachman.

They followed the hansom, staying a discreet pace behind it. At last the cab came to a stop, and the woman got out. As they watched through a slit in the curtain, she walked up the steps to an elegant white Georgian mansion and entered.

Megan glanced up at Theo. "Any idea who lives there?"

"Oh, yes," Theo replied. "I do indeed. That is the home of the late Lord Scarle."

Megan stared. "Lady Scarle? Your Lady Scarle?"

"I must point out, she is not mine," Theo responded.

"My, my, my. So all the while she has been chasing you, she has had Coffey dangling, too."

"It would appear. Very interesting." He looked at Megan, light dancing in his eyes. "I think we shall have a number of calls to make tomorrow."

They drove home, talking over what they had seen that evening and speculating on what it all meant. When they reached Broughton House, they found it not dark, as they had expected, but with lights blazing.

"What the devil's going on here?" Theo murmured, and they quickly disembarked from the carriage and hurried inside.

They were met by the butler, looking rather less composed than he usually did. "Lord Raine!" he exclaimed, looking relieved, and strode forward to meet them. "I am so glad you have returned."

"What's wrong?"

"I'm afraid, sir, that someone attempted to break into the house."

"What?" Theo glanced over at Megan, then back to the butler.

"They were lurking in the rear garden. One of the footmen saw a man peeking in a rear window. He gave chase, setting up a cry, but by the time he and the others got outside, the intruders were gone." He paused, then added, "I thought it best to wait until you or Lord Reed came home and inform you of the attempt."

"Yes, that's good. No point in worrying my father." Theo politely ignored the fact that his father, far from worrying, probably would have forgotten about the whole matter by morning.

"Quite so." The butler was equally aware of his father's propensities. "The intruders did drop something, though. Simms found it beneath the window where he had seen the man peering in. Doubtless he used it to try to pry the window open."

The man held out his hand, with a slender rectangular object about four inches long held carefully between his forefinger and thumb, as though it might contaminate him.

"Excellent." Theo reached out for the object, and as he brought it closer, Megan saw that it was a folding pocketknife.

The butler, having accomplished his mission, bowed and left. Theo looked down at the knife, and Megan, watching him, saw the color drain from his face.

"Theo! What is it?" She moved to his side, alarmed.

Theo was staring at the knife as though it had turned into a snake in his hand.

"Are you all right?" Megan asked. "Do you recognize it?"

"Yes. Oh, yes, I recognize it, all right. It belongs to me." He turned his stunned face to look at her. "But ten years ago I lent it to Dennis."

18

A shiver ran down Megan's back.

"My brother?" she asked. "Dennis had it?"

"Yes. He had lost his, and he was cutting something, and I gave mine to him and told him to keep it till he got another one. But then . . ."

"This is absurd," Megan said crisply, dismissing her moment of superstitious fear. "It can't be the same one. It probably just looks like it."

"It is," Theo insisted, holding it out to her. "Turn it over. There are my initials scratched on the back. I did it when I was ten. I got it for Christmas, and Reed got one just like it, and he was forever picking mine up. So I scratched my initials in it. It was a good knife. I carried it for years."

Megan looked down at the knife, her thumb rubbing absently over the crudely carved *TM* on the handle.

"Coffey must have taken it from Dennis when he killed him," Megan said at last. She looked up at Theo. "It is the only thing that makes sense. No doubt Dennis tried to defend himself when Coffey attacked him, and when he killed Dennis, he pocketed the knife. God knows why — it would have given it all away if you had ever seen him with it."

Theo nodded. "You're right. Of course. It gave me a turn when I saw it — but of course that is the only way the knife could have gotten here. It must have been Coffey who tried to break in — well, it couldn't have been Coffey himself. But he must have sent someone to break in here tonight. Do you suppose he left it purposely? As some sort of warning?"

Megan shrugged. "It makes no sense. It only makes it clearer that Coffey killed Dennis."

"I cannot imagine what sort of game he is playing at," Theo mused, taking the knife and turning it over in his hand thoughtfully. "What could he hope to gain by breaking into our house?"

"I don't know. Perhaps, as you said, it is a kind of warning. Mayhap he is threatening to kill you the way he did Dennis."

"Yes, but usually a threat implies doing

harm if one doesn't do what someone else wants. But what is it Coffey wants? For us to stop digging into the past? This only makes me want to dig more."

"Perhaps he doesn't understand your personality."

"Or yours," Theo commented.

"There is something more going on here," Megan mused. "There has to be. Why were those people at the museum tonight? They were obviously acting in secrecy. They had no lights outside to guide their way, and there were no lights visible in the museum. They dressed all in black, and slipped in and out on foot, not in their carriages or cabs — yet their clothes indicated that they are a well-heeled group, the sort who have their own vehicles. The women were veiled. The men wore their hats low."

"Yes. They are clearly hiding," Theo agreed.

"But why? My guess is that whatever is going on, it is in the cellar."

"Because we could see no lights?" Theo asked. "That is what occurred to me — that they were holding their meeting below ground, where no light could shine through any windows."

"Exactly. That is also where someone hit

me over the head."

Theo smoothed his hand over her hair. "That is another thing Coffey will have to answer for," he murmured, as he bent and pressed his lips against her hair.

The stir of his breath, the gentle pressure of his lips, sent a shiver through Megan. Theo had to do very little, she thought, to melt her inside.

She smiled, stepping back from him a little to look up into his face. The soft light in his eyes stirred the flicker of desire into a flame. "You shouldn't do that here," she said softly. "Someone might see."

"Then you should not look at me like that," he replied. "For now I want only to do even more."

He slid his hands down the length of her arms and slowly back up. Megan thought about how his fingers would feel on the rest of her body. She swallowed, her eyes darkening.

She glanced uncertainly toward the stairs leading up to the bedrooms. "It — doesn't seem right — I mean, with all your family —"

He grinned and bent to nuzzle against her ear. "It seemed right enough last night."

Megan blushed. "I was . . . not using

reason last night."

"Then do not use it now." He kissed her earlobe and the sensitive spot on her neck right below it, returning to take the lobe between his teeth and nibble tenderly.

Megan let out a low moan, and her knees sagged a little. She curled her hands into the front of his suit jacket, unconsciously turning her head to the side to give him better access to her throat.

He lifted his head. "I have an idea."

Megan looked up at him somewhat dazedly. "What?"

"Come. I'll show you."

Theo took her hand and led her down the hall, stopping in the library to pull the afghan from the back of the comfortable leather couch there. Tucking it under his arm, he whisked Megan out through the conservatory and onto the terrace.

"What — where are you — Theo, what if the men who tried to break in are still out here somewhere?"

"Shh." Theo silenced her with a quick kiss. "They are long gone by now. I'm sure of it. Coffey would not risk being found in our garden. Now, come . . ."

He wrapped his arm around her waist, pulling her down the steps and along the path into the garden. They wound through the garden and finally reached the rose arbor.

Latticework frames arched over an earthen pathway, and rose bushes, years and years old, grew up and over the lattice-work, thick with flowers of all sizes and colors. In the day it was a cool, pleasant re-treat. At night it was dark, lit only by the pale moonlight filtering through the climbing roses.

Theo laid out the afghan upon the earth floor, and he pulled Megan down upon it with him. Petals were scattered all over the earth around them, and their heady aroma filled the air.

They knelt, facing each other, and Theo reached up to take the pins from Megan's hair, letting it tumble in soft curls around her shoulders. He slid his hands into her hair, and leaned forward to kiss her, his lips soft and tantalizing on hers.

"Is this all right?" he asked, his voice husky with desire.

"It's perfect," Megan answered, sliding her arms around his neck.

And so they made love there, amid the rose petals, the moonlight dappling their naked skin, their sighs and moans lost in the soft darkness, their passion flowing, circling ever higher, until at last they were lost together in a final, shattering explosion of pleasure.

Afterward, Theo wrapped the thin blanket around them, and they lay together, legs entwined, Megan's head cradled on his shoulder, as they talked and dozed, sated. Megan did not know what lay in the future, or even what the morrow would bring, but there and then, cocooned in the soft summer night, she knew she had never been happier.

Megan went down to breakfast late the next morning. Indeed, she realized, with a glance at the clock on the sideboard, that it was closer to luncheon than breakfast time. She flushed, remembering the reason that she had slept so late that morning — she had gotten little sleep the night before, slipping in the back door of the house with Theo only a little before dawn.

She found no one but Theo in the breakfast room, and he rose with a smile, his eyes lighting up.

"Hello," he said, coming around the table to pull out her chair for her. Bending down, he murmured in her ear, "I have been hanging about drinking coffee until I am sure the servants think I am mad, hoping that you would come in."

Megan smiled to herself and cast a glance toward the sideboard, where a footman stood ready to serve her tea.

Theo went back around to sit down across from her. "I told the twins to go ahead with their lessons alone this morning," he went on. "I think we have too much to do today for you to work with them."

Megan nodded and took a sip of tea. "We need to talk to Mr. Coffey."

"And I would like a closer look at the basement of the museum."

"Yes." Megan got up to browse through the chafing dishes lined up on the sideboard and chose what she wanted. When she returned and set her plate on the table before her, she went on, "Most interesting of all, perhaps — we need to interview Lady Scarle."

Theo grinned wickedly. "Ah, yes. I thought that would be the highlight of your day."

Megan nodded as she tucked into her eggs with gusto.

"The only question is, what shall we do first?"

They discussed the matter as Megan ate and had still not made a decision when another of the footmen came to the door and paused on the threshold.

"My lord?"

Theo glanced up at him, something in the footman's voice alerting him. "Yes? What is it?"

"There is . . . a person here who claims to know you," the footman said carefully.

Even Megan, unused to the subtleties of the English servant's demeanor, caught the tone of disapproval in the footman's voice. Whoever was requesting admittance was clearly someone whom the servant did not think belonged here — or shouldn't be speaking to Lord Raine.

"Who is it?"

"I do not know, sir. He refused to tell me his name. He said that he wanted to speak only to you. He is . . . well, rather oddly dressed."

"Indeed? You intrigue me, Robert. Show him in."

"My lord . . ." He paused, polite distress clear on his face.

Theo said, "Perhaps I should go out to see him."

The footman's face cleared. "I think that would be best, sir."

Theo glanced at Megan and smiled. "Care to come?"

"After that? You couldn't keep me away."

Megan joined him.

They followed Robert's rigid back down the hall and into the large formal entryway of Broughton House. A man and a boy stood there, with another of the Morelands' footmen eyeing the two as if they might at any moment make off with some of the furniture.

The man and child were indeed an odd sight. They wore leather sandals on their bare feet, the straps wrapping up around their calves halfway to their knees. Above the sandals, their legs were bare to a bit above the knee, where the fringe of their brightly colored tunics dangled. The tunics hung straight from their shoulders, with holes for their arms, and were woven in a checkerboard fashion, each square containing geometric designs in orange and brown. The man wore a wide gold band around one bared bicep.

The boy looked to be about eight or nine. His skin was tanned, and his large, liquid eyes were a deep, dark brown. His thick black hair hung straight as a board down to his shoulders, with short bangs adorning his forehead. The man's hair was also long, but was pulled up to the crown of his head and caught in a leather thong wrapped around it for three or four inches, with the rest of his hair spilling out from it. His coloring, however, was different from the boy's — his skin several shades lighter, and his eyes not the color of chocolate but a light brown with an undertone of cinnamon. His hair, too, was lighter, with a hint of red, and it curled rather than hung straight. He looked to be perhaps twenty.

The younger visitor regarded Megan and Theo with stony suspicion. The older one smiled as he looked at Theo.

"Hello, Th—" His gaze shifted to Megan, and his jaw dropped. "Megan?"

Megan felt as if her stomach had turned to ice. She stared at the man, unable to speak.

"Bloody hell!" Theo rasped out. "My God — Dennis? Is that you?"

The man smiled a little crookedly. "Yes. It is I. I came because, well, you always said you would help me if I ever needed it. And I need it now."

"Dennis!" Tears shimmered in Megan's eyes, and suddenly her locked knees were able to move again. She flung herself forward, straight into her brother's arms. "I thought you were dead!"

The young man wrapped his arms around her and squeezed her tightly to him. "Ah, Megan, it's good to see you."

Theo stepped forward, exclaiming, "So it was you in the garden last night!"

"Yes," Dennis admitted, looking somewhat abashed. "I wanted to reach you without anyone knowing. But clearly you are a difficult man to sneak up on."

For the next few moments, there was nothing but hugs and handshakes and claps on the back, along with amazed exclamations, while the two footmen looked on with great interest.

"But, wait," Theo said at last, stepping back and looking at his friend. "What am I doing? You must be hungry. We were just finishing breakfast. Come in and eat."

The four of them walked back to the breakfast room, Megan's arm linked through her brother's as though to make sure that he stayed right there with them. Her gaze kept sliding over to the boy who walked on the other side of Dennis and who regarded her with a solemn, unwinking gaze.

When they reached the breakfast room, Theo dismissed the footman, telling him that they would serve themselves, then closed the door. There was a moment of awkward silence as they stood, looking at each other. Then the boy tugged at Dennis's tunic and said something in a tongue

Megan did not recognize. Dennis responded, putting his hand on the boy's shoulder, and turned to Megan and Theo.

"I am sorry," he said, his words coming somewhat awkwardly. "I forgot — I wish to introduce you to my son, Manco. Manco, this is my good friend Theo. And this is my sister, your aunt Megan. You have heard me speak of them."

"I am honored," the boy replied formally, his words slightly accented, his manner stiff.

"Your son?" Megan's eyes began to fill again with tears as she looked at the boy. She felt as if her insides had been turned into mush. "Oh, my." She blinked away the tears and bent to look the boy in the eye. "I am very happy to meet you, Manco."

She turned back to Dennis. "I — I cannot take this in. Da and Deirdre will be so thrilled. Oh!" She turned to Theo, then back to Dennis. "We must tell them at once! We must go to them! You have me so rattled, I am scarcely able to think."

"Da is here? And Deirdre? What of Mary Margaret? And Sean and Robert?"

"They are still in New York. Only Da and Deirdre and I came to England. Mary Margaret and Sean are married. Oh,

Dennis!" Megan raised her hands to her face. "I can scarcely believe that you are alive. We thought you dead ten years ago. All this time . . ."

Guilt covered her brother's face. "I know. I am sorry. I hope you can forgive me. I wasn't sure what had happened. I feared you would all think I was dead. I wanted to let you know, to send you word, but — well, I could not."

"Why?" Now that the shock was fading somewhat, Megan's temper began to rise. "Do you realize how we all felt? How we mourned for you?" She fisted her hands on her hips and glared at him. "And all the while, you were fine. Fit as a fiddle and raising a family. And not bothering to even drop us a line?"

He began to grin, and Megan scowled at him.

"What? Do you think that's funny, then?"

"No, no," he hastened to say. "It is just — seeing you with your temper up — it is just so wonderful. I have missed you, Megan." He reached out and took her hand, squeezing it. "I will explain it all to you, I promise. But first . . ." He glanced toward his son. "Manco is tired from our journey. It has been very long, and he has had no time to rest or play."

"I do not need to rest," the boy put in, his chin tilting up proudly.

Dennis smiled down at him. "You have been strong, Manco, and I'm proud of you. But you need to eat, and then I think it might do you good to run around a bit and be a child for a little while."

"Yes, please, have something to eat." Theo gestured vaguely toward the sideboard. "I shall send a servant for my brothers. They are a bit older than your boy, but I am sure they will be happy to see him."

Theo stepped out to send a servant to fetch the twins, and Megan guided her brother and his son to the sideboard, helping them pile up plates of food. Manco looked rather distrustfully at the strange foodstuffs, but he sat down at the table and picked up a piece of bacon, sniffing it, then taking a bite. He smiled and finished it in two quick bites, then settled in for some serious eating.

Dennis, too, tucked into the food, and for a few minutes there was nothing but silence as they ate. The quiet was interrupted by the clatter of feet, and then the twins burst into the room.

"Robert said —" Con began, snapping

his mouth shut when his eyes fell upon Dennis and Manco.

He came to a dead halt, and his twin stumbled into his back, letting out an exclamation of irritation before his eyes, too, fell on the visitors, and they widened.

"Hullo," Alex said at last. His gaze swung toward his older brother. "Robert said you wanted us."

"I did, yes." Theo carefully kept his lips from twitching into a smile at his younger brothers' amazed expressions. "Constantine, Alexander, I would like to introduce you to our visitors. This is Miss Mulcahey's brother, Dennis, and his son, Manco."

"The one who's dead?" Con blurted out, then clamped his lips shut, looking abashed. "I — I mean —"

Dennis eased the moment by smiling. "Yes, I am the one who was dead. Only, as you can see, I wasn't very much so. How do you do, Master Moreland?"

"Very well, thank you," Con returned politely. "I am Con and this is Alex."

Both of them stepped forward to shake Dennis's hand manfully, then turned toward Manco.

The boy, younger and quite a bit smaller than the other two, had crossed his arms across his chest and was staring balefully at Con and Alex. His chin lifted proudly. "I am Manco."

Alex and Con nodded. They glanced at Megan, then back at the boy.

"We thought you might show Manco around the house and grounds," Theo suggested. "Show him some of your animals and toys."

Manco looked scornful at that suggestion. "I am not a little boy," he enunciated carefully. "I am a prince."

"A prince!" Alex and Con chorused in disbelief and exchanged a glance. Megan started to step in to try to save the deteriorating situation, but Dennis spoke before she could.

"His mother is one of the Chosen. His grandfather is a high priest, his uncle the ruler of the village," Dennis explained. "He will likely assume one of those positions when he is grown."

"Oh. Where do you live?" Con asked.

"Why do you wear those clothes?" Alex added.

"Boys, don't be rude," Megan cautioned.

"They're not rude, just curious," Dennis said easily. "We are from South America, where your brother Theo and I went."

"Up the Amazon?" Alex looked intrigued.

"Yes."

"The jungle?" Con added. "Are there parrots? And jaguars?"

Manco unbent a little. "Yes. I have seen many of these. You have not?"

"No. But we do have a boa constrictor," Con offered.

"Would you like to see?" Alex asked.

"Very well." Manco turned to his father, offering him a short, formal bow, then followed the twins out of the room.

Theo and Megan turned to Dennis expectantly. He sighed and ran his hands over his face.

"I hardly know where to begin," Dennis sighed.

"How about with what happened to you?" Theo asked. "I thought you were dead when we left."

"I was near enough to it," Dennis agreed. "I don't know exactly what happened. The last thing I remember was fighting with Coffey."

"Then he *was* the one who stabbed you?" Megan asked.

Dennis nodded. "Yes. I could tell that he wanted the things we had discovered in the cave. I could not keep watch on him, because I was tending to you. I was busy with the villagers, too. Trying to find out everything about them." He paused, then added a little sheepishly, "And talking to Tanta."

"Who?"

"The woman who healed you, Theo. She was one of the Chosen — a sort of priestess and healer. Only the best and most beautiful are admitted into their company, and they remain there at the temple until they marry, usually to a priest or warrior. I — she was beautiful. And I spent too much time with her." His expression turned grim. "Time I should have spent paying attention to what Coffey was doing."

"Did you catch him trying to steal something?" Megan asked.

"Yes. I found a sack beside his belongings, and I saw that there were goblets and bowls in it. I heard him in the inner cave, and I went in there to confront him. He — when I saw him, I realized how far gone he was in his desire for their gold. He had draped that golden cloak about him, and when I walked in, he was trying on a magnificent mask. It was gold, a jaguar mask, with an elaborate headdress attached to it. The eyes were emeralds. I told him to stop it, to take it all off. I told him he would anger the villagers, that they would hurt him for mocking their religion. He looked at me and said he was not mocking it."

Dennis gave a little shiver. "Even now, it unnerves me. It was so eerie, looking at him in that unearthly mask. He scarcely even sounded like himself. I went forward to jerk that mask from his head, and that is when he picked up the knife and attacked me. I was so stunned, I didn't move quickly enough. He had slashed me before I knew what he was about. Of course, I fought back. We stumbled back into the main cave in the course of our struggle. You came to." He nodded toward Theo. "You tried to help me, but he pushed you away and you fell. Hit your head or passed out from your illness, I'm not sure. He had cut me several times. I was growing weaker. I stumbled and fell, and he was on me. He stabbed me, and that is the last thing I remember. When I woke up, he was gone. So were you. Hell, I wasn't even in the cave anymore. I was down in the village. The villagers had carried me there and tended to me. They saved my life — pulled me back from the very brink of death."

"I thought you were already dead," Theo repeated. "God, Den, I'm sorry. I — when

I came to, Coffey told me you were dead. You looked gone, and I never doubted him. I was so weak. I didn't want to leave your body. I wanted to take you with us, but he insisted that we did not have the time. I regretted it a thousand times that I let him rush me off. I should have stayed. Or taken you with me."

"It is just as well that you did not," Megan pointed out crisply. "Mr. Coffey would have finished Dennis off if you had taken him with you."

"She's right," Dennis agreed. "The villagers healed me. If I had been with you, I would have been dead by nightfall."

"But I don't understand, Dennis," Megan said, moving closer to him and looking intently into his face. "Why did you stay there? Why did you not come home after you recovered?"

"Because I had fallen in love," he answered simply. "I married Tanta."

"But you could at least have told us!" Megan flared. "All those years we thought you were dead. Don't you know how Da grieved for you — how all of us grieved for you? We blamed Theo for your death. And he labored under a terrible guilt because he had been too weak to save you or even to take your body with him. Why couldn't

490

you have sent us word? Just a letter to let us know you were alive?"

"It is a very remote place, Megan. It's not that easy to get mail in or out."

"In ten years? You could have made one trip out of the jungle, couldn't you? Couldn't you have gone to a less remote village and given a letter to someone to send?"

"Yes, yes, of course I could have. I am sorry for your worry, Meg, and your pain. It's no surprise if you and Da and everyone hate me."

"Of course I don't hate you," Megan replied. "Nor will they. We could not hate you. But I don't understand why you didn't think about how we must have been feeling!"

"I did!" He looked at her with tortured eyes. "You must not think I did not care. But I could not tell you. I was sworn to secrecy." He looked toward Theo. "You know how we had taken an oath, the three of us, not to reveal the existence of that village. We could not let it be destroyed by outsiders."

"But that would not have happened!" Megan exclaimed. "I understand that this village was untouched, but just because you told Da about its existence, that wouldn't

491

have meant the whole world would have found out about it. Even if people had learned of it, surely it wouldn't have brought hordes of visitors to such a remote place."

"No. You don't understand. It isn't just that it is pristine and beautiful, though it is. Very. It isn't just that the people have not been subject to our diseases, have not been corrupted by the greed of the outside world. It is — well, even Theo doesn't know just how special the village really is."

He hesitated, looking from Megan to Theo and back again. "I must have your word," he said finally, "that you will not reveal what I am about to tell you."

"Of course we won't," Megan said in some irritation. "Theo has known of it for ten years and told no one until he revealed it to me the other night."

"I don't know if Theo told you about the people who lived there, the villagers. We thought that they were the descendants of the Incas who fled with their treasure from the Spanish invasion."

Megan nodded. "Yes, he told me that they still spoke the old language, still lived as their ancestors had done two or three hundred years ago."

"Well, it was more than that. We did not

realize . . . the fact is, they are not the descendants of those people. They *are* the people who fled the Spanish."

For a long moment, neither Megan nor Theo said anything, just stared at Dennis. Finally Megan looked to Theo, then back at her brother.

"Are you telling us," she said slowly, "that the people in that village are three hundred years old?"

"Not all of them," Dennis answered. "Only the older ones."

"They cannot die? They're immortal?" Theo asked skeptically.

"No. They can die. They can be wounded or grow ill or simply die from old age. But they do not age as quickly as we do. My wife, who, I promise you, looks to be no older than I, is a hundred years old. I didn't understand when she first told me, and then I didn't believe. But as I remained there and learned their language and grew to be able to communicate better, I realized that what she had told me was the literal truth. Her father was one of the men who escaped from the Spanish with the gold."

"How is that possible?" Megan asked, still unconvinced.

"I don't know the answer. The villagers

believe that the valley in which they live is magical. They think that because they fled from the Spanish with their treasures, and protected the religion of the old gods and saved their sacred objects, those ancient gods blessed them by showing them to this valley."

He looked at his sister and smiled at her expression. "I know," he said. "I could not accept that explanation, either. But neither could I deny the evidence that I saw with my own eyes — and I doubt that you can either. Look at me. Do I look any older than I did the last time you saw me?" He glanced from Megan to Theo.

"No," Megan admitted somewhat reluctantly. Except for his manner of hair and dress, Dennis looked exactly as he had when he left New York ten years before — like a nineteen-year-old man. Yet he was almost thirty now. He was three years older than she was, though she realized with some dismay that he looked several years younger than she.

"Once I started living there, I stopped aging, too. I don't know what it is. I have thought of several theories. There is what they call a cenote, a well, in the village, from which they draw their water. They believe that it is part of the magic. I wonder if perhaps it has some special property that slows the aging process. Or perhaps it is due to the herbs they use in their medicine. Their medicines do have unusual healing capabilities. I should have died from my wounds — I would have, I think, if I had had to depend on the care of European or American doctors. Yet my wounds healed, and with very little scarring. And they were able to pull Theo out of that fever. He was gravely ill. I was very afraid he would die, as Captain Eberhart had, from the fever. Tanta says that her healing power flows into her from the gods, and that it is her chanting, her spiritual connection, that brings about the healing. But I cannot help but think that there are superior healing qualities in the herbs they use in their salve. And in that tea they gave you."

"It was a foul-tasting potion," Theo commented, making a face.

"Yes, it is. They give it for any illness. And they drink that tea at all their religious ceremonies. After drinking it, one can see visions. I am inclined to believe that the lack of aging is connected in some way to the religious ceremonies, because the children grow rather normally. Manco looks much like a nine-year-old should, does he not? It is only after they reach puberty and begin to participate in the religious ceremonies that their aging begins to slow so dramatically. Is it in the water? The herbs? The wonderful air of that high valley? Or some combination of those things? Or, perhaps, as they think, it is a gift from their gods, some powerful magic that turns water and herbs into an elixir that protects one from disease and aging."

"The 'fountain of youth,'" Theo murmured.

"Exactly. That is what anyone who learned of this place would say," Dennis assented, nodding emphatically. "There are some drawbacks to their lack of aging. Again, I do not know for sure what causes it, but births are rare in the village. So there are few children. Ours is the only family that has produced two children, and I suspect that the major reason for that is that I grew to majority outside of the village. Manco was born soon after we were married. It was three more years before our daughter, Caya, was born. Since then, there have been no others. There are few pregnancies, and many of them end in miscarriage. But that fact would not stop the rest of the world from wanting to take that elixir. And you know what that would mean."

"Yes. The world would beat a path to their door," Theo answered.

"Without a doubt. Everyone would want to acquire that drink, that water, those herbs. People would swarm there, engulf the villagers, ruin that wonderful, beautiful place. I could not let that happen to them. I could not be the cause of their destruction."

"I see." Megan nodded, looking thoughtful. "But we would not have told anyone about it. You could have written to us and let us know, sworn us to secrecy."

"Maybe it would have been safe," he agreed. "But I could not be sure. What if my letter had gone astray? What if some curious person somewhere along the way had decided to open it and see what it said? What if the news had seemed so extraordinary that Da just had to mention it to someone? Or had felt he had to tell Aunt Bridget that I was all right, and she had to tell Mrs. Shaughnessy about this miraculous place. Or Mary Margaret carried the tale to the priest in confession? I just could not risk it, Megan. It wasn't for my sake. I had a duty to protect all those innocent villagers. I couldn't risk them, even to save you grief. And I didn't know that you thought Theo had killed me — why, in the name of all that's holy, did you believe that?"

"Because that is the tale that Coffey told," Theo explained.

"But why?"

"To keep the suspicion off himself," Megan replied. "Why do you think?"

"But Theo knew the truth."

"No. I didn't. I did not know that it was Coffey inside that mask. I had no idea who it was, and he convinced me that you had been killed by a village priest. That you had violated some religious practice or other, and so the priest had killed you and was after us. I was ill and weak, and he whisked me out of there. Then, though I did not know it, he told Barchester that I had killed you, and Barchester was kind enough to tell your parents that."

"Coffey!" Dennis sneered, his face twisting with contempt and hatred. "When I get my hands on him, it will be the last lie he'll ever tell." His fists knotted, and he went on, "That is why I am here."

"To kill Coffey?" Theo asked. "But why — I mean, after all this time?"

"Not for what he did to me." Dennis made a dismissive gesture with his hand.

"Not even for what he has done to us over the years. But now he has taken my daughter from me. He has kidnapped Caya!"

19

"Your daughter?" Megan repeated, stunned. "He stole your daughter? Oh, my God, that is the something precious that was taken from you!"

"What?"

Both Theo and Dennis looked at her in confusion.

"Deirdre had a dream," Megan said.

"Ah." Her brother nodded, understanding.

"What are you talking about?" Theo asked.

"My sister Deirdre. She has these dreams. . . . She sees things in them. Things that other people can't see. I didn't tell you, because I was afraid you would think I was crazy. That my whole family was."

Theo's eyebrows vaulted upward. "After *our* dream? Besides, the Morelands are always having . . . unusual dreams."

Megan shrugged. "Well, *I* had difficulty believing it. But Da has always believed that Deirdre has special abilities. She dreamed about Dennis. She dreamed that he was asking her for help, that he had lost something precious. Da was certain that you had stolen something from Dennis. We thought that you two had perhaps argued about it. It was why we came to London — to find out what had happened, to recover this 'precious' object so that Dennis could find peace. It never occurred to us that the something precious was a person."

"I have to get her back," Dennis said earnestly. "That is why I came to you, Theo. You were the only person I could think of who could help me. I'm desperate."

"Why has he taken her?" Theo exclaimed. "Has he gone mad?"

"I fear he has," Dennis replied. "He has become obsessed with whatever keeps the villagers from aging."

"He knows about that?"

Dennis nodded wearily. "Yes. Coffey came back. I noticed over the course of the next two or three years that other treasures went missing. That cloak and mask, for one thing. He was not able to take them with him the first time — he wouldn't have

501

had room for more than a few small items. But two years later, the cloak and mask disappeared. I suspected that Julian had taken them. The villagers were inclined to believe that the gods had simply used some of their belongings." He shrugged. "But eventually I persuaded them to put guards in that cave, at least in the dry season, when Julian was most likely to come. And they caught him."

"What happened?"

"We let him go." Dennis's expression hardened at the memory. "With his treasure. He threatened to reveal the existence of the village. That is what they fear most — the outside world discovering them. They think it will anger the gods, and they will lose all their magic. And I know it would destroy them."

"So he blackmailed the whole village."

"Essentially, yes. The villagers thought it would be easier and more pleasing to the gods to pay him a 'tribute' every year than to have the secret revealed."

"Why didn't they just put him in jail or something?" Megan asked. "I mean, he tried to kill you. He was stealing from them."

"The years of peaceful living in that place have changed the villagers. They live without war or fighting. The ancient Incas used to sacrifice animals and even people as part of their religious ceremonies. But these people have grown to believe that they are blessed in part because of the lack of violence in their lives. They don't even sacrifice animals now. They believe that the gifts of goldwork and food and such that they give the gods are sacrifice enough. They don't have a jail. They could not bring themselves to harm Coffey, and they had no facility for locking him up. Jail is a foreign concept to them, anyway."

Dennis stood up and began to pace. "Frankly, I thought about killing him myself. I am not sure if I could have done it, but I was sorely tempted. I suppose he had some inkling what I was considering, because he informed me that he had left a letter behind for his assistant at the museum. In it he detailed the location of the village and its treasure trove of Inca gold. If he did not return by a certain date, the assistant had instructions to read it and publicize it. I could not risk it. So, much as I hated it, I agreed with the others to let him take things. The best I could do was try to keep him from wholesale looting of the caves."

"So that is how he has turned the

Cavendish into such a fine museum."

"Oh, yes, he is quite proud of the job he has done with it. He has apparently gained some degree of acclaim and respect among the academic world. But that is only part of what drives him. The fact is, he has used what he brought back here to gain wealth and power. Not just his increasingly important position as the museum's director, but also power over people."

"What do you mean?" Megan's mind went back to the evening before, and the number of well-dressed men and women who had slipped secretively out of the museum.

"He didn't keep all of what he stole for the Cavendish. He sold some pieces to collectors. Got a good amount of money for it. Enough to set him up in the lifestyle he prefers. But there is more. He attracted a following. He began to exercise control over them."

"How?"

"Pieces of the treasure are not the only things he took from the village. He realized, of course, that the villagers must have an unusual ability to heal. He was stunned when he saw that I had recovered. Visiting the village as often as he did, seeing the people and beginning to pick up on their language — well, eventually he realized what I had, that these people have an enormous ability to resist injuries and diseases, that they live an amazingly long time. First he took some of the herbs. Apparently he was able to improve the health of his benefactor, Lord Cavendish. Others came to him. He helped them and charged them a great deal of money. He also started practicing a sort of religion. He was fascinated with the Incas and everything about them, including their spiritual beliefs. He began to combine what he knew about their religion with his own special touches. He burned the herbs and brewed them into tea, which he and his followers drank."

"So they saw visions?" Theo mused.

"Yes. And, according to Coffey, this 'religion' helped to bring them more power and wealth. I am not sure how much of that is real and how much is simply his followers' perception. I am fairly certain that he gained enormous power over Lady Cavendish, her wealth and the museum by ultimately speeding up her husband's demise. Used improperly, some of those plants he uses can be very dangerous."

"So he made the old man well, thus gaining trust and power, then he killed him and gained even more," Megan commented.

Her brother nodded. "He is a wicked man, but he is clever. He does not miss many chances."

"How do you know all this about him?" Megan asked curiously.

Dennis grimaced. "He told me. Bizarrely enough, I was the only person to whom he could speak freely. He couldn't boast to his followers about what he was doing to them, and he feared putting himself under the power of any underling. But there I was. Unlike the villagers, I spoke his language, and I had some idea of the world in which he lived. And I was too far away from England to do him any harm with the police or his followers. He wanted to brag about what he had done, the things he had achieved. So he told me about them."

"But why did he take your daughter?" Theo asked. "I don't understand. Does he plan to hold her over your head, so you cannot do anything to oppose him?"

Dennis's face grew dark with anger and fear. "He plans to kill her."

Megan let out a wordless cry and went to her brother. "Oh, Dennis. No!" She slipped her arms around him. "How can even he be such a monster?"

"There is nothing that is beyond him," Dennis said roughly, giving Megan a hug before he turned away and sat down, burying his face in his hands. "Power and wealth are no longer enough for him. Now he wants immortality. He wants to live forever."

"Like the villagers," Theo commented.

"Exactly. He wants to live an enormously long life himself. Also, he sees it as an opportunity to gain even more control over his followers. But he could see that even though he drank the tea and applied the salves, it was not keeping him young. Every year when he returned, it was obvious that he had aged and I had not. So he kept trying to discover the specific formula that keeps us young. He already had the herbs, so next he took some of the water from the sacred cenote back with him. When that didn't do the trick, he decided that it must be because he had not put the tea in the goblet that the villagers use. So he took that a year ago. Obviously that did not work, either.

"I didn't tell him that his efforts were probably useless. The villagers believe that if they leave their secret valley, if they go out beyond the caves into the world, they will become their true age very quickly. They will wither and die. That is why only Manco and I could pursue Coffey after he kidnapped Caya. My true age is still young, and Manco has not started the sacred rituals yet."

"But what does any of that have to do with taking your daughter?" Megan asked.

"The last time Coffey came to the village, he talked to me about the religion he had made up, part the worship that the Incas used and part his own crazy additions. Truthfully, I did not pay a great deal of attention to what he said. I hated having to listen to him, allowing him to steal from my people. But he talked about the ritual of human sacrifice that the Incas employed. He wondered if perhaps it was not following this ritual that kept his 'youth potion' from working. You see, at certain important times, the Incas would sacrifice children to appease or praise the gods, or when a new emperor took the throne. They used only the most beautiful, the most perfect child, and they would give it a ritual wine to drink, intended to make their end less painful. Then they would bury the child high in the mountains. It was considered an honor, and the child was dressed in the finest clothes, buried with a toy or doll. Oh, God . . ."

His voice broke, and he hunched over, his face in his hands. "I should have explained to him that the villagers no longer employed that ceremony, that the potion did not need blood. I should have made him understand that it worked only there in that valley. But I did not realize that he meant to kill a child!"

He raised his head, his eyes wild with pain. "If only I had killed the bastard then, when I had the chance! But it wasn't until after he took Caya with him that it occurred to me what he intended to do. She is the most beautiful child, the daughter of one of the Chosen. She would doubtless have grown to be chosen herself. He must have decided that the sacrifice should be of an Inca child, not some child here in London." He let out a little groan. "God, for all I know, he might have tried doing this ceremony before with an English child, and it didn't work. Now he is going to kill Caya!"

"He won't," Theo said firmly. "We will stop him." He put his hand on Dennis's shoulder, gripping it firmly.

"Yes. You are right. I cannot give in to panic. I have to stop him." Dennis stood up. "Coffey will not have done it yet. He would wait for the full moon. There would be ceremonies leading up to it. But I cannot predict exactly what he will do. He has changed the ancient rituals to suit himself in many instances." He looked at them, his hands knotting into fists. "Tonight is the full moon."

"We shall move on it immediately," Theo promised. He looked from Dennis to Megan. "We need to make plans."

The others nodded, and Theo went on, "I think the most likely place for him to be hiding your daughter is at the museum." He glanced at Megan. "That is probably why you got knocked on the head the night of the benefit. Caya was probably being held down in the cellar somewhere, and Coffey was afraid you might stumble upon her."

Megan gasped as a memory flashed into her brain. "Yes! I just remembered. Oh, my God, how could I have forgotten?" Megan put her fingertips to her temples, pressing in. "I heard a noise. I was creeping along after Barchester when I heard a faint sound. I turned around, and that is when someone hit me over the head. But the sound I heard — it was crying. Faint and weak, but I am sure that is what it was. She must have been locked in a room nearby!"

Anguish filled her as she thought of how close she had been to her brother's daughter and had not even known it. "If only I had done something!"

"You couldn't have done anything," Theo reassured her, taking her hand and bringing it tenderly to his lips. "Someone hit you and dragged you away. It is no wonder you did not remember every detail. Besides, by the time we found you, Coffey had probably whisked her away from there to a more secure hiding place. I doubt we would have found any sign of her."

Megan squeezed his fingers in gratitude, then said, "But we cannot fail her now. We have to get her out. We should go to the authorities and tell them about this. They could search the museum."

"Tell them what?" Dennis retorted in a scornful voice. "You think anyone else would believe this tale? Inca sacrifice? People who do not age? The police would laugh in our faces."

"You're right." Megan nodded. "I would not believe it myself."

"We must do it ourselves," Theo said. "The question is whether to walk straight in and confront Coffey now with what we know and seize your daughter, or wait until tonight and sneak in and surprise them."

"If we talk to him this afternoon, we run the risk of alerting him and letting him hide Caya someplace else," Dennis pointed out.

"But if we wait until tonight, then we have to be completely certain that we have the right time and place. We cannot get there too late," Megan put in.

"How many men will we be facing?" Dennis asked.

"I'm not sure. I would say there were perhaps fifteen to twenty people leaving the meeting last night." Theo glanced at Megan for confirmation, and she nodded.

"And we are two," Dennis said heavily. "But we will be armed and have the element of surprise."

"We will be four," Theo told him. "We can count on my brother Reed and Tom Quick to help us. Unfortunately, Rafe and Stephen have gone to the horse sales at Newmarket."

"We will be five," Megan corrected. "You did not count me in the mix."

Dennis stared at her. "You cannot go!"

"I most certainly can, and I intend to. Surely you don't think I'm going to let the two of you run off on your own and do this."

"Megan!" Dennis expostulated. "It is too dangerous."

"I am quite grown up now, and you

don't have to play the big brother any-more," Megan retorted.

They began to talk over each other, and Theo crossed his arms and settled down to watch the two of them with an expression of amused interest.

But before they had gotten into a good wrangle, there was the sound of a commotion in the hallway and a footman's voice raised in exclamations, and above it all floated a voice, with a thick Irish accent.

"Don't you be telling me what I can or cannot do, you puffed-up, pompous little British —"

Another voice entered the fray. "Papa! Please. I am sure that Megan is all right."

"Mr. Mulcahey." This was an educated English accent, somewhat anxious sounding.

"Da!" Megan and Dennis exclaimed softly.

"And Barchester," Theo added grimly.

"Devil take you, you'll not be hiding me daughter from me!" Frank Mulcahey burst out.

"Bloody hell!" Theo muttered.

"It is better if Barchester does not see you," Theo told Dennis. "He may be an innocent pawn, or he may be in it up to his eyeballs. You stay here. Megan and I will do our best to settle this."

Taking Megan's arm, Theo swept her out the door and into the hallway, closing the door to the breakfast room behind him. At the other end of the hall they saw the footman Robert, under siege yet again today, backing up slowly before Deirdre, Barchester and an enraged Frank Mulcahey.

"Da! What are you doing?" Megan exclaimed. "Stop attacking poor Robert."

Robert turned, relief written clearly on his face, "Miss. My lord. I am terribly sorry. . . ."

Theo's mouth curved up into a half smile. "No need to apologize, Robert. I understand perfectly. It's all right. You may go now." His gaze turned to Frank Mulcahey, and he strode forward, extending his hand. "Mr. Mulcahey, I am pleased to make your acquaintance at last."

Red flooded Mulcahey's face, and he clenched his fist. For one anxious moment Megan was afraid that her father was going to launch himself at Theo. Instead, he shook his fist and roared, "Don't you 'Mr. Mulcahey' me, you spawn of the devil. You murdered my boy, and now you've sweet-talked my own daughter into turning against her family! Don't think I don't

514

know your game! You won't get away with it while I've breath in me body. I'll —"

"Da! Hush!" Megan exclaimed, coming forward to join them. "No one has turned me against my family. No one could. You don't know the facts, and you're talking nonsense. Deirdre . . . help me." She turned her gaze in appeal toward her sister.

"That is what we are trying to do," Deirdre answered, looking troubled. "Mr. Barchester came to us and told us that you —"

"Ah, yes, Barchester." Theo turned cold eyes on the man. "Clearly I can count on you to stick your hand in."

"Aye, and it's a good thing he did!" Frank retorted. "If he had not told us you had filled Megan's head with nonsense, we wouldn't have known to come rescue her. Let me tell you, you're not holding my daughter here against her will. I am taking her with me."

"Da! No one is holding me against my will. And no one has filled my head with nonsense. I'm not a child. It is Barchester who has been telling you lies. Theo did not kill Dennis."

"Bah! Just like Andrew said you would say," Frank retorted darkly. "How could you believe that murderer?"

"Because he told me the truth," Megan replied simply. "Da, Deirdre, you know me. Am I the sort to swallow whatever lies anyone tells me?"

"No," Mulcahey admitted. "But 'tis obvious that he is a canny bastard."

"That is twice that you have insulted my parents, sir," Theo said calmly. "In my own home."

"Theo! Don't you get up on your high horse, too," Megan protested. "Da, I want you and Deirdre to sit down and listen to me. I don't know what Mr. Barchester told you, but —"

"I went to Julian," Barchester interrupted. "Miss Mulcahey, you have to listen to me. Julian told me what happened. He explained how Raine was probably drugging you."

"Drugging me!"

"Yes," Barchester replied earnestly. "You probably do not even realize it. It is easy to put something in one's food or drink, and —"

"Yes, or in the tea one ingests during a ceremony," Megan retorted.

Barchester paled. "What? How do you —"

"We know it all, Barchester," Theo said firmly. "We know about the supposed 'religion' Coffey has been operating the past

516

few years. About the tea you drink that produces visions — or does he keep that to himself, making you think his hallucinations are some special link he has to the otherworld?"

"You don't know what you are talking about," Barchester protested, but his voice was weak. "Julian is an extraordinary man. . . ."

"What the devil are you talking about?" Megan's father looked from Theo to Barchester, frowning. "What is all this blather about religion? The point is that you murdered my son, Moreland, and I am here to see you pay for that."

"Julian Coffey is the one who stabbed Dennis and left him bleeding," Theo replied. "Not I."

"That's a lie," Barchester snapped.

"No," said a voice behind them, and they all whirled around. Dennis was standing in the doorway. "No, Da, it is not a lie. Theo did not kill me. I am here and alive, as you can see. But Julian Coffey did his best to kill me. And tonight he intends to kill my daughter, unless we stop him."

There was a moment of blank silence. Megan's father and sister stared at Dennis, their faces paling visibly. Barchester looked almost as astonished. None of them could say a word. Theo spun around.

"Blast it, Den, Barchester could go to Coffey," Theo told him.

"Not if we tie him up," Dennis retorted. "I could not just hide there and let this go on."

Dennis strode toward Frank and Deirdre. "Da. Dee. It's me. I swear to you that Theo did not try to kill me. I came here because I trust Theo more than anyone else."

With an inarticulate cry, Deirdre threw herself into Dennis's arms, and Frank wrapped his arms around both of them. Andrew Barchester continued to look at the man as if he had been poleaxed. Theo circled around the group, positioning himself so that he was between Barchester and the door.

Finally the Mulcaheys released Dennis and stepped back, smiling and wiping away their tears. Frank turned and sent a sharp look at Megan. "You knew about this, and you didn't tell us?"

"No! No! I was sure that Theo did not kill Dennis, but I did not know he was alive until just a few minutes ago, when he walked in the door," Megan hastened to assure her father.

"I don't understand," Barchester said

faintly. "Dennis . . . how . . . what . . . ?"

"Why are you dressed that way?" Frank Mulcahey put in, puzzlement seeping into his happiness.

"I will tell you. I'll explain everything. Let's go in and sit down."

Theo gestured toward the closest room to them, which turned out to be what the Morelands called the French salon, a large formally decorated room with an ornate marbled fireplace and furniture in the style of Louis XIV. The group shuffled into the room, with Theo carefully bringing up the rear. He closed the double doors behind him and, as they did not lock, stood with his back to them.

Everyone else sat down on the sofa and chairs in the center of the room, then turned expectantly to Dennis. He started his story again, telling them how Julian Coffey had tried to kill him, then had left him for dead.

"Are you sure it was Julian?" Barchester asked, frowning. "I mean, if he had on a mask . . ."

"It was Coffey," Dennis told him flatly. "I spoke to him. I recognized his voice. It could not have been anyone else. The villagers did not speak English, and Theo was flat on his back with a fever out in the main cave. Besides, I have spoken to him several times since then. Obviously he wanted you to continue to think that I had died. That Theo had killed me. But Julian has known for years that I am still alive."

He went on to describe Coffey's continuing thefts from the village, though in a somewhat abbreviated version, leaving out much of what he had told Theo and Megan about the people of his village. He was interrupted frequently by exclamations and questions. When he reached the end, detailing his frantic trip to rescue his daughter, his father jumped up with a loud oath.

"That murderin' bastard!" He glared at Barchester. "Have you no sense, man? Has this fellow Coffey pulled the wool over your eyes? Or are you in league with the devil?"

"No! I — I promise you!" Barchester looked shaken. He stared around the room at the others. "I had no idea! I cannot believe it. Julian is — he seems to be a great man. He has helped me, helped all of us. He has — I thought he had powers that no ordinary man could, that he was . . . *sent*." He looked at them pleadingly. "He has talked about tonight, of course, how special and important it is. He — he even spoke of the possibility of sacrifice. In the past we have brought objects of value to give to the gods — gold and diamonds and things of that nature."

Frank Mulcahey let out a snort. "Ah, you're a green one, aren't you? Gifts for the gods, in a pig's eye. Gifts for Coffey."

"He healed Lord Cavendish of pneumonia," Barchester told him stiffly.

"And how did Lord Cavendish die?" Theo put in harshly. "Your great man Coffey told Dennis that he helped the old man along at Lady Cavendish's request."

"What?" Barchester's eyes widened and he looked from one to the other. "No! That is impossible. Cavendish was old. Ill. It was a blessing that he finally died."

"A blessing to Lady Cavendish," Megan responded dryly.

Barchester turned to Dennis. "Are you sure? He told you that?"

"Yes. He told me a great deal about what he was doing. He is proud of the way he has deluded all of you into thinking he is all-powerful. The worst thing, though, is that now he is beginning to believe his own nonsense."

"Oh, my God." Barchester sank his head into his hands. "What have I done?" He raised his head and gazed at Dennis bleakly. "He said the gods required blood. But he intimated that it would be an animal. A goat, like the Incas used. Surely he cannot mean to kill a child!"

"He can, and he will," Dennis returned coldly, "if we do not stop him."

"We will stop him," Frank told him firmly. "We will go over there and get the girl from him."

"Sorry, Barchester," Theo told him. "I am afraid that we will have to lock you up. I will make sure you have a cot to lie on and water to drink. But we cannot let you loose to tell him."

"I wouldn't," Barchester protested. "What kind of man do you think I am?"

"That I'm not sure of."

Barchester looked abashed. "I know I have given you no reason to like me. I have been naive. Worse, I guess. I have gone along far too willingly in my own deception. I — let me try to make it up to you. Let me help you."

"How?" Dennis and Theo regarded him with identically guarded expressions.

"I can get you inside. I will sneak you into the museum before the ceremony starts. I know where Julian keeps the keys. We can go down to the basement and find the room where he is keeping the girl, and get her out of there before the ceremony."

Theo shook his head. "How can we trust you? How can we be sure you will not tell Coffey about our plans and help him hide the girl somewhere else?"

Barchester stiffened. "I give you my word as a gentleman."

Theo arched a brow. "I don't think that is good enough. Not when a girl's life is as stake."

"It would be helpful if he sneaked us in," Dennis pointed out.

"Lock him up," Frank suggested. "Don't let him out until we are ready to go over there. That way he cannot give away our plans to Coffey. We can make sure that he leads us to your daughter."

For the next hour or so, they hashed over their plans, until finally they settled on Frank's suggestion of locking Barchester in a room until it was time to rescue Caya, then taking him with them to guide them. They decided to leave right after dark, when they would be less noticeable sneaking into the museum, but before the other participants started arriving for the ceremony.

"Do you have guns for us to carry, Moreland?" Frank asked. "We should be armed."

"I have a couple of revolvers," Theo said, eyeing him askance. "But surely, Mr. Mulcahey . . . you are not planning on going."

"Of course I am. Why the devil wouldn't I?"

"Da, no, you might get hurt," Megan said without thinking.

"Oh, I might, might I?" he replied, putting his fists on his hips pugnaciously. "So it's feeble I am now?"

Megan sighed, realizing she had said exactly the wrong thing. "No, I don't think you are feeble. But we cannot have too many of us there or we shall be too easily noticed."

" 'Us'?" Frank raised his eyebrows so high that they threatened to disappear into his hair. " 'Us'? So you're saying that you are planning to go in, but I am too many?"

Megan scrambled to think of the right way to phrase her words to keep her father from objecting, but Theo was there before her, saying smoothly, "We need all the help we can get, Mr. Mulcahey. But Megan is right. We cannot have too many people entering the house, or someone will be bound to notice. But we will need to have someone in reserve — in case we get into trouble. If you and Megan could wait on the grounds or in the carriage, where no one could see you, then if we don't return in a reasonable time, you could sound the alarm."

"Hmm." Frank frowned, glancing from Theo to his daughter somewhat suspiciously.

Over her father's head, Theo sent Megan a significant look. She knew what he was trying to do. She could keep her father out of harm's way by standing watch with him outside, away from the actual fray. Of course, that would also serve the purpose of keeping *her* out of harm's way, a factor she was certain was not lost on Theo. He had caught her pretty neatly, she thought.

The idea rankled, but Megan was also sensible enough to admit that, much as she would have liked to be in the thick of the fray, it made more sense for her and her father to remain outside and the men to enter the house. Theo's brother Reed and Tom Quick would be handier with their fists if the need arose than either she or Frank.

Sending Theo back a sharp look to let him know that she was aware of exactly what he was doing, Megan replied, "Yes, I suppose you are right. We should wait outside, Da. In reserve, so to speak, in case they run into trouble."

"I will give you one of my revolvers, sir," Theo promised her father, leaning forward to say in a quiet voice, "if you will stay with Megan and watch out for her, it would be a great help to Dennis and me."

"Aye, I understand," Frank agreed. "I'll do that. No need for you and Den to be worrying your heads on that score."

With that matter arranged, they settled down to making plans for the evening raid on the museum. First they tucked Barchester away in one of the guest rooms of the house, the door locked to make sure he could not get away to warn Coffey if his expressions of remorse and willingness to help were merely playacting.

Theo sent for Tom Quick, then went upstairs to engage his brother's aid for their project. Dennis and Megan took the other Mulcaheys upstairs to meet Dennis's son.

The afternoon was a quiet, loving interlude in the action of the day. Despite the worry over Dennis's daughter, Megan and her family could not help but rejoice in this time spent together. For years certain that their brother and son was dead, murdered, they were filled with elation to be able to be with Dennis, to talk and laugh and, for this little while, to be the family they once were.

While Deirdre and Frank were talking to Dennis's son, Dennis took Megan aside, saying, "Let's walk for a bit, shall we?"

"All right." She led him down the stairs and out into the garden behind the house.

Theo had lent Dennis some of his clothes, and except for his longer hair, he now looked very much like the brother she had once known. He was silent at first, and Megan glanced over at him, wondering what had made him pull her away from the others.

"You and Theo . . ." he began slowly.

"Yes? What about us?"

"He is a good man," Dennis said quietly. "I want you to know — if I could have chosen someone for my sister to marry, it would have been Theo."

Megan smiled, unaware of the trace of sadness in her eyes. "I am not marrying Theo. Don't be absurd."

"Do you love him?"

Megan's eyes flew to her brother's. "Dennis . . ."

"Well, do you?"

"What if I did? It would not matter. You don't understand. I wouldn't have, really, until I had been here for a while. Theo is going to be a duke someday. He has responsibilities. There are certain expectations."

"I never thought I would hear you spouting such poppycock," Dennis retorted.

Megan grimaced. "I am being realistic. That is all."

"No. You are being foolish. Either that or you don't really know Theo."

Megan's eyes flashed, and she opened her mouth to retort hotly, but Dennis went on hastily, "The Morelands marry as they wish. All you have to do is look around you to know that is so."

"I know that his brother and sisters married to suit themselves. But they are not going to be the ones to carry on the title. It's a different thing."

"And what about his father?" Dennis asked quietly. "Theo told me how his parents met and married. The duchess was not a titled lady. Or even anyone that his family or peers would have considered suitable, I imagine. She was a reformer. A bluestocking, Theo called it."

Megan simply looked at him, whatever she might have replied dying in her mouth. It was true. The duchess came from a good family, but her father had been merely a scholarly gentleman, with no title.

"I think you are trying to prepare yourself for the worst because you are afraid," Dennis went on. "Afraid that he does not love you enough to marry you."

His words pierced her, and Megan's hand went to her chest, as though to protect herself from the wound. *Was he right?* Megan knew, had known from the moment she remembered her dream, that she loved Theo beyond anything, that she was fated to love him the rest of her life. He loved her in return, she had told herself; he could not have made love to her in that way if he had not.

But Theo had never uttered the words. He had not said, *I love you.*

And Megan knew, with a pang, that Dennis had indeed touched upon her deepest fear. *When this was over, would she lose Theo? He was the love of her life, but what if she was not the love of his?*

20

They set out on their mission in the early evening. The sun had set, and dusk had fallen, deepening the shadows that pooled around the bushes and trees that surrounded the museum.

It took two carriages to carry them all. Deirdre had remained behind with Manco, despite both their protests. Barchester rode in the first carriage, with Tom Quick and Reed watching him. Dennis and Theo followed, with Megan and her father.

The carriages stopped around the corner from the front entrance. They disembarked swiftly, moving along the dark street to the drive and onto the grounds of the museum. They melted into the shadows of the trees that lined the drive, walking around to the back of the old house.

Theo took Megan's hand in his and squeezed it gently. She looked up at him, her heart in her eyes. "Be careful," she whispered.

He smiled down at her and raised her hand to his lips. "I promise I will." He leaned closer, murmuring, "I'm not one for speeches. But I swear to you that I will be back."

Then he was gone, slipping out across the yard behind the others.

Megan watched, her heart in her throat, as her brother and her lover followed Barchester and the others to the rear door of the museum. Barchester opened the door, and they slipped inside. Megan and her father waited, watching.

Time stretched out painfully. Frank kept taking out his pocket watch and studying it as though it would give him the answer to the universe.

Finally he whispered to Megan, "It's been fifteen minutes. How long do we give them?"

Megan, who had been fidgeting in place and telling herself that it had not really been very long since they left, frowned, her stomach tightening. "I'm not sure. They probably had to hide. They may have had to wait for Coffey to leave. Theo said they would be out within twenty minutes, but . . ."

She knew, as she felt sure her father did, that the two of them were there more to keep each other out of trouble than for any other reason. No one, including Megan herself, had really thought that she and Frank might have to go in to rescue the rescuers. But now, as she stood there, a feeling of dread was burgeoning in her stomach.

Something had happened to Theo.

She waited, watching the house, hoping for some sign that Theo and the others were all right. She glanced at her father and found him studying her as anxiously as she was staring at the house.

"What is it?" he asked. "What are you thinking?"

"I'm not sure. It's just . . . I feel . . . anxious." There was a sudden, fierce stab of pain in her chest, and her vague, generalized fear changed to something compelling and dramatic. Megan looked at her father, alarmed. "Something has happened to Theo. I can feel it."

Her father was not one to question such a feeling. "Then we had better go in. They'll need us."

Megan nodded and started toward the house. But Frank grabbed her arm and pulled her back into the shadows, nodding meaningfully. She turned and looked where he was indicating. There were two men hurrying along the driveway.

They looked, Megan thought, as though they were late. *What if the ceremony had started earlier than Barchester thought? What if Theo and the others had walked in on a house full of people instead of an empty one, or one occupied by only Julian Coffey?*

What if Barchester had lied to them, and had led Theo and Dennis into a trap?

Her stomach twisted nervously, and she had to force herself to wait, watching the two men enter. She and her father held back for another long moment to give the men a chance to move out of earshot.

She looked at Frank, and he nodded, and they slipped across the driveway and up to the rear entrance. They hesitated for a moment in the shadows, looking carefully all around. There was no sign of anyone coming up the path that ran from the drive to the back of the house.

Megan moved forward to the door and twisted the knob. It was locked. The last men to enter must have locked it behind themselves.

Frank touched her arm and moved around the shrubs to the window that lay beyond it. It, too, was locked. The anxiety in Megan was building almost to a fever pitch.

"There is a window down there." Frank Mulcahey pointed to a long opaque window set low in the wall, almost on the ground. "I'll bet it goes into the basement."

Megan nodded. "Let's try it."

That window, too, was locked, but Megan was too worried to search for an easier ingress. Instead, she picked up a rock and rapped it sharply against the glass near the catch. Careful to avoid the jagged shards, she reached in through the hole she had made, then found the catch and released it.

They lay down on the ground and peered inside. It was dark in the room below, but they could make out, dimly, boxes stacked below them. Across the room there was an outline of a door, light coming in around the cracks. Megan looked at her father, raising an eyebrow. He nodded back and turned around, wriggling feetfirst into the space. He hung for a moment, then dropped down.

Megan peered in. He had landed on the crates and boxes, and seemed unharmed. He stood up and motioned for her to enter. Megan nodded and followed his example, twisting around and crawling backward through the window. There was a stomach-churning moment when her feet dangled in the emptiness and she clung to the sill of the window, but then she drew a breath and let go.

The drop was not far to the crates, and though she crumpled onto them, she did not hurt herself. She turned and scrambled off the box onto which she had fallen and onto the floor. Her father was waiting for her, and they made their way across the room. Though they could see very little in the dark, they could make out the thin line of light around the edges of the door. Frank stumbled against something low on the floor and cursed softly, but they moved on.

She was glad to find the door unlocked, and Megan opened it a crack, peering out into the hallway. They were, indeed, in the basement of the museum. The hallway was lit only dimly by light coming from a corridor that crossed it. Megan opened the door wider and slipped out. On tiptoe, she and her father went lightly down the hall to the crossing corridor, which, she suspected, was the main hallway of the basement. When they reached it, they edged forward and took a peek around the corner.

This was the hall in which she had been knocked unconscious, Megan thought. It was empty at the moment, but she could hear the sound of voices coming from one of the rooms down the way.

The two of them crept along the corridor, the sound of voices growing ever louder, until they reached the door from which they issued. Carefully, Megan pushed the door open a crack, and she and Frank put their eyes to the slit between the doors. Megan had to clamp her mouth firmly shut to keep from gasping aloud.

They were looking at a large room, empty of furniture. Around the walls were brackets into which flaring torches had been lit, lighting the room with a reddish glow. A group of people stood in a loose semicircle, facing a slightly raised dais. They were all dressed in brightly colored cloaks made from layers of long feathers. They wore elaborate headdresses, hammered from gold or silver, with feathers stretching high up from them. They were, Megan realized, the same sort of cloaks and headdresses that she had seen on the walls upstairs in the museum. Perhaps they were the very same ones. In addition, each participant wore a mask. Some were half masks and others full. Some were more elaborate than others, but they all served the purpose of rendering their wearers both exotic and anonymous.

On the dais, where they were all gazing reverently, stood a marble altar, about three feet high, and on it lay a child. Megan's breath caught in her throat, for the child was very still. But then she caught the slight rise and fall of the girl's chest, and she let out a silent sigh of relief. Caya was still alive.

She was dressed in a long garment of finest white linen, and her arms were decorated with gold bracelets. A small headdress had been placed on her head, and the colorful feathers were a bright contrast to the long black bob of hair below. Her eyes were closed, and Megan suspected that she had been drugged.

At the four corners of the table stood iron stands with small braziers sitting on them, and strong-smelling incense curled up from them, perfuming the air.

A man stood chanting, facing the wall beyond the altar. Bright plates of gold hung on the wall, inscribed with geometric designs and stylized figures. His hands were raised, arms spread out, as he intoned something in a harsh, guttural language Megan had never heard before.

He was dressed, she could see, in a long tunic that covered him almost to his feet. It was made of row upon row of thin golden plates, brilliant in the light of the torches. She could see the back of his towering headdress, the arch of feathers stretching up.

The man turned — she felt sure it was Julian — and she saw the elaborate front of the headdress, which was attached to a mask of gold. It was the stylized head of a jaguar, the sort she had seen on one or two of the stone statues upstairs. The eyes were huge emeralds. The mouth was open in a wide, square shape, and it was through this that the man inside looked out at the room.

The figure, glittering and hard, inhuman in aspect, was enough to send a ripple of primitive fear down her spine. This, she thought, must have been what Theo had seen struggling with her brother in the cave. It was no wonder that, feverish and drugged, he had been uncertain of exactly what he had seen.

The man raised his arms again in a benedictory manner and began to chant.

Megan eased back, letting the crack in

the door close. She turned to Frank. "We need to find the men," she whispered. "We will need to have their help with that many people in there."

She could not, would not, think about the fact that Theo, Dennis and the others might be lying dead somewhere in the museum.

Frank nodded, and they scooted back and started down the hall, looking into every room they passed. Just around the corner, they found a large room with an open door. Lit by an oil lamp, the place was full of cabinets, shelves and tables, with various vases, bowls and other museum objects stacked upon them. It seemed to be a sort of storeroom. They also saw, in one corner of the room, several bound bodies. Megan sucked in her breath sharply.

It was Theo and her brother and the other men, tied hand and foot. Fear stabbed through her, fierce and paralyzing.

It took a moment for reason to reassert itself. Surely they could not be dead, or Coffey would not have bound them head and foot. They must have been knocked out, or perhaps drugged.

She ran to them, Frank right beside her, and dropped down on her knees beside

Theo. Her finger went to his throat, and she let out a sigh of relief when she felt the steady beat of his pulse. "He's alive."

"Aye, they are," Frank agreed, starting to work on the knots that bound Dennis's hands.

All the men were, including Barchester, and as Megan began to work on Theo's bonds, she said, "At least we know that Barchester did not betray them. They must have been discovered."

"Aye. Big group like that, it's no wonder." Frank cursed as his fingers slipped on the hard knot. He let out a low cry of triumph when he managed to undo it a moment later. He slipped the rope off Dennis's wrists and chafed at them, trying to restore life to his no doubt numbed hands.

"Theo!" Megan whispered as she worked. "Theo, wake up!" She paused in her work to pat his cheek. "Wake up. We need your help."

She was just sliding the rope off when Theo moaned and turned his head. "Theo! Wake up." She leaned closer to him.

At that moment there was the sound of footsteps slapping along the corridor. Megan glanced at her father in horror. What if they were coming in here to check on their captives?

Frank and Megan darted behind one of the large cabinets, and Frank pulled out the revolver Theo had left him, holding it ready in his hand. They waited.

A cloaked figure came into the room. The person was small, and from that fact and the sway of her hips as she walked, Meg assumed that it must be a woman.

Megan and her father held their breath, afraid the woman would turn and see that two of the captives had been untied. But she did not even cast a glance at the bodies as she walked over to a table. There was a tray on it, and beside it some bottles and small bowls. The woman set a bowl on the tray and poured a dark liquid from a bottle into it.

A scheme began to form in Megan's mind. She glanced around her for a weapon, and her eyes fell on a small Aztec head carved out of onyx. It would do nicely, she thought.

Picking up the head in both hands, she hurled herself out from the cover of the cabinet and straight at the figure. The woman whirled at the last moment, and her eyes widened behind her mask. She opened her mouth, but before she could draw breath to scream, Megan swung, hitting her on the side of the head. She crumpled without a sound.

"Good girl," Frank commended her and started back to the captives.

"No, wait, help me get this costume off her," Megan told him. "I am going to put it on."

She knelt beside the prone figure, and pulled the mask and headdress from the woman's face. It was Lady Scarle.

No surprise there, Megan thought. They had, after all, seen her in Coffey's embrace after she left the museum the previous night. She was probably his confidant and closest assistant.

"Are you going to go in there?" Frank asked, crouching down beside her, frowning.

"I have to. With these clothes on, maybe I can get close enough to free Dennis's daughter."

Frank hesitated for another moment, then nodded. "You're right. It's the best way. I will untie the men and wake them up if I can, and we'll join you."

"I just hope they haven't been drugged."

Together, they twisted and pulled, managing to get the cloak off the limp body of Lady Scarle. Over in the corner, the men were stirring, and one of them let out a groan. Megan glanced over and saw that

Theo was blinking, his face dazed. The knot in her chest loosened some more, but she did not let herself go to him, however much she wanted to. She had to get back into that room as soon as possible, before the group of worshippers began to wonder what had happened to Lady Scarle.

Frank helped Megan pull on the heavy cloak and tie it in place, then settled the headdress on her. "You are a mite shorter, but that's good. It will let this heathenish feather robe hide your shoes."

"There. That's good." Megan slid her arms through the slits in the cloak and picked up the bowl of noxious-looking liquid.

Was this the brew that they would drink to induce hallucinations and the proper co-operative spirit? she wondered. Or was it a poison that Coffey intended to administer to her niece? Whatever the man intended, she was going to stop him first.

With a last nod to her father, she picked up the tray and left the room. Behind her, Frank hastened over to finish untying the captives.

Megan glided down the hall, trying to imagine how an acolyte in such a religion would walk. Solemnly, she thought, to match the gravity of the occasion. With pride, of course. She would be proud that she was the woman chosen by Coffey. And, if she was Lady Helena Scarle, she would love having every eye in the place on her, so she would milk every last bit of drama from the moment that she could.

She reached the opened doors into the altar room. Her eyes went first to the altar on which the child lay. She was still stretched out, motionless, and there was no sign of blood on her. Megan let out a sigh of relief. She had thought that there would be no sacrifice until Lady Scarle got back, but she had not been absolutely sure.

The high priest stood behind the altar, his arms spread out, his hands placed on the little girl's head and ankles. When he saw Megan pause at the threshold of the door, he broke into a loud chant, raising his arms and lifting his eyes to the heavens. Megan lifted her tray higher and strode toward the altar.

She wished she had some idea what she was supposed to do. The more time she could buy her father and the other men, the better. She reached the altar and stopped beside the priest. She kept her face turned down, thinking that surely this was the way Coffey would expect to be approached. It would also serve to keep him from looking into her eyes and seeing that they were not the vivid blue of Lady Scarle's.

He turned to her, reaching out and taking the bowl from the tray. He said something she did not understand. Megan hoped she was not supposed to answer. He turned back to face the audience and, lifting the bowl over his head, began to declaim.

"Hear us, oh, Inti, god of the sun. We are your children. We are chosen to carry on your blood. Your life. Come to us, and show us the way. Accept this, our sacrifice, the purest of the pure. Bring us the gift of your immortality. And make us your own."

He brought the bowl down to his lips and drank from it. Megan realized that next he would probably turn to her to offer her the drink and then to his followers. She was not about to drink the foul-smelling stuff, whatever it was, so she had to act now.

Grasping the metal tray on one side with both hands, she stepped forward, lifting her arms, and brought it down with all her strength on the back of Coffey's head. There was a satisfying clang, and Coffey crumpled, the bowl falling from his hands and hitting the altar, then rolling off onto the floor beyond.

There was a gasp of horror from the people before her, and in that instant, Theo, her father and the other men burst in.

Megan didn't spare a glance for them as they poured into the room. She leaped forward and shoved Coffey's sprawled form off Caya, then started to work on the straps that held the child bound to the altar.

The room rang with the sound of flying fists and shouts as the occupants reacted to the sudden appearance of the band of men. Megan ignored the sounds of the fighting, concentrating solely on setting her niece free.

Her fingers fumbled at the knots, but she managed to undo the strap around the girl's chest, and she moved on to the cord around Caya's legs. That, too, gave way after much tugging, and Megan bent to scoop the girl up in her arms.

At that moment an arm went hard around her waist, pinning her arms to her sides, and the cold blade of a knife was pressed against her throat. The hard plates of the high priest's costume bit into her back.

"Halt!" Coffey's voice roared out.

"Cease, or she is dead!"

Megan had been so intent on freeing Caya that she had not noticed that Coffey had regained consciousness. Silently cursing her carelessness, she looked out over the room. The fighting had stopped, and everyone was standing still, staring at her and Coffey.

Theo took an involuntary step forward, and Coffey pressed the knife more tightly to her throat. Megan could feel a thin trickle of blood run down her throat. The movement stopped Theo in his tracks, still several feet away from them.

"Let her go, Julian," Theo ordered, his voice tight. "You have not hurt anyone yet. You can still get away with it. But if you kill her, you will go to jail, and nothing, no one, will be able to save you. You will be hanged by the neck 'til you're dead. I am told 'tis a long, slow way to die. Not exactly your style."

"You think you can stop me?" Coffey asked, his voice smug. "That your puny efforts will bring me down? I am favored of the gods! I will be immortal."

"That is the ceremonial tea talking, Coffey," Dennis said flatly, coming up toward Coffey from the other side of the room. "You won't be immortal. You cannot.

There is one thing I never told you — the magic does not work outside the sacred valley. That is why you have never been able to keep yourself from aging, no matter what you did."

"You lie!" Coffey shouted. "You are trying to trick me."

He had turned his head to watch Dennis, and he did not see the way Theo was edging closer to the dais, but Megan did. She began to weep, sagging against Coffey's arm, so that he had to take more of her weight.

"Stand up, blast you," Coffey hissed in her ear.

"I can't!" Megan wailed, letting loose with loud sobs and leaning even harder against him.

"Bloody woman!" Coffey burst out, shifting his arm to get a better hold of her.

As he did so, his other hand moved away from her throat. Megan seized the moment, thrusting up and back with her head as hard as she could. She connected smartly with Coffey's chin, snapping his head back and sending pain bursting through her own skull.

Theo threw himself the last few feet at Coffey, and the three of them went down with a crash. The air whooshed out of

Megan's chest as she hit the floor, Theo's weight half on her and half on Coffey. Struggling for air, she tried to squirm away as Theo grappled with Julian.

A hand grabbed her arm and jerked her away from the men. She looked up to see Dennis. He pulled her to her feet and thrust her away toward their father, then turned back to go to Theo's aid.

But even as he turned, Theo's fist thudded into Julian's face, knocking the golden mask back and exposing his chin. Theo took advantage of the target by slamming his fist into Coffey's chin, and the man went limp.

Megan's beleaguered lungs began to work again, and she drew in a grateful gasp of air before Theo jumped up from Coffey's prostrate form and whirled, pulling her into his embrace.

"Megan! Thank God!"

If she was smothered in Theo's embrace, Megan did not seem to mind. She clung to him tightly as he wrapped his arms around her.

"I was so scared! I thought I'd lost you!" He rained kisses over her hair and face. "I love you. I love you."

"Theo . . ." Megan sighed, burrowing against his chest, warmth spreading through her. She was, she thought, home at last.

Dennis's daughter, to everyone's relief, awakened a few hours later from her drugged sleep, groggy and frightened but physically unharmed. She threw herself into her father's arms and let loose a torrent of tears of joy and relief. She did not move from her position in his lap for the entire time that they sat and related the adventures of the evening to the Moreland family. Megan, sitting beside Theo, with her hand firmly clasped in his the whole evening, could understand how the girl felt.

Not surprisingly, the duke and duchess took everything in stride, undismayed by the sudden addition to their household of a group of strangers. A large collection of cheeses, cakes, cold meats and breads soon appeared on the sideboard in the breakfast room, and the participants in the evening's raid remembered suddenly that they were starving.

Much later, after the tale had been told and retold many times, and Reed and Barchester had returned from the police station with the news that Julian Coffey was languishing in a cell, charged with a variety of crimes ranging from extortion to kidnapping to attempted murder, the party began to break up.

Dennis and his children left with Deirdre and Frank Mulcahey, and the various Morelands began to make their way toward their own beds. Even the twins were at last calmed down enough to agree to sleep. But Theo, instead of starting toward the stairs, took Megan's hand and led her toward the conservatory and the door into the garden.

They went down the steps, and he curled his arm around her shoulders. Megan leaned into his side, resting her head against his chest. She would not think about the future, she told herself. She would just revel in the present. Theo had said he loved her, and for the moment that was enough. It would have to be enough.

"Do you think Coffey will get out of jail?" she asked.

Theo made a scornful noise. "Not any time soon. The Morelands may be considered odd, but our word still carries weight. And Barchester told the police the whole story, even the parts that made him look rather foolish. All the followers are now scrambling to shift the blame for their actions onto Coffey, claiming that they were all drugged and unwitting." He shrugged. "Who knows? It may even be true."

He bent and kissed the top of her head. "He will pay, believe me."

"Good. When I think of what he did to Dennis and to you . . . Of the way he lied — and all those years that we thought you had killed Dennis! I don't think he could possibly pay enough."

"What about Dennis?" Theo asked. "Is he going back to South America?"

"Yes. He loves Tanta too much to remain here. But he said he would stay with us for a few days. Not long — his wife is at home, not knowing what has happened or if her daughter is dead or alive. He can't let her remain in suspense. But he has promised he will visit us in New York and bring his children, too. He believes that it is important that they come to know the outside world, as well as the beauty of their village. We will just have to work very hard to keep their village a secret from the world."

"Megan . . ." Theo stopped and turned to face her, taking both her hands in his. The light of the full moon slanted across his face, washing it with pale light.

"Yes?" Megan's heart sped up at the serious look on Theo's face, and suddenly her stomach tightened. She was not at all sure that she wanted to hear what he was going to say. *Surely he could not send her away, not after what had happened tonight!*

"Wait," she said quickly, holding up a hand to forestall his words. "I want to tell you something first. I love you."

"I love you, too. That is why —"

"No, let me finish. Loving you is enough for me. I understand you have responsibilities and . . . I can accept that. I am not saying I like it, but I can — I want to be with you in whatever way I can. I don't care about your title or my reputation or any of that. All I care about is you."

"Are you finished now?" he asked patiently, a smile lurking at the corners of his mouth.

She nodded.

"Good." He bent to kiss her lips quickly. "I am glad you don't care about my title, because, frankly, I don't, either. But I do care about your reputation. And mine. Most of all, I care about you and our life together. Megan, I love you. I want to spend the rest of my life with you." He paused, then went on, "Will you marry me?"

Megan could not stop the smile that

burst across her face. "Oh, Theo!" Her throat was suddenly choked with tears. "I love you, too. More than anything. I can't tell you how much it means that you want to marry me."

She reached up and curved her hand lovingly against his cheek. "But you will be a duke. You can't marry a commoner. An American one, at that."

"Believe me, you are anything but common," Theo retorted. "And what difference does it make that you're American? You act as if I'm royalty or some such thing. I'm not. I'm merely me."

"But your family — you owe it to them to make a good marriage."

"It *will* be a good marriage. I promise you that."

"You know what I mean!" Megan exclaimed in exasperation. "The sort of marriage a duke should make. Your parents —"

"My parents love you. They could not be happier."

Megan looked at him in surprise. "You mean — you told them?"

"Of course. I talked to Mother yesterday. She gave me this ring."

He reached into his pocket and pulled out a gold ring with a magnificent ruby set in its center.

"It belonged to my father's mother. She left it to my mother when she died — not because she liked my mother, you understand. Grandmother was something of a harridan and believed that my father had married very much beneath him. That is one reason my mother stuck the ring away in a box and never wore it. But it is tradition that this ring passes from duchess to duchess. And, as you will be the next duchess, she agreed that it would be the perfect engagement ring for you."

Theo extended the ring to Megan. She saw that his fingers trembled slightly with nerves, and all her insides went as soft as melted wax at the thought.

"Oh, Theo!" Tears glimmered in her eyes, and she raised her fingers to her lips, unable to say more.

"Please take it, Megan. Tell me you will marry me. If the title bothers you that much, I will give it up, make Reed take it. There must be a way I can do that."

"Oh, Theo!" Megan cried again, the tears spilling out now and rolling down her cheeks, and she launched herself at him, her arms encircling his neck. "Yes! Yes! Of course I will marry you!"

He let out a gusty sigh of relief. "Thank God! You were beginning to worry me."

He hugged her to him tightly, nuzzling into her hair before he pulled back and took her hand, slipping the ring upon it. "I thought you might insist I move to New York and go to work or something."

Megan let out a watery chuckle. "I don't care where we live or what you do. I will go wherever you go — China or Africa or the North Pole. All I care about is being with you."

"Then we are agreed," he said, adding with a grin, "for once."

"Don't get used to it," Megan warned.

"I won't," he promised, bending close and looking into her eyes. "But I plan to get used to loving you."

With that, he pulled her close, and their lips met in a long, slow kiss.

About the Author

Candace Camp is the bestselling author of over forty contemporary and historical novels. She grew up in Texas in a newspaper family, which explains her love of writing, but she earned a law degree and practiced law before making the decision to write full-time. She has recieved several wrting awards, including the *Romantic Times* Lifetime Achievement Award for Western Romances.